The Road To Grandeur

Brandt Trebor

Brandt Trebor [signature]

Haiku for An outdoorswomen
Anne Marie Vanvleet
A hiker extraordinaire
Let's take a nice walk

Clever Publications

This is a work of fiction. Names, characters, places, and incidents either are the product of the author's imagination or are used fictitiously, and any resemblance to actual persons, living or dead, business establishments, events, or locales is entirely coincidental.

Copyright © 2015 Brandt Trebor

All rights reserved.

ISBN: 099663570X
ISBN-13: 978-0996635707

For Mom

4

Chapter 1: Running

Jayde sprinted across the wet rooftops of Haynis; three men in black pursued her through the darkness. An arrow smashed into the nearby stone wall, causing sparks of light in the rainy night. The flat-topped buildings were separated by only a few feet. One slip and she would fall three stories to the street. Her mind raced as fast as her feet.

She glanced back and saw the trio of silhouettes against the horizon fifty paces behind her. They had fallen back, less reckless in their jumps from rooftop to rooftop. She needed a plan. Over the sound of rain, Jayde heard a clank of metal as another arrow whizzed past her head and collided into the stone building. She had a small lead. Only three buildings were left till the end of the street.

Jayde saw some buildings with rope ladders but not on the buildings she had passed. She looked down and saw none of the canvas awnings that appeared on the streets during the day. Only the hard-packed ground below would break her fall. The town of Haynis was made of clay, stone, and broken dreams. The buildings and houses were built quickly and close together, with an overriding color scheme of brown, gray-brown, and tan. She heard the *thoomp* of another arrow disappear past her into the darkness, and she sprinted on.

Jayde jumped to the second-to-last building on the block. She glanced back at the ground. Nothing. Not even a hay pile to break her fall. She sprinted onward to the last building, much farther away, but Jayde had no intention of stopping. She leaped.

As soon as she left the edge of the roof, she realized the distance was too great. She flailed between buildings, reaching as far as she could. Her palms collided with the roof's hanging edge at full speed, but her desperation allowed her to maintain her grasp on the slippery, wet roof. She thought about crying for help, but there was no one on the street. It was the middle of night in Haynis.

She tried to pull herself over the edge, but her arms were not strong enough. With her arms extended, Jayde slowly slid herself along the edge of the roof.

Hands cramping and in pain, Jayde focused on survival as she worked her way along the edge. The corner seemed impossibly far away, but she gritted her teeth and kept sliding. She looked behind her. The men had not caught up to her yet. They had to be close. Hanging in midair, with her back to her pursuers, she forced her hands to move.

Jayde felt a rush of wind pass right above her. She looked and saw nothing. Jayde expected the men to appear any minute.

With aching arms, Jayde made it to the corner and was able to look along the edge of the building.

No ladder.

Jayde looked down. Still nothing below but bone-breaking ground. She tried again to pull herself up, but her arms were rubber. Jayde closed her eyes, willing a ladder to simply appear.

A growl of conversation came from above, followed by the metallic clash of weapons. Could they not know where she was?

A horrible scream erupted, followed by more sounds of weapons colliding. Jayde strained for a glimpse of the building behind her. She saw a figure in a billowing long black coat standing at the edge of the other building. One of the pursuers had finally caught up.

Jayde braced herself for an arrow in the back, but it did not come.

"C'mon, Jayde, think!" she muttered, hoping she could conjure a miracle. Somehow the man in black had not seen her. Yet.

She closed her eyes tightly. A *pop* came from the edge of the roof, away from the action occurring above. Jayde opened her eyes and saw a glint of metal through the rain. A ladder had appeared, where before there was nothing. She could not will her arms to move one more inch, much less the entire distance of the roof.

"Need a hand?" a voice said from above.

Jayde dared a look. Her arms were burning. She glared at the man.

"I'll take that as a yes."

Jayde felt her body being pulled upward. Relief flooded her. She allowed herself to be laid on the roof, as she caught her breath.

The figure hid in the shadows. He blended into the darkness and sat on a squat bench, oblivious of the rain. His hair was jet black and pulled into a long ponytail. His angular pale face was outlined in the occasional lightning strike. He drank from a wineskin, a small amount dribbling from the corner of his mouth. In the wet blackness it looked like he was drinking blood.

"You're fine," said the figure, more of a statement than a question.

Jayde did not answer. He had just saved her life, but she was not sure if she liked what she saw. He appeared relaxed, but he had moved like a wraith. He watched her. She stared back.

Jayde glanced again at the ladder she had somehow missed. She turned back to look at the man and yelped. He was right in front of her, gliding to her, though she had not even realized he had moved. He sat next to her for a full minute, apparently comfortable in the awkward silence. His smooth angular face made his age difficult to guess—possibly late thirties.

"What's your name?"

"I'm Lisa," said Jayde, the lie already prepared.

"Real name?"

"Lisa **is** my name," said Jayde. Few people knew her in town, since she spent most of her life in the shadows. She had learned long ago to have aliases at the tip of her tongue with a different backup story for each. Rarely did she give her real name.

"Fine," the figure said. His tone made it clear he knew she was lying.

Jayde stared at him.

"I figured we could drop the act, considering you were about to give the street a three-story hug. My nurse is coming, and I have to return to work."

"What about the bounty hunters?" Jayde asked.

"You won't have to worry about them anymore."

"Right. I'm sure they'll just go home and forget everything. I might have been better off on the ledge."

"That could still be arranged. For what it's worth, they weren't bounty hunters. Why were they after you?"

Jayde frowned. "I don't know."

"Fair enough."

They sat in silence. The rain had resolved, and lightning flickered on the horizon.

"So what did you steal?"

"Who said I stole anything?" Jayde answered.

"Men were chasing you, and you assumed they were bounty hunters. What else? I suppose you could have killed someone, but you're not the type."

"No. I've snitched a few things. I once made amulets out of clay and sold them to travelers, claiming they had protective magic. I don't think that someone would hire bounty hunters over that though."

"Either way, you're safe for now."

"How can you be sure?" Jayde asked.

He stood up and nodded at a heap on the ground; three shapes created a motionless mound.

Jayde yelped in surprise. "You killed them!"

"I merely did what they planned to do to you."

He stood up and walked to the middle of the roof. A hatch appeared directly in front of him. A middle-aged female popped her head out the trapdoor. She wore a simple gray robe, but Jayde could see muscular arms hiding in the sleeves. The trapdoor appeared heavy to Jayde, yet this woman lifted it effortlessly.

"Hey, Cam. There's an idiot here whining about his foot. He looks like a nobleman of some kind, so I figured—" She stopped midsentence when she noticed Jayde. Immediately her voice and demeanor changed.

"Oh, my! Who is this? What are you doing on the rooftop in this weather? And how did you even get here? You're soaked! Cam, why didn't you get her inside? No matter. I'm Marie. Come here right now, and let's get you warmed up."

Jayde grinned. The woman had a stern face and commanding voice, but her smile came easily.

The man had already started down the hatch.

"I hope he didn't scare you or, even worse, talked about philosophy or some other drivel. Once you get him going, I tell you, he can be impossible to stop."

Jayde then looked at the man in black. "Wait! What's your name?"

"Cameron. Cameron Sangre."

Jayde made her way to the trapdoor on the roof of the building. She normally would be hesitant to follow someone unknown anywhere, but, unless she wanted to jump across rooftops again, she had no other choice. She looked over the city before heading down. In the distance she saw a door open, the light from inside the house illuminating a man about to start his day. He kissed his wife good-bye, and Jayde saw a small child behind the woman wave as he headed out. The man smiled and waved back.

They were just a normal family on another normal day. Jayde sighed and headed down the ladder.

Chapter 2: Noble

A balding rotund man with his left boot off sat on a cot in Dr. Sangre's clinic. Nobleman Thaddeus Gumble had left the mayor's house during the fourth night of a week of parties. His enormous nose beamed red from too much ale, and his pale thin lips gave him a carplike appearance. He complained loudly to his servant, Sarah Tanner, while she swiftly organized his belongings.

Sarah expertly folded his clothes heaped in the corner of a room. Her sinewy frame, caramel-colored skin, and effortless efficiency contrasted the nobleman's crass behavior.

"Sir, this is the best doctor in all of Haynis, not to mention the only one open at this time of the night," said Sarah, knowing her logic was likely wasted on Thaddeus.

"Most likely this 'medicine man' wouldn't know proper healing if it bludgeoned him in the face," Thaddeus muttered.

"Well said, sir," replied Sarah.

"This is the worst case of firefoot I've ever had. He's lucky I have such an incredibly high pain tolerance. Sarah, did I ever tell you about the time I fell off the front steps a few years back?"

"It was last year and, yes, several times."

"Yes, well, there I was, minding my own business. I had recently received a fine new pair of leather shoes as a gift. I was about to go outside, and some worthless servant had forgotten to salt the top of the stairs in the middle of winter, if you can believe that."

"I had salted the stairs, but, in your genius, you went outside in a snowstorm in new shoes as a challenge," Sarah answered too quietly for him to hear.

Thaddeus continued, oblivious. "And do you know what happened then?"

Sarah straightened one already perfect corner of the pile of clothes and waited for him to answer his own question.

"I fell down the entire flight of jagged stone stairs. If not for my incredible pain tolerance, well, I could not have made it back up those two flights and into my house, where the doctor came in and rushed me off for immediate surgery."

"It was three steps, sir. You just skinned your knee—"

"'Barely clinging to life,' they said. The surgeon himself said, if I had not had my nearly inhuman tolerance for pain, why, he did not know if he could have even performed the surgery."

Dr. Cameron Sangre heard the nobleman's bluster, while descending the ladder from the roof. He took a long drag from the wineskin flask and then hooked his stethoscope on his neck. In the corner of his shop, he saw two tiny pixies fluttering and chatting among themselves. He winked at them on his way down the steps, and they both broke into giggles.

Cameron always loved pixies, though he had not seen any in years and never in Haynis. Since the city was located in the northwest corner of the country of Tenland, a country almost entirely composed of humans, their presence in his small clinic seemed odd. He would have to find out what brought them here.

But first he had to make his way to his patient, who was not waiting patiently.

"Hello, sir. How can I help you?" asked Dr. Sangre.

"How can you help? You can find me the doctor or the soothsayer or whatever you imbeciles call the healer in this bloody rattrap of a city," answered the nobleman.

"I'm Dr. Sangre," Cameron said.

"*You* are the doctor here? You couldn't be more than thirty years old. Have you even tended an ill person before in your life? What are your qualifications?" said Thaddeus.

"My most important qualification is that I'm the only doctor you'll be able to see before tomorrow noon. My other qualifications include seven years spent at Vladimir University. If you need further proof of my abilities, your servant can drive your team of horses the twenty-seven-day journey to the university, where I'm sure they'll be glad to help you," said Cameron.

"I have a rare and unique disease that you probably have never heard of. You see, I have what is called—"

"You have firefoot or gout," said Cameron, examining the nobleman's red foot. "It can be quite painful, especially if you indulge. Been to any parties recently?"

The nobleman glared at him. "Actually, yes, but I don't see what that has to do with anything."

Cameron continued. "Your life of excess seems to be catching up with you, but I can help you nonetheless."

Sarah held in her laughter. No one ever condescended to Thaddeus. She watched his face change to a dark shade of red. She had been hired as a servant years ago. Gumble paid well because no one could tolerate him. Sarah could put up with anything. Her father had been a general in the Great War and had brought her up to be hard-working, diligent, and fierce.

"Marie, could you grab some indometh and a gout poultice, please?" Cameron said in the direction of the back room. To the nobleman he said, "My nurse will be right in with some medicine. I'll return in a few minutes to check on you."

Cameron walked to the rear of the clinic where Jayde sat quietly, sipping some hot chocolate Marie had provided. Jayde's bright green eyes darted, taking in the surroundings. She seemed content, but, then again, she had just been dangling from a rooftop.

"How are you holding up, Jayde?" he asked.

"How do you know my name? I never gave it to you."

"Do you always answer questions with questions?"

"Do you?"

"Fair enough," Cameron conceded. "You were talking to yourself while dangling on the ledge. I was listening then, remember? Now how are you holding up?"

"Fine."

Cameron noticed her trembling hands, as she sipped.

"Excuse us a minute, Jayde," said Marie.

Cameron got up and walked to the counter.

"Our noble patient has taken the indometh, and the poultice is set. Why don't you just heal him and get him out of here? His royal fatness really just rubs me the wrong way," Marie whispered.

"Why's that?" he asked.

"He takes sadistic pleasure in the discomfort of his servant. Though, to her credit, the servant ignores his blustering. Personally I just want to punch his blubbery face through the wall," she said.

"Why don't you?" he asked.

"Why don't you take another drink and smile for him?" she retorted.

"You think that he would even notice anything if I did?" Cameron asked.

"He wouldn't, but his servant is sharp. She feigns a lack of interest, but I have a feeling that very little gets by her. Just heal him, and get him out of here. Did you notice the duo on your trip down the hatch?"

"The pixies? I did. It's a long way from Suliad. We'll ask them, after I get 'Nobleman Gumble' out of here," he said.

Dr. Sangre returned to Gumble, who was complaining loudly about the terrible service, and how he could not wait until he got back to Grandeur, where they had competent doctors.

Cameron ignored him as he eyed the poultice Marie had applied to the puffy red side of Gumble's foot. After securing the salve in place, Cameron held his hands over the joint and concentrated.

Slowly Cameron willed himself into the nobleman. He felt what the nobleman felt. He saw through Gumble's eyes. As he had done many times before, he allowed himself to feel the pain and know what truly flowed through Gumble's body.

"A poultice? You think a poultice will heal me? No one has ever used a poultice before, you idiot," said the nobleman.

Cameron's eyes glazed over as he relaxed. He felt Thaddeus Gumble's foot and sensed a mild tingling pain along the first metatarsal. No fever, no infection, just gout. He delved deeper, concentrating only on the joint, magnifying and increasing his sensation of the area, until that was all he felt and all he knew. He could sense the tiny, nearly invisible crystals that caused the gout.

Cameron released a small, focused portion of his will and pushed energy into the inflamed joint. The nobleman's face relaxed. Cameron felt the inflammation oozing out of the joint. He saw the small crystals dissolving.

The inflammation dissipated. The warmth and redness disappeared. The entire process happened in about fifteen seconds.

The nobleman looked at Cameron with a wide-eyed stare.

"It's … it's gone." The nobleman's voice betrayed his disbelief. "That is the most amazing poultice ever! How did you do that?"

"Your foot should not bother you for quite some time. However, you need to cut down on the fatty foods and ale, or it will return," said Cameron.

"Maybe you aren't a quack after all," muttered Gumble, as Cameron walked away.

"That's a beautiful necklace," Marie said to Sarah. "Pixie made, right?"

"Yes," she answered, offering no more in the way of conversation. Sarah paid Marie and caught up to the exiting Thaddeus Gumble.

"Come back if your gout returns," called out Marie from the front door. She watched as they walked down the street toward the mayor's house and the weeklong party still in full swing.

"Now on to the next problem. What to do with the little girl?"

"What do you mean? She's a clever girl. She'll be fine. She goes back on the street and disappears into the crowd," replied Cameron.

"We've waited years for something to happen. Maybe this is it. She's what? Fourteen years old? And someone hired a triad of assassins to take her out?" said Marie.

"Marie, they were after me," Cameron insisted. "They had to be. It's the only logical conclusion."

"Maybe. But a triad? We've been keeping an eye on many people in this city. You have your suspicions about everyone, and I *know* that girl was one of those you mentioned as having quite a bit of potential," said Marie.

"Not our problem, Marie. Just because one seer paid for her healing by divining our future does not mean we have to uproot all our hard work over the last ten years because one girl fits the description. We've been silent caretakers for how many street urchins? I have enough difficulty staying out of trouble without help from a seer's vague predictions," he said.

"I know you felt the same flux of power I did the second she came into the shop," she said.

"She has Talent, that's for sure. You're better than I am at judging that though. So you want me to avoid trouble with one person," said Cameron, looking at the nobleman walking away, "but then you want me to invite in trouble with another."

"Fat, pompous noblemen can solve their own problems. I have a soft spot in my heart for homeless little girls. Especially one fleeing for her life, who happens to be brimming with Talent," she said.

"Fine. What should we do with her?"

"*Excuse me*!" came a protest from behind them. Jayde had snuck up on them. "I can take care of myself. Thanks for the drink, but I'm getting out of here." Jayde then pushed her way between them and through the door into the street.

"Problem solved," Cameron said.

Marie peered out the door, as Jayde disappeared into the rainy night.

Two creatures whizzed by in a flash.

"Thank you for the delicious chocolate beverage!" chirped one of the pixies, as they flew through the open door. They turned in the direction opposite where Jayde had vanished.

"I think our problems are just starting," answered Marie.

Chapter 3: Happy Smyle Inn

The city of Grandeur had 298 registered inns, most of which barely scraped together enough coppers to survive. The Happy Smyle Inn thrived in the darkest cesspit of the city.

The city was located in the southeast corner of the country of Tenland, near the borders of the four great countries: Suliad, Zantia, Verrara, and of course Tenland itself. Like all cities, Grandeur had levels of intricacies hiding just under the surface. Grandeur boasted unparalleled commerce. The Merchants' Order thrived, the Order of Transportation moved everywhere, and the Communications' Order corresponded brilliantly.

The Happy Smyle Inn was not near any of these prominent orders.

In Grandeur, knowledge of all the orders was a way of life. For some people, only the most secretive of orders could help them with their problems. The Happy Smyle Inn was located equidistant from the Thieves' Order, the Wizards' Order, and the Assassins' Order.

Esmeralda Smyle, who owned the Happy Smyle Inn, had initially trained at the Enchanters' Order. But, after practicing her craft on the fringe of Grandeur for years, Esmeralda realized that she hated enchanting. She started the Happy Smyle Inn and never looked back.

Esmeralda did, however, use her Talent to design three enchantments for her inn. The first was a spell of *intent*. This spell ensured that anyone within a one-hundred-yard radius of her inn would not hurt another individual. This spell did not prevent injury from happening; it simply changed people's minds. If someone planned to hurt someone else, the instigator would stop if they were within one hundred paces of the Happy Smyle Inn. A suspicious number of fights occurred just off the property.

The second spell Esmeralda enchanted was one of *privacy*. She realized her clientele had a strong desire to keep their private matters private. The inn's location between the three covert orders in particular made for frequent visits from people who went there to partake in business, not just pleasure. The spell of privacy was set over each of the small booths around the inn. Those inside the booths were the only ones who could understand their boothmates. The other people around the inn would hear only a babble of disconnected sounds. When sitting casually at the Happy Smyle, private business could be conducted without worrying about spies or other eavesdropping ears of dangerous people.

The third spell was one of *truth*. This meant that any agreement verbalized within the walls of Esmeralda's inn would be binding. Very few people would trust the words of a thief. Fewer still would trust the words of an assassin. Nobody trusted wizards. But, when someone tried to lie about an arrangement in the Happy Smyle Inn, only the truth came out. This made for some very awkward conversations when the Happy Smyle Inn first opened.

Four years ago, a wizard had wanted to hire a new, unknown assassin to kill a merchant who had betrayed him. The assassin responded to this offer by saying that he would instead kill the requesting wizard and steal his money since that was easier. The wizard looked at the assassin questioningly. The assassin tried to cover his mistake by saying he did not mean to say that, but the truth spell was too strong, and he stated that what he meant to say was that he really could not wait to get the wizard outside so he could slit his throat. The assassin then turned red and excused himself from the table. The wizard looked over to Esmeralda, complimented her on her spell, and left a hefty tip before he followed the assassin. No one ever saw that assassin again.

The Happy Smyle Inn became the hangout for the most ruthless, clever, and devious individuals in Grandeur. But, with the enchantments in place, people were always on their best behavior. On top of this, only Esmeralda and her staff were immune to her enchantments. Thus, if anyone got on *her* wrong side, they would find themselves in a tough predicament, one where the inn's guard could punch them but they could not punch back.

In one of the Happy Smyle Inn's private booths sat three men in dark cloaks, drinking their ale and speaking in hushed tones. The front door opened, and a surly-looking tree stump of a creature hobbled in, holding a metal box under one arm. It waddled over to the table where the three shaded figures sat.

"Is you the purchasers for the bozrac?" it said, while sitting in the empty space in the booth. Its voice sounded like broken glass was caught in his throat, and its breath smelled like rotten meat.

The three glanced at each other, clearly surprised by the appearance of the intruder. They had expected to meet a wizard or possibly a Dark-Man, not a gnome. The creature before them was grizzled, two feet tall, unkempt, smelled of sewage, and looked most untrustworthy. Only the last was expected.

The gnome snorted. "You got my stuff, or did I trundle this whole way for nothin'?" said the gnome, articulating his stance by spitting what looked like a dark brown garden slug on the ground.

The trio glanced at one another. The gnome had a metal box with the appropriate markings on it. Who were they to deny him?

"All right, here's the staff, the amulet, and the gold," said the smallest of the three men, handing over the items. The two other dark figures never made a noise. "And we have your guarantee on these?"

"I don't makes no deals that go bad. I gotta reputation to keep. You got your doom-critter. Just don't do nothin' dumb for at least three days," said the gnome, yet holding up two fingers. The gnome set the black box on the table, collected the items in payment, and left without saying another word or checking the authenticity of the items.

The three stared at the box, hardly believing they had done it. They had the most powerful weapon that had ever been invented. The brutes had no idea what a bozrac actually was.

"Mrs. Crass will flip. I can't believe we actually got it," said the second grunt.

"Shut up!" said the third, a giant of a man, as he looked around. Every face here looked shady and suspicious, but this was the norm in the Happy Smyle Inn. The largest of the three carefully picked up the box. The thug slipped it into a nondescript satchel, and the three left the Happy Smyle Inn to bring it to their boss. None of them noticed the low growl coming from the box.

Chapter 4: New Friends

Sarah and Nobleman Thaddeus Gumble walked on the muddy street away from Dr. Sangre's building. Thaddeus marveled at how well his foot felt. Sarah marveled over his lack of whining. Sarah walked a few steps behind Gumble, as he blustered. She knew all his stories, but she never interrupted him when he drank. Out of the blackness two tiny pixies zipped up to her and landed, one on each shoulder. She thought about all that had transpired to get her to this point.

Three years ago, before her employment with Gumble, Sarah had lived in quiet isolation with her parents in Suliad, a country located to the south and east of Tenland. The country of Suliad was thought of by most humans as a magical land with enchanted creatures everywhere, but the only creature Sarah ever saw was the occasional deer in the forest nearby, and it was not enchanted.

Her father had been a general in the Great War, fighting against the Dark King for decades. Despite her father winning many battles, the Dark King continued his slow progression, expanding the border of Zantia north into Tenland. After retiring honorably from his service in Tenland's army, her father had met a beautiful woman in his travels. Sarah's mother was half dryad and had been banished shortly after being born. Dryads had the ability to transform themselves into trees and gain strength, nourishment, and energy from the land. Her mother could perform this magic, but Sarah had never been able to perform any magic herself.

Sarah's parents desired a peaceful life in the country for her, yet her father still ruled the house with a general's authority. Sarah had her mother's dryad height, warm caramel-colored skin, and deep brown eyes. She also had her father's stubbornness and resolve.

Her life changed forever when sixty soldiers from Zantia surrounded their house in the middle of the night. Sarah remembered a voice calling out from outside, "If everyone in the house exits calmly, your deaths will be swift and painless."

Sarah's father lived by the motto that "Preparation lives longer than luck." Thus, when the army arrived, he immediately ushered Sarah into the small hidden cellar of the house. He closed the stone trapdoor, only to return a minute later, quickly throwing in a small satchel, and then closed the door again.

Though brazen, brave, and stubborn, Sarah respected her father and stayed concealed under the stone door in the floor.

Sarah overheard her father yelling with the soldiers from Zantia, who broke into the house shortly thereafter. In the blackness of the small room, she heard the sound of items being broken and screams. She overheard the soldiers accusing her father of guarding a Chosen creature from Suliad. After that, the fighting commenced. Her father was a strong man and a gifted fighter, but even he could not defeat threescore soldiers.

A short time later, Sarah heard a steady roar above her head and realized her house was on fire. The ceiling of her small stone room felt warm, but she remained cool, hidden within.

The sounds of her house burning and the resultant crashes continued for hours while Sarah wept. Eventually she fell asleep.

She was shocked to wake up later to sunlight coming through a small hole along an edge of the stone trapdoor. This made sense when she pushed open the trapdoor to reveal only a shell of her former house. The ceiling and most of the walls had been burned to ash. Everything she owned had been destroyed, except for what she had in her hidden cellar.

She opened the satchel her father had given her. Inside was a small pile of gold coins and a note.

Honeybun, your mother and I knew this day would come. We were told of it a long time ago.

Unique you are. We wanted to tell you years ago. But what would that accomplish?

Nobody lives fearlessly, but we had hoped to keep fear out of your childhood.

Tests are coming, my daughter, but you are amazing, strong, and we love you deeply.

Enjoy your memories, but know you must move on, survive, and, for now, run.

Remember your lessons. We locked your skills deep inside to keep you safe.

Show this note only to someone you trust with your life.

Love, Mom and Dad.

Sarah cried.

Hours later she realized that, despite her years of happiness and comfort, she had to leave.

The closest city was Grandeur. The gold would provide both traveling fare and provisions for at least a year, but she needed a plan.

Being her father's daughter, she had practicality almost oozing through her pores. She walked the first day and ultimately joined a baker on his way to Grandeur. While riding in the back of the baker's wagon headed to Grandeur, she made a list of short- and long-term goals.

Food, shelter, and a job, Sarah thought to herself in the rear of the wagon. Also she needed to figure out whatever the note from her parents meant. While riding, Sarah munched on an oversize pastry, storing the rest for later in the day.

Sarah vividly remembered entering the expansive city of Grandeur the first time. The main road was made of bricks that snaked through the city, while countless dirt side roads veered off from the main thoroughfare, all bustling with activity.

After leaving the bakery cart, she encountered three trolls, walking down the road. Sarah asked for help. She received a shove into the dirt for her troubles. A creature made entirely of mud appeared out of a trough that ran along the road.

"Whoa, rudeness! Sorry, miss. Not all people in Grandeur aim to please," said the man made of mud.

"Can you help me? I'm trying to find a place to stay and possibly a place to work," Sarah replied, surprised at her own calm while talking to the mudman.

"Normally I'd have to charge yah, but, since you just got planted by some punks, this one's on me. Check out the post in midtown, six blocks down. It'll steer you in the right direction.

Check yah later," said the creature, as it disappeared back into the trough of mud alongside the road.

She arrived at the ad post, which looked more like a giant tree covered with hundreds of slips of paper. She found a position as a servant which offered food, lodging, and pay. Perfect.

Sarah arrived a short time later at a large gate to a fenced-in residence. She pulled a string which ran into the house. She heard the distant ring of a bell from inside. While she waited, two creatures, each about three hands high, approached her. They looked like small green humans with tails, blending into the tall grass next to the fence.

"Pardon, ma'am, but could you spare some food for a sprite in need?" asked the creature.

"Oh," Sarah exclaimed, surprised to understand the creatures. "I have some leftover bread. Let me get it out."

"You can understand me, thank goodness! You are so kind, you see we have—" began the sprite.

"Get off my land!" yelled a rotund, balding man, who waddled quickly down the walkway, swinging his cane at the creatures. The sprites scattered, disappearing into the grass.

"Filthy creatures, probably trying to rob me blind. Filled with diseases, you know. And what do you want?" the man asked.

"I'm here for the assistant position," Sarah replied.

"Fine, you're hired. My previous imbecile had to be let go. If you can follow directions for more than a day, maybe you'll last longer," said the man, returning to the enormous house without looking back.

This was Sarah's first interaction with her employer of the last three years. Thaddeus Gumble came from Zantia, the country directly south of Tenland. Zantia had been waging war against all other countries for two hundred years. Thaddeus had renounced his former country, stating he disagreed with King Zolf and the war. He claimed to be a humble refugee, who had bravely fled for his life. However, like most humans from Zantia, he despised all nonhuman life forms. Granted, with Thaddeus, most humans received his scorn as well.

As Sarah walked toward the house, she glanced back. Seeing the green sprite looking at her, Sarah smiled and casually dropped the rest of her pastry. The creature bowed, then snatched the pastry, and disappeared into the grass.

Over the following months, Sarah quickly learned Gumble's quirks. Thaddeus called "mistress" any woman who leeched onto him for his status. It helped him not to have to remember names. He also hated going outside; thus, any purchases he left to Sarah to gather.

Many months later Thaddeus requested that Sarah obtain a necklace for his current mistress. As always Sarah left immediately to perform her duties. While walking from the winery across town to the bakery, she saw the Picky Pixie Jewelry sign.

Sarah had never noticed the store before. The second she walked through the door, she gawked. Scores of beautiful small winged creatures buzzed around, carrying intricately decorated items. Glass counters displayed glittering jewelry. She saw necklaces of gold and silver inlayed with elaborate designs and etch-work so small and detailed it was hard to believe possible. Beautiful rings, amulets, and medallions were adorned with precious gems and displayed in clear cases. In one corner there were elaborate chains for individuals with tentacles. In another display were glittering cone-shaped rings that were labeled Antennae Cones.

Amid all the different adornments, small beings zipped around, continuously adjusting and organizing. Sarah looked at a wall display and saw velvet belts of various colors and styles, ranging in size from those twice as tall as Sarah to a small piece of fabric that would barely encircle her little finger.

She realized the store must be new, though the location seemed odd. A jewelry store located this close to the thieving guild seemed like a recipe for disaster. Not that this was a dangerous part of town, just that valuable objects in this area of the city had a way of being discreetly relocated without the owner's knowledge.

"Greetings!"

The speaker's high voice squeaked, startling Sarah. A scantily dressed creature zipped right in front of her, wearing spectacles and carrying what looked like a tiny notebook. After catching Sarah's attention, the creature gently drifted down to the expansive display case.

"Something of elegance to suit your fancy? I am the proprietor of these premises."

"Something of what?" asked Sarah.

"Elegance!" she chirped, her voice perky. "I am Zanna-Nix-Nazarri. Er, sorry, I mean, I am Jenny. Yes, you may call me Jenny."

"Ah," Sarah said, trying to hide her amazement. "The gold necklace in that intricate braid, may I see that?"

"Oh, something of unique style for a lady of exquisiteness like yourself?" Jenny said, a grin spreading on her small face.

"It's for a friend," Sarah answered.

"I see. Well, that is a sophisticated and graceful piece. You have excellent taste," said the creature. She then blew into a small flute that materialized out of nowhere. Three tiny creatures flew into the display case and lifted the piece, gently laying it on Sarah's outstretched hand.

"It's beautiful. How much?" she asked.

"How much?" Jenny asked, puzzled.

"Yes. What is the price?"

"The price? Ah, yes, of course … the price." Jenny paused, speaking quickly and quietly to the three who had assisted her. "I'm sorry. What do you mean?" she asked again.

Sarah found her puzzled expression adorable. "Well, what would you like in exchange for the necklace? I have a few silver, but a piece of this quality, well, I'll be honest, I'm not sure if I have enough."

Jenny looked at the three who had arrived to help her with the necklace with a confused expression. They spoke quickly and all landed on the display case. Their faces showed frustration and anguish. The owner pulled out the flute again and blew a very quick, intricate tune. From the back of the shop, scores of creatures flew out, all landing on the display case around the one who had spoken to Sarah. They chattered in what Sarah assumed was their native tongue. It was an incredibly fast language with clicks and a musical intonation, occasionally accented with the buzzing of wings. She could not tell if they were arguing, fighting, or singing.

After a short time, the owner turned back to her with a sheepish grin on her face.

"I suppose I have to explain. You see, this is actually our first day, and we unfortunately have a plethora of inexperience. Prior to purchase, I had expounded to the dictator of this city about our competence. He then pontificated that such problems as this might arise. Our self-confidence seems to have overridden our common sense." She sighed. "I dismissed his sage advice. Such capriciousness flaws some pixies. The dictator had advised a consultant prior to opening shop to prevent such problems."

Sarah summarized it in her brain. The owner went to the city dictator. The dictator told her to get help with the business. Jenny had ignored the advice. Oh, and the creatures were pixies!

"We lack knowledge in pricing our wares. We have always made jewelry, but we have never actually sold any," Jenny said, the distress clear on her face.

"How is that possible? How could you make such incredible work but never sell it?" answered Sarah.

"Well, in Suliad's forests, interactions are quite different. The various vagabond travelers, the boisterous barbarians, etc., etc. Adventurers would randomly come across us, and we would exchange our jewelry for favors. Though I doubt it has escaped your countenance, but our sizes differ vastly. Thus, by performing tasks for us that would take us an insurmountable effort and time, we would exchange our jewelry. But I now believe we have made an error of incalculable idiocy."

During the speech her face had changed from that of the continual perkiness she had originally exhibited into that of outright despair.

"I don't know what we'll do!" she said, on the verge of tears. "You are our first customer, and we have utterly failed you! And now I am sure you will tell everyone of our disappointing shop, and we will become outcasts bound to failure and—"

"Wait! Stop right there," Sarah interrupted, hiding a chuckle behind her hand. "So you are telling me that you have an entire store of merchandise, but you do not know how much any of it is worth, correct?"

Jenny wiped away a small tear. "Correct."

"What you guys need is a manager."

"A what?" Jenny asked.

"Someone who can tell you what things are worth, how much to charge, how to anticipate changes for seasons. You know, all that stuff," said Sarah.

"No, I do not know 'all that stuff.' But you seem to know. Yes! You have brilliance beyond your years and experience in our areas of weakness. We will have to discuss, but I believe we can accept your proposition."

"What proposition?" asked Sarah, perplexed. For the amount of words Jenny used, the pixie made little sense.

"You are a human with experience in merchandising and purchasing interactions. You simply must consider a mutually beneficial correspondence! I assure you that my troop will be most accommodating," pressed Jenny.

"Something like that takes a lot of time and effort," answered Sarah. Then again, the more Sarah thought about it, the more she liked it. She could secretly work with the pixies during all her idle time sitting around waiting for chores. She worked for Gumble a few days a week and yearned for interactions with magical creatures. How could she refuse?

"All right," Sarah said, "what's in it for me?"

Again the pixies began rapidly speaking in their language. One popped up by her head, looked at her, and ducked back into the conversation. After a brief conversation they all suddenly stopped.

"What would you like?" asked Jenny.

"How about five percent of the profits?" Sarah answered.

The pixie looked blankly at her. "What does that mean?"

"Well, for every twenty of something you earn at the shop, I would receive one," she answered. "If you earn twenty gold pieces, I would get one. That way, if you don't make any profit, neither do I."

Jenny then looked back at the pixies on the display case. Her flute rematerialized, and she blew a surprisingly loud and shrill twittering note.

Pixies appeared from everywhere. Sarah had not realized how many were present, since so many fluttered around the large shop, plus more of them must have been in the back. Hundreds of pixies gathered in front of Sarah.

Jenny waited for them to settle, and then they rapidly spoke in their musical language. Every so often, Jenny would flutter her wings and point at Sarah. She thought she could almost understand some of what they were saying.

Sarah quietly bit her lip, eyes darting. After Jenny's speech, a few of the pixies buzzed their wings, and flew up and down rapidly. The owner pointed to each in turn as they melodiously spoke. She answered each of their questions, as they arose. She then addressed Sarah.

"All right, we would like to acquiesce but with certain prohibitions," Jenny said.

"Huh?" asked Sarah.

"We agree, but we would like to place a few caveats, more specifically in regard to linguistics. We would like you to teach us your language. Currently I am the only one in this troop who can converse fluently with humans. Some pixies can understand a bit, but most cannot speak your language. Would you be willing to teach it?" Jenny asked.

"Sure," Sarah answered. "I work as a servant currently, but I do have some free time. I would be happy to teach you 'human.' I won't be able to be here every day. In fact I may not be able to be here sometimes for weeks at a time. I'm my master's favorite traveling companion."

"If we fail, then you would be failing as well, correct?" Jenny asked.

"Well, yes, but that is not the point," Sarah answered.

"Do you promise your truthfulness and dedication?" Jenny asked.

"Yes."

The flute came to Jenny's lips instantly, but Sarah heard no noise. She felt a warm wave flow over her whole body. For an instant she felt sleepy, content, and giddy. Then the feeling disappeared as quickly as it had started.

"We have found you to be honest and do not believe you to be one who would attempt to capitalize from our misfortune. Our bargain is struck," the pixie said.

Jenny then played a short tune. The crowd of pixies concentrated while listening to the music. As soon as the melody stopped, cheers rose up from all the small winged creatures. They flew into the air and surrounded Sarah, zipping by closely, kissing her on her cheeks and landing on her shoulder to hug her neck. Sarah became very nervous and blushed, not knowing what to do. The pixies then lined up on the display case in many neat rows.

Sarah looked at them. They looked at her.

"Well?" Jenny asked.

"Well what?" Sarah answered.

"What would you have us do?" Jenny asked.

Sarah's mind raced. Her military upbringing filtered the pros and cons of the situation. The shop simply could not be opened. No prices, no place for money exchange. No system of organization. Not to mention the fact that the only security would be a polite request not to steal from a pixie. This would not do.

"Close the store." Sarah paced, while thinking out loud. "We don't want people to know there is an entire building loaded with jewelry. At least not yet we don't. We need some muscle for security. Also we will need a secure place to put the money." Sarah continued to rattle off ideas, while Jenny dutifully wrote down everything in a tiny notebook.

A flurry of pixies disappeared outside, and the sign was down in a matter of minutes. Everything Sarah said was written down on Jenny's small pad of paper.

After an hour of discussions and planning, Sarah left the Picky Pixie to go home. As she walked out, two small shapes quickly darted after her, each landing lightly on a shoulder.

Jenny fluttered in front of her.

"This is Zizunni-Zax and Ni. Oh, sorry. I meant, this is John and Lucy. They are to be your first two students. They already understand human language relatively well, so they volunteered to be your first educational undertakings," Jenny said.

Sarah looked closely at the two pixies now hovering in front of her. When she looked closer, she could see that one definitely had slightly masculine features. She had earlier assumed that they were all female. Apparently male pixies were part of the troop as well.

"Wait. You mean they're going home with me?"

"Yes, of course. The best way to learn a language is to immerse oneself. They will be of no trouble to you. Both John and Lucy are very well behaved, demonstrating the utmost propriety. Correction, I suppose I should say they are well behaved for pixies."

"Thanks, I guess," Sarah replied.

The storekeeper blew into her flute one last time, and a small fleet of pixies brought an intricately designed necklace and gently placed it around Sarah's neck. Jenny smiled. "A gift, as a token of our agreement and our gratitude."

"Oh, I couldn't! It's too beautiful!" Sarah exclaimed.

"It is yours! Good day!" Jenny said, then zipped back into the fury of reorganizing and closing down the shop. A large iron gate came down from the awning of the shop. Apparently the previous owners at least had acknowledged the dubious district that the shop was in.

"What have I gotten myself into?" Sarah said under her breath. She slowly walked toward the bakery with John and Lucy, her two new pixie companions humming right behind her.

Sarah snapped back from her reminiscing.

She had been lost in thought while walking back from their late-night trip to cure Gumble's gout attack. He continued telling one of his stories, never pausing to see if Sarah listened. She had met the pixies two years ago, but it seemed like yesterday. Gumble still remained unaware of her secret life with the pixie troop, despite her two companions never being far away.

John flew close to her head.

"He was a nice doctor. Such a kind and knowledgeable vampire! I wish we had a splendid doctor for us back home!" John said casually.

Sarah paled at this remark. She had grown accustomed to the pixies appearing out of nowhere and making comments. Most of the time she had no idea where they were, but she knew they accompanied her at all times.

As they walked down the street, they passed three limp bodies piled on top of one another. Thaddeus turned white upon viewing the dead and hurried past them. Sarah remained white after finding out Dr. Sangre was a vampire.

Chapter 5: Secrets

Seven days had passed since Jayde's escape from the three assassins. She spied on Cameron Sangre's clinic on the edge of town. Her years living on the street had honed her skills of blending in and observing from afar. Despite this, both Dr. Sangre and his nurse, Marie, periodically looked out and waved at her.

Jayde had noticed the faint blue nimbus that had surrounded Dr. Sangre when he had healed the fat man one week prior. She had seen such a glow before and knew it meant magic. After a week of surveillance, even after hearing the new rumors about a vampire in town, Jayde snuck onto the roof of Dr. Sangre's clinic and waited.

Surviving on the streets of Haynis required a decent level of cunning, theft, and ingenuity. At one time Jayde wanted nothing else but to become the best thief in town, swiping extra coins from rich merchants. Her goals had changed four years ago, on Jayde's tenth birthday.

Jayde woke early on that day four years ago and hid in brush alongside the main road. Some merchants had stopped in Haynis on their way north. She had patiently shadowed them, waiting to snatch any valuable item, if the opportunity arose. Unfortunately all had remained vigilant. Then she saw a small silver statue fall from a saddlebag. There were three horses, all of which continued to slowly walk away. It practically was not even stealing; it would be the easiest job she had ever done, but she saw more horses coming up the road, so Jayde had to act quickly.

Jayde sprung from the bush and sprinted to the statue. The motion caught the gaze of one of the horses, which spun around. Jayde heard shouting, but, by now, she was committed.

She grabbed the statue and ran. After a dozen steps, a sharp pain blazed through her legs as she collapsed to the ground. Jayde looked up and found herself surrounded by three horses and three angry, smirking men. One of the men had used a whip to snare her legs.

"We killed the last whelp who thought to steal from us," said the man.

Another man took out his whip, which he snapped down, circling her wrist, and wrenched her arm. He sneered at Jayde, lifting her next to his horse.

"I don't know. I'm feeling merciful. What say we just take back what's ours, and cut off the loose ends and call it even," he said, pulling out a wicked foot-long blade.

"Enough!" spoke a stranger, his voice coming from a nearby inn. An ancient man dressed in a simple gray robe ambled over.

"This doesn't concern you, traveler," said one horseman.

"Accosting children is always my concern. Release her," he said.

The man holding the whip and blade paused for a second, then swung his blade toward Jayde's arm. She braced for the inevitable.

Jayde opened her eyes and saw that all three men had a blue light surrounding them, and all remained perfectly motionless. Their eyes were open; they were awake but motionless.

The gray-robed man slowly walked to Jayde's side and unwrapped the leather whips on her. He permeated the same bluish light that bound the men.

"You were lucky today, child. You have potential, quite a bit actually. Perhaps you should pursue something other than petty thievery, eh?" said the man.

"If I could do magic like that, maybe I would," Jayde said.

"Child, with your potential, you could do much more. Now get out of here before the spell wears off, and I have to save you a second time."

Jayde ran. From that time on, she took every opportunity to learn whatever she could about magic. Haynis offered little opportunity for magical education. Jayde stole the only book that she could find on the topic, but she craved more.

Months later, a trained fool came and spent a week at the local inn doing magic tricks for coppers. His flowing multicolored robes dazzled in the torch light. Jayde attached herself to his side, to glean information, but he only had sleight of hand and no true magic.

When a witch came into Haynis to sell magical potions and spells, Jayde tailed her relentlessly, until the witch tired of her incessant questioning. The witch turned her weathered face suddenly to Jayde, the witch's eyes gleaming with crafty intelligence. "Bother me again, and you'll spend the rest of the day as a hermit crab."

Jayde nodded, her eyes wide, searching for words. She cleared her throat and, even with her trepidation, asked, "Just out of curiosity, how would you do that?"

Thus, four years later, when Haynis's doctor had magically healed a man, she could have screamed. Cameron Sangre had amazing power, though obviously he wanted to keep it hidden. Otherwise Jayde was sure she would have found out about him years ago. Her only concern was for the rumors circulating around town, but she was about to find out about those right now.

She waited on the roof.

An hour later, Cameron Sangre climbed out the trapdoor, looking over the darkness of the city before it transformed into the mayhem of a bustling town. He took a slow, deep breath.

"Hello, Jayde. What can I do for you?" he asked, never even looking in her direction.

"You're a vampire," she said.

Cameron remained silent for a moment.

"Yes. And?"

"And you can do magic. And you saved my life, didn't you?"

"Yes. And?" He took a drag from his flask.

"That's blood, isn't it?"

"Yes again."

Jayde walked around the edge of the rooftop. "I remember you drinking from that flask. You were sitting right where you are now, and you watched everything. But what I can't figure out is why."

"Why what?"

"Why did you do it? What was the point? Why save me? Why did you even care what happened to me? You had nothing to gain. You had no idea who I was or why I was being chased," she said.

"Didn't I?" he answered.

"No! Stop answering questions with questions. Just answer me. Why did you do it?" she asked."

Cameron drank again from his flask. "Jayde, you think you came to my clinic out of sheer luck and desperation, but I've been following you much longer than you've been following me. I know you grew up on the street after living in the orphanage for the first seven years of your life. You steal on occasion, but you have impeccable morals, considering your upbringing. You don't know anything about your parents, and that bothers you, yet you have an uncanny knack for making friends with the right people."

"I don't understand," she said.

"Jayde, people don't tend to stick around too long when they find out I'm a vampire. The only real friend I have in Tenland is my nurse, Marie. Usually, when people find out the truth, they disappear."

"Why? I knew you were a good guy after meeting you," said Jayde.

"Well, I did just save your hide. And not everyone can tell that much about someone after a first meeting. Most people judge after discovering my little secret."

"But, but, but you're a vampire! Couldn't you just, you know?" She made a hissing noise, pulling her fake cape around herself.

"What do you know about vampires, Jayde?"

"Not much, I guess."

"And yet you came, alone, to the rooftop to confront one? One that you knew could possibly make you disappear? You came in the middle of the night, all alone, to confront a creature you knew little about? And what, exactly, did you hope to accomplish?"

"All I wanted to know is why you saved me in the first place and maybe to learn a little about magic!" she shouted.

Cameron looked over the fog in the city, but he did not answer.

"Jayde, you are either very brave or very stupid."

"I'm curious and a thief, that's all."

"Marie believes those three men could have been after you instead of me. Years ago, an injured seer came into the clinic. Instead of paying for her treatment with money, she offered to give us insight into the future."

Jayde looked at Cameron suspiciously.

"Most seers are sham artists who just tell you what you want to hear and expect a silver for the effort. This seer, however, was authentic. She told us to stay here. She told me about a girl who would come who would have potential. Marie thinks that is you."

"Potential for what?" Jayde asked.

"Potential to be somebody different. Someone who could make a difference. Someone who could maybe stop the Dark—"

"And possibly have magic?" Jayde interrupted.

"Well, in the past, nearly all of them had magic. Powerful magic in fact," Cameron said.

"Who did? And what did the seer say would happen after that?"

"She never told us what to do, just to be aware. The seer said this person could change the world. That happened almost five years ago. So Marie and I have been watching many people in Haynis, but we wondered the same thing. What now? When I saw you running toward me on the rooftop being chased by three men, I intervened. Was this the event the seer spoke about? Who knows? Now I have a question for you. You knew I was a vampire before you came up here. How did you know?"

"The whole town knows," she said, matter-of-fact.

"What? How?" Cameron asked with a hint of anger.

"Ever since that royal fat guy came to town two weeks ago, people were talking. I don't know how these things get started. People were saying there was a vampire in the town. Then I thought how sometimes these things have a hint of truth to them. Then I guessed just maybe it was you. I told a few friends about it, but nobody believed me."

"I suppose it's time Marie and I packed for our move," he said.

"What do you mean?" she asked.

"Jayde, I've been through this before. It always ends the same. A mob with pitchforks and torches comes and demands I leave town. I'm just a scary monster who they want to get rid of before I can corrupt them with my presence. It's really too bad. I liked this town. I liked most of my neighbors. How long ago did you tell those friends about me?" he asked.

"Yesterday morning," Jayde said.

"Hmm, I would have expected them to be here by now."

"Who?"

"The angry mob," he said. "Well, nice chatting with you, and I apologize for being rude, but I do want to salvage the majority of my medical supplies, so I really have to pack before they get here. Maybe saving your life was what the seer wanted Marie and I to do. Maybe you're destined to be a seer one day. Who knows?

"Thank you for the roundabout warning, and best of luck with whatever it is you decide to do with your life. For what it's worth, you have a brilliant mind. If you would just apply it to something other than stealing, I'm sure you would go quite far. Oh, and feel free to use the trapdoor to get down, but I would try not to be seen with me. Who knows what people might think?"

"I don't care what people might think!" Jayde yelled.

The passion in her voice halted Cameron, as he pulled open the trapdoor.

"It's not fair if you have to leave! You're the first person—or vampire or whatever—who has ever taken the time to talk to me. Then you tell me that I might actually amount to something or be special. And then you say you're just leaving?"

"Life's not fair. I don't make the rules. Why does everyone automatically hate vampires? I don't know, but it seems to be a fact. You want some advice? Try not to think like everyone else but judge from your experience, not rumors. Can you do that?" he asked.

Jayde sniffed. "I'm here, aren't I?"

Cameron disappeared through the opening and woke up Marie. As Jayde came down the ladder and into the clinic, she heard quite a racket. Marie was running around packing vials like a madwoman.

"You have to leave before anyone sees you here. Best of luck to you. I'm sorry we couldn't get to know you better. Here, take this. It brought a smile to your face, and you need more smiles in your life." Marie handed over the large canister of hot chocolate.

Jayde did not know what it was worth, but she would never sell it. No one gave her anything without expecting something in return. Actually, now that she thought about it, this was the second time Marie had done that.

Jayde looked at her blankly. "Thanks."

"You really need to go now, Jayde, before anyone sees you here. People will come—maybe not tonight, but soon—and you can't be associated with us," she said.

"I don't care what other people think."

"Sorry about this," said Marie.

"Sorry about what?"

In response Marie lightly pushed both hands against Jayde's chest. Jayde felt a coldness flow into her. For some reason she felt terrified. She had to get out of their clinic right away.

Jayde ran down the empty street in the predawn darkness. The cold feeling diminished slowly, and she again felt normal. After a few blocks, Jayde realized Marie had used magic on her. They both could do magic! And, for some reason, they were kind to her. Who were these people?

Chapter 6: Rumors

Sarah wanted to scream in frustration after being dismissed for an entire week. Gumble spent the days either with his mistress or drinking or both. Sarah had told Thaddeus that the doctor was a vampire, though she realized she had little support for her accusation other than the word of a pixie. Over the following week, she spoke with townsfolk about Dr. Sangre and her suspicions, but few offered support for him being a creature of evil.

On their last day in Haynis, Gumble and his mistress went out to breakfast. Thaddeus Gumble retold the story of his vicious battle with firefoot. Sarah stayed close by, in case he needed anything. She rarely added to his conversations, unless he spoke to her, but she had to voice her concerns about the vampire doctor. Thaddeus responded with a chuckle.

"How could he have been a vampire?" Gumble asked.

"Well," Sarah began, "did you notice that he never showed us his teeth? Probably hiding something right there. Also who has a clinic that is open all night? I'll tell you who. A person who never sees the light of the day, that's who!"

Sarah continued mounting her evidence, while the nobleman and his current mistress pretended to listen. During meals was one of the few times Sarah could actually be heard, since Thaddeus loved to eat even more than talk.

"Why, if your allegations are true, I was lucky to get away with my life," said Thaddeus, eagerly inhaling a second helping of bacon, ham, eggs, toast, flat cakes, and mango juice. "I'm lucky I have a seventh sense about these things. My sixth being my inhuman attention to details," he said, while Lucy, the slight pixie, waved at Sarah from behind his shoulder.

"Of course," Sarah said.

"Well, we'll just have to do something about this. I know my friend the mayor doesn't have my attention to details, but I'll not have him losing face while a vampire sucks the life out of his quaint little horse-apple pie of a city," he said. "We'll march up there immediately. Now! Right away! Just as soon as we finish breakfast."

"Oh, and we want to visit the little market," his mistress chimed in.

"Yes, yes. Of course, immediately after breakfast and the market. Oh, and we wanted to see the play in the park. And then we planned to go to that bakery for a little snack before we go to the Mighty Mutton for lunch," he said.

"But after all that?" asked Sarah.

"But immediately after that we'll talk with the mayor."

The server came and gave them their bill, lingering to chat with Sarah.

"I could not help but overhear you mention a vampire. Where were you when you saw such a dreadful creature? Were you visiting the country of Verrara?" he asked.

"No, no! It was just down the road," Sarah answered.

"What! You *must* be mistaken. No vampire could possibly live here," he answered with a nervous laugh. "That's a dangerous thing to say, miss. Dangerous indeed." He paused. "Are you sure? I mean, could it be possible?"

"Oh, I'm pretty sure," Sarah responded. "And thank you for a wonderful breakfast."

Sarah continued pleading all day, but Gumble ignored her. Around midnight the group made its way back to the governor's house, where they were staying during their visit. The governor was already asleep, so Gumble would not be speaking of the vampire tonight. Sarah excused herself and went to her room to brood in frustration.

In her room, she changed into her nightgown and padded barefoot to the sink to wash up before bed. Thaddeus irked her daily, but how could he have no concern over a vampire's presence in a small town? Granted, she knew little about vampires, but she had heard terrible things, and she hated to think of the people in the city acting as cattle to a monster. Sarah balled her fists and repeatedly punched her pillow in frustration.

"Did the face cushion offend you?" asked John in a quiet voice. John and Lucy appeared in the open windowsill.

Sarah flopped on the bed, sighing loudly into her pillow. "No, it's just that Gumble won't listen to me. I warned him that the doctor was a vampire, but he didn't care!"

"Warn? What is a *warn*?" John answered.

Sarah looked at them. The pixies truly wanted to learn; thus, impromptu language lessons arose all the time. "To warn is to bring attention to. To tell someone that danger is near. Remember *danger*?" she asked. Over time Sarah had learned some of the more difficult aspects of teaching pixies. They remained eager to learn and understood secrecy very well; however, despite their diminutive nature, they seemed completely fearless. Thus, *danger* remained a difficult concept to explain. After weeks of examples, she thought she had finally made the point clear.

"*Warn.* I see. A *warn* means that a danger is not currently in our present location, but a danger may soon be within our area, yes?"

"Exactly, John," she said.

John beamed as he flew from the windowsill and landed on her bed. He appeared to be pacing in thought, though the thick comforter made movement difficult.

"But, Sarah, what was the warn about?" he asked.

"The *warning*. The warning was about the vampire of course!" she answered.

"The nice doctor?" John asked again.

"Yes! You were the one who told me that he was a vampire in the first place!"

"I see. I remember telling you that he was a vampire. Some action of his must have missed my attention. Did he threaten? What made him into danger, requiring you to make a warn?" he asked.

"Well, isn't the fact that he is a vampire enough?" Sarah asked.

John looked at Sarah, and then Lucy flew from the window as well. They quickly conversed in Pixish, as Sarah called it, and then looked at her, confused. Sarah understood much of their language already, but, when they spoke quickly, it was difficult to comprehend.

"I think we are both confused. Through our actions *we* created, by some unintentional manner, a warn for you?" she asked.

"Let me explain again. I wanted to *warn* the people of this town that they had a vampire living right under their noses." She paused to see if that made sense to the small creatures. They continued to look blankly at her. "Doesn't a vampire living among humans seem like a danger to the humans to you? Doesn't that seem like something that requires a warning?" Sarah found speaking to the pixies was not helping her already short temper.

"Why would this require a warning? Vampires rarely cause danger to humans of the degree you specified requiring a response in terror," said John.

"What? Vampires drink blood. Vampires fear sunlight and lurk only at night. How is this not a danger?"

The pixies again chattered to one another, intermittently flapping their wings.

"You are correct that vampires fear the sun and drink blood. However, they have coexisted with humans over countless years, and, for the most part, this has been without conflict," said John.

"Even the humans in Verrara live happily with vampires," said Lucy.

"Of course. Humans in Verrara need no warnings, even with the majority of the population being vampire. Vampires rarely kill. From our experience vampires kill much less frequently than humans do. It would be more befitting for you to warn humans that there are other humans in the town than a vampire," John said.

Sarah wanted to contradict them but stopped herself. The pixies had much more experience than she did with vampires. She considered their advice.

Could it be possible? Could he be a doctor who really was helping people but just *happened* to be a vampire? Sarah had studied magical creatures in books for many years, but the pixies had real-life experience. When she thought about it, the doctor provided excellent care. She rubbed her pixie necklace and felt a faint warmth flow through her. She was not ready to accept that vampires were good, but possibly one could be an exception. Thank goodness she had caused no harm.

She looked over her few belongings. They were going back to Grandeur tomorrow. Sarah found she missed the city and was glad the trip was ending, even if they took the long way back. She looked over as her two companions pushed against the glass.

"What are you doing now?"

"Just looking for the second," Lucy replied.

"*The second?*" Sarah asked.

"Of course," John answered. "Anytime we are in a new place we attempt to distinguish at least two ways to escape in order to hastily accomplish departure, preferably three."

Sarah unlocked another window and cranked it open. "There you go, guys."

"Thank you!" Lucy responded. John also expressed his gratitude, and the two pixies disappeared out the window.

"Just be sure to be back before morning. We're returning to Grandeur, and I don't want you guys left behind. Oh, and stay out of trouble," Sarah said.

The two pixies laughed and disappeared into the night.

Chapter 7: Defiance

Jayde spied on Dr. Sangre's clinic. She never saw them leave, though she thought she might have dozed momentarily during the day.

The day came and went, but the clinic showed no activity. The night came, and Jayde still saw nothing change. She worried she might have missed their escape from the city, but she dared not enter the clinic.

Jayde kept pondering her interactions with Cameron and Marie. Both had helped her out without asking for anything in return. Jayde wondered if that was what it was like in a family. Did everyone just look out for each other, not really needing a reason other than being family?

Several hours later, in the blackness of very early morning, Jayde spied a glow coming from the end of the street. She decided to walk toward the glow, only to realize that the glow was coming toward her as well.

Hundreds of people marched in her direction. She had the advantage of darkness, while they were illuminated by the torches they carried. She ducked into an alley and watched the processional pass. Any good thief knew how to disappear before trouble got too close.

"Living right under our noses! Well, we'll show him a thing or two. We're not scared of him. We can take care of our own—we can."

"My brother-in-law actually said the doc fixed his arm up good. Probably put a curse on him without knowing it, he did."

"And who knows what a vampire can really do, you know? Sure he might have fixed my little Ann's gash on her face, but who knows what he was thinking? He probably wanted to suck her dry right in front of us. Oh, and he took his sweet time too. It was like he was being all careful and whatnot with the gash on her face. Probably wanted just to figure out how much blood she could spare."

Jayde could not believe it. A mob. Jayde slipped into the crowd to see what would happen. Maybe she could change their minds. Maybe Cameron could magic them away, and he would not have to leave town.

The crowd advanced toward the clinic. Jayde worked her way to the front. The discussions remained the same. All spoke of the danger of vampires. Many in the crowd had been treated by Dr. Sangre. All the stories centered on someone being cared for and what the doctor could have done.

The mob arrived at Dr. Sangre's clinic.

The crowd quieted upon reaching their destination. The mayor of the town had apparently helped organize the group. He knocked on the clinic door.

"Come on out!" he shouted. The mob added shouts at the closed door and the blackness inside the clinic.

The door opened, and Cameron walked out, accompanied by Marie at the front of their clinic. The mob seemed somewhat unsure how to react. The hunted person was supposed to cower or flee in terror. Several of the veterans shouted "Vampire!" at Cameron to rekindle the anger, but most in the group seemed taken aback at his unassuming and calm demeanor. The mayor took control again.

"Okay, Sangre, your secret is out. We know what you are! You are to leave this town at once," he said. A few in the group yelled obscenities. Others just yelled.

Cameron looked over the crowd with regret and took a deep breath. He glanced at Marie, her face clearly revealing disdain.

"You know," Cameron began, "I've been here for quite a few years now."

Someone in the crowd shouted, "Too long," and another yelled, "Not anymore," but Cameron continued through the interruptions.

"I've been here ten years to be exact. I know you recognize my face. But the thing is I know your faces as well. By the way, Mrs. Brown, how is that giant cut that you had on your thigh from that slip last week?"

Mrs. Brown, one of the few women in the front of the crowd, looked embarrassed to be singled out, but she said quietly, "It's just fine. Just. Fine." The light before dawn had intensified, and people in the crowd were distinguishable from one another.

"Good, good," he continued. "You see, I've done nothing to justify any of this. I cared for every person who came into my clinic. Not just to improve health but to improve lives. Oh, that reminds me. Marcus, how is your sore throat doing?"

Marcus was the best baker in the town, and most in the mob were heartbroken when he had to close shop for a few weeks because he was suffering from a horrible case of "glass-throat." By now the mob was quiet, and all eyes were on Marcus as he meekly stated, "Much better now."

The faces that had been gray were showing more color in the early glow. People began glancing at their fellow neighbors, surprised by the number they recognized in the crowd.

"Good, good. I thought my treatment would work. I'm sorry that I have somehow broken the trust of those who I have treated in town. I never lied to any of you. But I did not come out in the open with my little secret. I suppose it was wrong of me to not be completely honest with you."

Immediately persons in the crowd shouted, "Dang right!" and "Murderer!" in response, though without their earlier enthusiasm.

Cameron continued, this time actually walking into the crowd of people holding pitchforks, torches, and bludgeons. "You see, I was worried. I was worried that if I was completely honest with you, perhaps some of you might see me in a different light. Oh, Phil, I haven't seen you for six weeks. Did that broken bone I set for you mend?"

The man he had just walked by folded his hands behind his back, hiding the large cudgel he was holding. "Better than ever, Dr. Sangre."

"Good, good. Great to hear. You see, I thought if you knew that I was different than all of you in some way, perhaps you might treat me differently."

A voice rang out. "You never told anyone that you kill people and drink their blood!" The crowd chorused its agreement.

Cameron paused in his slow walk through the crowd. "You are right. I never said that. But since I arrived, have there been any unexplained deaths? Can anyone here tell me of a single grisly murder or dried-up corpse?"

"What about Susie?" came a cry from the crowd.

"Ah, you mean the Dundermans' little girl who fell off the roof? Do you mean the adorable child who appeared in my office nearly dead, coated in her own blood? The one who was rushed to my clinic at midnight, after looking at stars in the middle of the night? Yes, I will admit, that I did have to use some of my"—Cameron paused, picking his words carefully—"less human attributes on her. She definitely was nearly dead when she got here. She had already lost one-third of her total blood volume. She was surely going to die, and I guess the group who brought her in knew it. How is little Susie doing now, Jack?"

Mr. Dunderman solemnly walked to Cameron. He dropped his torch. "She just turned eight last month. She wants to be a doctor," he mumbled.

"Oh? Well, I will leave that decision up to her, though being a physician can be quite a demanding job. Sometimes your efforts go unappreciated. But I suppose you are all correct. I am sure, if I was honest with you, then you would have treated me with kindness and lovingly incorporated me into your community. I am sure that would have changed nothing. Maybe next time I'll try to be more honest from the beginning."

The crowd was quiet. The last few torches were extinguished. Hushed murmurs went through the crowd, as the people dissipated. The mayor, realizing what had just happened, spoke up for the crowd.

"Dr. Sangre, maybe you did help many people, but that doesn't change the facts."

"And what might those be?" Cameron answered.

"You *are* a vampire. Do you deny it?"

The crowd awaited his answer in perfect silence.

"No."

"All right then," the mayor said. The fear that had left his face while Cameron had spoken returned. "I want you to leave the town, Dr. Sangre, and I don't want you to come back."

Cameron looked over the large mob. People gazed back at him with kind but nervous faces, many in complete terror. The mayor seized the moment.

"All those in favor of kicking him out of town?'"

At first, only a few ayes were heard. Then more added their votes. Eventually nearly all in the crowd had stated their desire.

"All those in favor of allowing him to stay say nay."

Marie barked out nay in a scornful voice. One small nay was heard in the back of the crowd, as well as a quiet nay from Mr. Dunderman.

Cameron looked over his neighbors and patients with a grim face. He stood his ground and folded his arms while surveying the crowd, his face a mask of disappointment. The predawn twilight at his back made him appear gray in color.

The first edge of the sun peeked over the horizon and illuminated the crowd. Instinctively the people in the mob blocked some of the sun while they looked at Cameron. He remained unmoving in front of them, his arms still crossed, a grim expression on his face. He stood defiantly.

Only after a few minutes had passed did someone in the crowd realize that Cameron had not moved. Jayde ran up from the back of the crowd and looked at him closely. With the sun at his back his features were hardly discernible. He looked gray, and only when she actually touched him did she realize what had truly happened. He had turned to stone.

"All he wanted was to live in peace with you!" Marie cried out. "He helped nearly every one of you ungrateful wretches, asking little in return, and yet you still could not accept him. You could not accept the fact that maybe he wanted nothing more than to be part of a community. Well, to hell with all of you. You lost out on having one of the most brilliant, talented, and kindest doctors ever in your lives. Well, it is not us who are losing out by leaving town as much as you. Be gone! All of you! Your job here is done."

With that, the crowd dispersed. A few stragglers touched the doctor, thinking his stony appearance a trick. Marie shooed away the few remaining people, leaving only the Cameron statue staring in the direction of town. His expression was etched into a mixture of betrayal and frustration.

Jayde watched, shocked. Living on the street had cemented toughness into her core. She had not cried in years, yet now she could feel the tears falling down her face. She watched Marie return to the clinic, and Jayde followed her. The clinic looked empty. Marie was nowhere to be found. Jayde walked to the back and saw a door leading outside. A horse and cart had already been joined, but no Marie was here. In the cart, behind the seat, rested a large chest.

The chest was about five feet square covered with drawers on all sides. From her vantage point, Jayde could see that drawers were even on top of the chest. It shimmered like heat waves on the horizon. As Jayde got closer, the wardrobe grew in size, and the hundreds of small drawers now changed in size as well. Jayde got nervous, backing away from the chest. It shrank in size, and the drawers again looked unassuming. She walked toward it, and once more it expanded in size, this time a different drawer enlarged in size and shape. Yet, as she walked away, it shrank to normal size.

"Weird," Jayde said to herself.

"Isn't it?" replied Marie.

Jayde yelped in surprise. She had not heard Marie sneak up behind her.

"Did you enjoy the show?" asked Marie.

"Not really," she mumbled.

"That makes two of us. What a bunch of ingrates."

"It's not fair," said Jayde.

"No, it's not. It never is. I can see why Cameron likes you so much. You saw the same reality as the rest of the village, yet you came to a different conclusion."

Jayde sniffed and gazed at Marie with a puzzled expression.

"You're not the only one he's helped. He's been helping people since he got here. Some just can't see past the word *vampire*. Yet you came to the conclusion that a great injustice has just occurred. Someone good, honorable, and compassionate was just condemned for reasons out of his control. *Vampires are bad. Witches are evil. Trolls are mean and kill people for fun. Mermaids lure you into the water to kill you. Werewolves rip off your limbs. Gargoyles will swoop down and steal your children.* All these are stereotypes, nothing more. Yet you see Cam's virtues."

"But people are smart. How come he didn't just come out with it and tell everyone that he is a good vampire?" Jayde asked.

"He did, in his own way. Jayde, one person can be smart. Unfortunately people in a group are usually stupid. I have never understood what happens when angry people get together that causes their brains to turn into mush, but it seems to happen every time." Marie hoisted a heavy examination table onto the chest. The table shrunk in size and slipped into one of the drawers in the cabinet.

"How'd you do that?" Jayde asked.

"This?" Marie answered, grabbing a bundle larger than her leg. She made a gesture, the bundle flashed white for an instant before shrinking into another drawer.

"Yes. That," Jayde said, gaping.

"It's just a simple modification spell. The chest has all the imbued magic. I just channel it."

"Whoa. I don't suppose you could show me how to, you know, learn some of that magic?" Jayde asked. She then realized Marie would not be around long enough to teach her anything. "Where will you go?"

"Oh, I have wanted to live in a big city for some time now, but Cameron said he always got nervous in big cities, so we never tried one. I think I would like a place with a little more diversity. I need to see if Grandeur can live up to its name. And, yes, I would have been happy to show you all sorts of insights into the world of magic, but you have your life here, I suppose."

Marie finished packing in minutes.

Jayde looked down at the container of chocolate that Marie had given her. It was her only possession. Marie picked up the large stone statue that was Cameron last and secured him onto the back of the trailer. She looped stout ropes around what had once been Dr. Sangre. She threw a large canvas tarp over the entire contents of the cart.

"It was a pleasure getting to know you a bit, Jayde. Best of luck to you in the future," she said. "I think I will just have one last look through the clinic to make sure I didn't forget anything."

Jayde watched Marie walk toward the clinic, then looked back at the cart, hiding a smile. Marie glanced at Jayde through a window, doing the same.

Chapter 8: Bozrac

Three men, two enormous and one small, waited in their hideout for their boss to arrive.

"We should call our gang 'the Slashers.'"

"Nah, we should go with 'the Thunder-Killers.'"

"There are only three of us, and you're both idiots, I don't need a special name for two stupid idiots," said the third, a small, slender man.

"But when we get famous, we gotta have a name, right?"

"No."

"How 'bout the 'Jail Breakers'?"

"What? We ain't in jail. Not yet at least."

A knock came at the door, and, before they could answer, a frail old lady let herself in.

"Would any of you like some cookies and milk? I brought them over, since I know how hungry you get," said the heavily wrinkled woman.

"Thank you, Mrs. Crass," they said in unison.

Mrs. Crass was their landlord, cleaning lady, cook, and the leader of the small gang. As far as the men could tell, she was also completely insane. She tolerated no vulgarity. According to her, she absolutely abhorred violence. She enforced her rules by slapping offenders with her wooden cooking spoon, cursing, and plotting the occasional murder. The men had learned to tolerate their crazy leader, since she had never steered them wrong.

"Did you get it?" she asked.

"We got it, Mrs. Crass, just like you said," the huge thug answered, dumping the box onto the floor with a *thump*. The smaller grunt winced, as the big thug laughed. The box let out a loud growl.

"Oh, my, isn't it lovely," she said, looking at the blackened box, as if it were a delicate vase. She then casually walked over and soundly smacked the thug across the temple with her wooden spoon.

"Didn't you think that it should be handled with care? Hmm? You dimwitted worthless sack of vomit." She smacked him across the head with the spoon again for good measure.

The sight of the elderly lady reaching up to hit the monstrous man with a wooden spoon caused the other large man to snicker, which rewarded him with a spooning across the knuckles.

"Well, at least you got it, and you managed to get it here without breaking it or opening it. That, in and of itself, is a miracle," said Mrs. Crass with a broad grin.

She put down her spoon and brought the thugs milk and cookies on three separate small trays. All three sat in a row on chairs a bit too small for two of them. They each dunked their cookies in the milk. She really did make fantastic cookies. Even street thugs could appreciate that.

"So whatcha gonna do with it, Mrs. Crass?"

"Do with it?" squeaked Crass. One could never tell when she would have a mood swing or just smack someone with a spoon for no reason. She smacked the man for no reason.

"I'll find out if this weapon is worth three years of searching, hiding, and stealing. If it is, then I'll kill the man who ruined my life. I've spent decades hunting him, but he always gets away. Well, now I finally have something that he can't squirm away from," she said.

The three goons looked at each other. They all shrugged. They rarely understood their leader's actions.

All three thugs watched as Mrs. Crass carefully handled the black box. She opened it and pulled out a cage. The cage appeared to be made of silver, but the bars glowed faintly as well. The thugs pushed against each other behind Mrs. Crass, trying to peer in the cage. Despite the fact that they could see through the bars, no light penetrated the cage. A pair of half-crescent slits peered from inside.

"Kill the candles," she said.

The sudden blackness made even the hardened thugs nervous. As their eyes became used to the darkness, a nervous feeling oozed into all of them, like spiders inching down their backs. It took a while to identify the phenomenon, but it finally dawned on them: the thing absorbed light. Normally the goons were too stupid to get nervous, but something felt wrong, very wrong. All four of them continued to stare.

Mrs. Crass collected herself first. "Do you agree that you are trapped?" she whispered to the cage.

The thugs looked at one another in the dim light. She looked at the cage when speaking.

A voice came from the darkness of the cage. "Aye" was all it said.

"Do you agree to transfer your servitude to me if I release you?" she asked, sweat trickling down her temple.

"What be your demands of servitude, mum?"

"Three tasks of my choosing," said Mrs. Crass.

"One!" shot back the caged thing.

"Two tasks, then you get your freedom," said Mrs. Crass.

A low growl came from the cage. The cage strained outwardly but remained intact.

"I agree."

"Do I have your oath? Your oath as a bozrac that you will obey until the tasks are completed?" she asked.

"Yes."

Mrs. Crass trembled as she slowly unlatched the box. Two glowing small golden crescent-shaped eyes came out of the cage.

The eyes then moved in a blur of speed and appeared next to one of the small glasses of milk. A lapping noise ensued, though they could see only the strange golden glow of the two half crescents.

"It's been a bitter year of entrapment. It's a long year when you can't have a spot of milk." It sounded almost cheery.

Mrs. Crass uncharacteristically gasped. The thugs had never seen her scared or excited. She seemed both. She had always acted like a senile, crazy, cantankerous old biddy as long as they had known her. For some reason, her excitement made them nervous.

"You are the bozrac?" she asked reverently.

A strange purring noise came from the direction of the milk. "I am *a* bozrac. I don't believe I am the last, but, even for those of us from the abyss, we are few. I am Finneus. My friends call me Finn. I can't say that gnome was all that friendly to me. He kept me in that bloody box for over a year."

"Well, Mrs. Crass is surely your friend, Mr. Finn," she said.

The eyes blinked.

Mrs. Crass felt an icy chill pass through her chest and stopped breathing for an instant. The creature had passed through her.

"Well, don't you just have the nicest of words, Mrs. Leynstra Crass? But why use me for the schemes you've planned?"

Mrs. Crass croaked out a nervous "Oh." No one had used her first name, Leynstra, for years. She had worked quite hard to make that name disappear. She had not uttered her own first name to a soul in over three decades, yet the creature had plucked *Leynstra* out of her mind as easily as an apple from a tree. She collected herself. The creature continued.

"I agreed to two requests, and then you'll release me. I'm bound by oath, however much I'd like to break it. So tell me your two requests, or shall I extract them myself?" Finn asked.

The thugs sat quietly in the back of the room, too anxious to breathe. The darkness and confusing conversation was more than one of the thugs could handle. He ran to the fireplace, stirred up some embers, and relit a candle. He then relit the rest of the candles and let the glow grow till again he could see everything in the room. Neither Finneus nor Mrs. Crass said anything. The room looked exactly the same, except for the bozrac. When they looked at it, all but his glowing eyes remained hidden in blackness. The bozrac seemed to create its own darkness. Slowly the darkness around it dissolved and blurred. The inky darkness coalesced; a small black cat remained.

"Ah, material form, how quaint. You seem to know enough to keep your skin on the right side of your body. For now."

"I have always thought it is better to prevent trouble than to deal with it once it is upon you," said Mrs. Crass.

"Really? Obtaining me is a poor way to avoid trouble. Though you do seem to be cloaking your thoughts much better now. Perhaps you do know what you're doing, but nobody is perfect. Right, Leynstra?" said Finn.

The goons stood dumbfounded, as the small cat and Mrs. Crass conversed. The cantankerous old lady never showed respect to anyone. The bozrac was nothing more than a cat? All that work and sneaking around for a stupid cat? Granted the cat could talk, but, still, it looked like an inky-black kitten, nothing more. Normally anything that even hinted at a lack of respect toward Mrs. Crass got a wooden spoon to the skull. Yet here she tried to walk quietly through a field of dry sticks with this creature.

"The instructions are to come only from me, not from these idiots," she added quickly.

"I certainly hope so. They have only blank sheets where thoughts should hide," he said.

"And you won't hurt me as long as you are here?" she asked.

"I'll try to play nice, but one oath a day is my limit," he said.

"I'm serious, Finn. You may be out of your box, but I could make one request for you to go back inside, and that would be that. I'd ship you right to that gnome or worse. Now I want you to promise that you won't hurt me," she said, her voice quavering slightly.

The small fluffy cat vanished in a blur of black smoke, then appeared behind the thugs on the table, where it finished off another of their glasses of forgotten milk.

"As I said, I gave you an oath to release me, unless you would like me to bind it in blood?" asked the creature.

"With the promise you agree to all the conditions I've listed," she said.

"Which one for the seal? Or did you bring three for me to have a selection? I'll assume you're not choosing yourself."

"I have to choose now? But you haven't done anything yet," she said.

The thugs looked at each other nervously.

"I'll make it easy on you. Which one of the louts dropped the crate on the ground?" he asked.

The thugs looked at one another. Two pointed at the largest of the three.

"Thanks, boys. Yah just saved your skins," Finn said. The bozrac then pounced.

The man swatted at the little kitten, but his arms went directly through the creature. It was as if he were repelling fog. The head of the small cat melted directly into the man's chest. The man screamed in agony and flailed on the ground. Each time his body rolled over the bozrac, its body would disappear in a puff of smoke, then reappear when he rolled onto his back again.

The thug rolled on the ground. The creature occasionally appeared from inside his chest, a sinister bloody smile on its face. The bozrac purred while killing the man, who gasped for air. Tears poured from his face. His body twitched in agony. He could not breathe. The other two goons normally would have thought it humorous—a grown man crying because of a small black kitten—but neither laughed. After two minutes, the small fluffy face of the bozrac emerged from the man's chest. Blood dripped from the bozrac's mouth.

"The deal is struck," said the bozrac.

Mrs. Crass took control again, her usual anger pouring out at the two remaining thieves.

"You two just let Mrs. Crass do the thinking. Do what you're told, and you'll get everything you deserve. In the meantime, I have to figure out what to do."

Chapter 9: Ambush

The first day of travel crawled by for Marie. After a terrible morning of betrayal by the entire town, she forced herself to drive her wagon for twelve hours, only stopping to rest, feed, and water the horses.

Marie stopped briefly at a roadside inn for directions and supplies. Grandeur was several days away, and she had no desire to be on the road longer than necessary.

She directed the horses down a dark pass, traveling into thick woods, and she could feel the forest envelop her.

The horses whinnied as they took the narrow path through the trees. The woods itself seemed to be waiting for something. Despite the size of the forest, only the cart made noise.

The darkness loomed. The crescent moon provided little light to guide her path, yet Marie pushed on without difficulty.

Marie extracted some dried meat, bread, cheese, and a large flask of water. From the back of the cart, she heard a loud gurgling noise. In the silence of the woods, it echoed eerily.

"You know, Jayde," Marie said, "I have plenty of food, if you would like some."

Jayde froze.

"I know that hot chocolate is good, but it really is not proper nutrition."

Jayde poked out her head from under the canvas. Marie looked right at her.

"Hello, Jayde," she said.

"Hiya," said Jayde. "How long have you known?"

"Long enough," Marie answered.

"And you didn't kick me out because … ?"

"Cameron wouldn't have wanted me to. Have some food," Marie said. She broke off a large piece of cheese and bread.

Jayde eagerly wolfed it down.

"How long were you and Cameron together?" asked Jayde, her mouth full.

"I've traveled with him for nine years now. Before you get any ideas, I'm a human. He's a vampire. *That* type of relationship doesn't work," said Marie.

"I didn't say anything," Jayde said.

"You had a look."

"A look?" Jayde asked.

"Yes, a look. To understand me and Cameron, you have to understand what happened. I'm a sage, more specifically a war sage. I found out at an early age that I had more Talent than most," said Marie.

"Talent?"

"Talent is one of hundreds of terms all meaning one thing. *Magic*," said Marie.

Jayde jumped to the front seat next to Marie, eager to learn more. Marie continued to guide the horses forward while they talked.

"All people have some minute ability. A rare few have more natural ability than others. I'm blessed—or cursed, depending on your perspective—to have a Talent for essence bending. This means I can manipulate anything I touch for a very short time. In battle that means, as long I can put my hands on something, or someone, I usually win the fight."

"So where does Cameron fit in?" Jayde asked.

"A long time ago I worked as a mercenary, taking a variety of random jobs. I was hired by the Tenland army to research Verrara, the country to the distant east. Rumors about thousands of vampires dying—more important, the vampire king's death—had reached Tenland. The city of Haynis is far in the northernmost part of Tenland, but our country has been at war with Zantia for nearly two centuries. Vampires, and all of Verrara, the country to our east, flat-out refused to join in the war. But with the death of the vampire king, many people thought this could change.

"Unfortunately no emissaries from Tenland to Verrara had returned after a year. They hired me to find out what had happened. I had no desire to become one of the missing humans in the land of vampires, but I had been hired to obtain information, not as an emissary. I simply needed to stay in the shadows and observe.

"In less than a week after arriving in Verrara, despite my considerable fighting ability, a group of vampires captured me.

They held humans captive, using us for our blood and bleeding us frequently. I became part of their 'flock.' We had a dismal existence, until Cameron rescued us. I found out that Cameron had been trying to help maintain order and peace in Verrara for nearly a year. After the death of the king, the country of Verrara had exploded into chaos."

"I thought Cameron was just a doctor," said Jayde.

"Cameron is more than just a doctor and more than a normal vampire as well. He never told me what had caused thousands of vampires to die in one day, but apparently a human had been responsible. It had something to do with the war between Zantia and the world, but I don't know any more about that. This single event shattered the trust that had been forged for years between vampires and humans living together in Verrara. Groups of rogue vampires—like the ones who had captured me—had appeared all over Verrara.

"After a year of failure trying to reunite humans and vampires, Cameron had made many enemies. The newly elected king enjoyed having humans subservient, and Cameron's continued involvement created trouble. Thus, Cameron had a bounty on his head. He had planned on leaving Verrara but luckily rescued me before he left.

"I traveled with him from then on. He saved me from a fate worse than death, and there is *nothing* I wouldn't do for him. Cameron is special, even for a vampire.

"After fleeing Verrara, Cameron needed to stay away from any place with vampires. He has been attacked several times, as he moved from place to place. Ultimately we ended up in Haynis, which seemed perfect, until a seer predicted he would save a young girl with potential, who we believe is you."

"What is so special about me?" asked Jayde.

"We believe you may be one of the—wait, I heard something. Get out of the cart. Quick," Marie said. They had just entered a large clearing in the pass through the forest. She led the horses to a huge tree and quickly secured them. She pulled Jayde into the woods away from the cart. Marie held a finger to her lips. Marie sat on a log and motioned for Jayde to do the same. They sat side by side, just under the cover of darkness.

Minutes passed.

"Stay here, stay quiet, and DO NOT leave this area, okay?" Marie whispered to Jayde. Her voice indicated this was not a question.

Jayde nodded. Marie put her hand on Jayde's shoulder and gave her a reassuring squeeze. Warmth flowed into the girl, after Marie had squeezed her shoulder. Jayde sat obediently on the log, hidden in the darkness. Marie disappeared into the black woods.

Jayde watched the cart. She strained her eyes but could not find Marie. After a few minutes, movement appeared on the clearing's edge. A man appeared. He paused. Six more men materialized and walked forward. They all had clubs, except for the leader, who held a sword. They slowly surrounded the cart. The horses nervously stomped as the men approached, pulling against the line securing them to the tree.

One of them lifted the tarp with his cudgel and grinned.

"Big haul, boss," he said, his voice gravelly in the darkness.

"Marl, be quiet. The cart didn't get here by itself," said another.

"Ain't no one around. They heard you stomping around and left ages ago," said a third.

"Quiet," said the leader. He peered into the forest.

Jayde was sure he must have seen her, but his glance continued past her. He looked back at the cart. The others busied themselves untying the various knots holding down the tarp.

"All right, you louts, pack up everything you can carry and get out of here. Something ain't sitting right with this," he said.

Jayde saw Marie walk to the edge of the clearing and whisper something to herself. A faint glow of light surrounded her. She walked into the clearing, making no effort to conceal herself. She made it halfway to the horses before she was spotted.

"What have we here? Boys, looks like we might have a bit more fun than we thought, eh?" said the leader. "Lady, you should've just stayed in the woods."

"She just wanted to meet some new friends, boss. And we're real friendly," said one brute, walking toward Marie. His grin broadened, showing yellow teeth at odd angles.

"I'll say this slowly with small words, so all of you can understand it. Get. Off. My. Cart. And. Leave. Now!" Marie said.

"We're not letting one little waif tell us what to do! Listen, you little wench, you should've stayed hidden in the forest. Coming out of your hole was your last mistake," said the leader.

The other men seemed emboldened by their leader's confidence. They formed a half circle around Marie, with the forest and Jayde to her back. Marie made no effort to prevent their move.

"Rough her up, but don't kill her. I think we could all have some fun with her," the leader said.

"Get back in der woods," the largest man with the gravelly voice whispered to Marie.

Before she could respond, two of the men came at Marie with their clubs. What they lacked in skill they made up for with their massive bulk. One swung a spiked club toward her head. Marie casually leaned to the side and dodged the blow. The second swung right behind the first with his staff, and Marie did the splits. The staff barely cleared her head. The two looked at each other and laughed, clearly surprised by their prey's agility. The one with the club held out his arm in a gesture to allow the guy with the staff to go first. The other shook his head and indicated they should go together.

Jayde glimpsed a broad smile on Marie's face.

The two came at Marie with renewed vigor. One swung his staff quickly in broad passes. She moved little, yet each blow missed. The thug became frustrated with his inability to connect, and swung harder and harder, but she continued to sidestep every attack. He then ran next to her and swung a crushing overhand blow. Marie dodged, stepped close to him, and pushed against his stomach; the brute flew twenty feet straight back and collided with a tree, falling unconscious—or dead.

The other men observed this, and their laughter ceased.

"No more one at a time?" Marie asked with a grin on her face. "Come on. Surely a rock troll and five grown men can take a little waif like me, right?"

The men formed a large semicircle around her.

Marie again made no effort to prevent herself from being surrounded. She crouched in front of the group with her legs apart and knees slightly bent. "Next."

The remaining men glanced around, apprehensive. The same large man pleaded with her again. "You run now. Go in woods. No come out. You be safe. Me no like hurt you," he murmured. The other men seemed not to notice.

"Just kill her, you idiots!" said the leader, still behind the fray and close to the cart.

Marie backed into an immense oak directly behind her. Jayde could not see her as the monstrous tree blocked her vision. Marie had to be in trouble. Jayde grabbed a tree branch and began sneaking up to the clearing.

Two of the men had entered the forest to prevent Marie from escaping into the woods. The other three blocked her escape from the front, but Marie did not try to run. She waited.

One lunged in and swung a sideways blow at her chest. Marie dove to the ground and kicked out one of his legs at the knee. A loud popping noise was quickly followed by a bellow from the man who went down in a shriek. The rest of the men attacked. Jayde saw a whir of clubs. Marie continued to dart and dodge. Her movements were erratic yet graceful. The men came from all sides, but Marie continued to spin and dodge every strike. The cudgels repeatedly came inches from braining her, yet Jayde heard a feminine laugh again and again. Marie was amazing, avoiding the four in a small area, with the leader hanging back. She seemed to dance while she fought—and she still had a grin plastered on her face.

The men rushed her. Jayde saw only a blur of punches and kicks. Bodies flew out of the clearing, and only the leader and another remained. The last man stood up straight. Jayde thought, if this guy had any brains, he would figure out that he was outmatched and run.

"Why you not leave? Why you make Marl have to smash you? Go now! Run now an' leave, then me not have to kill you," the last man said. He threw down his cloak. His visage changed right in front of Jayde. The skin on his face chipped off. Parts of his face fell to the ground like a broken mask. Under the mask, his features became jagged and angular. His hands similarly cracked and fell to pieces around him. They lost their flesh color and became ashen. His fingers lengthened until they were each about a foot in length. His arms hung down and touched the ground, though he was still erect. His fingers dragged across the dirt. All around him were pieces of what appeared to be skin-colored ceramic.

Jayde had lived her entire life in Haynis. She had heard of vampires, werewolves, and elves, but, until recently, she had thought they were mostly stories. Cameron had put a small crack in her understanding of reality. The thing in front of her shattered it.

The monster slowly walked toward Marie. "Why you no leave?" it said to itself. It let out a sigh that sounded like distant thunder. "You die soon. Tell me how you know me troll?" the thing asked, its voice impossibly low and grating.

Jayde winced just listening to it.

Marie seemed unruffled by his transformation. She lightly bounced on the balls of her feet.

"It's obvious," she said. "First, the gravel, your food, which came out of your cloak was marble, and there's really no marble anywhere near here. Second, though your disguise is actually quite good, your teeth still look like a perfect row of rocks in your mouth. Granted, that is exactly what they are, but, in this group, you were the only one with more than three teeth, and all of yours were gleaming white and square. Finally you still walk with the hunched gait of a rock troll."

"Ah," said the troll. "T'anks a lot!" he said. To Jayde he actually sounded sincere. "It sad I have to kill you. I not want to kill you. You fight good. You best man-t'ing I fight."

"Thank you," she said, continuing to circle. Her eyes darted around. The leader of the group had disappeared into the woods. It was just her and the troll. Marie continued her slow circle, but now a group of trees flanked her back.

The troll exploded at Marie. His long arms enveloped her and the tree behind her. Marie jumped up six feet and shot over the troll. The stone appendages crushed the tree to splinters and spun. It launched at her in a flurry of whipping punches. The long appendages gave the troll an extended reach, as it swung in lightning rapidity. Marie danced backward, bouncing off her hands and feet with equal dexterity.

"*Oi!* You quick! You hard to catch. You run now? I not be able to kill you, if I not catch you. Boss won't get mad if you just go now. Go now please?" asked the troll. The creature truly seemed to not want to kill her, though its actions suggested otherwise.

Marie ran to her cart, disappeared under the tarp, and reappeared in a blink, holding a small vial in her hand.

"You get arms?" the troll asked. "Dat good. You need all help you get." It laughed. "Me get arms too." It swung at a tree and felled the large sapling in one strike. It picked up the tree and hurled it at Marie.

Marie dove away and bounced back to her feet. She approached the troll and shattered the vial on the ground at his feet.

"What dis?" it asked.

As if in response, vines shot out from the ground and surrounded the troll. The clinging vines grabbed at its arms and legs. The troll pulled and twisted, snapping the vines repeatedly, yet more instantly replaced the ones he snapped. In seconds the troll was wrapped in the clinging vines and unable to move, struggling in vain. Only the creature's head remained uncovered by the vines.

"*Oi*, dat be good trick!" it said, sounding happy, and in fact the troll had a broad grin on its face. "Me not have to kill you now."

Jayde ran toward the clearing with a cheer. "You did it!" she yelled, running for Marie. She looked over at Jayde from across the clearing. Marie's smile disappeared and a look of horror covered her face.

"Jayde, look out!" she yelled.

Jayde had run from her concealment and then tripped on a root.

While Marie was distracted, one of the vines from the rock troll extended and wrapped around her ankle and held her fast.

Jayde stopped and looked from her place on the ground. The leader had been hiding in the shadows where Jayde had emerged. He was on her in an instant, sword poised to kill. Jayde saw him swing the killing blow.

The sword halted its descent halfway down. A black blade had stopped the swordsman's killing blow. A figure materialized behind the swordsman, who seemed as surprised as Jayde.

"Even for pathetic scum like you, that's pretty low," said the newcomer.

The figure in black wrenched the swordsman's arm behind his back, and Jayde heard the crunch of bones. The leader screamed in pain and tried to pull away, but the person held him fast. The figure in black grabbed a hunk of the leader's black hair and wrenched the thief's head to the side. He then bit deep into the neck of the man. Jayde was immobile, transfixed by the horror in front of her. Jayde could see the color slowly drain away in the face of the leader, till he turned a shade of sickly white and then groaned as he collapsed to the ground.

Jayde turned from the corpse in front of her and ran toward Marie. She had unraveled herself from the vine and quietly watched.

"Well now, wasn't that exciting?" Marie said calmly.

"Marie," Jayde said, "what should we do? Do you have any more magic potions? Can you stop that thing?"

"Oh, I doubt I could stop *that* thing," Marie said, stepping away from another vine.

Jayde turned to look, but the figure in black had disappeared. "Where did it go?"

Marie still seemed unconcerned as she rummaged through her cart, pulling out a small cloth. She poured water from a pouch over the cloth, all while occasionally looking at Jayde.

"She'll figure it out sooner or later, you know," Marie said to the back of the cart.

"I know."

"Oh, just come out. We can't leave her behind either way," Marie said.

"Toss me the towel first," he said.

Marie threw the towel to the darkness, where it disappeared behind the cart. The voice sounded familiar. Jayde ran around to the back of the cart. There stood Cameron, his face and shirt completely soaked in blood.

Jayde watched him clean off the blood and peel off his bloody shirt. Marie threw him a fresh one, and he quickly dressed. He scrubbed at his face till most of the blood was gone and looked at Jayde. He appeared nervous.

"Cameron?" she asked.

"Yes, Jayde, it's me," he answered.

"Cameron!" she said and launched herself at him, hugging him tightly.

Cameron's face beamed, as he returned the hug.

"I told you that she was a special kid," said Marie.

"Okay. Okay, you were right, Marie. She's a thief and a schemer. But she's a keeper."

Chapter 10: Flee

Sarah set up her small tent, while chatting with John and Lucy. Thaddeus's caravan had finally stopped for the day. The pixies' language skills had improved immensely over the weeks, although they enjoyed teaching Sarah their musical Pixish more than learning Sarah's "human talk." Sarah understood quite a bit, which surprised the pixies. The smallest changes in intonation or gesture greatly changed the meaning. The pixies quickly realized that, in "human talk," hand gestures meant nothing. On the other hand, Pixish involved the entire body, including their wings. Sarah tried her best, but speaking it required her to occasionally jump in the air flapping her arms, which meant she only practiced in the company of her small friends. Also she had become quite careful only to have conversations far from where people might overhear.

John spun in the air in front of her, laughing. Lucy was giggling too. Sarah waited to find out what she had accidentally said. She had supposedly asked if they would like her to get them some food. However, in Pixish, "food" was always "foodstuffs," for some reason. The pixies' musical laughter slowly faded.

"Oh, I readily accept your offer, Sarah. Though I do think that your lifetime aspirations should be elevated," John said. Lucy just laughed more in response.

"Okay, what did I say this time?" Sarah asked.

"I assume you were proposing to John that you would obtain delicious foodstuffs for him?" asked Lucy.

"See! Lucy understood what I said," Sarah said.

"Yes, yes, indeed," John said, while laughing. "However, you paused at the wrong time, and you spun to the left, not to the right."

"Ha, ha, very funny, John. Now what did I say?"

John smiled at Lucy. "You just proposed that I can eat on you, and you would be my food-stool," he said.

"Hilarious," she said sarcastically. "Are you two hungry?" The pixies nodded, and Sarah left her tent to get some provisions. The journey home had taken longer than Sarah had expected, though, as always with Thaddeus, the food remained plentiful.

She set up a few tiny plates and bowls for the small creatures, and dished out helpings she had pilfered from Thaddeus's table. John flew over and sat on the edge of her bowl while they ate.

"Hey, Sarah, what's it like being a human? You guys are always inventing devices and changing your environments. And what's it like to be so big all the time?" John said, hovering in front of her face.

Sarah laughed, the pixies' odd questions had become a natural part of their interactions.

"Well, John, I'm not sure how to answer that. Humans like to create. I suppose some more than others. We also learn from our predecessors, so that each time we make something, it is hopefully better than before. But humans are driven by more than objects. Emotion plays huge roles in what drives us. Emotions and experiences shape us. Two humans can experience the same tragedy, yet react completely differently," Sarah said.

Sarah thought back to a few years earlier. At first anger had fueled her. She had thought becoming the servant of a refugee from Zantia would have helped in her goal toward revenge. She had come to dislike Thaddeus but so did nearly every other individual who came in contact with the man. He was not forthcoming with any information about Zantia. She had tried, but he never gave her any indication that he knew anything about the war or how she could fight against whatever evil had taken her family from her. She had no clue why her house had been targeted or how to find more information. Her desire for vengeance faded with time. However, she continued to feel a pull toward something unknown. She could always sense a longing within her that was difficult to describe.

Sarah felt a twinge of sadness, thinking about her parents and the house fire. She loved her new pixie friends, but emotional complexities seem foreign to them. Pixies trusted everyone implicitly. If some creature came to a troop of pixies and devoured half, Sarah figured the surviving half would move on, never looking back.

At first Sarah wanted to find out who had destroyed her family and to make them pay. How do you explain the desire for revenge to creatures who barely understand the concepts of danger and deceit? Her family, her safety, and what remained of her innocence had been ripped and burned from her that night.

Sarah no longer desired revenge. But she could not deny the tugging sensation she felt. Sometimes she thought it was loneliness, sometimes homesickness, but other times she could feel a specific direction she should go. She had felt this especially strongly in Haynis. Maybe it was just wanderlust. She had lived most of her life in a small cabin near the woods. Now she could finally go out and explore the world. Sarah realized how deeply she missed her family and smiled to herself, seeing her two pixie friends were still staring at her.

Sarah swallowed, realizing she had zoned out. She glanced back at the two pixies. "What's it like being pixies, always zipping around all over the place? Don't you guys ever get tired?"

"Well, the more we fly, the more ambient energy we absorb," John said, as if this explained everything.

Sarah looked blankly at him.

John continued. "Pixies have to fly. It circulates our magic, but we really cannot use our magic till we are maxed out. Also, after we use it, we are utterly exhausted. We are as helpless as—how do you put it?—as helpless as infant canines. You know, most people do not even know that we can …" John paused.

"Wait, you can do magic?" Sarah asked. "What can you do?"

John looked at her. Maybe he had revealed too much, but then he decided to continue.

"We can give whatever Talents we have to another creature, though not permanently. Much like humans, pixies have greatly varying abilities which, through magic, we can imbue temporarily. Pixie magic only lasts a short time, maybe an hour or so. Also there is not a pixie I know who can really control it," John said, hovering. "Pixie magic rarely happens as planned."

"What do you mean?" asked Sarah.

John paused, drinking deeply from his thimble of punch.

"You know, to humans, pixies seem to have acquired a unique reputation. Humans see pixies as curious, mischievous, unpredictable, and at times ridiculous," John said.

"*Wheeeeeee!*" cried Lucy, flying around Sarah's head. She flew in a few tight circles, then accidentally caught a leg in Sarah's hair, losing control and colliding with the side of the tent.

"I don't know where pixies could have gotten such an unfair reputation," Sarah said ironically.

"Exactly!" agreed John, not catching Sarah's sarcasm. "Yet I must admit that, in regard to our magic, this reputation is quite correct. Our magic is always unpredictable. The intention is not always the result. Feelings that we might not admit even to ourselves become revealed in our magic. Pixies cannot hide their true emotions when using magic."

"So if you cast the same spell for someone you liked and for someone you hated, you might get different results?" Sarah asked.

"Exactly, but pixies do not have 'spells' like human wizards practicing magic. We concentrate on desires and release the accumulated energy, and then something happens. The result is rarely the anticipated expectation, but customarily the general intention is usually fulfilled," he said.

Sarah laughed. "The 'general intention' usually happens? You make it sound like you never know what will happen when you use your magic."

John smiled. "What would be the fun in knowing all the consequences in our engagements?"

"*Wheeeeeeeee!*" Lucy repeated. She then flew down and landed on Sarah's bent knee. She extended her arms to her side and fell back, landing on the blanket with a laugh.

"I know. I'll use my magic to convey precisely to you what it is like being a pixie!" said Lucy, who was still on her back on the blanket, staring straight up at the top of the tent.

John suddenly became much more serious and flew over to Lucy and spoke quickly in Pixish. Sarah had a difficult time understanding it when they spoke so fast, but she caught that John thought it might not be a good idea. Lucy ignored him.

Lucy flew up to Sarah and hovered, holding her hand out, palm up. Sarah held out her palm, and Lucy landed on it. Lucy then held both arms straight. At first, nothing happened. Then a small pinprick of pink light appeared between Lucy's hands. The pinprick slowly grew into an intensely bright glowing orb. It continued to expand until it surrounded Lucy. It kept growing, and the light overlapped Sarah's hands.

Sarah could feel the warmth flow through her. The sensation grew to incorporate all her senses. She could smell the freshness of a forest after the rain; she could feel the love of a friend, and she could see thousands of pixies on the edges of her vision smiling at her. The glowing pink orb continued to grow until it enveloped Sarah completely. Warmth flowed through her whole body. She felt light as air and happy.

Suddenly the light exploded into her, and she felt as if she had taken a large gasp of freezing air. Sarah opened her eyes in surprise. The tent looked exactly the same, yet in sharper contrast. Colors jumped out at her, and she could see auras around most of the objects in the room. She could taste the air and clearly hear the sounds of the conversations of the other servants in the distance outside. The sensation of happiness still bubbled through her. Sarah felt fantastic. She felt more alive and vibrant than ever before. Suddenly she began noticing a cramping discomfort in her back, which progressed quickly into pain.

Sarah tore off her shirt and felt her back growing outward.

She had wings!

They took up the entire tent. Four clear gossamer wings spread from the center of Sarah's back. Sarah looked down at her tiny friends.

Lucy was lying on her back looking up, exhausted. She noticed Sarah looking down at her and gave her a quick thumbs-up before her arm flopped back to the ground. John just stared at Sarah.

John looked down at Lucy and quickly rattled in Pixish, "What were you thinking? You made her into a giant pixie? You could have altered her spirit! You could have caused her to shrink to our size!"

"She's fine," Lucy said from the ground. "I like her too much to endanger her, and how else will she ever really know what it's like?"

Sarah, on the other hand, had run out of the tent and stretched her wings. She buzzed them tentatively and found herself floating upward. The shock of being off the ground startled her so that she stopped and quickly fell. She suddenly realized, if she were seen outside her tent with giant wings, Gumble would fire her on the spot. Sarah figured she must have also inherited the pixie tendency to act first and think second. She looked around with a bemused grin on her face and ran back into the tent.

Sarah looked down at them. "This is amazing! I finally get it!" Sarah said in rapid Pixish, her gossamer wings fluttering appropriately for the first time.

John gaped at Sarah. "That was perfect Pixish," he said quietly.

"I know! I can finally understand the intricacies and inflections!" Sarah said. "Whoa, did I just say that in Pixish?"

"Well, when one's entire body is involved in communication, efficiency naturally follows," Lucy said, still on the ground. She had not moved from the spot on the floor where she had fallen. Sarah reached down to her small friend.

"You look terrible," Sarah said, gently lifting the tiny pixie.

"Using magic exhausts us entirely. I just need to rest."

Sarah set Lucy down on a bed of linens. John buzzed over, floating near Lucy.

"All right, it's official. Lucy is insane. But, to your benefit, it seems her magic has provided you a unique opportunity. Shall we go?" asked John.

Sarah smiled. "Absolutely."

John led her away from the encampment to a small field they had passed earlier. The lush grass felt wonderful under Sarah's bare feet. The smells seemed to be alive.

"I have never actually taught anyone how to do this. Pixies fly without trying, and you are not really a pixie, but you have similar attributes. Just remember to trust your wings. Try to stay low. Normally pixies can crash pretty hard without any damage, because we are so light. You on the other hand have significantly more weight—"

"Hey now!" said Sarah laughing.

"—and if you crash, you could cause significantly more damage as a result," he finished.

"I cannot believe I am receiving words of caution from a pixie. You two are about the most reckless pair I have ever encountered. I can't count the times I thought one of you two nearly came to your untimely end, the way you fly and crash and zoom so erratically," she said.

"I know it might appear that way, but our reflexes are more honed than you realize. For example …" He grabbed a handful of rocks and rapidly threw them at Sarah. The speed at which he sent the projectiles made his arm appear as a blur, and the pebbles flew straight at her.

With little effort she caught every single pebble with her open hand.

"Whoa! How did you do that? On second thought, how did I do that?" she asked. She looked down at her hand and counted them. Thirty-three pebbles in about three seconds.

"Well, it seems you also gained increased reflexes as well. Let us see how well you fly, shall we?"

Sarah's face beamed. She concentrated on her new appendages on her back and willed them to move. They lamely bent forward and back slowly, responding to her thoughts. *Okay,* she thought, *I can do this.* She then tried to flap her wings, as she had earlier outside the tent. The four wings responded by flapping up and down, but Sarah remained on the ground. She attempted again while John watched.

"What am I doing wrong?" she asked.

"You are not a bird. You need to buzz, not flap. Let your wings work independently of your thought. Relax and let them pull you up on their own accord. Manually forcing independent motion is an exercise in impossibility," John said. He quickly flew over to her and held out his hand. Sarah held out hers, and he landed in her palm.

"Watch closely," he said.

Sarah brought the small creature close to her face. John slowed his wings. She could see his face relax and watched the wings go from a slow flutter to a fast blur, as he rose a few inches off her hand. He repeated this twice and then hovered in front of her, smiling.

"Think of a dragonfly. Try not to overly involve your consciousness. Let your instincts override your actions," John said.

She relaxed her body. In doing so, the feeling of happiness again bubbled through her. She took a deep breath and let it out, smiling to herself. The warm feeling rushed through her again. She thought of her two friends and of any number of their various antics. She thought about Lucy flying for the sheer joy of it.

John flew in front of her face. "Maintain that emerging state of mind, Sarah. Now open your eyes."

Sarah opened her eyes. She was hovering ten feet off the ground. She looked at John with a grin, and he grinned back. John flew backward. He then picked up speed, and Sarah followed, laughing.

They continued to work on turning and hovering in midair. She began to understand how her emotions altered her control, and she started relaxing and trusting her wings.

They worked on flight for twenty minutes, when suddenly a scream pierced the silence of the night. A shriek of absolute pain and despair shocked Sarah. She plummeted to the ground. More screams followed. Sarah looked around in confusion. She had inadvertently flown two thousand paces from the camp.

John flew down to her. "Sarah, those are *wivari*! Get into a tree now. I have to retrieve Lucy! Go now!" he said, and she saw the blur of him flying toward the camp.

Sarah followed her friend's advice and quickly ran to a large tree. She tried to relax and fly up to the first branch, but her wings would not listen to her. She looked around and saw that the next closest tree was about one hundred paces away. She again attempted to relax and let her wings lift her to the lowest branch.

Screams continued to escalate from the direction of the camp. The horrible howls echoed in the trees. Sarah jumped up to the lowest branch, but she could not even touch it with her fingertips. Over and over she tried, but the bough remained out of her reach. Screams of agony and terror continued from the camp. Along with the howls, Sarah now heard a sickening laughter, repetitive and barklike, filling her with fear.

Sarah ran at the trunk and pushed off for extra height. Her dew-coated bare feet made for a slippery purchase. Her palm touched the lowest branch before slipping off. Sarah fell to the ground and landed on her back, knocking the wind out of her. She leaned over, catching her breath. The howls sounded much closer than before. She looked toward the campsite and saw a blur of movement, and then quickly realized it was John. He flew in bursts.

He would ascend in the air, then drift downward, only to repeat the burst of flight again. He arrived shortly, holding Lucy in his arms. She appeared to be asleep or unconscious.

"Get into the tree now!" he yelled to her in rapid Pixish. "The wivari are coming!"

"I'm trying! I can't fly!" she responded.

Sarah looked at the edge of the woods and saw it. The body looked like a giant wolf, but that was where the similarities ended. Two large yellow eyes protruded on each side with a mouth that opened vertically instead of horizontally. Even at this distance Sarah could see the glowing eyes. The pupils of its eyes made a sinister X instead of a circle. Four rows of teeth layered the bizarre vertical mouth that split the beast's face. The mouth gaped widely, and the horrible laughing howl struck Sarah like a blow. It then tilted its head to the side, appearing to see her for the first time. The large eyes focused on Sarah, and she could actually feel its gaze. Sarah felt short of breath, as the beast stared at her from across the field.

The wivari, at first, appeared to be covered in black ink. Sarah realized that the creature was drenched in blood. The laughter echoed again from its mouth. It turned its head sideways, and the mouth that bisected its face now appeared in a horrible grin. Sarah saw movement on the edge of the forest as other creatures slowly walked toward her, yet she could not move. The strange creature just stared at her, and Sarah stared back. Somewhere in the distance she thought she could hear John pleading with her, begging her to get into the tree, but her thoughts were jumbled.

Sarah could see the specks of other wivari galloping toward her, but they were impossibly far away, just dots in the distance.

Only the one in front of her was close. She continued to stare at the creature. Intelligent eyes stared through Sarah. The chattering laughter continued to bounce all around her, and she let out a barking laugh of her own.

A small flying creature suddenly appeared directly in front of her face. Sarah looked at the thing in front of her, blocking her vision. The tiny creature was trying to communicate with her. She leaned to the side to see the interesting wivari, but the flying creature continued to block her line of sight.

Go away, she thought.

The harder she tried to look around it, the more the annoying creature would fly right in front of her face. Sarah shooed it away, but it would not leave her alone. Finally she lost her patience and soundly swatted the pest. She looked back to the howling creature coated in blood. It nodded its approval and laughed again. She looked to her side and saw the other wivari were much closer than before. They had been on the edge of the horizon just seconds earlier. How had they come so far so fast? She looked down at the little flying pest she had swatted to the ground. The annoying creature appeared dazed, as it shook its head and looked up at her in confusion.

A thought entered her mind. For a split second she felt filthy, as if she had been horribly violated. She looked down at the dazed creature trying to communicate with her. Sarah felt nauseous and weak. She pushed against the feeling, but it returned. She tried to remember something but could not. Again a thought flowed into her mind. Sarah flinched again in response, as the thoughts pushed into her consciousness. *Just take one step. That flying pest will recover soon and begin annoying you once again. Just be rid of that little mosquito once and for all. It is just a bug. You know what to do with pesky tiny bugs, don't you? Of course you do. You step on little bugs and end their interference.*

Sarah lifted her foot and then put it back down on the ground right next to the pixie. Something felt wrong. Then she felt the push in her mind again. *Just step on that bug. Don't let a puny insect tell you what to do!* Sarah lifted her foot and placed it over the small form on the ground, pinning it to the ground. Something in her desperately urged her to stop. Another mental push came, stronger this time. Sarah could feel the little worthless pest struggling. She could feel the tiny hands pushing in vain against the bottom of her foot. It wriggled, trying to get away, but Sarah held her foot firmly, enjoying the struggle. *DO IT!* the thought commanded. Something deep in Sarah's mind screamed at her to stop, but, for some reason, squashing the struggling little bug under her foot seemed like the right thing to do. All she had to do was step forward and crush the life out of that annoying little flying thing.

"Sarah, no!" Lucy cried from above.

Lucy's voice shattered Sarah's trance. Sarah snapped back to reality and looked around. She was nearly surrounded by wivari. She quickly lifted her foot, and John flew up to her. Wivari were bounding toward her from all sides, too fast for her to escape. They were only a dozen paces away. Their vertical mouths gaped with row upon row of bloody teeth ready to embrace her. John hovered in front of her with both of his hands extended. A brilliant flash of light surrounded both Sarah and John. She felt herself exploding upward, as the wivari rushed in, snapping a hand's length from where she had just been. She landed hard onto the upper branches of the tree, twigs and leaves flying everywhere. She looked up and saw John spinning out of control rapidly toward the ground. She quickly leaned over the branches and snatched him from the air. An open-mouthed wivari had been sitting twenty feet below, waiting to catch him from his fall.

"Nice catch," John said and then collapsed.

The wivari howled at the base of the tree. They paced back and forth, angry to be denied their carnage.

Sarah glanced at the one at the edge of the woods. The creature appeared to be in pain, but it loped to the base of the tree to join the others. Four hounds circled below, but Sarah saw no way for them to reach her.

"What do we do now?" Sarah asked.

The two pixies looked exhausted. John was unconscious in Sarah's hand. Lucy looked over at her. "We stay up here, until they leave," she said.

"What if they don't leave?" Sarah asked.

But the pixies had both passed out. The creatures below laughed and laughed.

Chapter 11: Rock

Cameron walked back to the rock troll ensnared in vines. Jayde watched in wonder from the cart till Cameron indicated that he wanted her to come over. Despite being completely stuck, the troll appeared quite happy.

"And why are you so happy?" Cameron asked.

"Me not have to kill," it said, indicating Marie with its chin.

"And *not* killing her makes you happy?" Cameron asked.

"Oh, sure. Me no like to kill, but Boss said we have to. He take from rich and give to help all. He say dat he did," said the troll.

"Right. I am sure his compassion was only outclassed by his chivalry. Out of curiosity, did you ever see him give away any of this money to the needy?" Cameron asked.

"No, me no see him. He go on trips. He say, on trips, he help lots of dem. But he have wine on clothes when he get back," said the troll.

"Your boss is officially out of work," Cameron said. "He tried to kill this young girl," he said, putting his hands on Jayde's shoulders, presenting the girl in front of the troll. The troll looked right at Cameron, and his face melted in shame. A growl like thunder came from deep within the troll. Cameron held his gaze. For a long time their gazes remained locked, and then the rock troll came back to himself.

"Yah. Me see him. Boss not nice man like he said," said the troll. "Me mad that me join him. Make rock troll seem dumb. Me know you think trolls dumb. Me just not want to prove dem right." The troll sighed. "Me dumb. Me know not to hurt nice girl. Me so dumb."

"You were tricked," said Cameron. "Even the cleverest of us can be tricked from time to time. What will you do now that you are unemployed?"

"Me not know. Most no hire rock troll. That why me want to know how she know me rock troll," said the behemoth, looking to Marie.

Cameron gazed deep into the eyes of the troll. The troll took a deep breath and appeared paralyzed. Cameron smiled. He broke his stare with the troll. The troll seemed confused.

Cameron looked over at Marie. Marie shook her head. She jumped off the cart and sprung to his side.

"Cameron, I know you have a soft spot for the downtrodden and all, but I did just barely escape with my life. Not to mention that his employer nearly skewered Jayde. What do you think he would do with us?"

"Marie, I've looked into him. He is clean. Cleaner than most humans I know. He really thought he was doing good. From what I hear, Grandeur can be a pretty rough city. Wouldn't it be nice to have a little added security?"

"You're serious?" she asked.

"What are you talking about?" Jayde said, trying to decode the argument.

"Well, Jayde," Marie began, looking at Cameron scathingly, "Dr. Sangre is thinking of adding the rock troll to our party."

"Marl," said the rock troll.

"What?" asked Marie.

"Marl. My name. Marl," it said.

"Fine," said Marie. "I vote he stays here."

"And I vote he comes with us," said Cameron.

"All right then, Jayde, it's up to you," said Marie.

Jayde looked at the massive troll. It was completely immobile trapped in the vines, but it smiled broadly at Jayde. She had had few friends while growing up. Most of the acquaintances she had known had either used her, beaten her, stole from her, or worse. But all those people were human.

"Is he really safe?" Jayde asked.

"She asks the vampire," Cameron said. "No, Jayde, he is not safe, but neither am I. Neither is Marie. Neither are you, to be honest. All of us make choices all the time on the limited information we have, which can drastically change lives in ways we can't comprehend. But his heart is in the right place, and that's more than I can say for most."

Jayde looked at the troll.

His broad, flat head and angular face gazed at her with uncertainty.

"Can I trust you?" Jayde asked the troll.

"Me no lie," said the troll.

"Will you keep me safe?" Jayde asked.

"You fight like her?" he asked Jayde, indicating Marie. "You not need me to keep you safe, if you fight like her."

"No, I can't really fight much at all. I'm more of the run-away-from-danger type. I think what I need is a friend," Jayde admitted. "Could you be that for me?"

The troll appeared struck. It looked at Jayde, then at Cameron, then Marie, then back at Jayde. Marie arched an eyebrow at Cameron but remained silent.

"You mean it? You no trick me, right? No?" Marl asked.

Jayde shook her head.

"Real man-thing as friend. You have my oath," it said.

Marie and Cameron gasped simultaneously. Another silent glance between the two of them implied something had just happened, but Jayde did not catch it. A long pause ensued as Jayde seemed to be thinking. She looked at the troll; his angular face stared at her, hope in his eyes.

"I say he's in," said Jayde.

Both Cameron and Marie let out the breath they had not realized they had been holding. Cameron recovered first.

"Well, Mr. Marl, since you are currently unemployed, would you like to join us and work with us in Grandeur?"

"O!! Work in big shop place? Sure, sure! Me want go there long time, but me scared. Most man-thing get scared of rock troll. They throw rocks. Rocks not hurt me, but it make me sad, so me not go. You think, if me go with you, they no throw rocks?"

"From what I've heard, Grandeur is quite the melting pot of all races and creatures. You might even blend in," Marie said.

"Hah! Dat be first time for me," said the troll. In his happiness he threw up his arms, snapping the vines.

Marie jumped backward, landing in a defensive crouch.

"Wait! You could have broken the vines all this time?" Marie asked.

"Oh, sure," said Marl. "But me not want to fight or hurt you. You make it seem like me caught in trap, so me stop fight, and Boss not get mad, if he see. Me glad you found way to trap, since me no like to hurt," Marl said.

They reloaded the cart. Some of the men that Marie had dazed were stirring. Their leader, however, remained quite dead.

Marie drove the wagon back to the road and continued their slow pace; the night was still young. The rock troll insisted on walking. Despite Marie's reassurance that her cart would not break under his weight, he remained skeptical. They ended in a compromise: the troll would ride, if he could not keep up.

Marl periodically disappeared into the woods, only to appear later a good distance down the road. He would then wait for them to catch up, only to repeat the process. Sometimes he would disappear from the road, and they would not see him for nearly half an hour. After he left the group the next time, Jayde had to ask about what he was doing.

"He's scouting," Cameron answered. "He's taking his new role quite seriously."

"His new role?" Jayde asked.

"Marl did more than just agree to come with us, Jayde. He gave his oath as a rock troll. That may not sound like much to you, but, to a rock troll, his oath is everything. That is a pledge of heart and soul from most humans. And while I have known many humans to break their word, I have never known a troll to do so," Cameron said.

"Wow, really? What would he have done if I had not chosen to have him join our group?" she asked.

"Most likely he would have journeyed to the nearest desert to find the Great Chasm and jumped in."

"What! He would have killed himself?" Jayde asked.

"Well, they don't view it as suicide. They view it as rejoining the trolls of the past. But essentially, yes. Fortunately you chose to let him join us," Cameron said.

"You could have told me!" Jayde said.

"Yes, but then you most likely would have had him join us out of pity or guilt, not because you thought he would be a friend and good for the group as a whole. I had confidence you would choose as you did," he said.

"So you think we can trust him?" Jayde asked.

Marie answered, "He will *never* break that promise. Rock trolls rarely make friends. He had tried to camouflage himself as a human, so that he could be part of this group of thieves."

"But why didn't he leave, after he realized that the leader was just spending everything on himself?" asked Jayde.

Marie pulled next to a large boulder in the road and halted the cart momentarily. "Like Cam said, once a troll gives his oath, he won't break that promise. After the leader lied to Marl to get his promise, it was too late."

The giant boulder in the road unfolded itself. He looked at Marie. "*Oi*, dat be right. Me be sad to say it. Me know it be wrong, but an oath's an oath, and me not break word."

"No matter what?" Jayde asked.

"You got it," said Marl. He then left to explore far ahead of the cart, scouting for anything or anyone who might be a threat to the group.

Traveling at night provided few scenery changes. Jayde filled the time peppering Marie with questions, mostly about magic. Her explanations often created more questions than answers.

"How did you punch a guy twenty feet into the air?" Jayde asked.

"Endless hours of training, Jayde," Marie answered.

"I met a witch once in Haynis. Do you think I could be a witch?" Jayde said.

"You're not ugly enough," Cameron answered.

Marie laughed. "You would make an excellent witch but a better necromancer. There are a wide variety of magical abilities. I trained in essence bending, which allows me to greatly affect anything I touch. Cameron can use his energy to feel exactly what other people feel. In cases where they are injured or sick, he can use his energy to heal. He also has many other skills. Every person has a natural aptitude toward one field or another.

"I trained so I could detect magic and snuff it out before it caused problems. But I'm getting ahead of myself. What other fields are there? Let's see." She began ticking them off her fingers. "There's Wizardry or Witchery, which deals with a wide variety of studies. There are enchanters, who cause large field effects. Others study elementalism, such as firecasting or icecasting and the like, usually affecting anything that comes within range. There's Necromancy, talking with or reanimating dead things, or even Zombimancy. It's a smelly, rotten field. Not good if you want to have many friends."

Cameron looked over at Marie with a frown. "My friend Mort is a zombimancer."

"And I'll bet that he smells terrible. Then there are seers and divination. Diviners can look into your mind, and see your past and your true self. Cameron has some skill in Divining, which is how he judged Marl to have such a pristine character. But many diviners are crackpots who tell you stuff about yourself that you already know," she said.

"What other fields are there?" Jayde asked.

"There are hundreds. Voodoo, Monkeymancy, and Conjuring to mention a few," Marie said.

"Monkeymancy, war sages, Conjuring ..." Jayde shook her head in awe.

Cameron continued. "Conjurers can create and alter the substances around them. It takes a great deal of imagination and a powerful mind to will something into existence. Not only that but most of them burn out after a few years. Conjuring takes more self-control than any of the other branches of magic, that's why Marie could never go into it," he said.

Marie smirked at him. "I don't have the imagination for it. But not to worry, you don't need to concern yourself about any of this if you have no interest," Marie said, glancing down at Jayde, who was still gaping. Cameron laughed.

"Do you really think I could do"—Jayde wiggled her finger in the air—"stuff like that?"

Marie shrugged. "I think so."

Jayde rode in her seat, quietly contemplating for a few minutes. "So what does a war sage do exactly?" she asked.

"Most of our missions were reconnaissance."

"So dat how you learn to fight so good. You train at good school, so you fight good. It make sense." Marl smiled. "Me have to learn just by me bash rocks and trees. You train Marl to fight more good?"

Marie looked at Cameron.

He nodded. "I see no reason not to, as long as he doesn't kill you in the process."

"Wait, what about me? Can you teach me magic too? Which field is the best?" Jayde asked.

"Most of my training centers on fighting, but I'll show you what I know. There is no *best* field, just different types. But remember, mastering magic will greatly complicate your life. Magic makes your life unique but also problematic. It provides incredible power, but the choices you make still determine who you are," Marie answered.

"Right, I got it. So when can you show me how to punch through a tree?" Jayde grinned.

Chapter 12: Relief

The wivari attempted in vain to run up the tree trunk. They howled in frustration, but their prey remained safe. Some gnawed at the tree. Another rammed into the trunk at a high rate of speed, but it bounced off harmlessly. The other wivari released their characteristic laughter in response.

Hours passed until they finally galloped away. Sarah could not see them in the darkness, but she heard their howls in the distance. John remained unconscious for the entire time. Sarah had placed him inside her pocket and buttoned it closed, just in case she fell asleep. Lucy flew around the tree to make sure the hounds were really gone. After rounding the tree three times, she stated simply, "All gone. Finally."

Sarah's recollection was fuzzy. She remembered running in the field and trying to get up the tree. She remembered seeing the wivari across the field, but, after that, her memory remained muddy. Sarah could not explain her actions, and Lucy seemed confused as well. As far as she knew, wivari did not have magic or any ability to control minds. But, after Sarah described how the thoughts had been pushed into her head, Lucy said she knew exactly what they were facing.

Sarah leaned against a branch of the tree from her perch near the top.

"That hound that you gazed upon for numerous moments was unlikely a wivari at all. I believe with great certainty that it was a shayde," said Lucy.

Sarah just looked down at Lucy, waiting for further explanation.

"It looks like an upright shadow, and it gains strength by overtaking other creatures. It does not really alter its own countenance itself. It just claims the body of another creature and replaces that creature's consciousness with its own," Lucy said.

"Is that what that thing was doing to me? Was it taking me over?"

"That specificity is difficult to determine. My understanding of shaydes is based primarily on legends and less so on experience. Even the strongest shayde lacks the necessary fortitude to overpower a human. The higher the intelligence and willpower of the human, the more difficult it would be for the shayde to overpower the human. However, a shayde could likely implement principles of transference of will to influence decisions. They can temporarily push themselves into your thoughts and make irrational thoughts seem plausible and logical," Lucy said.

"Like me not recognizing John and wanting to hurt him," Sarah said.

"Exactly. It takes a tremendous amount of effort to overtake the will of an individual even momentarily. Such an act could likely destroy the shayde's host body. This can be extremely dangerous, since the death of the host body would ultimately result in the shayde perishing. Unless the shayde translocated to another creature before the host died, the shayde would guarantee its demise. The shayde took a risk to influence your decision-making capacity, but it almost exterminated both you and John," Lucy said.

"I know. If I would have hurt John, I—" She stopped, tears coming to her eyes.

"We're all safe with little injury. Neither John nor I had the awareness of what we truly faced. Also the happenstance of pixie magic I imbued likely weakened your natural defenses," Lucy said.

"How so?"

"My magic gave the shayde an alternative entryway to your consciousness. A shayde's attack is strictly magical in nature. Normally you would maintain only miniscule openings through which his magical attack could penetrate. But after I spelled you, with your new unmastered pixie aura effervescing through you, you were—how do you say it?—pickings of easiness," Lucy said.

"Then how did I stop it?" Sarah asked.

"The shayde capitalized on magic I created in you. I realized this, flew down from the tree and removed all the magic I had imbued in you. This removal of my magic severed its connection and broke your hypnosis. To be forthright, I'm perplexed by your resistance against the shayde's magical assault. You should have squelched John and allowed the wivari to devour you. I do not understand how you resisted the attack without having monumental magical abilities of your own."

"You got me. I'm new to the whole magic game," Sarah said.

The first rays of sunshine peeked over the horizon. Lucy went off on another scouting mission, this time expanding her search to a much broader area. She disappeared into the forest for a brief period of time and then quickly zipped back to Sarah.

"No sign of them?" Sarah asked.

"No. Wivari never voyage in the sunlight. The destructive remains of their nocturnal attack are strewn all over the campsite."

"What about the shayde?"

"I saw no trace of the shayde either. Even if it escaped before sunrise, it will lack fortitude to pursue for over a week. Attacking you likely taxed the host body to incapacitation. It will probably require shifting to a new host soon."

"Great," Sarah said. "Why don't we go back to camp and see if anyone needs our help?"

"I don't think that is a good idea. It's a gruesome sight," Lucy said.

"People might need our help," Sarah answered, climbing down the tree.

"But who will help us?" said Lucy.

Sarah hardly recognized the campsite. Bloodied body parts had been strewn everywhere in unidentifiable pieces. No one responded to her yells. Thaddeus Gumble's carriage remained locked, but no noise came from it. Sarah pounded on the side of the carriage. Silence. He must have died, along with his mistress and the rest of the servants.

She had been a good servant, yet treated as a necessary nuisance. She supposed someone with her years of experience and common sense might be of some use, but other than the jewelry store …

"No one is here. Sarah, what will we do?" asked Lucy.

Sarah took one last look around the former campsite. A single horse had escaped the bloodshed. The pixie looked at Sarah, waiting for her to determine their next step. Sarah realized she had been taking orders her whole life. First from her parents and next from Gumble. She had immediately placed herself in a position where she would not have to choose. Sarah paused to think.

"We go back to Grandeur," Sarah said. "We make the shop the best shop in the city and try to leave all this behind us. Do wivari normally come back?"

"Wivari kill for sport and revel in the terror they convey in their victims before utterly devouring all in their path. However, Wivari normally don't attack campsites. Fires and noise usually dissuade their violent tendencies. I suspect the shayde influenced the wivari and overwhelmed their normal hesitance to provoke the attack," said Lucy.

"We need to get away from here," Sarah said.

Pointless destruction, thought Sarah. She reminisced about her mother and father, anger burning inside. For some reason she felt the familiar pull deep inside her growing stronger. Someone had to be held accountable for this, but Sarah had no idea who. But, for now, she had to get to Grandeur.

Chapter 13: Hatred

Mrs. Crass had grown to hate the fluffy black bozrac. She knew its lethality held the key to all her dreams. Her power had been stripped from her, but, if she could kill one person, she would gain back all that she had lost. If she failed to kill that person, however, the rest of her life would be that of a mindless zombie slave.

The creature seemed annoyingly happy to be out of imprisonment. It behaved just like an irrational, cute, fuzzy kitten. The only difference was that this kitten could consume souls.

Thirty years ago she had power, real power. She had been the first advisor to Solomon Glass, the dictator of Grandeur both then and now. Solomon became dictator because of his cunning, intellect, and morality. Mrs. Crass was promoted for her cunning, intellect, and lack of morality.

Grandeur did not have a mayor, like most other cities. As the capital of Tenland, the ruler of Grandeur also ruled as dictator of Tenland. Being a dictator provided power, but power brought enemies. Over time, other countries changed to monarchies, with kings and queens. Tenland did not.

Thirty years ago, the dictator at the time—DATT—who had initially hired Mrs. Crass had had an unfortunate accident. Accidents happened with great frequency to dictators, especially around Leynstra Crass. The replacement DATT, Solomon, continued where the previous had left off. Leynstra Crass remained a close advisor, as she had with the previous DATT. Through careful planning, tactful bribing, and a few discreet murders, she had climbed to First Advisor. She had a reputation, class, and her own fleet of servants. Not to mention power second only to that of the DATT. Life had been good, until Kafe Mean had appeared.

Solomon had invited all the royalty throughout the country to an elaborate party. The DATT had spared no expense. Thousands ate, drank, danced, and enjoyed the elaborate feast Solomon had provided. He had hired a storyteller by the name of Kafe Mean, who would be the pinnacle of the evening's entertainment. The dictator insisted that everyone be present for Mean's performance.

Leynstra knew little about the storyteller, which made her nervous. She knew that Kafe Mean had the DATT's ear, and that was worrisome enough.

"You've made quite a nuisance of yourself, Kafe. I understand you are here as entertainment for the Wintertide Ball, but Solomon has other obligations beyond listening to your idle prattling," Leynstra said.

Servants scattered as Leynstra entered the room, double-checking that everything in her presence was perfect.

"Leynstra, let the man finish his story," said Solomon.

She had been known only as Leynstra, dropping the Crass last name. At the time, she enjoyed the anonymity and uniqueness of having the single sinister name. Leynstra demanded respect. Leynstra had great magic and powerful friends. Leynstra could make your dreams—or your nightmares—come true.

"No worries, Your Grace. First Advisor worries that I command more of your ear than she does," said Kafe Mean.

Leynstra would never admit it, but his statement held more than a sliver of truth.

"Save your stories for the festival tonight, jester. Solomon and I have business to attend to."

"With your permission, sir," said the storyteller, bowing to Solomon.

"I await tonight's tale with great excitement."

"I guarantee I will not disappoint. Your Grace, Leynstra," Kafe Mean said, briefly bowing to both and leaving the room.

"I don't trust that man," said Leynstra.

"I do. That's all that matters," said Solomon.

Solomon never showed fear. Leynstra found it annoying, considering everyone else in the city feared her. She assumed his lunacy kept him free of fear. They had heated arguments, sometimes ending with her yelling that she should just turn him into a snowflake and let him melt to nothing. With time she found herself agreeing with his points of view more. This bothered her.

"We need to readdress the problem with the hundreds of lazy—"

"Yes, yes, Leynstra. I know how you feel about the homeless in Grandeur. We have been over this before," Solomon said.

"If you would just be firm, we could have already eliminated this problem," she answered.

"Seeing people as a problem is *your* problem."

"Not seeing them as a problem is your weakness. They are using you. They are wasting money and resources. How can you not see this? I have many ideas on how to not only fix these drains on society and use them for something that—"

"*Enough!* We've been over this, and I have given you my decision. Now, unless you plan to turn me into a newt, I do have other matters to attend to," said Solomon.

Leynstra realized that he had not only changed the country, he had changed her as well. She did not know how he had altered what she wanted. She never used to discuss problems she saw with the country and her decisions. If she wanted something from the old DATT, she simply took it. Now she discussed and argued with Solomon about matters before acting. He took her advice into consideration but acted independently.

They regularly discussed the worthless peasants. The DATT was tough on the drunk and lazy, the unmotivated, and those who had been unemployed for long periods of time. But he continued to offer resources to help those who were willing to try. Leynstra knew such people for what they really were: hopeless. Wasting time, energy, and money on people like this would drain Tenland's treasury, and those resources were better spent elsewhere.

Solomon sent the lazy to Frock, a small farming community too far away for them to cause trouble. Most sent to this place considered it a form of forced exile. Leynstra had seen people transform quickly from laziness to hard workers after being transported to Frock. If a person chose not to work in Frock, they would not eat. Some citizens in Grandeur improved out of fear of exile to Frock. What she mostly saw, however, were people avoiding work and sucking the life out of the country. If it were up to her, she would exile people by the thousands to a much harsher environment than a work community.

Leynstra realized that Solomon had to go, and she had carefully planned for his disposal at the Wintertide Festival. His beloved Kafe Mean would provide the entertainment, and, shortly after his grand tale, she would end Solomon's reign as DATT.

Later that evening, with the grand ballroom full of nobility, Kafe Mean arrived at the ball. He entered the center of the enormous room, and the talking died down, as the man took the stage.

Storytellers were common for royal parties, and many present had favorite tales they enjoyed. Most wanted to hear "Revelc Sly, the Clever Fox," but instead Kafe Mean told a lesser known tale, "The Story of Stanley, the Smiling Snake That Never Lied." He told of a serpent that gained the trust of the other animals.

As the fable commenced, Leynstra could feel the web of magic being released, as Kafe Mean wove his story. Images appeared and disappeared in front of the giant crowd. Kafe's magic flowed into the crowd. Smells of the forest and the sounds of the animals surrounded them all, as his story unfolded. Leynstra felt herself drawn in, just like the rest of the crowd.

His voice changed for each character, and soon the room became lost in a world of his creation. Everyone present hung on his every word, each magically enchanted in a story. His words were so wrapped with his magic that he hardly seemed to be talking; the crowd simply was watching it in front of them. By the time Kafe came to the end of his tale, all eyes in the room had become entranced by the vivid magical world Kafe had created.

"Stanley the snake came to the forest as a small snake. He gained the trust of the animals, despite animals disappearing over time. Stanley planted seeds of doubt among the animals, causing the animals to distrust one another. Who could blame them? Stanley had been nothing but helpful. He had consoled those animals who had lost a friend or family member. Stanley the snake had led the group to search for the unknown entity and bring him/her to justice. Not only that but, as Stanley grew in size, he volunteered to move animals to a safe place he discovered. In this place Stanley guaranteed no animal would ever have to worry about disappearing again.

"As time passed, the amount of creatures in the forest declined. By now Stanley had become a very large snake. Finally Stanley called the remaining creatures together. At this meeting only one creature remained in each of the main six groups. Stanley said this was a very serious meeting, since he was to reveal what had caused all the disappearances. One mole, one rabbit, one bird, one squirrel, one mouse, and one rat were here, and none of these creatures trusted one another. Stanley dwarfed all the other creatures in size, but he smiled and welcomed them into his den.

"He advised the squirrel to block the outermost hole, so that none could get out. The squirrel did so dutifully. He then advised the rat to close all the innermost holes, so that none could easily escape this large den. He then asked the mole and bird to also create a barrier in front of all the escape routes, so that none could easily get out. All the creatures did so eagerly, since they wanted nothing more than to be sure that the fiend that had caused all the trouble would finally be caught.

"The last of these six creatures were in a circle. The snake then went to each creature and quietly asked a question, so that no other creature could hear it. Each creature answered the question by pointing to the creature to its right. The snake then went to that creature and asked another question, till the snake had made a full circle. All creatures had pointed to the animal on its right, making a full circle.

"The snake then stretched its long body, easily surrounding all the creatures in the room. Stanley addressed them all and hissed with a smile. 'You are all correct.' The creatures appeared confused. At first they squabbled among themselves, and then they realized something was very wrong. They looked at the snake and said, 'You *lied* to us.' The snake then smiled one last smile and said, 'I never lied, but that does not mean I told you the truth.' The snake then ate them all and slithered away, never to be seen again."

Kafe Mean paused in his presentation. The crowd exploded into cheers and applause. The vivid images that he had created faded. The smells and sounds of the forest were replaced with the interior of the castle. He slowly looked around the audience, grinning broadly.

"So what was the question the snake asked the animals at the last meeting?" Kafe Mean asked his audience. "Stanley asked each animal the same question. He *did* always tell the truth, so what did he ask?" Kafe said.

Whispers in the crowd grew into murmurs, which ultimately found their way back to the storyteller. Kafe Mean grinned and allowed his control over the crowd to momentarily slip away, as the discussions became heated. Finally he clapped his hands three times and silence reclaimed the room, as if lightning had struck.

"I have heard many answers floating around the room," said Kafe. "I have heard many of you say, 'The snake asked each creature who they thought he should eat next.' This seems a perfect question for the snake to ask, but it was not Stanley's style. Stanley never even admitted he had eaten a single creature. Also how could he answer this with 'You are correct?' I have also heard it guessed that the snake asked each creature, 'Which creature should go to the safe place next?' Also a good answer, since, by this time, none of the creatures truly knew where this safe place was, and no one really wanted to go there. But, alas, this was not the question the snake asked either."

Kafe paused, glancing in a long circle around the room, feeling their eyes begging him for the answer. "No, my friends, the snake asked a much simpler question. All he asked was 'Who is responsible for the disappearances?' Each creature pointed at the next in line in answer to the question. Thus, all the creatures were responsible. It is the responsibility of the whole to look out for one another. Sometimes a giant snake might be in the room, yet all we can do is blame one another and lay helpless as it slowly devours us all. Scary situation, no?"

The crowd shifted uncomfortably, but no one said a word.

"But what were the animals to do? In truth, at the final meeting, there was *nothing* they could do. By that time it was far too late. The snake had grown too large, too powerful, and knew too much to be stopped. By that time the snake could destroy any of them at a whim. None of them had a chance. The animals had stopped trusting each other. Not only that, the one they did trust was the creature that should have been avoided. Stanley said it himself, 'I never lied, but that does not mean I told you the truth.'

"What did the snake mean by this? I'll tell you. We see what we want to see. The one that deceives us easiest is ourselves. It is *this*, and not the obvious thieves and scoundrels out there, that is truly dangerous. It is the snake that tricks us into ruining ourselves for their benefit that scares me the most.

"Stanley the snake could have been stopped. But the only way was for someone to say from the very beginning that something was wrong. The creatures pretended nothing was happening. They ignored the problem and hoped it would go away. But what happened? The problem, the snake, continued to grow in size, influence, and power. Creatures disappeared until it was too late to stop him. So how could you stop a snake like Stanley? The trickiest and most evil creatures like this can only be stopped before they get started, before it grows too powerful."

The crowd continued to yearn for his every word. He turned, looked straight at Leynstra, gestured with a grand wave, and said, "I give you, your snake."

The crowd gasped, unsure of how to react. Guards appeared on all sides of her. Leynstra worked a few spells, but the DATT had many wizards on his security force that squelched the effort before she had a chance. A truth enchantment was cast, and her confession followed shortly thereafter. She admitted to the plans of slavery, deceit, and even to the backup plans to kill the DATT. She admitted to all the people she had killed on her road to the top. She admitted to all her actions to maintain her appearance of innocence. Nothing was left behind. After the whole confession was out, Leynstra was stripped of her titles and political power. From then on she was only known as Mrs. Crass.

Kafe Mean suggested her punishment, and the DATT agreed. Several wizards working together removed all her magical power. She had brimmed with natural magic, but, after the spell took hold, she could only feel the faintest hint of magic. She had just enough to remind her of all that she had lost. Only by luck did Mrs. Crass manage to escape without being executed. She had hidden hundreds of gold coins, which she exchanged for her freedom with her jailer. The act lacked her normal level of intrigue and class, but bribery for freedom saved her from an ax to the neck.

Her exile and fall from greatness fueled her lust for revenge. But, despite her multiple attempts to find and destroy Kafe Mean, she never succeeded. After a decade of plotting revenge, she looked for answers in darker corners.

Mrs. Crass had turned to the Dark King, Zolf Heller.

Zolf Heller ruled Zantia, the country to the south of Tenland. He had gained power over the centuries. No one knew his age, only that he had a one-track mind of taking over the world. He was fearless, and either ignored or killed all who disagreed with him.

The Dark King surrounded himself with the strongest and smartest in the land. If he had one flaw, it would be that he loved taking chances. He loved any form of gambling, and the higher the stakes, the better. He often gambled with lives, though never his own of course. He also hated losing; thus, the odds, more often than not, were stacked in his favor. Countless people had been enslaved to King Zolf after a wager that went awry.

"I know this storyteller," said Zolf Heller.

"How?" replied Leynstra.

"This man has traveled the world and used his gifts to hide any children with ample Talent from my agents. He has many names. I know him as the Great Traveler, but I am sure he is the same man. So far his efforts have accomplished nothing, but I think our goals are similar enough for me to propose a wager to you," said Zolf.

The king offered to return half of her power immediately. All her power would return if she succeeded in her revenge. If she failed with her one chance to kill Kafe Mean, her free will, her freedom, and her very soul would belong to Zolf. But, if she won, *when* she won, all her power would return and her obligation to Zolf would end. A small gamble for the king, but Leynstra Crass's entire life depended on her success. She signed the blood-bound contract, and the necromancer performed the ritual on her. She could feel the weight of the spell to her core.

Years later she returned to Grandeur, still never locating Kafe Mean. She had aged horribly. No one recognized the once proud Leynstra as the decrepit Mrs. Crass. She was still no closer to killing the man who had destroyed her life. But now, by obtaining the demonic black kittenlike bozrac, she had acquired the means to do so with ease.

Mrs. Crass woke from her reminiscing.

Her shirt was damp with tears, even after all her years of exile. She cried for her loss of power and reputation. She cried for the decades lost to anger and bitterness. She cried because the chance to destroy the man responsible had arrived, and she was scared.

She had plotted to kill Kafe Mean for years. He had tricked her years ago and had made her an embarrassment in front of the entire country. Since then, she lived only for revenge. Yet he continued to elude her.

Finneus, the bozrac, lapped some spilled wine. She called the creature, and it bounced over to her.

She did not even know if Kafe Mean still lived. If he had already died, then she would get her powers back and her freedom.

If he lived, not even his most powerful spells could save him from a bozrac. Kafe Mean was a storyteller with a great deal of magic. A man who, according to King Zolf, traveled around the world putting spells on children to protect possible Chosen from harm, was about to die.

She had to have her vengeance; her very soul depended on it. She swore to the Dark King that she would kill Kafe Mean. That time had finally arrived.

"Finneus, go kill Kafe Mean."

Chapter 14: Grandeur

Jayde enjoyed the early evenings when she still had enough light to see the passing countryside. As the trees faded in the twilight and the colors slowly ebbed into blackness, sightseeing became impossible. Cameron emerged shortly after dusk from being undercover and took over the reins. Then the teaching began.

Jayde's formal schooling had ended at age seven, but her fascination with magic had never wavered. She continued to try but remained unable to perform any magic herself. Marie restated her thought that Jayde brimmed with potential, despite her lack of results.

The team took occasional breaks for food and rest, during which Marl received combat training from Marie. Marl took Marie's word as law. During their breaks, they would disappear into a nearby field, and Jayde would watch them spar in the moonlight.

Marie bounced as easily off her hands as she did her feet. She lunged at Marl and pummeled him into the ground. Although frequently hit, Marl smiled and thanked Marie, eager to learn more.

Marl attempted back handsprings for nearly an hour. The forward hunched frame of the rock troll made it impossible. Over and over he jumped backward and landed on his head.

"Rock trolls won't need handsprings," said Marie.

"Me need to learn. If me not try, me no learn," said Marl, landing on his chest. Instead of turning over, the back of his head morphed into a face and his arms simply rotated around.

"Wait, you can morph your body to the other side?" Jayde said.

"Yah, all rock troll can," said Marl, looking embarrassed.

"Marl," Marie said, "we need to train you to stop working on perfecting human techniques and start working on techniques that only you will be able to perform."

Marie and Marl discussed new techniques while traveling. She discovered he could throw a punch with one arm, and then have that arm split into two arms while he punched. Marl explained that the amount of rock in him stayed constant, but the ability to change shape was nearly infinite, except in his chest which always stayed the same. He learned to retract one arm into his body while punching with the other. This effectively doubled the punching distance. Having a single exceptionally long arm looked quite odd but was remarkably effective in fighting. Marl learned the importance of versatility. With Marie's help they created a wide variety of attacks only a rock troll could do. He still remained unable to strike Marie even a single blow.

Jayde learned magical concepts but had little success in practice. Tonight they were discussing Conjuring.

"I still don't get what the components are," Jayde said.

"Well, try thinking of it in a different way. I know I have talked about elements and the various states of confluent forms, but—"

"But that just sounds like goop to me. I don't *get* it," Jayde said.

Cameron looked over. "Jayde, did you ever see a baker in a window?"

"The baker in Haynis was one of the few guys who didn't mind when I nicked the occasional roll or pastry. I think my sneaking in and stealing amused him for some reason," she said.

"You know how a baker makes a cake?" he asked.

"Not really."

"Well, a baker begins with flour and mixes in other ingredients. He has to add butter, eggs, sugar, and milk. He then stirs it all together to get the right consistency, but too much of any one ingredient ends in a cake that tastes bad."

"Conjuring is the same thing," Marie said. "For inanimate objects, you can make anything out of the ingredients around you. The best conjurers can change what they have around them into what is required. Like turning dirt into the flour, sugar, eggs, and milk they need. Then, after creating all the ingredients, they combine them and conjure up a cake. Before you conjure anything, you need the right ingredients."

Jayde thought about this for a while. "What about animals?"

"What do you mean?" Marie said.

"Well, you said 'inanimate' objects. Can a conjurer make animals and people and stuff like that?"

Marie looked at Cameron. "It's possible. But that is advanced Conjuring. It is not something you should even be attempting. True masters of Conjuring can create familiars."

"What?"

"A *familiar* is a creature that is part of you. You have to give part of yourself to the creature, and the creature behaves as you desire. It is completely loyal to the conjurer because it *is* part of you. I have been told that conjurers can see through their familiars' eyes and control them from across an entire country. However, if a familiar is hurt, you lose that part of yourself. It takes quite some time to rejuvenate lost parts of your soul. Thus, it's a terribly dangerous Conjuring, even for the most gifted."

"Why?" Jayde asked.

Cameron jumped in. "Think of it this way. Let's say to make a familiar you had to shave off all your hair. If you used that energy to make a mosquito, and someone absently swatted that mosquito, you would still have lost all your hair. It takes a long time to grow your hair back. Familiars have similar properties, only, instead of your hair, the part that you give to the familiar comes from in here," he said, pointing to his chest.

"So you can grow that part of yourself back, even if it is lost?" Jayde asked.

"Well, yes and no. Some conjurers fall into the trap of Conjuring too much or making too many familiars. If you split your spirit into too many parts, and all the parts are killed before you can regenerate them, you would die too," Marie said.

Jayde pondered. "So it's kind of like I'm an icicle. I could use really small parts from the bottom of the icicle, but then I would not be able to make as cool of a creature. I could use a bigger part of the icicle and make a better, more complicated creature, but it would be at risk of destroying the whole icicle. And, if I use too much of the icicle, it would break off, and there might be nothing left," Jayde said.

Cameron looked over at Marie, who seemed shocked by Jayde's explanation.

"Actually," Marie said, "that's a better explanation than I've ever heard before."

"So, if I wanted to, I could make a whole bunch of small mosquitoes, as long as I used just a little bit of my soul-spirit-Conjuring icicle and let it regrow, right?" Jayde asked.

"She understands the difficult concepts better than I do, and she can't conjure dirt," Marie muttered.

Jayde grinned. Over the days of travel she had become close to Cameron, Marie, and Marl. Previously she had to steal information or food. Marie seemed not only willing but also happy to educate Jayde about magic. Both Cameron and Marie shared their food and possessions freely without question. Jayde knew better than to trust them completely, but she did not know why they continued to help her while requesting nothing in exchange.

The road became more congested as they traveled. Most moved in the same direction as Marie, Cameron, Jayde, and Marl. The variety of travelers increased as well, including elves, a group of intelligent oxlike Bosks, and even a couple merfolk, who had some contraption surrounding them which allowed them to move on land while being surrounded with water.

Jayde pointed and yelled, "Look, a dwarf!"

The dwarf then pointed at her and yelled, "Look, an idiot!"

Jayde blushed, and they carried on past the dwarf. Marl glared at the dwarf as they passed. After passing, Marl began scouting again.

Five days later, Cameron halted the cart along the side of the road. Jayde looked up at Cameron, but his face remained impassive. Jayde guessed that Marl might be hiding. The rock troll could change his shape so well that he always resembled whatever rocks happened to be nearby. Jayde heard Marl's whisper from his hiding spot, right next to the cart. Despite being just past midnight, Cameron had found the rock troll and had pulled to a stop next to the boulder that looked like all the other rocks nearby.

"Big man place be where we go, right?" Marl asked.

"Yes. How far do you think till we get there, Marl?"

The rock troll paused. "Me think four or five."

"Four or five days?" Cameron asked.

"No. Four or five rocks," he said, and the boulder on the side of the road cracked into a grin.

Cameron looked at Marie, who shrugged. He advanced the cart to the edge of the bluff and gasped at the enormous metropolis spreading out before them, roughly four or five rock throws away.

Even in the middle of the night, the city teemed with light and activity. The place unfolded for leagues. Even from their slightly elevated position, they could not see the other side of the city. A few hundred paces ahead of them, a large, well-fortified gate stood in the middle of the road. An expanding city wall showed the gate to be the only entrance in sight. They made their way to guards armed with crossbows and stopped at the guard post.

Though they arrived at midnight, they still had to wait in a line behind various creatures to enter the city. The wall surrounding the city towered twenty feet above them. It continued in both directions as far as they could see.

"Whatcha need?" said the guard.

"I'm looking to set up shop in Grandeur," Cameron answered.

The guard laughed. "You should pick a different entrance next time. This is the Thieves' District. I suggest riding straight through half a league till you get to the Merchants' District. But if you need a place to stay, stop off at Gummy's. Safest place in Grandeur. Fairest prices too," he said.

"Thanks," Cameron replied. They rode on into the city. Flickering flames from lampposts illuminated the street. The street still buzzed with activity in the middle of the night. The city of Grandeur did not sleep.

Cameron took in everything with casual ease. Marie scanned her surroundings continuously. Marl slipped into the cart and curled up into a rock, not wanting to be seen. Jayde stared at everything. Her head swiveled continuously, trying to take in all the sights.

As she looked back at the guard post, she saw what looked like a giant pile of mud wave at her, then it collapsed into a trough that ran alongside the road.

Jayde's brief education over the last two weeks helped her identify some of the creatures prowling in the streets at night. She saw some large black bats zipping around. She saw goblins, golems, and griffins, all moving about their business down the side streets. Mostly she saw people in every sort of garb that could be imagined.

A group of goblins hunched over a small sprite. They looked up at Jayde, threw the sprite to the ground, and disappeared quickly in the night.

Jayde saw a cartful of mothlike gypsies being pulled by giant birds with reptilian heads. Everywhere she looked, creatures of all shapes and sizes went about their business. Jayde glimpsed two creatures with whiskers and feline features under their hoods darting onto a rooftop. She tried not to make any noise and also tried not to point, after learning her lesson from the dwarf. But when she saw the giant spider, she could not help herself; it was three feet tall with eight hairy legs stretching far as it scurried down the road. Jayde covered her mouth to muffle her small scream. It had on dark brown pants that allowed the multiple legs to move. It passed their cart briefly and scurried about its business.

A sidewalk ran parallel to the main road in front of the multiple houses, inns, and shops. The few people present walked on the sidewalk. Next to the walkway ran a low trough of mud about a foot wide. The mud continually churned, and sloshed back and forth. No wind nor outside force caused the motion. Jayde pointed it out to Marie, and she just shrugged and shook her head.

Eventually they made it to an inn with bloodred letters that read Gummy's. Broken glass littered the front of the inn, and cracked paint drifted from the sides. The smell of rank ale and urine flowed from the front of the inn.

"This is the place," Cameron said, as he pulled up the cart.

"You dudes new here?" asked someone in a cheery voice.

The voice surprised all of them. Cameron disappeared right before Jayde's eyes. Marl jumped in front of Jayde, creating a substantial rock wall between her and the speaker. The voice had come from the area of the mud trough.

"Whoa," said the speaker, "you're like totally freakin' out over nuthin', man." The voice sounded like a school of dead fish being dropped from a building. The creature splurtched into the dim light. It looked like a big upside-down bowl made of mud. It was about four feet tall, which made it about four feet wide as well. The creature had no arms or legs but oozed toward them, a large pair of eyes peering from the sides of the blob.

"Didn't mean to frazzle yah, brahs. Sorry about that. I just thought you dudes and dudettes might like the Happy Smyle Inn a bit more. It's totally more your style," said the mud creature.

"And what exactly is *our* style?" Cameron asked from somewhere behind the creature.

The creature's face melted away and appeared on the other side of its body, facing Cameron. "Oh, you know, dude. The style that lets you hold on to all your worldly possessions. Wicked bad karma in this part of the city, brah. Hard to hang onto the things you've grown attached to, you know? Things like this cart, the magic cabinet, your kidneys, those sorts of things."

"And why should we trust you and not the guard who recommended this inn?" asked Marie.

"Well, probably since that dude works for Gummy's, and I work for myself. Check that. I work for the dictator, but Solo's a cool dude, dude. Other than that, use your own noggin, brah. Just being helpful. See yah around," said the mud creature. It oozed back into the trough and disappeared.

"What do you think?" Cameron asked Marie.

"Happy Smyle Inn sounds better, and it can't be worse than this," Marie said.

Cameron materialized next to Jayde again, sheathing two black blades he had drawn the second he had been startled by the mud creature. The horses seemed as eager to get away from Gummy's as Jayde. They made their way to the Happy Smyle Inn.

The instant they came within a hundred paces of the Happy Smyle Inn, Jayde felt something odd. Marie later explained to Jayde that that sensation was an enchantment. Many inns had enchantments to prevent violence cast on them, so it was not abnormal to feel an enchantment near an inn.

A stable boy was sleeping on a small cot on the side of the inn. Next to him was a sign that read Think About a Bell Ringing for Assistance. Marie walked over and looked at the sign. She thought about a clanging bell. The young man jumped up out of a dead sleep. Marie spoke briefly to him, and he then led the horses and cart into the stable, as they went into the inn. Before they went in, Marie took Jayde aside.

"When we are inside, I don't want you to say anything to anyone."

"Why?" Jayde asked. Even though she had been brought to this new place, she was hesitant to let anyone have control over what she did or did not say.

"Trust me on this. I'm pretty sure the owner of this place is an enchantress. We don't want to cause suspicion while we are here, so just let me do the talking, all right?"

Jayde frowned but nodded.

It took some convincing to get Marl to enter the inn, but his reluctance was overruled by his desire to stay at Jayde's side.

As they walked inside, an odd sensation washed over them. Many small groups dressed in black spoke in strange hushed voices. Jayde tried to understand but could only hear a bizarre low murmur. Serving girls sped by with tankards of ale. It seemed that the Happy Smyle Inn never closed.

A plump woman in a bright purple blouse smiled and greeted them, as the foursome walked to the bar. Her garb seemed more appropriate for a jester than for a barmaid in a shady part of town.

"Welcome to the Happy Smyle. What can I do for you, with you, or to you?" asked the lady.

"We'd like a room for the night," Cameron said.

"For the night? You mean the next two hours?" she asked.

"How about till tomorrow night?" he said.

"No problem. You hungry? We have stew," she said. She nodded toward Marl. "If you prefer, we do have some good granite. I've been told our limestone's not too bad either, though I'm not really one to judge."

Marl's face beamed. "Me have the first."

"Granite it is," she said.

"Anything special you need for your daughter?" she asked.

Jayde started to respond but stopped when Marie grabbed her shoulder.

"She's fine. Just some milk instead of ale with the stew please," said Cameron.

"No problem," the plump lady said, winking at Jayde, while she pointed toward a booth.

After they finished eating, the woman handed Cameron the room key, and they all went upstairs together. Marl collapsed into a rock and quickly fell asleep. Marie and Jayde took one bed, and Cameron took the other. Before going to sleep, he made absolutely sure the windows were completely covered without a chance of sunlight coming through. Then he locked the door and lay down. It had been a long night.

Jayde lay in bed and waited for Marie to fall asleep.

She had initially planned on leaving once she got to the city. The part of her from Haynis told her to leave. She just got a free ride, free food, and, in addition to that, she had learned more about magic in two weeks than in all the time she had spent on her own. If she left now, she could disappear into the city. She could continue researching magic and be happy.

Jayde got up, walked to the door, and stood still. The lady at the bar thought she was Marie and Cameron's daughter. Jayde smiled; maybe she would give Marie and Cameron just a few more days before Jayde left. They likely had money as well. She would need something to get started in a new city like this.

Jayde walked silently to her bed and crept back under the covers, drifting quickly to sleep.

Chapter 15: Rescuing the Shop

Sarah slept fitfully, haunted by the nightmares she had witnessed at the campsite after the wivari attack. It had been over a week, but she could still see the slaughter vividly in her mind.

Sarah mounted her horse and tucked her two pixie companions safely in her pocket. Fortunately one horse had escaped the slaughter. Nearly everything else they owned had been destroyed. Thaddeus Gumble may have been an ignorant, self-centered lout, but no one deserved to be torn to shreds by a pack of wild wivari. Her memories flooded back to the horrific scene at the campsite. She tried not to think about the carnage, but she could not control her thoughts.

The road became more familiar with every passing league.

Her mood elevated upon seeing Grandeur on the horizon. It looked beautiful at dawn. The perfectly straight main roads lined the troughs for the mudmen. The city entailed the business of thousands of creatures scurrying on a multitude of errands. Lines of shops selling everything imaginable spanned throughout the bustle.

Sarah stopped on the roadside to let out her two companions. The pixies could easily keep up with the horse for a short while. They were elated to know their journey was finally ending. They had been away from their troop for weeks, something quite rare for pixies.

Sarah thought about her small house on the edge of the forest and about her parents. A twinge of homesickness swept through her, and she felt a pull, though oddly she could feel the sensation leading her to the city. She rode into Grandeur.

She hitched the horse outside Gumble's house. She took off the saddlebags and carted the gear to her small servant's quarters. She flopped into her bed in her empty room. What would she do next? She had no one to tell her what to do. She had no one to tell her where to go or how to behave. She had nobody to say who she was allowed to speak with and who she had to avoid. Her entire life she had always followed orders. Her father had run the house as any military man would: with orders. When he said *run*, she had better sprint, if she did not want her hide tanned.

She supposed her upbringing may have been one of the reasons she had excelled as a servant. She followed directions perfectly, without question. Often she knew better ways to do her orders, yet she followed through dutifully, since that was expected. Sarah stopped abruptly. The two pixies resting on her shoulder were flung forward and caught themselves in midair.

"Problem, Sarah?" they asked in unison.

"I can do whatever I want. I can do whatever I want, *whenever* I want. I don't have to take any orders anymore," she said. Slowly a smile crept over her face. It had not dawned on her until now. She had always looked for different ways to approach what happened in her life. She had wanted to explore Suliad, but her father had said no, and she had obeyed. She had wanted to see magical creatures, but her father wanted to keep her safe. Even after her house had burned down, some part of her sought out an existence where she had others making decisions for her. Never again.

"I am in charge now," she said.

The two pixies looked quizzically at each other, shrugged, and then landed on her shoulder once more.

"How is this discovery a novelty of understanding?" Lucy asked.

"Well, I always took my directions from Thaddeus Gumble. I had to do what he said," Sarah responded.

"Really?" the pixie said. John and Lucy spoke in rapid Pixish quietly to each other.

Sarah picked out "bumbling ineptitudes of masters" and "character beyond reproach to coexist with imbecilic ingrates." Finally Sarah asked what they had thought her relationship with Thaddeus Gumble was.

"We always thought he had intellectual deficiencies requiring your assistance," said John.

"We thought you had volunteered to assist, due to his lack of mental and physical fortitude," said Lucy.

"He was disgustingly corpulent," said John.

"And he interacted like an ungrateful juvenile," said Lucy.

"We assumed that you were master, since he could not take care of himself. You went out of your way to help, despite the fact that you had greater mental, physical, and emotional depth," said John.

"Our lack of experience with humans faults us again, I suppose," said John.

"Is it a sign of status and power for humans to be pudgy, slothful, and obnoxious?" asked Lucy.

Sarah pondered their conclusions. "Not exactly. Granted, I guess it sometimes seems like that. For humans, power and wealth often go hand in hand. Humans can be powerful and wealthy without being intelligent. I suppose he was obnoxious since he could afford to be obnoxious. He had more money than most, so perhaps he assumed that equaled superiority."

She heard some more rapid Pixish.

"So if you become wealthy, then will you be required to act as he did?" Lucy asked.

Sarah laughed. "No, I will still be just as I am now. Humans come in all levels of greed, desire, stupidity, and brilliance. That's what makes us fun. Humans have stereotyped one another for centuries, but, when you get down to it, you have to judge each human separately."

"We will try to take that into consideration," said Lucy, who seemed relieved that Sarah would not become fat and lazy the instant she obtained any wealth.

"It would not be fair for me to judge all pixies by the behavior of just you two, right? Humans vary greatly. Though I suppose you guys have not seen many human customs, have you?" Sarah asked.

"Our human experience is still quite lacking," John responded.

"I suppose we might as well tell you," Lucy said. John eyed her nervously but did not stop her. "We were assigned to follow you for more reasons than to acquire excellence in English. We were to obtain understanding of humans from a personal level. We were to better comprehend how humans interact to improve the troop as a whole."

"Oh? And?" Sarah asked.

"And I believe that we were extremely lucky to happen across you as the human that we decided to observe," said John.

"Well, let's hope the rest of the troop agrees," said Sarah. "Because I no longer have a job as a servant, and I think I know a shop in town that is about to really take off."

"You can make the shop levitate? I thought you indicated that you lack magical aptitude," asked Lucy.

"Oh, I have my own special type of magic," Sarah said.

As they approached the Picky Pixie, they saw a great crowd outside the store. A varied group of ruffians, cretins, and burly miscreants surrounded the entrance. To Sarah's relief, it appeared that the shop had not been opened in her absence. The gates in front of the shop were still down, protecting the store. Sarah cupped her hands and peered inside. Jenny the shopkeeper had diligently organized the wares. It was the sign outside the shop that worried her:

"LOOKING FOR HONEST PERSON(S) TO HELP GUARD PRICELESS JEWELRY COLLECTION. CURRENTLY ONLY GUARDED BY PIXIES, AND IT WOULD BE EXTREMELY EASY TO STEAL, SO WE NEED EXTRA HELP TO PROTECT. COME AND APPLY FOR THE JOB ON THE TWENTIETH OF THE MONTH. PLEASE BE HONEST AND DO NOT STEAL."

"Oh, wow, she's an idiot," Sarah said. "Is there a secret entrance up top that only pixies can get in?"

"How did you know?" Lucy answered.

"You told me that pixies always have a few entrances to any location, right? Fly in there right now and tell them *not* to open the door. As soon as these guys are let in, they will loot the place. They will take everything. Go!"

Lucy and John both disappeared over the roof of the building. A minute later they reappeared from the rooftop of the building with Jenny the storekeeper at their side. Sarah could hear John and Lucy warning the shopkeeper, but Jenny seemed indifferent to their warning. Jenny had a large grin on her tiny face upon seeing Sarah.

"Sarah! So wonderful to be revisited by you again. We diligently organized and isolated problems, as you had hypothesized would come. I conversed again with the dictator, and he advised hiring protection. I see that quite a crowd has accumulated. How wonderful!"

The crowd seemed uninterested in the small pixies. Sarah walked away from the crowd, so she could talk. It seems they had arrived just in time.

"Jenny, if you open the front door, those men will come in and take everything in the shop."

"But why would they do that? I most certainly would not tolerate employment if they pilfered merchandise."

Sarah held back a curse. "They are not here for the job. They are here for free jewelry."

"But I gained understanding about such interactions. I am not volunteering our merchandises without adequate exchanges of money or services. They would be stealing," Jenny said.

"Exactly," said Sarah.

"But my sign—"

"Informed them that they have an easy target filled with valuables that is currently unguarded," Sarah finished. "Now we have a bigger problem. We have every thug in Grandeur gathered in front of the store, drooling for the store to open."

"You mean they would just take it? They would take all our hard work and precious metals and leave? That's so very impractical, impolite, and impudent!" said the pixie.

Sarah had never seen Jenny angry. Sarah looked back at the crowd. A few of the thugs had grabbed the metal fence in front of the store and shook it. There had to be a way to stop them from destroying the store.

"I've got an idea," said Sarah. "Go inside and grab something flashy but not too expensive. Just be sure it looks like it would be worth a lot to humans. I'll need some pixies to bring it out and keep it in the air, out of reach of any of those cretins."

Jenny and Lucy disappeared above the roof. Sarah took a deep breath and walked toward the rough-looking crowd. John perched nervously on her shoulder but did not fly away.

"Hello! Attention! Please?" Sarah said. The crowd had gotten a bit more boisterous as the morning had worn on, and one young woman shouting did not change their attitude much.

"WILL YOU IGNORANT OAFS PLEASE SHUT UP!" Sarah bellowed.

They quieted. Dozens of eyes looked on the small woman in front of them, surprised that such a noise came from one so tiny. Others gave her stares that bordered on hatred.

"Thank you. I have invited all of you here to look for someone to guard our new shop. I knew that this sign would get the strongest, quickest, and best applicants for the job," she said.

She heard a few snickers in the crowd, as well as some laughs.

"I realize that some of you might actually be here to get some easy pickings. Sorry, we are not idiots. We put out this sign to get you here. Let me just tell you right now that that gate is not going up today nor is the store opening today. But I want you to know that we *are* hiring someone to guard the store. I'm sorry for the deception, but we wanted the best. I know that one of you in this crowd is truly the best, so we created a contest," she said.

The men in the crowd all talked at once.

"*Oi*, what's all this then, eh?"

"Why you bother to have all us come here?"

"What's this rubbish about a contest?"

Sarah continued. "Oh, I guarantee that it will be more than worth your time. Well, it will be worth the time of some of you. You see, we could not possibly hire all of you. So we just want the best. The competition begins at sundown. For now, anyone can sign up for the competition right here in the street. It is open to whoever wants to come. The purpose of this contest will be to hire two guards. So between now and sundown, all of you have that time to pick a partner. You are applying for the job together. If you win, you not only get the job but you win the prize," she said.

At that time, a small fleet of pixies appeared over the rooftop holding a large necklace. It was gold and studded with layers of sparkling gems. The sunlight reflected off the gems and caused the piece to shine with multicolored radiance. Sarah swore under her breath. The pixies remembered the part about it being flashy but forgot about the "not too expensive" part. Oh, well.

"This is the Nautilus. It is the shop's most valuable piece. It might very well be worth a small kingdom. The troop has asked me to help them with promoting their store. I am not a pixie, but I can only imagine a piece like this must have taken them months or even years to create. Also, as I am sure you all know, pixie jewelry always has a little bit of pixie magic in it. With a piece like this, who knows? Perhaps it can create its own wealth. This noble troop plans to open its shop soon, and, through great deliberation, they have decided that they want the two best possible guards for their shop. Thus, this is the prize for the twosome that wins the competition," Sarah said.

John whispered Pixish her ear. "The Nautilus? What is this Nautilus? That piece was made two weeks ago. I know since I helped make it."

The crowd, however, had gone mute. The crowd stared at the gleaming necklace floating above their heads. A few were actually drooling.

"Tonight's contest will be a simple affair. It will be battles in pairs. I only want those who are serious about getting the job. We'll see you and your partners at sundown. Good luck."

At this, the thugs looked at one another and grinned broadly. Several had already darted away. It seemed like many needed to find a partner they could trust, which, in that crowd, might be difficult. The rest of the crowd rapidly dispersed upon realizing the shop had no plans to open its doors.

After the crowd had gone, Jenny opened the front gate, and Sarah slipped in the shop. They locked the gate behind them. Only after she was inside did Sarah hyperventilate.

"OhMyGosh. OhMyGosh. OhMyGosh," she said.

A swarm of pixies brought over a tall glass of water that she gulped down. She slowly caught her breath. She heard many conversations in Pixish going on at the same time. Parts of what had happened echoed in Pixish throughout the troop.

"How can she deliberate acquisitions without consulting the whole troop?"

"She dispersed the ruffians utilizing human talk? Inconceivable!"

"Did she mesmerize via magic? Does Jenny know of her magical fortitude?"

"How can she partake of such actions without Jenny? Are we being betrayed?"

Sarah took a few deep breaths. When she looked around the room, the buzzing quieted. There were many more pixies than she remembered. It seems she had another speech to make today. John and Lucy smiled at her. Jenny did not.

"What just happened out there, Sarah?" Jenny asked, a hint of anger in her voice.

Sarah straightened and looked Jenny in the eyes. "I just saved the shop. That's what happened. Those men were planning on robbing you. Your sign was an invitation for thieves. They were not looking for jobs. They just wanted to come in and take your jewelry."

Lucy and John rapidly translated into Pixish. Sarah could hear the gasps of surprise through the crowd. Sarah explained how some humans think and how some prey on the weak for their own gain. Sarah then explained her impromptu plan. She explained that she needed to get the greedy crowd of thieves to disperse, which she had. She also wanted to get talented fighters to come and apply for the job of guards, which she had.

Sarah explained that the story of the competition would spread like wildfire through the town. She had seen such things happen many times before in Grandeur. The thugs would look for partners who could fight well, so they could split the prize. The fighters would talk to each other, and curiosity would rise. Sarah figured that, by sundown, double the number of competitors would come to battle. Not only would they get a good look at some of the best fighters but they got rid of the problem of the shop being robbed by the thieves. Also she had created free advertisement for the shop.

John embellished some of the finer details. He explained how Sarah had risked her own life for the good of the troop, confronting a horde of bloodthirsty ruffians, armed only with her quick wit. He went on to discuss how she had created the story of the Nautilus to add value to the piece. He stated that, other than naming the piece of jewelry, she had never lied, thus upholding the truthfulness of pixies.

"But what of the tournament?" Jenny asked.

"We have fighters coming here to compete. Let's figure out the rules for the tournament. We need paper and pen, rope, and something to make an arena. We've got a lot of work to do," Sarah said.

Sarah rattled off a list of needed items, Jenny translated, and the shop buzzed with activity. Sarah created flyers to promote the tournament in the first hour. She then sent out groups of pixies to post them all over the town. Within two hours, the first twosome approached the shop asking to sign up. It was still early morning.

Sarah had figured out the location right away. Thaddeus Gumble had owned plots of land all over the city. One of them happened to be an empty field. He had never used it, and it was a perfect location for the tournament. The rules of the competition created a larger problem.

She had toyed with the idea of one giant brawl, winner takes all. However, that seemed just plain wrong, and people would get hurt. After discussing logistics with Jenny, they decided on the rules. They would have a large ring where the competition would take place. Since they wanted to find guards, they would take their cues accordingly. Guards throw out unruly people. Thus, the competition would be all about throwing people out. Four go into the circle, and the twosome that remains inside goes to the next round. When a competitor is pushed out of the circle, he is out. If he happens to be unconscious at the time, so be it.

By noon they posted the rules and signup sheet in front of the shop. By this time twenty more twosomes had appeared. To Sarah's relief, the pairs appeared more like the typical guards she had in mind and less like cutthroats. The groups signed up and left without a problem.

After hours of groups signing up, Sarah realized that the popularity of her competition had grown beyond her expectations. She had thought a few people would show interest. She did not think that she would have over fifty teams competing. The free publicity would be great—as long as no one got killed.

Chapter 16: Assassin

Before the bozrac left, it asked Mrs. Crass, "If you had to sacrifice your life to end his, would you?"

"Absolutely," she answered immediately.

"Aye, I bet you would," Finn said.

"Find Kafe Mean and kill him!" she yelled.

The demon disappeared.

Mrs. Crass spent the following days pacing, terrified the bozrac might fail. She had never seen Kafe Mean again, and she only had a hint of her former powers. Her desire to kill Kafe was fueled primarily by revenge; the return of her power was only an added bonus.

Excitement flooded her when the small monster reappeared four days later. The demon purred as it approached.

"Your life is apparently worth as much as his," said Finn, still purring. "Some men don't die easily."

Mrs. Crass glared at the cat, not understanding. "So … is he dead?"

"The entity Kafe Mean is dead surely. But I don't think that was what you truly desired," said the bozrac.

"Is he dead?" she asked again.

"The thing named Kafe Mean is dead. Names have power, Leynstra, and sometimes people go to great lengths to protect that power. 'Kafe Mean' was just a familiar that the storyteller had created long ago just for you. As it died, the creature called Kafe Mean left a message for you."

The bozrac ran into a shadow, where it disappeared. Smoke rose from the outline of the creature, creating letters hovering in the air.

The letters *K-A-F-E M-E-A-N* floated in front of her. Then, ever so slowly, the letters moved. The *K* shifted right, and the *F* shifted left. *M-E-A-N* shifted as well, with the letters slowly drifting to different positions. Even before the letters had halted, Mrs. Crass began to wail.

"No. No! Noooo!" she yelled. "That's impossible! How? But, but, how? He didn't know! He couldn't know!" she said, tears pouring down her face.

"But he did. The storyteller figured you'd find a way to track him down. He thought of it from the beginning," said the bozrac.

She cried at the ease that the storyteller had twisted her plans. He had a Fake Name—Kafe Mean—from the very beginning. It was all part of his plan. He had figured that, just in case someone held a grudge against him, he would give out an alias. King Zolf had warned her that the man, this Great Traveler, went by many names. It was so simple, but she had been duped. The stupid simple trick had cost her the one chance she had at vengeance, her only chance. The bozrac had killed Kafe Mean, but that was not the storyteller she needed to kill for her freedom.

The creature continued to purr as it hopped onto the table, helping itself to some leftover chicken.

Mrs. Crass collected herself but continued to curse under her breath.

The bozrac chuckled. "He's clever, that one. But you agreed to a death, which I provided. Now, do you have my second task yet, or do you need more time?"

Mrs. Crass felt a jump in her heart. "Wait! You mean you saw him? Describe him to me!"

The bozrac described the man. It was him. It was the storyteller.

"But you told me to kill Kafe Mean, which was the name of the familiar that traveled with the storyteller. No one can hide their true self from a bozrac, as you know too well," it said.

"How could the storyteller create a familiar?" she asked.

"He didn't make it himself. Someone made that familiar for him. He must know a conjurer with massive power to create a familiar that complex," said Finn.

"No matter! You know then who the storyteller is? Right? You know who he is, so you can kill him? Right?" she asked.

"Is that your next request then? Would you like me to kill him? You could've saved me quite the legwork if you had mentioned this from the beginning," said Finn.

Mrs. Crass wanted to answer yes. She tried to tell the demonic cat that this was exactly what she wanted, but she could not. A flash of violet came from her eyes, and she groaned. She had failed. The Dark King had given her both her freedom and one chance for revenge. If she had succeeded, she could keep her powers and her freedom. If she had failed, her life and soul belonged to him. Her life and soul now belonged to him … unless.

The bozrac asked again.

She stood, unable to answer.

She fought in silence for three days straight. The bozrac sat, watching her struggle, often purring as she battled the curse that she had allowed to be placed on her by King Zolf.

Mrs. Crass knew her will had been tainted. She felt her free will tearing away from her. For three days she did not move. She did not eat nor drink. She fought against an invisible wall of will. She battled the spell Zolf's necromancers had placed on her, as it sapped her freedom. She cried, weeping without moving as she fought.

Finneus had periodically asked her about his second task during the three days. The bozrac knew she could not answer. The creature delighted in her suffering and her inability to utter the single word yes that would solve all her problems. Mrs. Crass gazed at the creature. The bozrac seemed patient with her. It happily bounced around the room. It had only occasionally disappeared, only to reappear and ask her again, "Have you decided what my second task will be?"

After three days of agony against the continuous pull of the spell, she collapsed.

Mrs. Crass's will snapped.

She had tried to ask the bozrac to kill the storyteller, but the words never came out. She had a frustrating dichotomy within herself. She could feel her old thoughts and still had her prejudices and quirks, but she could also detect the underlying drive of the Dark King's will flowing through her and becoming her entire purpose in life.

Late one night her goons came in after an evening at the tavern. One vomited in the corner, and she woke up to the retching noise. She knew better than to yell at the imbeciles. She was livid. She still had enough of herself to strike out against idiocy. Mrs. Crass had warned them repeatedly about her thoughts of overindulging in ale, yet they had continued to ignore her warnings. Her rage overcame her. She translocated them out of the city. She had not had power like that for decades. Her power had returned. They would have at least a four-hour walk back. More than likely they would pass out on the street before they made it home. *That would show them to have more manners*, she thought. Giving her will to the Dark King had returned her full powers.

It was then the witch realized her final request for the bozrac. The creature had failed her, but she could not fail the king. The demon taunted her with its very existence. She hated it, but it could be used. Finn listened to her second request with a blank expression.

"You need to kill the next Chosen," said Mrs. Crass.

"Aye. But I wonder, what's in it for you?" asked the cat.

"Nothing is in it for me, but everything is in it for him. The next Chosen has the potential to kill the Dark King. King Zolf has killed Chosen for the last two centuries. However, somehow, in the last twenty years, all the Chosen have eluded him. Whenever the next Chosen is discovered, you kill. No tricks. Just death. Once dead, I grant you complete freedom," she said.

That caught the cat's attention.

"When I find and kill this next Chosen of yours, you'll let me free? Are you willing to bind your words in blood? I won't kill you, but I need to be sure that you are not lying to me," asked the cat.

"Yes," she said.

The cat licked its lips and plunged into Mrs. Crass. Despite being over a league away on their walk back, the two goons could hear her screaming.

Chapter 17: Relocation

"Me not want you get killed," Marl said.

"Listen. I know you really want to look after me, Marl, but I've been taking care of myself for a long time now. I've lived on the streets my whole life," Jayde said.

The giant rock did not budge. Jayde knew Marl just wanted to keep her safe, but his overbearing parenting irked her to no end.

"Marie, can you talk sense to him? You know I can handle myself," said Jayde.

"Don't look at me, Jayde," said Marie. "We still have a few hours till sundown, so Cameron's not going anywhere for a bit. Why don't we see what we can learn from the innkeeper? Also keep quiet downstairs. I'm still not sure what is going on here, but there's an enchantment on this inn that I haven't figured out yet."

The threesome went downstairs and sat at the bar. Only a few patrons occupied the tables. Apparently most of the Happy Smyle's business occurred at night. The plump innkeeper greeted them, as they walked toward the bar.

"Well, good morning! Or should I say evening? Can I get you guys some fresh bread and pot roast?"

The smell from the kitchen washed over Jayde, and she realized she was starving. They ordered three servings of the roast.

Marl ate the man-food without complaint; he could survive on just about anything.

"So what're you doing in Grandeur?" the innkeeper asked.

"We're looking to set up a new business after running away from our last town," Marie said. Immediately her attention snapped into place. She knew better than to just blurt out information like that. What had just happened?

"Ah, trouble with the last town, I see. I see. Well, Grandeur is a great place for refugees. It has provided a second, third, or tenth chance to many," she said with a smile.

Marie looked right into the innkeeper's eyes. "What's going on here?"

"What do you mean?" she asked.

"I know there's an enchantment here. What game are you playing?" she said.

"Oh, that. First time in Grandeur? I'm an enchantress. And, yes, I did place some enchantments on my inn. First, only the truth can be told here. Try as they might, people are unable to lie while in my inn. I'm sorry if you already admitted more than you wanted, but that's part of the benefits of being the innkeeper here," she said with a smile.

"Humph," Marie said. "Well, we really *are* looking to set up a new business."

"You must be. You said so in my inn. Thus, it's the truth," Esmeralda countered.

"Oh, right."

"Listen. I can tell you have been burned in the past, but please let me assure you. What you want to do is talk with the DATT," Esmeralda said.

"What's a DATT?"

"The 'dictator at the time.' The DATT is the person who keeps the country in order, but I think just keeping this city from imploding is more than enough work," she said.

"A dictator?"

"We've had a few bad ones in the past, though Solomon has been here for a few decades now. Best one we've had in centuries, if you want my opinion. He takes a great interest in people setting up new businesses. He met with me before I set up this shop. I told him my idea, and he recommended setting up right here. I thought he was an idiot, but nonetheless I followed his advice."

"Why not here?"

"Well, this is a busy area for thieves, assassins, wizards, and all sorts of shady people. I thought that none of them would want an inn that required honesty. Yet, it seems that it is the perfect meeting place for people who are always suspicious of others. I mean, honest merchants don't need a place that guarantees honesty. It is the suspicious who needs a place like this. Not to mention the fact that some really shady people just happen to be some of the wealthiest people around. As it turns out, I have really done quite well."

"Interesting. How do I schedule a meeting with the DATT?"

"*Splurg* him a message," she said.

Marie looked at her blankly.

"Have you seen the mud troughs running along the main road?"

"Yes."

"Those are the Splurgs. The mudmen moved into the city shortly after this DATT came to power. The DATT allowed them in, only if they would get honest jobs and work hard. They suggested setting up the mudways."

"Mudways?"

"Those troughs through the city span *all* the main roads. A Splurg can go from one area to the next in a blink of an eye. It makes communication over the distance of the city incredibly easy. I don't know how they got along without the Splurgs before they were here. All you have to do is block the mud flow, and one will appear. For a copper he will bring your message to anyone along the mudways. Just tell the Splurg what you want, and he'll get the message there in seconds."

"Wow. The DATT must get a lot of messages," Marie asked.

"He probably has a fleet of servants filtering the messages for him, but he always gets the important ones."

"Esmeralda!" a man called out from the door, followed by several sneezes.

"Excuse me a minute," she said to Marie, while walking to the other edge of the bar. She faced the man who had just walked in. "What do you want, Waddle?"

"You seen Mullet?" he asked, sniffing loudly and wiping his nose.

"No. Last I heard, he was playing chess at Gummy's. What do you need him for?"

"There's some pixie place that's holding a tournament tonight! They'll let any two, who want to fight, duel for a huge diamond necklace. They ain't got *no* entrance fee! Something about a promotion or guard contest. I don't know. All I know is that I need a good second, so we can win that necklace. It's gotta be worth a load of gold, easy!"

Marie's ears perked at that. The long trip had drained much of their reserves.

"Any twosome can enter this tournament?" Marie asked.

"Sure lady. But it'll be pretty rough. Your buddy here might be good in a fight, because I think some really tough people will be there," he said.

"When is it?"

"Sundown at the field across from the Black Jack's Oddities," he said. "Es, if you see Mullet, tell him that I'm looking for him."

"If I see him, I'll let him know. But you realize, if he fights, it will be with Kevin. Just because Mullet beat you in chess a few times doesn't mean he'll want to get pummeled with you in a fight," she said.

The man ignored her comments. He grunted a response which was interrupted by sneezing. He then slipped back into the street. They heard the distant sound of someone losing their lunch.

Marie looked at Marl. "What do you think? You up for some sparring practice?"

"Me not let you down," he said.

Jayde grumbled. "I can't go out and explore the street, but he gets to fight everyone in sight. Sure, that's fair." Marie glared at Jayde, but it was too late.

Esmeralda let out a gasp. "Oh, my. OH, MY! This isn't your daughter. This isn't your daughter at all!"

Marie eyed the innkeeper. "You work in a place that sees every sort of lowlife imaginable, right? So I'll have to assume you can keep a secret," she said.

"Of course," Esmeralda said.

"I'll assume you can feel what I feel as well."

"Of course! Anyone with even a glint of Talent could sense it the second she talked. My goodness, child, have you decided?"

"She hasn't decided yet," Marie said. "And we're not deciding for her. Jayde is a bright kid. We figured the best way for her to decide is to let her choose for herself."

"Anyone want to clue me in as to what the heck you're talking about?" Jayde said.

"Child, you could go into anything. Well, I suppose you're right. It should be her choice. Considering I practiced as an enchantress for only a short time before changing careers and becoming an innkeeper, it's only fair. Yes, yes. Having it be her choice is really the best way," she said.

"Thanks?" Jayde said, glancing at Marie with one eyebrow raised.

They finished their meals and went to the mud trough in front of the inn. It looked like normal mud, except that it flowed in both directions at the same time. The right side of the trough flowed toward the entrance of the town; the left side flowed toward the inner city.

At the corner of the Happy Smyle was a large wooden slab. In the trough of mud was a slot that looked like a perfect fit. An iron chain attached to the wood prevented someone from stealing it. Jayde grabbed the piece of wood and gently slid it into the slot. She pushed down on the wood, but it only slid a little bit. The mud sloshed over the slot and continued its course in both directions. The mud bent around the slot, actually hovering over the ground but continued on its course. Though it hovered around the sides, not a drop of mud landed on the ground.

On the other edge of the porch of the Happy Smyle, Jayde saw a creature approaching. It looked like a giant spider, but it wore short pants with eight legs and had a beret on its head. Jayde hid behind Marie. The creature scuttled up to the trough, leaned over, and then slammed the wood into the slot with a *thunk*.

"Takes a bit o' muscles, ma'am," said the spider. It then tipped its hat and went on its way down the street.

Jayde released the breath she had been holding and shuddered. "Thanks," she said, long after the spider was out of earshot. She yelped as a voice spoke right behind her.

"Was'sup, brah?" said the mudman that had appeared.

"*Ahg!*" said Jayde.

"Was'sup? You dudettes need sumpin'?" said the mudman.

"Yes," said Marie, who collected herself first. This was the way to get a hold of the Splurg. Apparently they appeared quite quickly when summoned.

"We would like to start a business in Grandeur, and we were told that we should meet with the dictator first."

"Totally. Totally," said the mudman. "You gotta copper for the message to the DATT, dudette?"

"Um, yes," said Marie, as she dropped a copper into the outstretched blob of mud, which she assumed was the creature's hand. The coin slowly disappeared into the mud.

"Thanks, brah. I'll get it to him posthaste." It then lifted the piece of wood that obstructed the mud flow. The wood swung next to the trough, and the Splurg disappeared into the trough. Jayde watched as a small rise in mud zoomed down the mudways and vanished in less than a second.

"Well, that was easy, I guess," said Jayde. "I wonder how we'll know if we can meet with him?"

"I'm not sure," Marie said, as they walked back toward the inn.

"Where's Marl?" she asked. They saw him on the other side of the street speaking to a wood troll. It appeared that Marl had gotten over his earlier nervousness about being in a city. A voice surprised them from behind.

"All righty, dudes!"

They turned to see that the mudman had reappeared.

"The DATT says someone will come in twenty minutes."

"What? Already? But how did he get the message?"

The smear of dripping mud looked confused. "You just asked me to give him a message. You wanted a meeting, righto? You got your meeting."

"Give him points for efficiency," Jayde said.

"Where are we supposed to meet this person?" Marie asked.

"Here, of course. They all like Esmeralda's place. He'll, like, totally be here in twenty. Speak atcha later!" said the mudman. He then disappeared back into the trough of mud.

Jayde was laughing. "I love this place!"

"Let's see what the dictator has to say before we jump to conclusions," Marie answered.

Jayde saw Marl still talking with the wood troll. They spoke in harsh, guttural tones. All Jayde heard was "*Splank ka bak kak-ba-Splanksh!*" A short time later Marl walked back over.

"Nice guy. He want me to be with him to fight. Me have to tell that me got me a man-thing to fight with. He sad but glad to meet new troll in town. Me not see wood troll for long time. Most trolls just want to bash. Dis place not same at all. Nice to meet," said Marl.

"Aren't we all just making so many friends today," Marie said.

The group went back inside and joined Cameron, who was having breakfast at a table. Marie gave him a quick update of their activities. They sat in a corner without any possibility of direct sunlight. It was second nature to pick such places. Marie, Jayde, and Marl had been nervously watching the door ever since they sat down. Waiting for a dictator could make anyone nervous. Cameron, as always, seemed at ease. Eighteen minutes after sending their message via the Splurg, a man dressed in black with a pointy goatee and thick black hair entered the Happy Smyle.

The man went directly to Esmeralda and gave her a big hug. She poured him a wine glass of clear liquid, and he walked directly toward their table and sat down.

"Hello, ladies, and … the rest. I'm Loman. How can I help you?" said the man.

"Are you the dictator's assistant?" asked Cameron.

"Oh, heavens, no! The assistants are much too busy to leave the castle during the day," said the man.

"But you are here representing him, right?" asked Marie.

"Correct."

All but Cameron seemed disheartened by this.

"From what I was told, you are interested in doing business in Grandeur. What type of business would you offer?" asked Loman.

"A medical office," Cameron said.

The man paused and looked thoughtfully at the group. "What qualifications do you have?"

"Four years of medical training and a three-year residency over at—"

The man interrupted him. "Yes, yes. Fine. A simple, 'I'm actually a doctor' would do. Here in Grandeur we have hundreds of medical businesses. Most sell fake cures, panaceas, and placebos to the ignorant. It might be interesting if one clinic had a person who actually knew what he was doing."

"Thank you," said Cameron.

"No problem. Where?"

"Here. Here in Grandeur," Marie answered.

"Grandeur is a pretty big place. Would you be averse to me suggesting a location?" he asked.

"Suggest away," Marie said.

"I know of an abandoned building located on the main road. It would set you up across the street from a spirit healer, but that should not be a problem. As a doctor I expect you would have a different approach to medicine other than screaming at disease. After all, Grandeur's never short on injured or sick people."

"And why would you go out of your way to help us out so much?" Marie asked.

"What I am proposing is a bit of a symbiotic relationship. We help you. You help Grandeur. You pay us back, and everyone wins. The DATT would rather set up a business that adds value to Grandeur than another snake oil salesman out to steal dreams. There's too much snake oil going around these days. I mean, seriously, how much oil does one person really need?"

"Truly," Cameron said.

"So you accept the offer?" he asked.

"The price?" Cameron asked.

"Well, you'll have to buy the property. But since the previous occupants left the building without selling it to anyone else, it, of course, belongs to the governing body at the time. Five gold rents you the building for the year, but you have to take it as is," said the man.

Cameron paused and looked over at Esmeralda. "Miss, would you take this deal if it were offered to you?" he asked.

"Absolutely. I have learned to trust the DATT, especially in regard to his offers about businesses in Grandeur," she answered.

"Okay. Deal. But if we get to the building and find the offer unacceptable?" Cameron asked

"You may refuse the deal anytime in the first month. Just let the Splurg know, but no other deal will be made," said the man.

"Sounds fair," Cameron answered. "I don't know if we could have asked for anything more."

"Oh, you could have, but you wouldn't have gotten it. Your first payment will be due at the end of next month. Here's the address. Good luck and welcome to Grandeur," said the man.

They shook hands, and the man left.

Cameron rarely went out in the daylight, for obvious reasons. Becoming a giant stone statue until the following midnight really put a damper on the day's activities. He remained fully conscious the entire time he was a statue, which sometimes worked to his advantage. A statue often can obtain secrets if in the right location. But, the drawbacks greatly outweighed the benefits. On top of all that, turning to stone always had him craving fresh blood.

He had devised a way to travel during daylight, since he realized that sometimes it was inevitable.

Direct sunlight would change him to a statue very quickly. Sunlight through glass would cause him to change less quickly. As long as he had all his skin covered, he had little risk of turning to stone. Sunlight could permeate through just about any cloth, but Cameron had learned that a good druid robe covered just about everything. Granted, there were few places that one could dress in a full-length robe and not be seen as out of the ordinary, but Grandeur was one of those places. He had never actually tried out the costume, but, in theory, it seemed a sound idea. Marie, however, thought it was a stupid idea, since she would be the one who would have to haul his stony body over to the new place if the cloak did not work.

Fortunately for both of them, the cloak worked. Cameron could see little through the dark mesh. Admittedly, when they finally did get to their new business location, he felt a bit stiff.

"This is it," he said with a smile, as they all walked in the door, "our new business and home."

The foursome stopped and stared in silence.

"This building is a steaming pile of garbage!" said Marie.

The building was indeed a steaming pile of garbage. Large piles of waste with swarms of flies and crawling maggots buzzed angrily at the intruders. The air blurred with the atrocious stench of weeks of decaying refuse. Broken glass lay strewn all over the floor. It appeared that this building had been used as a storage location during garbage strikes. Large piles of rancid meat, leftover cabbage, and decaying fruit lay scattered through the large room. After a few seconds inside the building, all four quickly exited.

"I think I'm going to be sick," said Jayde, who ran into the street to prove it.

"Oh, I don't know. I think with a few weeks' hard work, dedication, and a lot of love, we could upgrade this place to a dump," Marie said.

"How can we turn *this* into a medical office?" Cameron asked to the sound of Jayde retching.

"I guess I can understand now how the DATT found it in his heart to spare us this building. If we only cleaned up the place, he would be ahead on the deal. By some miracle, if we turn it into anything profitable, the city would benefit. Though it really is in a great location," Marie said.

They looked around and saw that the street teemed with all sorts of busy people, who gave the reeking building a wide berth. Next door was a bustling restaurant wafting delicious aromas. Freshly baked bread could just be detected among the reek of decaying fish blasting from their building.

"What you all make noise for?" asked Marl.

"Are you crazy? Doesn't the smell make you gag?" Jayde asked. She had pulled herself together from the other side of the street.

"Smell? What smell?" he asked.

Jayde looked at him, as if he was crazy. But then she looked again and noticed that, on his angular face, he really did not have nostrils. He had a flat beak that looked like a nose, but no actual nostrils were present.

"Oh, I think we found a winner for cleanup duty," Jayde said.

"Sorry, kiddo," Marie said. "I need Marl. He and I need to do a little sparring, don't we? Time to sign up for the tournament."

"Try not to kill anyone," said Cameron.

"Don't worry about us. I think you guys are in greater danger staying near this building than we will be in the tournament," she said. "C'mon, Marl. Let's go register."

Marie and Marl then disappeared down the road. Cameron commented on how the sun was making him feel stiff and went back into the putrid building. Jayde reluctantly followed, her nose buried in a rag.

"How is that fair?" Jayde asked. "I mean, we get stuck cleaning, and they get to have fun?"

"Well, by 'fun' do you mean they get to risk their lives in a brutal tourney to make some money so we can turn this dump into a clinic? Marie looked into the tournament and found out that the winners take home a prize worth enough gold to completely remake this place. If she wins, we may actually have a chance at setting up shop here. If she doesn't, well, it will take more than just hard work to turn this place into a functioning medical office. Marie may make light of her actions, but her motivation is for the whole group, not for any selfish reason," said Cameron.

"I guess," said Jayde.

"Don't worry. We'll survive. Now see if you can find a broom," Cameron said. Then he looked around again. "On second thought, see if you can find a shovel."

Chapter 18: A Crowd Gathers

Sarah and a fleet of pixies made their way from the Picky Pixie to the large field where they had set up the tournament.

By sunset the list had grown to over a hundred competitors. Most groups had two large, burly creatures but not all. She had seen a group of two small dwarves, as well as a twosome of the spidery arachadons. Nearly all the competitors were male unsurprisingly. She had also seen the occasional burly female troll. One twosome was composed of a tough-looking rock troll with a slender female who looked familiar for some reason.

The pixies had worked continuously. Stout rope created a circle in the center of the field. The dirt outside the circle had been colored bright blue with dye. The dirt inside the circle remained brown. Several pixies cast a spell on the ground for the night. If anyone inside the circle touched the ground outside, the blue dirt would stick to them and make it obvious that they had been outside the circle. Thus, judgment would be easy.

As Sarah approached the tournament field, she gawked at the crowd. Thousands of people stared, as she entered the circle. People made a twilight picnic out of the impromptu competition. As she neared the center of the field, the crowd became silent.

Large torches blazed on the edges of the circle, illuminating the field. Sarah had never spoken to such a large group of people. She had created the tourney just to prevent the store from being robbed; now it had spiraled out of control. She took a breath to slow her racing heart, no help for it now.

"Thank you all for coming to the Picky Pixie Jewelry tournament," she said. The crowd erupted in cheers. She held up her hands, and the cheers died down. "This tournament is to find two guards for our new facility. But more than this comes with winning." As she spoke, a group of pixies flew into the circle with a sparkling golden necklace. It was much smaller than the Nautilus, but it had its own simple elegance that radiated beauty. The necklace had been polished to the point where it positively glowed.

A shocked silence came over the crowd as the necklace flew overhead. The pixies then made a sweep over the heads of the onlookers as a chorus of oohs poured out. Sarah was sure that the rumors about the Nautilus would have grown by now.

"As you can tell, this is quite a unique piece. It has a gentle intricacy and is imbedded with pixie magic, as is all jewelry from the Picky Pixie. This, of course, only adds to the value of the incredible pieces there," she said. "Certainly a great piece for the contestants getting second place."

Murmurs broke out instantly throughout the crowd; most had thought this piece to be the Nautilus. A second fleet of pixies flew over the crowd with the Nautilus. One of the pixies had used her magic so that it *actually* cast its own light. The luminescence from the piece of jewelry mesmerized the crowd. The crowd burst into applause, as the piece was paraded over their heads. The roar grew and made its way back to the center near Sarah. The buzz over the Nautilus remained in the air, as Sarah continued.

"This is how the tournament will work," she said, as the pixies unveiled a chart on a huge canvas. "Each team of two will compete against another team. The goal is to get the other team outside the circle by whatever means possible. However, there will be no weapons and no killing. Other than that, use whatever means you desire. As soon as a competitor is pushed from the circle, they are out for that round. But, the round continues until both members of a team are pushed outside the circle. If you win a round, you will continue. If you lose, you are out of the tourney.

"There are two judges. I am the first, and Jenny is the other," she said. In response to this, Jenny flew over their heads and zoomed around the periphery of the roped-off area in a dazzling display of flying. "Our ruling is final. Other than this, let the best team win!" she shouted, and the crowd again burst into a roar. Sarah announced the first two teams. Jenny flew into the center of the circle as four burly men came together. She gave them a "One, two, three" to begin, and they went at it.

The initial battles ended quickly. This was a good thing, since there were over a hundred teams competing. Shortly after the first few battles, spectators created a large board of teams that was displayed for the entire audience.

Seemingly from nowhere, booths popped up. Some sold trinkets; others sold food. One man kept screaming "Taters! Taters! Taters!" over and over. Somehow, despite the roar of the crowd, his voice could always be heard, and he had an endless supply of piping-hot potatoes that he sold out of his sack. On the back of his tunic was written Potato Man.

Many of the teams simply attacked the other teams, but brute strength often lost to cunning. Tricking opponents to attack and then tripping them out of the circle seemed a common tactic. As the competitors watched, teams quickly learned to adjust to different strategies.

The tourney began with 128 for the first round, and then 64 would be left. After that, 32, then 16, then 8, then 4, then the final 2 would remain. Thus, 7 rounds would be fought by the winning team. To get to this point, over 100 rounds of fighting had to commence.

The crowd cheered as a twosome entered the ring for the first time—a bear of a man named Mullet and a lanky, sinewy fellow named Kevin. Their competition consisted of one grizzled female wood troll and a young man of medium build.

Sarah started the round from the sidelines. Mullet walked deliberately toward the center of the ring, then turned and faced the troll. His lanky partner Kevin seemed almost uninterested in the fight and remained near the side. Kevin had a long stalk of wheat hanging from the corner of his mouth that he chewed idly.

Kevin held a cupped hand to his ear, and the crowd responded in cheers. Mullet ignored the crowd completely. In a flash Mullet sprinted toward the troll. He swept out the legs under his opponent with a fierce low kick. While the body fell toward the ground, he continued to spin and landed a kick to the dropping body. Though enormous, the man moved like a cat, swift and precise. The creature cried out in pain, as he landed in a heap outside the ring.

"Out!" said Sarah from the sidelines. The crowd cheered.

The remaining lad looked nervously at Mullet. He then charged Kevin, still relaxing near the edge of the ring. The man punched with rapid, desperate swings. Kevin easily avoided the blows. Over and over the man swung. Kevin hardly appeared to be trying, but the blows never hit him, despite his proximity to his opponent.

The man circled Kevin and continued to attack. Finally Kevin grabbed his opponent's arm in midpunch and gracefully pulled forward. The man continued to come at him, but Kevin smiled and pointed. His opponent was outside the ring.

The crowd clapped, as the duo smiled and exited the ring.

"Them be good," Marl said to Marie.

"Indeed. They dress like commoners, but both seem to be quite adept," she said.

"Me just say that," Marl said.

Marie and Marl had been placed at the bottom of the bracket. This gave them the opportunity to observe most of the competition. A duo of arachadons easily dispatched their opponents with rapid kicks, as well as some thread from their spinnerets. Having eight legs on the ground made it quite difficult to tell where they were going.

As Marie walked into the ring, several in the crowd jeered at her dainty frame. The crowd quickly became silent as the massive rock troll entered as her second. Two broad men stood opposite them in the ring. The silence was broken by a scream of "Taters! Taters! Taters!" from Potato Man, but the cheers immediately returned.

As soon as he heard "Fight!" Marl sprinted toward one of the men. His training with Marie showed. He landed a barrage of blows on the first man, before the second even had a chance to help. The first fell out of the ring in an unconscious heap, as the crowd came alive, seeing the quick rock troll. They had anticipated a lumbering fight, not the rapid staccato assault that Marl had performed. The second man rushed Marl. He bounced backward, before the man could land a punch. Marl charged, burying his rocky shoulder in the man's stomach. His shoulder then expanded outward as his arms disappeared into his body, heaving the man from the ring. He looked back and smiled at Marie. She had not moved. Marl seemed quite pleased with himself, winning the round without Marie's assistance.

Suddenly the first man out of the ring returned and swung a metal-tipped hammer into Marl's side. Marl bellowed in pain and collapsed to his side. The man stood above him. He tried to pull the weapon from Marl's side but was unable to do so. Before the man could land another blow, the lanky Kevin appeared out of nowhere. Kevin punched the man repeatedly and rapidly in the face. His arms blurred when he struck. The man lay in an unconscious heap on the side of the ring as the crowd cheered.

Marie ran to Marl.

"You okay?" she said.

"*Oi!* Why he hit me when round done? He be cheat, right?" he said to Marie, as she helped him limp out of the ring.

"He be a big cheat, Marl, but I think you've got bigger problems," she said, pointing at the hunk of metal sticking out his side.

"That not fair." Marl grunted.

"We need to go to the clinic. I'm sure Cameron can get you fixed up."

"We no have time for that. We have next round to fight," he said.

"Marl, I don't know if you're in any condition—"

"Me fine! You punch me more than that in field. I rock troll, not wood nymph!"

Marl gasped for air. A horrid sucking noise came from his side with each breath. Marie had seen him take blows before but not from a war hammer. She helped him to the sidelines, and they hobbled away from the crowd.

The weapon protruded from his side, oscillating with each breath.

"You stay here. I'll get Cameron. It's after sundown, so hopefully he can come without any difficulty," Marie said.

Marie ran toward the clinic. She guessed the clinic to be a league from the field, but she had no other way to get there.

Halfway to the clinic, she let out a sigh of relief. Jayde and Cameron had decided to come to the match, and she met them about a half league from the field.

"Hey there, Marie!" Jayde said. "How'd the fight go? Did you guys lose already or something?"

"Have a little faith in us, Jayde," said Marie. "We won our first match, but after that our opponent took a cheap shot at Marl." She then looked over to Cameron. "Our competitors thought having a rock troll that was not a lumbering idiot was unfair, so after the match they clubbed him."

"What'd they use?" Cameron asked.

"A war hammer. I didn't see the attack, but it's buried in Marl's chest," she said.

"I'll go grab my supplies. Take Jayde, and I'll meet you there," said Cameron.

Marie and Jayde ran back to where Marl rested. Despite having to run back to the clinic to grab his supplies, Cameron still arrived with them. He let out a low whistle, and Marl groaned. Jayde, who hadn't recovered from her garbage-induced nausea, immediately excused herself to the closest bush. A metal spike protruded from Marl's side. If that club had hit Marie as it had hit Marl, she would be dead. His natural stone armor deflected much of the blow. Marl's breathing continued to quicken.

"*Oi*, you kin fix it?" Marl asked, through his rapid breaths.

Cameron nodded.

A few people from the crowd had appeared to watch the scene. Kevin, the one who had assisted in dispatching the ruffian who had hit Marl, approached the group.

"Hey, y'all. How's he doing?" he asked, and then gaped at Marl's injury. "That's gotta smart! You better get to a doctor."

"Good idea," Cameron said softly.

The sinewy man continued. "I mean, I know y'all be good fighters, but that ain't right," he said.

Cameron, Jayde, Marie, and Marl looked at the lanky fellow staring at Marl's side.

"I'm sorry, y'all. Where are my manners? I'm Kevin," he said, sticking his hand out toward Cameron.

Cameron shook his hand. "Pleased to meet you, Kevin, I'm Cameron Sangre. As luck would have it, I *am* a doctor. I don't think the spike will come out very easily though."

Kevin took this as a challenge. He leaned forward and grabbed the edge of the spike. He heaved with all his might. Marl, who had been laying on the ground, was lifted off the dirt for a split second before landing with a groan.

"*Ol!*" groaned Marl, breathing very shallow and fast.

"Whoa, you're strong," said Jayde.

Kevin just grinned.

"Jayde, come here a minute, will you?" asked Cameron.

Jayde came close, still a little green in color.

"If you're going to work in a medical office, squeamishness is not an option," Cameron said.

Jayde took a deep breath. "Okay."

Cameron poured a small amount of sweet-smelling ointment in her hands and instructed her to vigorously rub her hands together. When she stopped, her hands looked gleaming clean. He proceeded to clean around the area of the spike carefully. The rock troll's skin looked like overlaying layers of scales.

"The thing about rock troll skin," Cameron began, speaking as if in a lecture hall instead of on the dirt in the middle of the night next to an incapacitated rock troll, "is how their skin is almost like a carapace, similar to what insects have."

"Hey! Me not bug," said Marl, gasping.

"Of course not, but insects do have some of the best natural body armor. The skin overlaps many times over and over. Human skin continuously sloughs off. Rock troll skin, unsurprisingly, has rock in it. Thus, it rarely sloughs off and is much stronger. In fact rock trolls actually start off quite small and simply keep adding layer upon layer of rock. The overlapping plates make an impressive barrier. But, if somehow it does get punctured, the skin folds inward," he said, pointing to the hole in Marl's side.

"Thus, the imbedded foreign object is actually twice as hard to get out, as it was to get in."

Jayde listened intently. She and Cameron had had many talks during their long trek to Grandeur. She loved the discussions about the differences in medical techniques and approaches for injuries with varying species.

Marie had been rummaging through Cameron's bag, while he was explaining all this. She had been with him long enough to know what procedure he was about to do.

"This appears that it might actually go into the thoracic cavity, causing a collapsed lung. Treatment is similar for rock trolls as it is in humans, but, fortunately for our friend, the pain tolerance for rock trolls is legendary," Cameron said, while he sprinkled a white powder around the edge of the wound. He then rested his hand against Marl's side. A faint glow came from his hand, and Cameron paused for nearly ten seconds, seemingly lost in thought.

Marie had prepared a bandage for Marl, while Cameron finished explaining, and handed the bandage to Jayde.

"Okay, Jayde. As soon as I pull out the spike, you need to put that immediately over the hole. Got it?"

"Got it," she said.

"One," he said, looking at Jayde. He placed his right hand on the spike and braced the other against Marl.

"Two," he said, looking at Kevin.

Kevin had a doubtful look on his face. Cameron *was* a good head shorter than Kevin was, and Kevin had pulled Marl off the ground. Kevin obviously did not think the spike was coming out so easily.

"Three," Cameron said. The spike slid out in one clean jerk.

Jayde immediately put the dressing over the hole. Marl did not budge.

"Woohoo!" said Jayde.

"Nice work," said Cameron.

"U*uuuurrrrrg*," groaned Marl.

"Tater?" said Potato Man, who had come over to the small group. Potato Man then left a hot potato with Jayde and disappeared into the crowd. Apparently this potato was free. It was hard to tell when the only word he ever said was "tater." Jayde put the potato in her pocket to keep her hands warm; an evening chill had set in.

"Take some deep breaths, Marl," Cameron said, ignoring the weirdness of Potato Man's appearance.

Cameron had tightly sealed three of the four sides of the bandage to Marl's side. As Marl took a breath, the dressing made a one-way valve. Air could leave his wound but would not be able to go back in. When Marl took a breath, air escaped the open side of the dressing, allowing his lung to expand. When he exhaled, the vacuum inside his chest cavity pulled the open side of the dressing closed. After a few minutes of deep breaths, Marl's breathing became much easier.

"You be good doc!" Marl said.

Cameron put his hands over the site of the injury. His eyes were closed in concentration. Kevin looked from person to person with a nervous half grin on his face. A faint glow again appeared over Cameron's hands. His forehead wrinkled in concentration, and he let out a little groan. A seeping noise came from Marl's side. Marl gritted his teeth and spat out a few guttural words in troll tongue.

After a long two minutes, Cameron leaned back.

"Well?" Marie said.

"Good as new," Cameron said.

"Uh, what did you do to him?" Kevin asked.

"I'm a doctor, so I healed him," Cameron said.

"But a pneumothorax with a probable rib fracture? I mean a busted carapace in a rock troll'll take a month to heal. You can't just heal that in a minute and be good as new," said Kevin.

"Pneumothorax, Kevin? You seem to know a bit about injuries yourself," Cameron said.

Kevin looked at him and grinned sheepishly.

"Cam has a bit of a gift with healing, you might say," Marie told him. She looked down at Marl. "How do you feel?"

"Me good. Me no feel no pain now. *Oi*, you good doc!"

"Thanks. Now don't let anyone else ram a spike through your side. I don't want Jayde to have to fix you up again," Cameron said. Jayde smiled.

"You got it," Marl said.

The second round had already begun. Kevin nodded goodbye and disappeared into the crowd. A short time later he reappeared in the ring with his partner, Mullet. An explosion of applause erupted as the crowd favorites entered the ring. Their opponents this time were two large men covered in scars. The match lasted less than thirty seconds. The two scarred men kept close together at the edge of the ring. Mullet again charged to the center. He lined them up and tackled both of them, dragging them out of the ring. He accompanied the men out of the ring, but Kevin sat in the middle of the ring, smiling. No other team had tried this strategy yet, and it worked perfectly. The two scarred men protested, but Jenny quashed their complaints.

"His partner remained in the ring. Both of you are out. He did not cheat. Next two teams, get up here!" she said. The crowd cheered.

The large board that had been assembled now displayed all the teams as well as their opponents. Behind each of the names were multicolored numbers with arrows. Groups of men in the back made complex wagers on the different teams. Jayde eyed this and made her way over to the jovial group of men. A pockmarked man with an eye patch grinned at her. She put on an expression of wide-eyed wonder. She had gambled in Haynis all the time, but Jayde figured that pretending to be a clueless little girl would be the best approach.

"Excuse me, sir. What's all this about?" she asked.

"Gambling Order. They had this going from the first. The red numbers are the odds for the round."

"I see," said Jayde, looking over at the display board. "Is that why the numbers by the Mullet-Kevin are so low? Since they are favored to win?"

"You got it, missy," he said. "I made a little bundle in the first round, before people knew who was any good." The man cackled loudly and then coughed harshly, until he caught his breath. "The odds will even themselves out after a few rounds. Some people want to get in after they figure out who the good ones are, but, by that time, the odds get quite risky. It's no fun to put down ninety-nine silver and only win one hundred in return."

"Gotcha," Jayde said.

"The crazy bearded guy is in charge. He's as honest a man as you'll get to run something like this. I ain't saying he's clean, just good enough to not rip yah off for no reason. Just ask for odds and the wager. Be sure not to lose your ticket neither, or the bet's off. Good luck, missy," he said.

"Thanks," Jayde said. She then ran back to the group. She figured the direct approach was best.

"Cameron, can I have some money?" she asked.

"What for?"

"Well, I was thinking about the best way for us to clean out the clinic. Personally I say let's have someone else do it," she said.

Cameron laughed. "I could agree with that."

"I need some money to do a little ... well, let's just call it hiring," she said.

"Would you like me to come along?" he asked.

"Nah, I think this will work better from the angle of a clueless, greedy kid. One thing I learned as a street thief, if people *think* they are taking advantage of you, it makes cheating *them* so much easier."

"That's terrible," Cameron said.

"So is cheating a wide-eyed little girl," Jayde said with a smile, grabbing Cameron's entire money purse. She disappeared into the crowd before he could protest. She quickly looked through the purse before she got to the gambler's booth. Seventeen silver pennies were inside. Jayde was shaking when she got to the booth. She had never seen that much money in her entire life.

Jayde looked up at the board and found Marl-Marie. Behind their name was a large red seven. That meant, for every silver she bet, she would win seven. Few groups had numbers that high. Many had fractions of numbers written on the board. Jayde assumed that everyone had seen Marl take the brutal attack to the side, and the odds reflected this.

Jayde wormed her way to the booth. The man behind it had a beard that looked like it was desperately trying to separate itself from the man's face. The black beard exploded in all directions, ending in sharp black spikes. But, behind the ridiculous beard, the man had shrewd eyes.

"Excuse me, mister?" she said.

"Aye, little lady. What kin I do yah for?" he said. His voice was as big as his beard. He smelled heavily of ale, but he had no slur in his voice, and he appeared to be thinking clearly.

"I would like to make a wager," Jayde said.

"Oh, would you now? Ye have a bit a string yah want to be bettin', do yah? Or do yah actually come with a copper penny or two?" he asked. At first Jayde thought the man was just making fun of her, but his face remained serious. Apparently the man would have allowed her to wager just a piece of string.

"I'll admit I don't have much, just these," Jayde said and poured out all seventeen silver pennies.

"Ah, that'll do, indeed," said the man. The man showed no surprise or curiosity about a young girl with a small fortune. Jayde had thought for sure the man would accuse her of being a thief or demand proof of how she got it. He did neither. He picked up a few of the coins and looked at them under a large lens, which made his eyes look enormous. He turned back to her.

"Now which do yah want to be bettin' on, young miss?" he said.

"That one right there," she said, pointing to Marie-Marl versus Berret-King.

"Aye, and who do yah think'll be the victor?" he said.

"Team Marie-Marl will win. I just know it," she said. She put on her expression of innocent ignorance.

The man smiled. He swiped the seventeen coins into one meaty palm. He counted the money again and then plunked the coins one at a time into a massive box. He filled out a piece of paper and put some red melted wax on top of it and stamped it.

"There ye go, little miss. Best o' luck to yah," he said with a chuckle.

Jayde looked down at the small slip of paper. On it read:

SINGLE BATTLE: 7–1 ODDS

MARIE-MARL VICTOR OVER BERRET-KING

RECEIVED WAGER OF 17 SILVER PENNIES

An ornate red *G* was embedded in the wax over the lettering. She could still read the wager through the wax, but she could not change anything written on the paper. Jayde read the sign posted behind the man. The sign explained the rules of wagering. The wax prevented tampering with the wager. If the wax seal came back broken, her bet was lost. Jayde carefully placed the wager slip in Cameron's purse, then slipped the purse over her head. She could feel the near-weightless purse hanging on the inside of her clothes. It was her only possession, except for the potato in her pocket.

Jayde bounced back toward Cameron to watch the matches. As she walked, she saw a cute little black cat slipping through the crowd. Jayde loved cats and followed it, but it vanished before she could catch it, so she made her way where Cameron waited.

Marie and Marl's next battle ended in seconds. Their opponents had thought that Marl was too injured to continue. Both opponents went to attack him immediately. He let them come, then grabbed both in an enormous bear hug and fell out of the ring, much like Mullet had done. Marie watched it happen and laughed, not having to do anything for yet another round.

Jayde ran over to the man with the poky beard.

"Yah got lucky that rock troll bounced back from such an injury," the man said. His grin shone under his bristly black beard. He seemed unfazed by her win. "Any more bets before yah collect?" he asked.

Jayde looked up at the odds board. Marie-Marl versus Fester-Fester.

"Looks like the odds went down," Jayde said.

"Aye. That troll be a fighting dynamo, he be," said the man.

"I think so too. But, since you are still offering five-to-one odds, I might as well bet on them again. How much did I win again?" Jayde asked.

"Seventeen silver at 7:1. It comes to 119, miss. How much of that ye be wanting to wager?" he said

"How about one hundred silver pennies on Marie-Marl, and I'll keep the change."

The bearded man counted off nineteen silver pennies and wrote out another wager slip for her. Jayde slipped the silver into Cameron's purse and the gambling slip in her own pocket.

"Yah really think that rock troll can take on the Fester brothers? I dunno if even Mullet kin take those two. Well, that ain't true. Mullet kin take anybody, but they be good," he said.

"So is Marl," Jayde said.

"G'luck to yah, miss," he said, as Jayde walked back to her spot in the crowd.

She again looked for the cute cat. She saw a faint outline of the cat at the very edge of the crowd, rubbing against an old woman's legs. The cat's gaze locked on hers for a split second, and for some reason Jayde felt cold. She hurried back to where Cameron and the others waited.

"Here you go," Jayde said, tossing the purse to Cameron. He hefted the purse a few times, and then stuck it back under his cloak without looking inside. That bothered Jayde. She was not used to people trusting her. Now the trust was expected, and anything else was considered abnormal.

Kevin and Mullet destroyed yet another duo with their brutal crowd-pleasing efficiency. Mullet again charged the two, but they were much quicker than their previous opponents. It took nearly a minute for the duo to overpower both opponents.

Marie had been watching all the previous events with great interest and knew they would be battling two unique fighters next. To become a battle sage, she had studied different cultures, animals, and strategies to use in every circumstance. She had watched the two they were up against and knew them to have assassin training. She explained to Marl how they would strike at pressure points and use their opponents' strengths to their advantage. Marie thought these two appeared to be journeymen assassins, not experts. Regardless, they had annihilated all their opponents in their previous rounds.

"So how we beat 'em?" Marl asked.

"They'll be too fast for you to block them. I doubt they could hit any pressure points on you though, with your troll skin. We should split up. If they come at you, don't try to avoid them, just get one good hit. Even if you have to let them hit you fifty times, just get in one solid punch. It'll be over. They're precision fighters, not endurance. One good bash should probably end them."

"How 'bout you?" he asked.

"Well, you've done all the fighting so far in our matches. Most here have assumed I've just won off your fighting skill. If they come at me, they'll get a big surprise."

The fight started, and Marl and Marie moved to opposite sides of the arena. This time both their opponents rushed directly toward Marie. The crowd had only seen her act in the background and thought her to be dead weight. The blows came rapidly from both men. Marie spun, blocked, and hand-sprung her way under the raining blows. The crowd gawked at the woman who appeared to be dancing with the two attackers, neither landing a single blow. Marl helped, but their speed never allowed him an opening.

Marie's body blurred. The assassins attacked furiously but only hit air. Marie laughed as she bounced around the blitz of punches. Finally she ducked a blow and struck an uppercut into the chest of one of the attackers. He bent forward briefly in pain. That was all the opening Marl needed. He landed a ham-size fist on top of the man's head. The man crumpled to the ground. The remaining assassin attacked Marl. Despite Marie's advice to allow him to get close, Marl attempted defense against him. The man landed ten jabs before Marie caught up. The man spun and swung in one motion with his arm straight. Marie dodged in an instant back bridge, holding herself up on the balls of her feet and the palms of her hands, avoiding the blow. She completed the bridge by kicking her legs back over her head with such speed that she kicked the man in the face. Marl planted his rocky fist into his chest. The man gasped for air, and Marl shoved him from the ring. Marl walked over to the first man, picked up his unconscious body, and dropped him outside the ring.

The audience cheered in response to the slight woman who had destroyed the trained fighters. Marie grinned.

They made their way back to their friends, waiting at the sidelines.

"Nice work out there, but your secret is out," said Cameron.

Marie looked into the crowd. Most eyes were still on her, amazed by her recent display. She locked gazes with Kevin, who gave her a thumbs-up and mouthed "Nice work."

"Way to go. See you around," said Jayde, as she disappeared into the crowd.

"Where's she off to?" said Marie.

"The gambling booth. I think she's doing all right," Cameron said, a wry grin decorating his usually somber face.

"Keep an eye on her, Cam. She has a knack for finding mischief, and, if she can't find it, she makes a fresh batch herself."

Chapter 19: Higher Stakes

The tournament progressed, as he watched from a nearby rooftop. He had failed his master in his previous assassination attempts of any potential Chosen, but that did not matter. So much time wasted, calculating, scheming, and pretending to be an oaf. Oh, well. What mattered was ultimately succeeding. He knew better than to check in with King Zolf. He had learned only to check in with good news.

His target had slipped through his traps twice already, through no fault of his own. He had decided to leave nothing to chance. He had hired excellent assassins, even though his skin crawled thinking of the dark creatures he had dealt with. Since no Chosen had been captured for twenty years, the king had become testy. A testy king desired results, not promises. The king had dispatched chaos agents everywhere throughout the four countries, yet the location of the next Chosen remained a mystery. He knew his target had potential. It was time to kill, and he would watch at a distance, where nobody would know he even existed, much less had orchestrated the madness.

He could feel another dark presence in that crowd. His gaze locked on a haggard-appearing woman with a black cat. These two had some connection to King Zolf as well; he could tell. One did not become an agent of chaos without the ability to feel the darkness in others. Perhaps it was time to work with another? He would have to stay hidden until he could assemble another method to kill his prey, if somehow his target wriggled through the trap he set up for this tournament. Though it was quite unlikely his target would live through the day, yet it always paid to have a backup plan just in case. For now, all he could do was watch, and hope for death.

Chapter 20: The Tournament Ends

The next two rounds of the tournament went by quickly. Since Marie's Talent was no longer a secret, she and Marl attacked as a team. They destroyed their opponents with an efficiency similar to that of Kevin and Mullet. Both teams had turned into crowd favorites.

Only four teams were left in the tournament. Cameron had moved to the other side of the field to keep an eye on Jayde. She had spent many rounds talking with the man with a black beard. Jayde and the man both had large grins on their faces, but Cameron tracked her just the same. He glanced through the rest of the crowd, and his gaze landed for an instant on an old woman and her cat watching from afar. The cat looked at him for a split second, then faded into blackness; only the old woman remained.

The crowd had doubled in size. Mullet and Kevin faced off against the two arachadons. The enormous four-foot-tall spiders darted all over the arena. They occasionally shot sticky strands of silk to snare their opponents. Mullet and Kevin had watched the spiders' tactics in earlier bouts, so the humans were ready with a strategy of their own. Shortly after the start of the match, Kevin sprinted through a wall of sticky silk to grab one of the spiders in a giant bear hug. He pulled both the creature and himself out of the ring, not daring to release it.

This left Mullet and the remaining creature in a one-on-one battle for the championship fight. In the end, Mullet had simply too much brute strength for the giant spider to overcome. Mullet landed blows through the silk. The creature could not trade blows with the massive Mullet and eventually was knocked out. The crowd grew silent, as Mullet approached the unconscious creature. Despite the crowd yelling for him to smash it to pieces or to kick it out of the ring, he gently picked up the giant spider and lightly placed it out of the ring, securing their spot in the finals.

"Taters! Taters! Taters!" screamed Potato Man in what sounded like a respectful voice to complement Mullet's gentle action.

Marie had been tracking their opponents quite closely, discussing strategy with Marl during the ever-decreasing time between rounds.

"We're fighting a pair of nekarions next," she said. Marl looked at her blankly. "They look somewhat reptilian in nature. Also they are much stronger than they appear. They are lightning quick and use their tails as an extra arm, so be ready for that. I'm not sure we could take them in a fair fight, but tonight the edge is in our favor. I'm interested in winning, not playing nice."

Marl continued to look at her blankly, so she explained more to him. "Nekarions have terrible eyesight. They can barely see anything besides shadows, but they can track movement very well. What usually gives them an edge is that they can see heat, as clearly as we see each other at noon. Thus, they can attack in absolute blackness without difficulty. Fortunately for us, we have the torches," she said.

"So how we use dat to help us win?" he said.

Marie described her plan. Marl grinned in appreciation. Marie ran off to find the closest rain barrel, and, a short time later, they entered the ring.

The nekarions looked like giant walking lizards. They had scales instead of skin, and their thin faces tapered into a snakelike snout. They flicked their forked tongues. Their eyes were orange with black crescent slits. Their heads swung back and forth in sweeping movements on long extended necks, taking in the battle arena.

Marie and Marl entered the circle, as a bubble of laughter slowly spread through the crowd. Marie was drenched in cold water, shivering, and walking on top of Marl's monstrous feet. She pressed herself into his chest. It appeared quite comical. Marl had altered the skin on his arms to give Marie handholds, so she could move as he moved.

Marl stood with his back directly in front of the closest torch.

"Fight!" called out Jenny, as she flew above the arena.

The two nekarions rushed directly toward Marl. Their skin blurred and reappeared, making them difficult to track, even in the brightness caused by the torches.

Marl glared at one, and the other appeared right next to him out of nowhere. It landed three quick punches before Marl could whip a crushing blow at it. It jumped backward, avoiding the blow.

Marl again repositioned himself next to the burning torch. Marie remained pressed close against his chest, continuing to move with him.

The reptiles rushed again and struck a barrage of blows. Marl spun with a quick strike, but again the creatures sprung backward before he could make contact. While Marl fought, Marie balanced on the tops of Marl's enormous feet and mimicked his movements. Marie shivered but remained balanced.

Over and over the two creatures worked in unison to keep Marl off guard. They landed glancing blows and slowly worked Marl closer to the edge of the arena.

Some people in the crowd yelled at Marie, believing Marl was simply protecting her. Marl moved himself toward the middle, but one of the lizards spun and struck Marl with his tail, like a whip.

"You ready?" Marie whispered, while the reptiles prepared for another attack.

"For long time," grumbled the rock troll.

Several things then happened at the same time. Marie slumped off Marl and crouched in a tight wet ball. Marl launched himself at the closest nekarion, which retreated from Marl's sudden assault. The nekarion's partner began sprinting toward Marl in response to the attack.

As the second creature darted toward Marl, it seemed unaware of Marie. Marl continued to attack the first with his back toward the second. The creature ran right next to Marie, oblivious.

Marie launched her entire body into an uppercut. The creature shrieked in shocked surprise, as the blow lofted it into the air. Marie rolled onto her back and kicked both feet into the creature as it descended. The nekarion bellowed a second time, as it flew out of the arena.

The crowd burst into cheers in response to Marie's attack. She quickly rushed toward Marl. He and the other nekarion battled viciously, but the lizard creature had the upper hand. She ran to Marl's side and whispered quickly to Marl, then retreated.

Marl attacked with multiple swooping blows that caused the nekarion to backpedal. Marl retreated as fast as he could. The lizard rushed at him again but stopped in midstride. Marl ran past Marie and stopped near the edge of the circle.

Marie looked over and heard a rasping hiss from the other nekarion that had already lost. The two creatures had a heated conversation. The nekarion in the ring shook its head back and forth rapidly, while the first continued to hiss, gesturing wildly with its arms. The remaining creature in the arena shook its head one last time, hissed vehemently at the other nekarion, and rushed at Marl.

Marl stayed next to the edge of the arena. The creature ran along the edge to get to Marl. Marie crouched in waiting, perfectly still. When the nekarion sprinted past her, she struck in a flash. Marie tackled the creature; it lost its balance and fell out of the arena.

Marie relaxed as they made their way from the arena to the cheers of the crowd. Marie warmed herself next to the closest torch. The finals would be Marie-Marl versus Mullet-Kevin.

"Pretty clever, Marie," Cameron said.

"How'd you do that?" said Jayde.

"At night, nekarions see primarily by the heat generated by creatures. We just warmed up Marl next to the torches till he kept in some of that heat. I stayed on the other side of him, protected from the warmth of the torch. After he spent so much time that close to the torch he was practically glowing to the nekarions. Me, on the other hand, my little body heat was hard for them to see," Marie said.

"Sort of like when you go inside a dark room after being in the sun. You can't see anything, since your eyes are used to seeing in the bright," Jayde said.

"Exactly," said Cameron. "Drenching herself in water before the match helped."

A squad of pixies fluttered into the ring along with Sarah. The crowd quieted when she reached the center of the arena. Sarah complimented all the competitors as the pixies flew around the ring one last time, showing off the two necklaces for the first- and second-place winners.

Marl spoke quickly with Marie about strategy. Marie thought they were pretty evenly matched. She knew Kevin and Mullet had more than just casual training. She felt she could match either one individually, but together they seemed flawless. Marl would not be a match for either based on speed or technique, but he had plenty of raw power.

The pixie yelled, "Fight!" and the final match began.

Kevin sauntered casually toward the center. Mullet stayed right at his side.

"Y'all're good fighters. Mullet even thinks so too, and that's rare. Best of luck to yah," Kevin said.

"Likewise," Marie said, crouched in her ready position.

Mullet glared at her, his face an unreadable mess of scars. Kevin looked at her stance. Despite the light banter, the match *had* already begun. "You fight like a war sage," said Kevin.

"Indeed," Marie responded. "How about you two? I'm guessing either paladins or knights of Xavier?"

Mullet looked surprised for the first time of the night. Kevin answered her question. "Paladins are rarely recognized, these days. This should be a good fight," he said with a grin.

"My thoughts exactly," said Marie.

Kevin and Mullet both held up open left hands and punched their right fists into it. They held their fists in place and bowed. Five seconds passed. No one moved.

Mullet darted at Marie and missed a crushing blow by a finger's width. His giant frame moved with impossible speed, yet Marie spun, twisted, and blocked every attack. The crowd roared. Marl stayed near Marie, but Kevin quickly split the two apart. He landed blow after blow to the rock troll's face and side, remaining nimble enough to avoid all the troll's attacks.

Mullet continued his assault with a seemingly endless supply of energy. Marie had landed a few quick blows to his stomach and chest, but he seemed unaffected. Marie knew her blows struck much harder than anyone in the crowd would realize, but he shrugged them off as if they were mosquito bites.

Marl continued to circle Kevin, moving from side to side to prevent the rain of blows from landing. After that did not work, he decided to launch himself at Kevin, to no avail. He rushed at him to tackle him. Right as he reached to grab him, Kevin dropped to the ground and kicked Marl forward. Marl fell, out of control. Luckily he collided into the back of Mullet.

Mullet spun for a split second. This gave Marie the opening she needed. She landed both open palms on his chest and released an incredible supply of energy. Mullet exploded across the entire ring in a graceful arc and landed in a heap. Unfortunately he landed within the circle. Kevin backed him up in a flash, and the two began circling again.

Marie pressed her advantage, but Kevin gave Mullet the little time it took for him to recover. The two switched, so Mullet again attacked Marie. Kevin slipped between the two, raining multiple blows on Marl.

Marl swung at Kevin who bounced backward. Kevin then jumped straight up in the air nearly ten feet high from a standing start. When he landed he pounded his fist into the ground. An echoing boom came from the punch, and a split second later the ground under Marl launched him straight up into the air.

In the air Marl pulled his arms and legs in tight, making a perfectly round rock. He came out of the ball facing downward. While high in the air, Marl had a unique view of the entire arena. He knew Jayde had been staying by the gamblers' booth. He looked over toward the booth while in the air and instantly became terrified. When he landed he struck the raised circle of earth with tremendous force. The circle of earth compressed back into the ground. Kevin fell head over heels spinning in the air.

Kevin landed in a tangled mess but bounced up immediately after the fall. He grinned and laughed. "Y'all fight well!" he said. The rock troll, however, had already disappeared. Marl ran out of the ring.

Mullet on the other hand continued his assault on Marie, showing no sign of tiring.

Marie looked over and saw Marl running out of the ring and through the confused crowd. She glanced in the direction he ran and realized why he had abandoned the tournament. Jayde was in danger. No tournament, prize, or any physical compensation was worth his friend.

Near the outer edge of the crowd Cameron was surrounded by three figures in black. Jayde hid behind him, terrified and bleeding. Behind her a man with a large black spiky beard occasionally peeked from under his stand.

Even in the dim light Marie could make out the glint of metal. She ran toward Cameron. As she made her way to the center of the ring, Mullet and Kevin flanked her on each side, not realizing that she had intended to give up on the tournament to help her friends. All she could do was block punches and kicks that came continuously as she backpedaled. Marie jumped out of the ring, then changed direction and sprinted toward Jayde. The crowd exploded as Mullet and Kevin remained in the arena.

Marl ran where the three men had Cameron pinned down. The attackers had surrounded Cameron from a distance of twenty feet. Their arms moved quickly over and over as they threw metal needles half a foot long. Cameron's long black cloak flowed and billowed, deflecting the needles as fast as they were thrown. The deadly needles created a nearly invisible barrage in the darkness. Barbs flew at his face, chest, and legs at the same time. Cameron continued to spin and flailed his arms while he pivoted, his cloak acting as a shield from the missiles. It sounded like metal rain as the small barbs continued to accumulate at his feet. Though Jayde was directly behind him, she could barely hear the slight tinkling of metal over the triumphant roar of the exuberant crowd. Two needles protruded from Jayde, one in her left forearm and another in her right thigh. She grabbed them to pull them out, but the blood made them too slippery.

Jayde remained crouched. She realized that this prevented Cameron from attacking any of their assailants, but she could not get away. Cameron's arms and body blurred with speed, and the vast majority of the needles landed on the ground. She could see his body was soaked with blood.

As Marl sprinted toward the attackers, he saw other black-cloaked bodies lying dead. He counted nine bodies that matched the three remaining attackers. Had Cameron been attacked by twelve people? If so, how could he be alive?

Marl finally made it to the nearest attacker and launched himself with deadly ferocity. The roaring crowd prevented the closest man in black from hearing his approach. The man's side collapsed, as the immense bulk of stone-skinned terror collided with him at full speed. The collision tore the man's clothes to shreds, yet the concave depression from the deadly blow remained. The man leaned forward once, gasping for air. Marl rewarded the killer's efforts with a bone-shattering blow to the face. The man died instantly. Marl turned back toward the remaining two figures and bellowed.

The other two continued to attack with the needles but realized that both their element of surprise and their advantage in numbers were gone. They exchanged quick glances as one rummaged inside his cloak. He pulled out what looked like a spiny sea urchin. It was a sphere the size of a fist, completely covered in long spikes. Connected to the spiky ball was a cord. The other nodded and pulled out a second spine-covered ball.

Marie sprinted toward the figures in black. She screamed at the still cheering crowd to run away.

Cameron saw the weapons. "Needle bombs! They shoot needles in every direction and explode if they hit anything hard!" Both assassins faced Cameron and whirled the wicked-looking balls. Jayde could see that he remained standing by the power of sheer will alone. He leaned forward, hands on his knees, as he breathed heavily, grateful for the halt in the attack, whatever the reason. A pile of needles that he had deflected lay on the ground in front of him; however, many needles had found their mark. Jayde saw that his entire body bristled with punctures. His arms, legs, and body were wet with blood.

Marl remained at his side, not sure whether protecting Cameron or attacking the two killers would be the best course of action. Cameron's voice was slurred with exhaustion, but he told the troll to run, since the needles would explode on his rocky hide. Marl did not move. He would sacrifice anything to protect Jayde.

The two assassins stood side by side, as they swung their arms and hurled the spike-covered balls into the air. Immediately after throwing them, they both turned to run. As they did, each received a foot directly in the chest from Marie. She had come back after warning the crowd, who had already run in the other direction. The men collapsed in a tangle of body and limbs. But the two spiky balls had already been launched. Marie shoved one unconscious assassin on top of the other one.

Marl hovered over Jayde, ready to envelope her in a rocky embrace.

Jayde glanced around the large arena. Time slowed to a crawl. She saw the collapsed assassins. Twelve men vanquished, nearly all by Cameron. Two now lay unconscious on the ground. She saw the pair of arcing balls of needles gliding upward over their heads. She saw the distant crowd, still cheering on Mullet and Kevin. She even saw Potato Man running through the crowd, selling his baked treats. Jayde reached into her pocket and pulled out the potato that she had received from the man. She threw it in the air. In the terror and chaos Jayde could feel an untapped energy flowing through her. She released her energy, focusing on the floating potato.

As the spiky spheres crested their arcs, they exploded, sending hundreds of spikes in every direction. The noise of the spheres exploding and shooting out their deadly missiles made a metallic snap, but this was overshadowed by a deep boom that emanated at almost the same time.

The two men who had launched the needle bombs became skewered by hundreds of needles. Under the two bodies hid Marie, who had used their bodies as shields.

The rest of the party had disappeared. They had all crouched to protect themselves from the bomb. Jayde was under Marl who was under Cameron, who was under something that had covered them all.

"Everyone okay?" Cameron asked.

"Me be fine," Marl said, "but where me be?"

"I'm okay. How about you, Cameron?" asked Jayde.

"I've felt better," said Cameron.

"What you do?" asked Marl. "We be dead now?"

"I didn't do this," responded Cameron.

They could still hear the cheers of the crowd, but it sounded muffled or distant. Marl, Cameron, and Jayde remained in darkness.

Jayde breathed heavily. "It can't be. It just can't, can it?"

"What did you do, Jayde?" asked Cameron.

"Well, I was thinking about what would protect us from the needles yet not squash us, but I didn't know of anything soft that would absorb the needles. Except maybe, well, ... Marl, see if you can just push up what's covering us."

Marl stood in the dark and bumped his head on the low ceiling. He pushed hard, and the darkness disappeared. They apparently had not been transported anywhere; they were just covered. Marl lifted their protection, and the threesome crawled out. The man with the porcupine beard glanced up from behind his booth.

"That's the biggest dang potato I've ever seen!" he said, gaping.

And it was. They had been saved by a giant potato, with a hole in the bottom—just big enough for them to fit under. Marie looked over at Jayde with a raised eyebrow.

"It was all I could think of. I don't even know how I did it," said Jayde.

"I think you just saved our lives," said Cameron, "with a potato."

A small crowd had begun to gather around the massive potato. It was nearly twenty paces around, and the top and sides of it had a thick layer of spikes. Potato Man looked at it with reverence.

The group took a few more looks at the giant spud and walked a short distance away to the stand of the man with the bristly beard. Cameron collapsed against the wooden side of the betting table.

Marie sprinted to Cameron and began pulling out needles. He could not bend his arms due to the vast number embedded within. His clothes dripped blood. His breathing took obvious effort. He even looked ashen, which was something, considering he was a vampire. Many of the needles were in too deep to be easily pulled out. Most were coated with blood, making them too slick to grip.

Cameron closed his eyes and concentrated, focusing on the multiple areas of pain throughout his body. A faint glimmer of blue light under the skin of his right hand slowly moved up his arm. The light crept across his body, down his legs, and then to the entire left side. His breathing became more relaxed.

"Jayde, reach into the bag and get the large forceps in there," Marie said.

"*Four sects?*" Jayde asked.

"The big metal tweezers. They'll be wrapped in clean gauze. Let's see how many quills this porcupine has."

Jayde grabbed the bag and rummaged through it quickly, pulling out the forceps, and ran them back to Marie. Marie unwrapped the forceps and quickly began pulling the deeply embedded needles from Cameron. Each time a blue light appeared under his skin after a needle was pulled. Some of the needles were buried so deep that the only sign was a slight glint in the skin.

Marie quickly and methodically removed the barbs. The blue light glowed after each removal, and Cameron's skin healed over. Jayde watched, fascinated. An impressive pile of needles littered the ground next to Cameron.

"Feel better?" Marie asked.

"Getting there," he answered.

"Did you manage to block any of the needles without getting them embedded in you?" asked Marie.

Marie looked down at Jayde and tended to the needle in her arm and leg. The girl yelped, as Marie gently pulled them out. Jayde had no idea how Cameron survived with the giant pile that had skewered him.

"I think I might not be all the way better yet," he said.

"You think?" Jayde answered.

"No, I mean, a few needles might still be lodged. I wish I had a magnet. I don't know how I'll get these things out," said Cameron.

"I got yah covered, friend," said the man with the huge pointy beard.

"I always keep me strongbox cemented down with a strong magnet. It makes it a bit harder for the casual thief to make the box disappear. First rule of gambling, yah gotta keep what you make," he said with a wink at Jayde.

He walked back to his booth and grabbed an enormous crowbar. He inserted the crowbar under the metal table and heaved. The entire table bucked, but nothing happened. He heaved again, and a loud *thunk* followed. He reached under the table and pulled out a large U-shaped hunk of metal.

"That'll do yah," he said, handing it to Marie with a grin.

Marie walked over to Cameron and held the magnet to his side. She felt the pull of the magnet and heard Cameron groan at the same time. Hiding just under his skin appeared the tip of a needle, pulled out by the magnet. She slowly moved the magnet away from his body, the needle following. She continued a slow survey over his chest with the magnet. She found nineteen more needles. Cameron concentrated while she performed each extraction. After removal, a hint of blue light appeared, and his skin healed over. Marie sighed in relief after pulling out the last needle.

The man with the porcupine beard paled after watching the needle extraction from Cameron. Marie walked back to him and returned his magnet.

"Feel better?" the bearded man asked Cam.

"You have no idea," Cameron said, taking a deep breath.

"Now what?" Marie asked.

"It no be fair, but we no win fight," said Marl, looking back toward the circle. Most of the crowd still had no idea that a separate battle had just taken place. Kevin and Mullet were receiving the Nautilus from the pixies, and the crowd showed its appreciation.

"Now we go back to the Happy Smyle. I don't know about you guys, but I really don't feel like sleeping in garbage. We'll figure out payment later," Cameron said. The group followed his lead, as they stepped away from the fight crowd. Jayde however, lagged behind.

Jayde looked at Cameron, walking slowly after the removal of hundreds of deadly barbs. Marie also lumbered along. After competing all night, she had had her fair share of injuries. Marl seemed sad but did not show any apparent injury.

Jayde had been a vagrant most of her life and a gambler for all of it. She looked over at the man with the bristly beard, who looked right at her but did not say a word. Jayde sighed. Cameron had almost been killed trying to protect her. If not for her, he likely could have taken all the attackers himself, but instead he had protected her. He had gone out of his way with no thought of his own safety to defend her.

"I can't believe I'm doing this," Jayde murmured. "Guys, wait one second." She walked back to the bristly beard man. She had not bet on Marie-Marl versus Mullet-Kevin, since she had no idea who would win. Jayde had a knack for knowing the odds. The bristly bearded gambler had held on to all her vast winnings till the tournament was over.

"You can pick up your winnings later," he whispered. "You don't need to do it in front of all them. With this much money, you could live like a princess for a year."

"Believe me, after living on the streets half of my fourteen years, I know. But maybe it's time I did something for someone else for a change," she said.

The man grunted and walked back to his gigantic storage box. He pulled out a leather bag and counted. He handed Jayde the bulging bag.

"You're a good gambler. Yah earned this. Especially after your family saved me from becoming skewered."

"Oh, they're not my—" and then Jayde stopped. She looked over at Cameron, Marie, and Marl trudging slowly in the direction of the pub. Her thief upbringing told her to bolt with her winnings and disappear into Grandeur. She had more money in her hands than she had ever seen.

"Sure," she said, "no problem."

Jayde ran and caught up with the rest of the group.

"What was all that about?" Marie asked.

Jayde explained how she bet on Marl and Marie and won a fair amount of money. They let Jayde finish her entire story, though Cameron wore a whimsical smile the entire time.

"I saw how good Mullet and Kevin were, so I did not bet on either of you to win the finals. But I did manage to make a little bit of money from you guys winning so many rounds," Jayde said and heaved the heavy pouch at Cameron.

Cameron grinned at Marie.

"What?" said Jayde.

"Oh, we're not as naive as you may think," said Marie. "We realized you were betting on us at the tournament. Cameron actually was planning on betting on us as well, but then he saw you doing it and figured he'd take a chance," said Marie.

"A chance on what?" asked Jayde.

Cameron looked into her eyes. "You, of course. You've led a troubled life, Jayde. You've had to fend for yourself at an age when little girls are supposed to be playing with dolls. Most people who grow up in such circumstances are quite reluctant to trust anyone and quite willing to betray anyone. You, on the other hand, seem to have acquired the skills of a thief without the mind-set and morality that normally go along with it."

"Thanks. I think. So now what?" Jayde asked.

"Now we sleep. First thing tomorrow we have a clinic to clean."

Chapter 21: Hobgoblins and Secrets

They ate a warm breakfast of oatmeal and rolls served by Esmeralda. She chatted with them and discussed the winnings of Mullet and Kevin. The tournament news spread fast. Then Esmeralda handed them a stunning necklace.

"You guys did get second place, so I believe this belongs to you. A small fleet of pixies came in the middle of the night and dropped it off for me to give to you. It's a nice piece. Congrats. So what's on your agenda today?" she asked.

"A miserable day of cleaning leftover garbage out of a building. Probably followed by several more weeks of the same," grumbled Jayde.

"Sounds fun. Though, if I were you, I'd get the hobgoblins to do it," Esmeralda answered.

"The who-with-the-what now?" Jayde asked.

"The hobgoblins. They're the garbage workers in Grandeur. Every day they go down a different route and put all the garbage into their giant containers. Then they take it out of town to their secret location and sift through it all. They use anything they find. Broken furniture, twine, week-old rolls—they find a use for all of it. The DATT pays them a small amount, and they get to keep all the garbage. Both groups think they are suckering the other, which is the best arrangement possible."

"Do you think they'd clean a building?" Marie asked.

"Well, that depends on how much garbage and what you'd pay them," she said.

"Well, the entire place is pretty much buried in filth, so they should do it for cheap," said Jayde.

"Not likely. They're great cleaners. Don't get me wrong, but they're tricky, and they *will* try to rob you blind. But if it's really that bad, it might be worth it," said Esmeralda.

"How do we contact the hobgoblins?" asked Cameron.

"Ask the Splurgs," said Esmeralda.

After eating, Cameron headed back to his room to apply a cream Esmeralda had suggested to keep the sun from penetrating his skin. The cloak he wore only helped so much. Along with being an innkeeper, she also sold a multitude of magical wares, and Cameron was not the first vampire she had come across.

They headed back to their garbage-filled building. It had a mud trough at the front, similar to the one at Happy Smyle Inn. Marie picked up the large wooden plank and shoved it into the slots. A Splurg appeared seconds later.

"Was'sup, dudette? How can I assist?" said the mudman.

"Could you tell us when and where we might find the hobgoblins?" Marie asked.

"Totally, *chicarino*. Gotta charge yah somethin' for it though, you know. I feel kinda bad for doin' it," said the Splurg, holding out a muddy arm. Marie dropped a copper into the arm, and it sunk into the mud.

"Why do you feel bad about helping?" Marie asked.

"Cause, like, they're comin' down this road in about an hour. But, if I don't charge yah, then I have to give favors to, like, everyone. It's not cool to play favorites, dudette. Rock on! You know how to get me if you need me. Peace out!" it said, lifting the wooden slat and disappearing into the trough.

Cameron stayed inside the house, but the rest decided to wait for the hobgoblins outside the smelly building. After an hour, an enormous wagon appeared. It covered nearly the entire road, as it slowly lurched down the street. Large musk-oxen hauled the cart forward, as a filthy hobgoblin guided the cart from a high seat.

A fleet of small gray horn-covered creatures pitched garbage into the wagon as it continued its slow procession. Most of the shops had piles of garbage out front. The vehicle and its odd inhabitants slowly made its way toward the clinic.

Marie and Jayde stood in front of the cart, signaling it to stop. It continued onward at its slow pace, nearly running over them both.

"*Oi*, I speak a bit of der talk. Dey speak like you, just with bad word choice," said Marl from the side. He then ran inside and came out holding a handful of silver pennies in the air.

"*Vas issa joobie* thinkin' *dare vissa* bling-bling?" said the creature leading the cart.

"Trash, cash, house, clean," said Marl, while jingling a big handful of silver pennies.

"Yoosah payin' mucha penny for us be takin' allsa dat trash outta yer house ands hauls zah masser of stinkin' rubbish awayz for goods now. Eh? EH?" said the leader in the cart.

"Yah," said Marl.

"After wezah finish, you gives eacha hobgobs that helps a halfa-silver penny fors zah job zat be well done. Right, yah?" said the hobgoblin, stopping the oversize cart in front of the clinic.

"Yah," said Marl.

The hobgoblin jumped down from his cart. He came up to Marl's knee. He spat a large amount of green mucous into his hand and held out his hand to Marl. Marl spat some white dust into his hand, and they shook. The hobgoblin nodded once toward the building.

The creature hobbled back onto his cart and pulled out a twisted wooden horn larger than his head and blew. In less than a minute, hobgoblins appeared from all directions and flooded the street. Filth covered their bodies. The road could hardly be seen outside the clinic due to the mass of small creatures. The driver barked some orders, and they all ran into the house screaming.

"Wow. They really take their job seriously, huh?" said Jayde.

In a matter of minutes all the windows facing the street were open, and garbage began pouring out. The wall of hobgoblins formed a mass of wriggling forms, each diving eagerly into the trash and heaving it out the windows toward the cart. Cameron joined the rest of the group outside. He was covered in trash. Marie made him stand downwind.

"What happened?" she asked.

"You try to get out of the way when hundreds of screaming hobgoblins run in, fill their arms with trash, and sprint out. They're maniacs!" said Cameron.

After twenty minutes, the loads of trash being brought out by the mass of creatures were reduced to small handfuls. The hobgoblins continued to sprint back inside after every trip. The driver waited another twenty minutes. Jayde looked into the mounting pile of odious slop in the gigantic wagon. Areas of trash were undulating with rats and maggots. Blurry waves of heat and odor hit her nostrils like a dead wet dog.

"That's the most disgusting thing I have ever seen," said Jayde.

Twenty more minutes passed, and the driver took out his horn and blew it again.

"Okee now. Yoosa block-o checken seeya iffin cleen enuff foryah, right?" said the leader to Marl.

"Uh ... 'Kay," said Marl.

The rock troll went into the building. They could all hear his loud footsteps, as he did a thorough sweep through the entire place. They heard multiple doors opening and closing. After five minutes Marl came back out.

"It look good. Way good. No trash to be seen. They do good job," he said.

"Let me check. No offense, Marl, but the whole 'no nose' thing is a strike against you in this matter," said Jayde, as she ran into the clinic. They could hear her running around, opening and slamming doors. Her head popped out the second story window. "I can't believe it!"

"Yahsir, wesah makers places soopercleaner, yah. I counts 218 hobgobs. That beesah two gold and nine silvers," said the driver.

Marl looked over at Cameron, who was already calming down Marie. She was fervently arguing that they were being gouged by the tiny garbage men. Marl stepped forward.

"We be say half per gob. Yar?" said Marl.

"*Oi*, meesah beezer getting allzah mixedupin. Dassah one gold, five silver," said the hobgoblin.

Marie still fumed about paying that much to the creatures. Cameron paid the money to the head hobgoblin, and they filed into the building.

The place was immaculate. All traces of filth had been erased. Somehow the hobgoblins had also eradicated the revolting odor as well. The place sparkled.

"Wow. Amazing how creatures so gross got it this clean," said Jayde. "I almost don't want to puke when I think about them now."

The group spent the rest of the day moving all their equipment and belongings into the clinic. Marie's amazing cabinet continued to produce supplies from its ever-expanding interior. Jayde spent much of her time exploring inside. Now that it was clean, she had fallen in love with the place.

The clinic was three stories tall, like all the other buildings on the street. The main floor was open, with a ceiling over fifteen feet high. Jayde finished exploring the large open room in minutes. Upstairs, however, rooms twisted and turned on top of each other. The layout was confusing, with curves connecting the rooms together instead of straight lines. The doors on the far sides were cemented shut. After investigating and taking a few trips outside the building to figure out the true location, Jayde realized that the doors must have connected to the neighboring building at one time or another.

In the front corner on the main floor was a small room that had a pole which extended upward into the ceiling. Jayde could not understand the purpose of this until she found the same pole upstairs. She then realized that this pole allowed someone inside to slide all the way to the main floor. The stairs were located at the very back of the building, and the pole allowed easy access to get to the main floor quickly. She also found a miniature elevator in the back of the building by the kitchen. Marie explained that this was actually a dumbwaiter, used to bring supplies to the other floors, without having to traverse the narrow stairs. Jayde found that she could fit inside, and pull herself up and down in the dumbwaiter with ease. It slid noiselessly, and she amused herself by pulling herself up the dumbwaiter and sliding down the pole.

By sunset, the clinic had been transformed from a rancid dump into a livable mess that no longer smelled like a sewer.

"We still have a long way to go," said Cameron.

"You really want a fully functioning clinic again here, Cam? I mean, you were attacked just yesterday," she said.

"I know. Maybe someone from Verrara recognized me and put out a hit on me. Those men from yesterday were definitely from the Assassins' Order, but were they connected to the ones in Haynis? I doubt the previous group of assassins could have tracked us here, considering I made sure each was quite dead. Also it has been just a few weeks. In a place this big, it could be decades before we are found, if ever."

"I hope you're right. I really do. But that just brings up the next question. Was it a random attack or did someone actually order an attack by a dozen assassins?" she asked.

Cameron looked out the window. Creatures of every shape and size made their way down the street, none of them stopping even to glance at the clinic. "I don't know. Who here would care about vampire hierarchy? Who here would even know? There is so little communication between Tenland and Verrara. Each time we pick up and move, it's farther and farther away from anyone who should know about such things, yet each time it seems I am discovered earlier. I'm done running, Marie. I wish we hadn't killed all twelve, so I could get some answers from one of them."

"You and me both. How could someone recognize your face out of the millions who live here, organize some assassins, and then attack when we decided to go to the tourney only last night? It seems so implausible. I just feel like someone or something must be tracking us," Marie said.

"The Assassins' Order wouldn't do that. They track you just long enough to catch up with you. Once they've found you, they attack. That spiky bearded gambler might have been the target, and we might have just been in the wrong place at the wrong time. He was right. We did protect his stand," Cameron said with a sigh. "Those guys were professionals. Granted, if I didn't have to protect Jayde, I think I could have ended their little assault pretty quickly. But they did have a couple needle bombs. I thought those things were outlawed everywhere."

"They are. That didn't seem to stop them. It was a pretty dumb choice for assassins as well, considering they explode and damage everything in all directions. Though, to their credit, they did receive the majority of the shards themselves."

"But it's not them I'm worried about. They were sent by somebody. That's what we need to find out."

"Should we tell the others? I mean, Marl's so happy to have a few friends, he would not care about you being on the run from your past. It's Jayde I'm worried about. She is used to being a little thief in a small town. She might leave us at any time, even though the poor thing's just getting a hint of happiness in her life. That was the second assassination attempt she's seen, and that's a lot to ask of a little girl, even one as street-hardened as Jayde. Sooner or later she'll find out the truth about your past," Marie said.

"True. But what if our suspicions about her are true as well? She conjured a potato twenty feet wide under incredible pressure with zero experience. She could kill herself accidentally if she had to fend for herself. Too bad we don't know any seers in this city, then we could just find out for sure."

"Are you joking? How would we know if a seer is working for Zolf? Why don't you just go flip a coin to see if you want to hand her right over to the Dark King? 'Here you go. One potential Chosen wrapped up with a bow,'" Marie said.

"I know. I know. But I'm sure there's a clean seer in a town this size."

"We'll just have to take it slowly. Hopefully we'll be able to figure out some answers before we're discovered. In the meantime we give Jayde some stability without terrifying her too much."

They walked out of the kitchen and back into the larger main floor of the clinic. After fifteen minutes the door to the dumbwaiter silently pushed open. Jayde peeked out to be sure no one saw her. She took a deep breath, but it did nothing to slow her racing heart. She felt happy that Cameron and Marie honestly cared for her, but what had just happened? Who were Cameron and Marie really?

Chapter 22: Orders

Despite moving all their worldly positions into the clinic, they lacked some supplies. Thanks to Jayde's winning wagers, they had more than enough money.

Cameron woke before any of the others to put on coats of the sun cream. After allowing one coat to dry, he slowly applied another coat, then another.

"I've got too much to do today to turn into stone," he said.

"What wrong with stone?" asked Marl.

"Nothing at all, if you can keep moving, Marl," said Cameron.

The group split up. Cameron and Marl went to buy supplies. Marie and Jayde explored the city.

Jayde and Marie made their way to the Merchants' District, where buildings had large signs that flashed their wares. Merchants also had their goods in carts and wheeled them down the street, shouting about special deals on sale just for today. People sold nuts, fruit, fish, and bread. Delicious aromas emanated from shopfronts and buildings. People performed on street corners with amazing acts of agility. Some sang songs; others played instruments, while the rest juggled and told stories. Wizards performed illusions for small crowds with a tip jar left out to reward their efforts.

Jayde grinned continuously at the sights. She had been waiting to explore the city for days, but, for reasons she did not understand, she hadn't ventured on her own. Jayde wanted to ask Marie a hundred questions after overhearing her and Cameron's conversation. But Jayde knew her eavesdropping might be a strike against her. She tried a bit of subtlety.

"Hey, Marie, what is an assassin?" she asked.

Marie stopped walking and looked at Jayde. She was startled to see that Marie's expression was not one of anger but more of a sly smile. She continued walking while she answered. "The Assassins' Order is one of the larger Order Halls in most cities. Usually assassins are trained to gather information, but people can train at their halls for a wide variety of skills. Some of the best trained soldiers had their start in the Assassins' Order. I actually trained at one of the Assassins' Order before becoming a war sage," said Marie.

They came to a large white stone building with an intimidating iron door at the front. The building towered over all the others on the street. The letters *EO* marked the outside of the building.

"Jayde, before we go in this building, I want to do something. It might make you feel a little light-headed, but it will help protect you."

"Sure. Will it hurt?"

"No. It will make you feel a little funny, that's all," said Marie.

"Whatever you say."

They walked inside. Marie put her hand on Jayde's shoulder. As they walked through the door, an eerie silence surrounded them. Jayde felt calmer and more relaxed than she had just seconds ago. She also felt slightly light-headed.

A young woman sat at a desk. A second iron door loomed behind her. The lady wore a lime-green dress and purple glasses much too large for her face. She looked up from her mass of disorganized paperwork.

"What do you want?" she said.

Jayde saw the woman's mouth move, but somehow all the sound come directly out her nose.

"Yes. We were wondering if you could—" Marie began.

"—could provide more information about enchanting, yes. I could if you were worth the time," finished the thin lady with a sneer. She worked on her paperwork, ignoring Jayde and Marie, creating an awkward silence.

"Anyway, yes. Jayde here, I believe, has great—" Marie said.

"—great potential for just about anything. Or so you think. But you really don't know, do you?" said the lady. This time she looked at Jayde. Again she paused, as if daring them to speak again.

"Right. Like I was saying, Jayde seems—"

"—to be positively brimming with raw Talent, or so you are convinced. And you don't think she even realizes this yet," she said. The lady sighed much too loudly and dramatically. She slowly pulled her spotless glasses off her face and began furiously cleaning them. "Listen. We get potential enchantresses here all the time. Each one thinks he or she could make it to Elite Enchantress in less than three years, but time and time again we see nothing but novices with the Talent of a kumquat. This little waif probably doesn't have enough Talent to walk across the street without holding your hand."

"Hey!" said Jayde. "Who do you think you—"

"Not now, little urchin. The adults are talking. Doesn't have much for manners either, huh? I can see that she was pretty much raised on the streets. Now isn't that a star on her report card? Undisciplined, unkempt, and stupid—a triple threat," said the lady.

"Now listen here," said Jayde, who could feel her anger pulsing, "you have no right to—"

"To what, little girl? To insult an urchin with no Talent who is wasting my time? Don't have any delusions of importance here. I can tell right now you won't amount to much," she said. While she spoke, she leaned over her desk and looked down at Jayde.

Jayde wanted to slap her smug expression right off her face. She willed her body to do so, but it did not respond.

"Oh? Can't do anything? No surprise there, urchin. You obviously are too dumb to know my enchantment prevents you from resorting to your usual violent, immature ways. You barge in here with ridiculous requests. What do you do? You waste my time. *Please* ..." said the lady.

Jayde stared right into the eyes of the woman. As the nasally woman ranted, Marie narrowed her eyes and took her hand from Jayde's shoulder. For several seconds nothing happened. Then her expression changed. The woman stopped her rant, as if someone had flipped a switch. "Oh, my, but what happened?" she said.

"I was just cloaking the amount of Talent she has," said Marie with a smile.

"I can personally guarantee that that child will *never* become an enchantress if she does anything drastic," sneered the woman, who now appeared less confident. She stood up and poked Jayde hard in the chest, as she did so. "Don't even think of it!"

"All we really want is the location of all the orders. Is that too much to ask? As the largest order, the Enchanters' Order is supposed to provide guidance for all the other orders, correct?" asked Marie.

The lady ruffled through a drawer, leafed through hundreds of pages, and threw a sheet of parchment at Marie.

"Now that wasn't so hard, was it?" said Marie.

"Don't strike that tone with me. You think you're smart, but that little mongrel still has—"

Jayde looked right at her and screamed "Stop it!" As she yelled, a sound like a thousand windows shattering cascaded through the room. Jayde suddenly felt much lighter and sensed the release of pressure she had not noticed.

Marie faced the rude woman, pulled her elbows to her side, and clenched her fists tight. She closed her eyes and concentrated. The color in the thin lady's face drained away, and she let out a tiny whimper. Marie opened her eyes wide and roundhouse kicked the desk. The desk exploded against the wall in a shower of splinters and papers. Seconds later three women in matching black dresses came out of the iron door leading deeper into the building.

"What is going on here?" one snapped. Her voice pulsed with steel and anger.

"Your receptionist insulted my friend here too many times. She has no respect and no eye for Talent. Not only that, she failed to recognize someone with a bit more strength than she thought," said Marie, her tone matching that of the first woman.

"Oh, my. My, my, my. Did you shatter the antiviolence enchantment?" asked one.

"Nope. Jayde did. I just smashed the desk out of frustration to get that idiot's attention. I'm sorry for breaking the desk, but she was hiding behind that enchantment with such an infuriating air of authority. It was all I could take," said Marie.

"Really?" said the second lady dressed in black. "Well, we thank you for teaching our novice a lesson," she said. She then looked at the thin woman in the glasses.

"Novice? But I passed all my novice exams months ago!"

"If you passed them, you would have learned the ninth tenet of Enchanting better than that, hmm? 'Always know strengths as well as weaknesses.' The enchantment let you see her weaknesses, but you failed to even test her strengths. Novice, you're lucky she only destroyed the desk. Most war sages I know would not have tolerated such disrespect."

"Sage? You're a war sage?" asked the thin woman, now trembling. "But, but why didn't you say so? Why didn't you think about it? You *knew* I was reading your thoughts. I know you knew. Why didn't you think about that?"

"Because I didn't want you to know. I wanted to see how you would treat someone who you thought of as your inferior. I found that you treat them quite badly. Not only that, I blocked Jayde's true potential from you for the same reason. I wanted to show Jayde how she would be treated, if she were to become an enchantress. I think I've accomplished that."

The three women in black dresses glared at the freshly demoted novice. She wilted and slunk through the back door, disappearing from sight.

"This girl is positively rippling with Talent," said the third woman, speaking for the first time. "Please at least give her an honest chance at Enchanting."

"Uh, thanks?" said Jayde. "Could one of you possibly do me a favor?"

"Certainly, child. It is the least we can do after slighting you so unfairly."

"Could one of you try to share, putting aside your feelings toward Enchanting, what you really think I would be best at?" Jayde asked.

"Jayde, you're asking more than you realize," said Marie.

"No, that is fair. This child has wisdom far beyond her years. Margaret, if you would be so kind," said one.

The stern-faced woman in black walked forward. She asked the rest of them to take a few steps back. She put both hands to Jayde's face and closed her eyes. She instructed Jayde to do the same. A golden glow surrounded the elderly lady and Jayde.

A rush of emotion mixed with dizziness consumed Jayde. She felt her body falling, yet also felt a surge of energy holding her in place. She felt shapes and designs and creatures unimagined pass in front of her with blurring rapidity. It lasted less than a minute and faded away like a dream.

"Well?" asked Marie.

"No doubt in my mind that she would make a gifted enchantress," said Margaret. The other two women nodded in agreement. "But," the woman added. She then looked right at Jayde.

"Yes?" said Jayde.

"But I think you would be a Conjurer of Excellence," she finished.

"What!" said the first lady.

"You're joking, Margaret. You have to be!" said the second.

"Have you ever known me to joke? Ever?"

"Those hacks will waste Talent of this level! Even in their upper echelon, there's hardly a master among them! Oh, sure, Yow is incredible, but he's really the only one," said the first.

"She asked for my opinion, and I gave it," said Margaret simply. "The girl is a born conjurer. Her imagination is untamed, nearly explosive. Her mind creates unique answers from angles yet unthought. Not only that, her will dwarfs even my own."

"Oh, but what an enchantress she would make!" said the first.

"Indeed. But that is not our choice. It is hers," said Margaret.

Jayde looked at the stern-faced Margaret again. Then she impulsively gave the old woman a hug. The woman seemed taken aback but returned the hug.

"Thank you," said Jayde.

"You're welcome, child. Good luck. You have a rough road ahead of you, but I think you can do anything you put your mind to."

They left the Enchantresses' Order, and Marie explained what had just happened to Jayde.

"Your inquiry, Jayde, asking an enchantress to give her honest opinion of you, was sheer brilliance. You may not have known it, but one of the enchantments in there was that of truth. Normally the enchanters have the advantage of knowing that people who come in can only speak the truth. You turned that on them by forcing the enchantress in there to give her honest assessment of you. It was exceptionally clever, even if you didn't quite plan it that way," said Marie.

"I just thought they might point me in the right direction."

"I thought we could go from order to order to see which one *you* like best. You have a recommendation for Conjuring, but we should visit some other orders to see how you feel about them."

The rest of the day was spent going to various Order Halls. The Necromancers' Order scared Jayde, regardless of their raspy encouragement that she would be "horribly skilled in the dark conversation," whatever that meant. The Wizards' Order seemed stuffy and overly fixated on books. The Philosophers' Order thought she was a bit flighty, and she thought they were nuts. Jayde liked the Witches' Order, even with their cackling laughter.

They also visited some of the minor Order Halls. They visited the Voodooism Hall, where a man in only a loincloth with a necklace of skulls greeted them. He threw some chicken bones on the floor and said the bones did not want her here. He then said the bones did want her to give him a silver piece for happiness. They left.

They tried to get into the Order of Abjuration. Marie explained how helpful a good abjurationist could be in battle. They could create wards of impenetrability and strong barriers of protection. Unfortunately, when they arrived at the Order, for some reason they could not get through the door.

They walked into the Seers' Order only to find a person waiting for them at the front door. She smiled and explained that they should continue their tour of orders elsewhere. Marie found this quite amusing, but Jayde seemed a little put off. They then went to the Alchemists' Order. To Jayde, it seemed like a boring version of the Witches' Order. They had bubbling pots in neat rows sorted by shapes and sizes; yet, where the witches had energy and spontaneity, the alchemists seemed cold, sterile, and dull.

Finally they made it to the Conjurers' Order. A portly goateed man swept the front porch of the Order Hall. He greeted them as they came toward him. A delicious smell drifted through the air, like freshly baked bread and simmering vegetables.

"Greetings, friends. I'm Yow," said the fellow with a broad grin.

"You *Meow*?" asked Jayde.

"No. I am Yow, Yow Li. But I do love cats," he said. Yow looked down at the ground and grabbed a handful of dirt. He winked at Jayde and made a strange gesture. Out of the dust came a small creature three inches long. It lacked shape at first, and then it shook itself and dust fell from its coat. It was a tiny cat, made of the brown-gray dirt. It blinked its eyes at her and gave the tiniest squeak of a meow.

"Oh, you're good, Yow," said Marie. The old man smiled at Marie.

Jayde reached down and pet the tiny kitten with one finger. The kitten rubbed its head against Jayde's finger and purred. It was so tiny, the purr was just barely audible, but Jayde looked up at Marie with a smile that could melt granite.

"Would you like to come in?" Yow asked.

"Can I take her with me?" asked Jayde.

"Of course," said Yow. "Though try to keep her off the counters. I'm not sure if she's potty trained yet."

Jayde put her hand down, and the dirt-kitten jumped into her outstretched palm. It pushed on her hand a few times with its front paws and then curled up in a tiny ball. Jayde cupped her other hand over the tiny kitten and walked into the Conjurers' Order. Yow held the door for her as she walked in, followed by Marie.

A flurry of activity greeted them as they entered. The order house was larger on the inside than on the outside. Flying creatures had room to fly since the ceiling rose to over three stories. A group of elderly conjurers—two humans, a creature with long catlike ears and whiskers, and four reptilian beings—sat in front of a fire, deep in discussion. Hallways expanded in different directions. Small creatures scurried around and then vanished into nothing. A herd of giant spiders ran along the walls and ceiling, carrying drinks. One would drop down from the ceiling to refill an empty mug from time to time. Occasional bursts of laughter could be heard throughout the enormous room. Explosions punctured the air as well. Something struck Jayde as unique; beyond the multitude of creatures of all shapes and sizes, something felt familiar. She could not see it, but she could definitely feel it. Jayde looked toward Marie.

"I don't know what it is, but it feels right. None of the other orders had this level of energy. I mean, I understand the allure of alchemy. They mix stuff together to make new stuff. That's fine. And I think I get Enchanting. They make spells that stay in one place and affect a certain area. All the other orders seemed so focused on studying and diligence. What does a conjurer do?" Jayde asked.

"What does anyone with Talent do?" answered Yow Li. "The orders offer channels to use Talent. Many people attempt to go to the order with the most power. Others go to orders where they think they can achieve fame or fortune. You could harness your Talent in any order. You are new to the world of magic, correct?"

"Is it that obvious?" asked Jayde.

He smiled. "Yes, it is. But that is a beautiful gift to the lucky order you chose. You come as a blank page, without preconceived notions of power, greed, or fame. Conjurers rarely have such desires. The fact that we accept anyone who wants to try Conjuring also might add to the chaos."

"Wait. You accept anyone to be a conjurer? Why? Doesn't that mean that you get a bazillion people who call themselves conjurers, even if they're awful?"

"I would say just under a bazillion, but yes."

"Do you think that's a good thing, Mr. Li? I mean, doesn't that dilute the population with a giant group of pretend conjurers?"

"Exactly!" said Yow.

"But why? Everyone hates being looked down on," said Jayde. Then she stared at the man and a thought came to her. "All right, I'm gonna try Cameron's approach on this one and break it down from your angle."

"Please continue."

"I presume you're a good conjurer. The clueless old guy sweeping out front seems a little cliché for me. You made a kitten out of nothing, so let's pretend that you're really talented. I don't know anything about Conjuring, but I read people pretty well," said Jayde.

Yow Li's face suddenly shifted to a serious expression. "Indeed you do."

"So why would you want everyone to ... oh, it can't be that simple," Jayde said.

"What conclusion did you reach?" asked Mr. Li.

"You *like* people to think of all conjurers as people with little Talent. You want the general public to think of conjurers as a joke. That way, when someone with a true gift for it comes along, they will be filed along with all the riffraff. A gifted conjurer is like a dragon among chickens," said Jayde.

Marie just looked at Mr. Li and smiled. He shook his head.

"You know, Jayde, for someone who has not even lived as a conjurer, you think like a conjurer," said Mr. Li.

"I don't know why everyone keeps saying that. Even Margaret the enchantress told me that I'd be a 'Conjurer of Excellence,' but *I still don't even know what one is!*" shouted Jayde.

The room became silent.

"What did you say, child?" asked a skeleton, who had been sitting at the bar. Despite being made of nothing more than connective tissue and bones, its voice seemed surprisingly upbeat and happy.

The sudden silence surprised even Marie. Jayde looked over at the skeleton. "I said, Margaret the enchantress thought I'd be good," repeated Jayde quietly.

"No. Say it exactly how she said it," said the head of a dragon mounted on the wall.

Jayde had assumed it was merely decoration; apparently it was not. Jayde looked helplessly at Marie and Yow, but neither would answer for her. Hundreds of stares locked on the young girl.

"She said I would make a Conjurer of Excellence, whatever that means. But I still don't even ..." Jayde trailed off.

All the heads seemed focused on Jayde and Yow. He smiled, stood, and motioned for Jayde to walk down one of the hallways. Slowly the buzz of the great room returned to its normal level of chaos.

"What the heck was that all about?" cried Jayde.

"Well, Margaret is more than just another enchantress. She is possibly *the* most powerful enchantress in the world. She rarely gives compliments," said Mr. Li.

"So some crazy old bird gave me some big compliment. I still don't know what everyone is talking about," said Jayde.

Yow just grinned. "Patience. Many of those in the great hall would give a fortune in gold or years of their lives to have Margaret give them just a nod of approval, much less marking them as excellent. I have known Margaret for a long time now. I have only heard her use the word *excellent* two other times and never about a conjurer. *Buffoon, idiot, imbecile, incompetent, delusional, horrendous*, and other such words flow like a river from her mouth. Ah, here we are," he said in front of a door that looked exactly the same as all the rest.

They entered a small room with a large sandbox in the middle.

"This is training sand. This room has an enchantment on it that helps bring out your latent Talent. The sand also has been altered by a few of my alchemist friends to be more pliable. This allows you to take large steps forward, well beyond your normal abilities."

"What abilities?" snapped Jayde.

"You want to see what Conjuring is all about. I think the best way to show you is to have you show yourself," said Mr. Li.

"Um, okay," said Jayde.

"Do you still have the kitten in your hands?" he asked.

"She's sleeping," said Jayde.

"Is she? That's nice. Why don't you put her in the sand? Cats love sand," he said.

Jayde put the tiny kitten in the sand. It looked up at her for a second and then pounced at something only it could see.

"Look closely at the kitten. Really look at it. Look at the kitten and concentrate," he paused. "Now close your eyes, Jayde." She did.

"Picture the kitten in your mind. See it right in front of you. See it walking around in the sand before you. Don't think about it, but actually try to see it in your mind," he said.

Jayde continued to concentrate.

"See it. *See* it. Now think about that little kitten."

"I see it," she said.

"Yes, I believe you do. Keep your eyes closed. Now what color is it?" he asked.

"Dust gray. I don't need to open my eyes to know that."

"Indeed. But, in here, it doesn't have to be," he said.

"It doesn't?"

"Not here."

"Hmm," said Jayde. The small kitten rapidly changed colors. It first morphed from a kitten made of dirt into an actual kitten covered in gray fur. The fur then changed color again. It became brown, then Siamese, then orange. Jayde smiled. The kitten changed to lavender. Then its ears turned pink, and its paws turned brilliant yellow.

The kitten shifted through a rainbow of colors, shades, stripes, and splotches. It changed from short haired to long haired, then into one with long whiskers and a short tail. The tail grew longer and longer, then again shortened. Faster and faster the tiny kitten changed shape, color, and form. The kitten seemed unfazed, continuing to happily pounce around in the sand.

The tiny cat mewed. Jayde opened her eyes. The cat currently had an orange head with a diagonal blue stripe, as well as a long glowing white tail and chocolate-colored paws. The kitten mewed happily again. It spun in rapid circles, trying to catch its brilliant white tail. It then stopped and looked right at Jayde again and licked its nose.

"Can anyone do this in here?" asked Jayde.

"No," said Yow. "All I did was imply the kitten's fur color might not be permanent. I never said anything about you changing the cat by just thinking about it, much less making it into an artist's palette of random colors. I didn't speak of fur or length of tail. And yet you have realized a few possibilities by yourself. Your imagination as a conjurer is your best and most valuable asset. Imagination is more important than facts. Imagination is change. Imagination is power. You must see things from a different point of view, find solutions in ways that have not yet been considered or attempted. That, Jayde, is the way of a conjurer."

"I guess, if you say so," said Jayde. "But it's almost not fair."

"What's not fair?" Yow asked.

"Forcing the poor thing to look like what we want. Though, I wonder," Jayde said and then slowly closed her eyes. The color in the kitten slowly drained away and the long hair shortened. It slowly changed into a short-haired gray tabby.

Yow looked down at the kitten, currently rubbing against Jayde's legs and purring.

"Jayde, what did you just do?" Yow asked.

"I ... I'm not sure. I just thought that, if it was so easy to have it change colors, it would seem fairer if the kitten could change colors whenever it wanted. I mean, it's her color, so she should be able to change it, right?" asked Jayde.

Marie looked at Yow. "Did it work?"

"Try it out," he answered.

Marie walked behind the cat, then quickly stomped her feet and yelled. The tiny kitten released a startled hiss. For a split second they all saw the kitten's hair stick up on end, but then it vanished.

"You killed it!" shouted Jayde.

"Patience," said Yow.

Jayde felt a small wet sensation at her ankle. She looked down but saw nothing. She reached to touch where the sensation was and felt a small form. The kitten rubbed against her ankle, touching its cold nose against her leg. She picked up the invisible cat. It purred right away and slowly materialized into view. This time it had a light pinkish color to its fur, as it purred.

"Jayde, I'd like you to keep her," said Mr. Li.

Jayde's face beamed, and she looked over at Marie, who just nodded.

"I love her!" she said.

"I'm glad to hear that, for she is your responsibility. If, that is, you want to become a conjurer," said Yow.

"Yes, definitely! And I'll take great care of her. I promise."

"Good to hear. But she requires Conjuring to flourish. The more you conjure, the stronger and healthier she will be."

"But I don't even know how to do anything yet," said Jayde.

"Well, you know how to change her colors. That's enough. You can try to vary her colors or make her fur longer or shorter—anything at all. You can't hurt her by trying, so don't worry about that. She can help you out on your trips too," said Yow.

"My trips?" asked Jayde.

"Yes, indeed. You are now a novice conjurer. All start off the same. Making deliveries."

"Deliveries?"

"Conjurers are on the bottom rung of the magical Talent ladder. Most regard conjurers as strange people with a few party tricks, though I suppose that does describe the majority of us quite well. Thus, we had to make some sacrifices to stay a flourishing order."

"What does that have to do with me?"

"The order stays in business mostly through the restaurant upstairs. One of the reasons the restaurant does so well is that we offer free delivery. That's where you come in," he said.

"Can she come with me?" Jayde asked, pointing to the kitten.

"She *must* go with you on your deliveries. You see, since I made this familiar, I will always have a link with her. If you ever get in trouble or have any difficulties, just tell the cat, and she'll let me know," he said. In response, the small kitten mewed in agreement.

"When do I begin?" asked Jayde.

"Tomorrow."

Jayde looked up at Marie, Jayde's bright green eyes beaming in hopeful expectation.

"There are still orders that we have not checked out yet. Usually one decides on which to join over years, not after a whirlwind one-day tour bouncing from hall to hall. I don't want you to do this just because someone told you to do it," said Marie.

"I'm sure. It feels right."

"I guess she'll see you tomorrow then, Mr. Li," said Marie.

"Call me Yow," said Yow Li.

Jayde and Marie walked out of the Order Hall. Jayde beamed in the early dusk. Before they could get more than ten paces from the hall, they heard a faint mewing. They both looked down to see the kitten trying to keep up with their long strides. The kitten appeared gray again, now that they were outside of the training room. Jayde grinned and picked her up.

"I guess she wants to come with me even when I'm not on deliveries," said Jayde.

The kitten attacked the frayed end of Jayde's sleeve but missed its pounce and landed in the sleeve instead. It popped its head out, as if surprised how it got there.

"You know, a cat should have a name, even if it is made of only dust and magic," said Marie.

They walked a short distance, while Jayde contemplated names.

"How about Jasmine? I was thinking of Grace, but I think that she might be a little clumsy for that name," said Jayde.

The kitten looked up at her and lightly bit her thumb.

"Ow! You little stinker!" said Jayde. The kitten gave a cute little meow and purred again. "That's it. I'll call her Fang."

Chapter 23: Trust

A month had passed since the tournament.

The endeavor had been a booming success, especially considering the original intent was to stifle a possible looting. People still approached Sarah about the marvelous tournament and her store.

The second result of the tournament had also been unexpected. The winners of the tournament had taken the jobs she had offered them. Sarah looked at the front of the store where Kevin and Mullet helped the pixies attach strong steel supports to the wall. She had been a little apprehensive at first about hiring the two fighting champions, but she kept her word and made them the promised offer.

The two men pointed out that nighttime seemed the most important time for them to be present. They suggested that they actually live in the store. This would give them not only a place to stay but also the ability to monitor the store during the most likely times for someone to break in. Sarah had initially been nervous to allow the two men to be unsupervised in the store. Granted, an entire fleet of pixies lived in the store already, but these two men had already proven how tough they could be. If they could defeat trained fighters in an arena, a few pixies could never stop them.

Sarah researched both men. She made a list of questions, background information she desired, and started searching. She found that the more she searched, the more she liked the two men she had hired. No one she talked with ever spoke poorly of the men. She reluctantly agreed to their request to stay in the shop.

The store's popularity blossomed, attracting interested new buyers as well as thieves. Allowing the men to stay in the store proved to be a wise decision. Two weeks after opening a foursome of novices from the Thieves' Order broke in. The robbery went poorly. Kevin ambushed the four. They were bound and gagged in less than a minute after their silent entry into the store.

Kevin left them tied together in the center of the store, upside down, dangling from the ceiling. When Sarah groggily walked into the store that morning, she yelped in surprise, which woke Kevin.

"I figured no need to bother the authorities in the middle of the night," he explained. Thus, he had left them tied together, so they would learn a lesson.

"But they are all beat up!" she said, pointing to the black eyes and bruise marks on the men hanging from the ceiling.

"Well, then I reckon they learned their lesson. Didn't you, boys?" he said to the dangling mass, while ripping off the gag he had applied to one of their mouths.

"Yes! Please, mister, please just let us down!" one pleaded.

Kevin put the gag back over the thief's mouth.

"Sure will, as soon as the local officer makes his rounds. He comes down this street quite regularly, usually about noon," said Kevin. Moans came from the mass. Sarah shook her head.

"Kevin, that … that can't be legal," whispered Sarah.

"Well, I don't really know or care. Stealing from here *definitely* ain't legal. I just want these boys to know that breaking in here was a really, *really* bad idea. I'm sure that they can spread the word when they get out of jail. Can't you, boys?"

Groans responded.

"We can't have this mass hanging here while people come into the store to look at jewelry," Sarah said.

"Why not? I know how you like free publicity, since you've been raving about how well the tournament turned out," he said.

Sarah started to disagree, but then she stopped. Any publicity was good publicity, right?

"You got a store of pixies making jewelry, run by a young woman. To me that sounds like bait for every thief in the city. Why don't we make it known that you also got the two toughest brutes in the entire city here too? People will come just to see the contrast," Kevin said.

Business continued to boom. A second group of thieves broke into the store. This group had more experience than the first. Mullet was on duty, since it was his turn to sleep downstairs. It took slightly longer to dispatch this group since one actually made it outside. Mullet ran him down and walloped the man on the head, then dragged him back into the store. The group awoke, upside down, the same as the first. This time, however, they had several angry pixies flying around their heads when they woke up.

Kevin had become friends with all the pixies who could speak human. Kevin had an open, simple, and likable demeanor. He explained to the pixies how thieves would steal all their hard work and give them nothing in exchange. Pixie culture thrived on fair exchange. The thought of taking something without an exchange was a baffling concept. Stealing never even entered their minds as a possibility.

The thieves thanked the police for taking them to jail. They did not mind the beating they had received; they figured they had earned that for being caught. They just wanted to get away from dozens of angry pixies buzzing in their face and screaming high-pitched ethics lessons.

The pixies trusted Kevin, but Mullet received nothing but anxious glares. He was used to this. Mullet's face had layers of scars, and his nose had been broken too many times to count, giving him a gnarled, fearsome look. On top of this, his giant bulk intimidated most large men, so the pixies remained terrified. Mullet seldom spoke; when he did, his voice grated like a mix of thunder and gravel. He moved quickly and quietly. These factors created a high level of nervousness. This lasted until Tali, an impulsive pixie at the best of times, got caught outside the shop with some unruly men.

Tali had mastered speaking human faster than the other pixies by spending her time with Sarah and Lucy. She had taken it upon herself to keep Mullet in check.

Late one afternoon Mullet was setting up some new security measures outside the shop. Tali watched him for two hours as he worked. The sun was setting, but the enormous man showed no sign of stopping. Tali had become bored with watching him work, so she taunted him. She just didn't trust him; he never said anything.

"You know, those abundant scars do not create the visage of supremacy," she teased.

Mullet said nothing.

"Did you receive them in battle? Doubtful. You probably misaligned your own feet and imprudently toppled on your face," she said.

Nothing, no reaction. He did not even stop working.

Above all Tali hated being ignored. She flew down and hovered right in front of the giant man's face, sticking out her tongue and flying away. He worked on, hefting another barricade into place.

She continued to needle him as he worked. He ignored her, working in silence. She pestered, taunted, and insulted the giant man. He never budged as the sun slowly drifted away.

Though Mullet ignored her, a couple men had heard the tiny pixie's taunts.

While Tali mocked Mullet, the two men across the street watched her actions. They had been at the tournament a month ago.

"Issat little fairy givin' you trouble, Mullets?" one said.

"No," he answered and continued his work.

"Oh, amazing, it communicates!" said Tali. "I thought you lacked sufficient competence to entwine two words together. Though, on second thought, that utterance remained a single word, so maybe you still lack the intelligence for multiworded sentences," she said, laughing loudly at her own joke.

"Hey! You leave him alone, little fairy, if you know what's good for you," said the second.

"First of all, I'm a pixie, not a fairy. The barbarian is fine. Just because he appears to shave with a misaligned pitchfork does not mean he lacks the ability to reciprocate. You don't require these inebriates' assistance, do you, dunderhead?" she said.

"No," he answered.

"You should stop calling him names, you dumb, stupid fairy! He's a hero. He's saved more lives than you've got in your whole ... wait. He's done more than you ever did," said one man. The other nodded in agreement.

"I am certain you are attempting to communicate, however rudimentarily," said Tali. "Did you two just leave the Wizards' Order after a long night of diligent studying? Why not just ambulate along and leave us. This troll must complete his engagements before disappearing beneath his bridge. Sorry, that was quite egregious, insulting trolls like that. Some are tolerable, and most are more attractive."

"You shut up! Shut UP!" yelled one, staggering across the street. The other joined him, not wanting to miss the chance to yell incoherently. The second of the two men reached into his pocket and pulled out something while crossing the street.

Tali zipped to the sign high atop the shop's storefront, out of their reach.

"You needs to appolifis ... appologish ... say you're sorry, dumb fairy," said the first.

"I. AM. NOT. A. FAIRY," said Tali.

"Yah," said the second, "a fairy's smarter. What're you? Some kind of poop-beetle that talks?" said the second.

Tali zoomed right in front of the face of the first one. "Let me tell you some—" She didn't finish.

The second man swooshed a net over her. He clenched his fist around the top of the fine mesh. She was trapped.

"Let me out! Let me out, oh, please! Please, please, PLEASE let me out!" she screamed. Her tone had instantly changed to a helpless plea. Her voice had heart-wrenching desperation in every word. The complete misery and agony in the pixie's voice halted the two men for a moment, but their stupidity returned quickly.

A dark voice rumbled nearby. "Let her go." Each word was slow and deliberate.

Tali stopped her wailing for an instant to see Mullet putting down the large grating. She stared, desperate for anyone to free her.

The two men showed no sign of granting her wish. One reached a dirty hand into the net and roughly grabbed Tali by her wings, pinning them together. She screamed in pain, as he pulled her from the net, ignoring her miserable wailing.

"Not so tough now, dumb fairy," he said, violently shaking the tiny creature by the wings. He reeked of stale ale and body odor.

Tali wailed in pain as he shook her some more.

Mullet's dark rumble from fifty feet away came again. "Let her go. Now."

"How good d'you fly without wings, stupid—" was all the man got out before he collapsed around Mullet's fist. Though Mullet had hit the man in the stomach, he actually went up in the air before coming back down. Mullet caught the pixie midair before she fell.

The other man looked at Mullet, then down at his buddy gasping for air, then back at Mullet. He shrugged; his brain had fired off enough warning signals to realize this was a battle to stagger away from. He disappeared into the night.

Tali tried to fly and screamed in pain.

Mullet carefully held her in one giant hand. She cried uncontrollably.

"You okay?" he asked.

Tali looked around for the first time since falling. She saw one man staggering away. She saw the other collapsed in a heap on the ground. She had been saved; she continued to cry in pain, but relief flooded through her. Mullet looked down at the small creature, waiting for her to regain composure.

She continued to sniff but got out a small "Thank you." She buzzed her wings and screamed out in pain again.

"Take me inside, please?" she pleaded. Mullet carried the pixie as if she were made of eggshells and walked to the front door, translucent fluid leaking from her wings.

Seconds after entering, pandemonium broke out. Several of the pixies accused Mullet, but Tali quickly relayed the story between sobs. Jenny, the head of the troop, blew a few notes on her magical flute. A male pixie with blond hair flowing to his knees quickly flew over. They chatted rapidly in Pixish, and he nodded.

He flew onto Mullet's hand and then pointed at the table. Mullet gently lay her on the table. Tali continued crying in pain. Jenny and Tali buzzed Pixish as the long-haired pixie touched her wings a few times. Each time he did, she let out a high-pitched scream. The normally gossamer wings oozed clear green fluid. The blond pixie chattered to Jenny, pointing to Tali's wings. He flew away, only to return moments later with a clear fluid that he poured on Tali's wings.

Jenny flew over to Mullet.

"She needs a doctor, one who knows pixies. She's injured beyond our abilities. Her wings are broken and not circulating gliae. I doubt you fully comprehend the intricacies of pixie life for her if she were to lose her wings," Jenny said.

"Like chopping off my arms," said Mullet.

Jenny raised her eyebrows in surprise. It was the longest sentence she had ever heard Mullet speak, and it showed his insight.

"Precisely," Jenny said. "Now the difficult task arises. It is after sundown, and we need a doctor who is not only open right now but also can handle severe pixie injuries," said Jenny. She blew into her flute again, and the room filled with pixies in seconds. Jenny made a quick speech in Pixish, followed by a long pause. No one spoke. "That's what I was afraid of," Jenny said to Mullet. "Not one of us knows where a physician is in this city, much less one who could handle pixies. I am so sorry, Tali."

Tali had been whimpering in pain before but now howled uncontrollably. "*Nooo!*" she said over and over. "My wings! Jenny, my ..." The rest was lost in her crying.

"I'll find one," said Mullet. Jenny looked at the giant with a raised eyebrow.

"Anything! Any chance, any chance at all, please!" said Tali. She limped over to the edge of the table and looked up at Mullet. "Please," she said.

He lowered his hand, and she stepped on. They disappeared out the door.

The closest mud run was five blocks away. Mullet cupped his hands over the pixie to keep her safe and sprinted. Giant bounding strides took him to the mud run in no time. He used his free hand to slam the blocker into place. A mudman appeared.

"Was'sup, dude? Oh, and dudette. How can I, like, help you on this fine evening?" he, or it, said.

"Doctor," said Mullet.

"You want someone in particular or just someone for plastic surgery, since your face could use, like, some major touch-up work, if you know what ah mean, brah?"

"Dr. Cameron," said Mullet. He had spoken with Kevin after the tournament. They had discussed their win at length, and Kevin had mentioned meeting not only Marie and Marl but also the doctor who had been with them—how the doctor not only pulled out a spike from a rock troll but had also fixed him enough to make it to the finals. Mullet figured a doctor who knew troll anatomy had a good chance of knowing about pixies.

"No problem, muchacho. I know right where the good Dr. Sangre lives, but, ah, do you have the payment?" asked the mudman.

Mullet threw a silver at the mudman. It hit him in the chest and slowly soaked its way into him.

"You know we don't ever carry change, right, amigo?" said the mudman.

Mullet glared at the creature.

"Righto, the good doctor is this way," it said. It pulled up the blocker and proceeded to ooze quickly down the trough. Mullet kept up with the creature's rapid sloshing.

Mullet ran continuously for fifteen minutes. The mudman looked back and seemed surprised that the big man never fell behind.

"Wow, dude. You're in some killer shape, brah. This is the shop right here, and, judging by the lights still on, I think you are in luck. Hasta la bye-bye, little dudette. Hope everything turns out okay," said the mudman to the pixie, disappearing into the trough.

Tali laughed weakly at the muddy creature as it disappeared. "Quite helpful, though I suppose most would be for a silver," she whispered.

Mullet said nothing. He pushed open the front door and encountered a roomful of activity. People moved from bed to bed, asking questions. He could see patients with tubes connected to their arms. He walked up to the front desk and rang a bell.

Mullet rarely experienced surprise. However, when the war sage appeared, dressed in a white nurse's outfit, he did a double take.

Marie looked at the giant man for a second and then dropped into a defensive posture. She crossed her forearms and bowed to Mullet.

"Greetings, paladin. May I help you?" she said.

"Help," he said and gently lay the tiny pixie on the counter.

Marie took one look at the pixie, then grabbed clean white towels, and gently picked her up and rushed into the clinic. Mullet followed.

"Dr. Sangre, you're needed in Room One now, please!" she said loudly.

Cameron appeared in seconds. He looked down with a frown at the pixie laying on the large gurney.

"What happened?" he asked, kneeling next to the pixie.

"Two men. I was stupid and did not watch my back. One caught me and crushed my wings," said Tali.

"Are you hurt anywhere else?" asked Cameron.

"I do not think so," she said.

"Do you have any other medical conditions?" he asked.

"No."

"No breathing problems, bleeding disorders, heart problems?" he asked.

"No, no, no."

"No hyperactive magical release, no pixie paralysis, no enchanted devices?"

"No, no, and no."

"Not taking any medicine, herbs, potions, or drugs?"

"No, but the pixie troop doctor put temporary gliae on my wings."

"Good. Any allergies to medicine? Last time you ate or drank?"

"No allergies. Lunch, about six hours ago," she said.

Cameron continued questioning the pixie; Marie used a small pair of scissors to carefully cut off her clothes and replaced them with a miniature paper gown. She explained that she did not want to risk any more damage to her wings by pulling them through the back slits in her clothes. Tali agreed.

Cameron then went to a drawer and pulled out a stethoscope; it had normal attachments for his ears, but the diaphragm end of the instrument came to a very tiny point, where he put it on her chest in different places.

"You sound fine, but your wings look terrible," he said.

"Are they broken?" she said.

"Yes. I need to set them and get your gliae flowing through your wings again."

"But, but I heard that, when you do that, pixies can die just from the pain!" she said.

"That's rare. Don't worry. I will put you to sleep before I set the wings," said Cameron.

Tali looked terrified. She stared up at Mullet for support. He nodded solemnly at her, as if to say, "What other choice do you have?"

"Doctor, I don't know if you truly comprehend. Pixies can DIE if they are overloaded with pain, and wing pain is the most severe," said Tali.

"I know," he said without hesitation. "You need to trust me. I'll give you a sleeping medicine. You won't feel a thing. It will make you feel a little funny, but then you will drift off. When you wake up, your wings will be all better."

Tali nodded.

Marie brought over a small scale. She carefully lifted Tali and recorded her weight.

"Marie, could you get 0.015 cc of Ketafol please, standard ratio mixture. Thanks," he said. Marie disappeared and came back with a very small syringe with a hair-thin needle as Cameron placed Tali on the center of the padded gurney once more.

"This is the medicine to put you to sleep. I know that we are really rushing you through all this, but time is a very important factor here. Your wings are leaking gliae badly. The longer we take, the worse the chances for your wings to recover," Marie said.

Mullet stepped between Cameron and Tali. "Can you really do this?" he asked.

"Yes," said Cameron.

Mullet looked into Cameron's eyes. He continued to stare into Cameron's eyes for an awkwardly long time. Cameron already had his surgical mask on. Despite the awkward glare from the behemoth, Cameron did not look away. A slight glint came from Mullet's eyes and then faded.

"Satisfied?" Cameron said to Mullet.

"Okay," said Mullet, stepping aside.

Marie eyed Cameron for a second, then continued to care for Tali. She cleaned a small area of her tiny thigh with a cotton ball moistened with a strong-smelling liquid. She then inserted the hair-thin needle and injected a nearly imperceptible amount of the fluid. Tali continued to lay on her side, but slowly she drifted to sleep. Marie held a tube connected to the wall above the pixie's face.

Cameron opened one of several vials he had prepared. He took some salve and liberally covered all four wings with it. He then gently pulled one wing with forceps until it was taut. It made a light clicking noise. He smoothed the wing over and over. He repeated the process with each of the other three wings. When all four wings had been straightened, Marie assisted him putting on his face a comically large pair of glasses. The glasses had many sets of lenses, one directly in front of the next. Each lens was slightly smaller than the one behind it. He started with just the large lenses, then put down the next smaller, then the next smaller, and so forth, until he had five lenses stacked in front of each other in a series of concentric circles. While Cameron adjusted his glasses, Marie went around the room lighting candles and focused the candlelight with mirrors, so that the tiny creature practically glowed from the illumination.

Cameron then took out a smaller set of tiny forceps and ever-so-slightly lifted the wings. With one hand he made minute adjustments to the wing; with the other he held a tiny stick which he dipped into a sticky gel. He used a small metal toothpick to apply minuscule dollops of the glue to the wings in different spots. As he worked, he spoke to Mullet, explaining what he was doing.

"When a pixie's wing is broken, it is different than a broken bone. Pixies have a blood supply, like we have, but, for their wings, they have gliae. Gliae is similar to blood in that it nourishes the wing, but the substance has nearly no weight to it. Gliae has high amounts of pixie magic in it, which allows them to fly as quickly as they do. However, if the wing goes too long without a supply of gliae, the wing dies."

Mullet grunted. He clenched his fists a few times, thinking about the men who had done this. Cameron continued.

"That's the reason we put on the gliae substitute first. We did it right away since that acts as a short-term gliae for the wings. The wings must be perfectly aligned to keep the channels flowing. What I'm doing now is gluing each wing precisely in place. It's tedious work, but, for pixies, if they lose their wings …"

"It's like cutting off our arms," Mullet finished.

"Well, yes and no. For pixies, flight is part of their identity. They not only use wings to fly but also to communicate and to do magic. Losing their wings is like losing their identity."

Cameron applied invisible amounts of the glue to each wing. After all four wings were finished, he allowed the glue to dry, which only took a few minutes. He flexed and extended the wings gently, looking closely for any leaking gliae.

"Looks good, Cam," said Marie.

"It's her wings, Marie. I really should …" he began.

"Cam, you can't do it for every patient. You'll wear yourself out, and you won't have any reserve left for when you really need it," she said.

"We're not having this tired old argument again, Marie," he said. "Besides, I'm only checking my work. I'm not changing anything, unless I need to."

Cameron carefully lifted the sleeping pixie in his cupped hands. His breathing slowed, and the room darkened despite the lighting. A faint blue glow appeared around his hands. Slowly Tali's wings moved up and down. One speck of blue light came from the wings, then another, then another. The wings sparkled with blue light for an instant and then slowly faded away.

Cameron opened his eyes and smiled. "She'll be fine."

Marie muttered under her breath something about not even using the glue in the first place if he was going to do what he just did.

Mullet quietly watched the pixie on the cot. The small creature breathed regularly and evenly while sleeping off the anesthetic. Marie monitored Tali until she regained consciousness. The doctor had already disappeared to another room.

After ten minutes Tali stirred. Marie removed the small tube she had been holding near the pixie's face. Tali groaned and opened her eyes. She leaned forward, but Marie gently pushed her back with an index finger.

"Not so fast there," Marie said. "You need to rest. Not only that, you have to take it easy for a few days. That means no flying."

"What? You can't stop me from flying," she said.

"No, I can't. But your wings need time to heal. After three days, the glue should be gone, and you can fly—but only short distances. Not too fast either. Also do not do any magic. That will put too much stress on your wings."

Marie looked at Mullet. "Are you staying with her for the next few days? Pixies don't usually take instruction too well. Will you help her to not fly for a few days?" she asked.

"Yes," said Mullet.

"Good. I want you to stay here for another half hour while the rest of the anesthetic wears off. The doctor will see you again and get you on your way," said Marie.

Marie left the room and caught up with Cameron.

"So what was the deal with the staring contest between you and the paladin behemoth back there?" Marie asked.

"He is actually quite a skilled diviner. He wanted to be certain that I really could do everything I said. He was just looking out for her, making sure I wasn't about to hurt her," he said.

"He got all that from staring in your eyes?" Marie asked.

"Like I said, he is quite good," Cameron answered.

"He didn't get anything else too important, did he?" she asked.

"I don't think so. I'm pretty good at keeping hidden what I don't want found," Cameron said.

A half hour later Cameron checked on the tiny pixie, who tried flexing her wings quite carefully but did so with only a slight groan of discomfort.

An hour later Mullet walked back home. It was midnight, but no one approached Mullet's bulk in the blackness of the night. He had both hands cupped around the pixie.

The normally talkative pixie still had the effects of the medicine in her. She fell asleep halfway to the Picky Pixie.

Mullet knocked on the door to the shop. The shop had been locked up, and, in his haste, he had not remembered his keys.

Kevin let him in. Shortly after their arrival, the entire troop had assembled. Mullet gently lay her on a towel. She continued to sleep.

"Well?" Jenny, the troop leader, asked.

"She'll be fine," Mullet said. "No flying for three days. Doc wanted me to watch her till then," he said to the hundreds of pixies watching from around the shop.

A flurry of pixies immediately disagreed. Others surmised that Mullet probably crushed her wings himself. Yet others looked at Tali's healed wings with a sense of awe. Jenny pulled out her flute and blew a shrill note. The pixies instantly became silent, and Tali woke up. Jenny looked down at her.

"He states your wings should be adequate and that flight is forbidden for three days. He also explained it was his duty to observe you during this time. What do you say to this, Tali?" Jenny asked.

Tali grinned. "He saved my life. I'll do anything he says."

"Yes. The doctor did some amazing work indeed. I truly thought your wings were beyond repair. However, what say you in regard to …" Jenny said, but quieted to Tali's shaking head.

"No. Mullet, Mullet saved my life. I will do anything Mullet tells me to do. If he says I am not to fly for three days or for three years, I will do as he says," she said. The rest of the pixies looked at Mullet, shocked.

"So be it. Mullet, you have not only Tali's gratitude but the gratitude of the troop as well. Are you willing to act as her guardian till she has recuperated?" Jenny asked.

The giant man nodded.

"Done. Now the rest of you get back to your bunks. We have another busy day tomorrow," Jenny said. The pixies zipped off in different directions, leaving only Jenny, Kevin, Mullet, and Tali. "Thank you, Mullet. You will have the troop's complete support. I just wish it did not take such an act of heroism to convince my troop of your valor."

He said nothing and carried Tali upstairs. After preparing a large mound of soft linens for the tiny pixie, and gently laying the miniscule sleeping creature on top, he collapsed onto his bed.

Chapter 24: Conjuring

Jayde woke just before dawn. In a month she had advanced greatly since becoming a novice conjurer in the order.

She could hear Marl snoring down the hall, as she quickly went through her morning routine. She slid down the long pole which landed her near the front of the clinic. Marie waited for her as she landed.

"Up early again, aren't we?" Marie said.

"It's the only way I can get time in the practice rooms. The older conjurers kick me out during the day, so I usually end up training by myself," said Jayde.

Jayde wolfed down a plate of eggs and juice. She had been training for four weeks. Yow Li had called her a prodigy, but she still had so much to learn. She woke up each day excited to learn more.

Jayde sent out a thought to Fang, who bounded down the stairs. During breakfast Jayde would dress and conjure Fang in new and interesting ways. One morning she had changed her fur to black, and had changed her size and coloring to make her look just like a panther. Fang and Jayde had developed a sense of communication. They could tell what the other thought, and both enjoyed a bit of mischief.

Jayde told Fang to hide behind one of the curtains in a patient's room, while Jayde went to tell Cameron that a sick patient was there. Jayde waited till the split second when Cameron opened the curtain and told Fang to jump. Even for a vampire it was quite a shock to see a jet-black jungle cat pouncing out of nowhere.

"*Jaaaayde!*" he yelled.

The black panther instantly changed into an adorable gray kitten and purred as it rubbed its tiny face against Cameron. Then it was Cameron's turn to disappear. He reappeared directly behind Jayde.

"Jayde," he said, his voice quite dark, "how much blood do you have?"

"Um, I dunno. A lot?" said Jayde, a quiver in her voice.

"Would you like to keep it that way?" he asked.

That was the last time Jayde and Fang snuck up on Cameron.

Jayde ran to the Order Hall with Fang at her heels. The cat received strange looks on the walk there, mainly because it was a purple-and-green cat with a full pink mane and an extraordinarily long tail with a poof of fur at the end, but Grandeur was a strange city.

Jayde walked into the hall and smiled at the familiar sights. Despite the early hour many creatures worked throughout the Great Hall. Beasts of all shapes and sizes attended to the chores to keep the Great Hall in order. A flying bird-ferret swept out the embers from yesterday's fire. A creature that looked like a purple pumpkin with five legs walked back and forth across the floor; wherever it walked, the floor became clean. An enormous brown praying mantis with huge hands stood behind the bar cleaning glasses.

Jayde now knew that all these creatures had been conjured and came from the imaginations of the order members. The conjured creatures had differing levels of intelligence, personality, and attributes. All of them seemed to be permanent members of the Order Hall.

"G'morning, Norris," said Jayde to the mantis.

"Salutations, Jayde. Here early again to train? Chocolate milk?" asked the mantis from the bar.

"That'd be great. Thanks, Norris," said Jayde.

"Yow indicated he would like to see you this morning," said the mantis, sliding a frosty glass down the bar, where it came to a halt precisely in front of Jayde.

"LINE UP!" came a yell from the balcony.

All the creatures stopped what they were doing and went to the middle of the room. They stood in a straight line. Jayde was confused but followed them, joining them in one of the lines.

Yow Li made his way down the stairs, smiling briefly at Jayde as he approached the line of creatures.

He walked in front of each of the creatures and then slowly ambled around the spotless hall. He mentioned an area here or there that did not have as much sparkle as the rest of the hall before he dismissed them. The creatures slowly dispersed. Most went out the front door into the streets; a few others went upstairs or into the labyrinth of the Order Hall. A couple remained to tend to their duties. Norris returned to the bar.

"So how are your Conjurings coming?" Yow asked, sitting in a cushy chair in front of the now cheery fire burning in the fireplace.

"Pretty good, I guess. I mean, every day I try to conjure Fang in different ways that I have never done before. You know, like you told me to," said Jayde.

"Good, good," said Yow.

"And it's kinda cool too. I mean, Fang and I know what the other is thinking. And I've been delivering now for a month, though they don't give me any deliveries anywhere near the Thieves' District, nor near the East Side—not that I'm complaining about that," she said.

"Good."

"And I have been getting up early every day so that I have time to come here and use one of the rooms to practice."

"Indeed you have. Very good, Jayde. You really have shown remarkable interest in Conjuring, despite what we've thrown at you."

"What do you mean?"

"Well, even though I saw the raw Talent within you, I still had to treat you the same as I treat every novice in the order, though it pained me to do so. Every new member to the order normally starts with a month of service to prove they are truly dedicated to their new calling. Not only that but they must also prove their loyalty. Most novices know this ahead of time and accept the first month as a sort of hazing ritual that must be lived through. You, on the other hand, took a multitude of deliveries, harder and harder work schedules, and less and less personal time, yet you did so willingly, so that you could become a better conjurer," Yow said with a grin.

"Oh, that's good then, right?" she said.

Yow Li laughed. "Indeed, that is quite good."

"So then why won't anyone teach me new stuff?" she asked.

Yow sighed. "To be honest, Jayde, many of the conjurers here are intimidated by you."

"Intimidated by me? But I don't know anything! I've seen all their cool tricks, and, every time I ask them to show me, they find some excuse to go somewhere else. I mean, I can conjure a few things, but the only thing I really seem to be able to do is change Fang. I can't create new things except in the practice room. I can't make something appear out of nothing. The only one here who ever talks with me is Norris, but he keeps saying, 'Not till you pass your novice test.'"

"Well, consider the test passed. As for your complaint about Fang, I must confess that I limited your Conjuring. You have too much raw power for you to try anything too advanced without guidance. So, when you came here the first time, I limited your abilities by using Fang," he said.

"What? You limited me? What do you mean?" she asked.

"Now don't be angry. I did this to protect you. You have an incredible ability to conjure. But, without training, you could hurt or even kill yourself or others quite easily. That is why I am training you myself," he finished.

Jayde tried to take it all in. "Really?"

"Really."

"But I still don't think I get it! I mean, it's cool to be able to change Fang into any color cat I want. But what's the point? I still don't think I get what a conjurer does. As far as I can tell, not even the good ones can do magic spells at all. The best I ever did was changing Fang to look like a panther which scared Cameron and—"

"Very good, Jayde. Completely wrong but very good," said Mr. Li.

"Uh, what?"

"Well, your insight is brilliant. You have shown remarkable patience for one of your age, so I suppose you deserve some straight answers."

"Finally!" she said, sitting down on a chair with her empty glass, all the chocolate milk gone.

"To understand Conjuring, we must define it," he began. "In the simplest terms it means to create. Conjurers are limited only by their imaginations, which can make them the most powerful of all the orders."

"Everyone I talk to says that wizards are the most powerful, then maybe enchanters or witches, but most just laugh when I tell them I am a conjurer," said Jayde.

"It's all situational. A water elementalist can manipulate all the properties of water. They can turn it into ice crystals and shoot shards of ice at you. They could make a cloud come down from the sky or create fog out of a nearby stream. Yet they would not be able to give you a drink of water in the desert. They have to have the water in order to manipulate it. A conjurer though …" He waved his hand. A small popping noise sounded near her, and she saw that her glass was refilled with cold chocolate milk again.

"Whoa! So why don't you just make giant piles of gold and be rich?" she asked.

"Cut right to the chase, don't you? First of all that would disrupt the entire global economy," he said.

Jayde shrugged. "I could live with that."

"And then there's the second part of Conjuring. Whenever you conjure, you must use your will. I slightly misspoke when I said we can create from nothing. We create from our wills and various components. In order to make that milk, I had to partition a small part of myself in order to create it. Most conjurers, when they start out, only have enough will to manipulate a very small object. Also the quality and weight of the object take substantially more will. This is the reason most conjurers use substrates. If I wanted to create a gold coin, that would take a remarkable amount of effort and use a large amount of my will. But if I wanted to make a clay bowl, and I already had a large handful of dirt, it would take much less will to make the bowl. For your milk, I just replaced the milk that was in there with some of the milk from the bar. I changed milk into milk, so it really did not take much will at all," he said.

"I think this is what Marie was explaining to me earlier," said Jayde. "I told her it sounded like everyone has an icicle inside them, and, in order to do any Conjuring, you have to chip off a piece of the icicle. The icicle will grow back, but it grows back slowly. Also, if you used too much of your icicle, there won't be enough ice left for it to grow back, and the whole thing stops working."

"A decent-enough analogy, though, in your case, it seems to be a bit different. Most people have quite small icicles of will. It takes every bit of the icicle to do any Conjuring at all. Most become good at Conjuring one or two things, and then they are done until they recover."

"What do you mean, *recover?*"

"Conjuring takes incredible power of will and mind. It also drains one's physical stamina. Conjuring large complex objects will mentally and physically exhaust the conjurer. Recovery times vary, depending on the complexity of what is conjured. You can think of it like running ten leagues, only you do it all in a fraction of a second. After doing so, the body demands time to recover," he said.

"Makes sense, I guess. Can you ever unmake something?"

"Like this," he said, pointing again to her glass.

Jayde watched, as she heard a strange sucking noise, and the chocolate milk vanished.

"Whoa! Where'd it go?"

"It was composed mainly of my will, so much of it went back to me. Granted some of the energy is lost in the transfer," he said.

"Wait. What would have happened if I had drank that, and then you sucked it all back again?" she asked.

"That depends. If you drank it quickly, it would have disappeared from your stomach. You would have gone from feeling full to an empty stomach in an instant. If I had waited an hour, the milk would have been absorbed and distributed through your whole body. I would not have been able to distinguish the Conjuring from you, so I would not have been able to undo it. Granted, undoing Conjuring is an advanced skill. When most people conjure, whatever they create usually remains permanent."

"Stop showing off and show her," said the giant mantis behind the bar.

"Yes, yes, you are right, Norris," said Yow. He got up and slowly made his way to one of the training rooms with Jayde following.

"Like I was saying, Jayde, most people only have an ice cube of latent Conjuring Talent in them. For you it is more like a glacier," he said.

"What's a glacier?"

"Oh, well, bad example. Most people have only a tiny little flame, whereas you are a brewing volcano," he said with a smile.

"What's a volcano?" asked Jayde.

"Jayde, your pool of will is enormous. Your potential is incredible. Not only that but your ability to regenerate is the best I have seen since Franky," he said.

"Who's Franky? One of the regulars around here?" Jayde asked.

Yow's face became serious. "No, Franky was the Elite Grand Master Conjurer who taught me."

"That's quite a title."

"Indeed. I'd guess only a few thousand people in the world can conjure at a master level. Of them, only a hundred could do so as a Grand Master. I only know of perhaps three people who could be Elite Grand Masters, my master being one of them," he said.

"Really? They are that rare? Who're the other ones?" she asked.

"Me and you," he said.

Jayde laughed. "Thanks, Mr. Li, but I haven't been able to conjure anything more than changing Fang's stripes," she said. The cat mewed in response to her name and then changed her stripes.

"Come with me," he said. He led her to a room similar to the one they had practiced in a month earlier. It was empty, but Jayde could sense something unique.

"You can feel it now, can't you? You might not have been able to put your finger on it the first time you were in here, but now you can feel the energy. You can feel the room helping you conjure. The other practice rooms don't have the enchantments like this one does. This room allows you to create without sapping your reserves. However, whenever you leave this room, whatever you conjure will disappear as well."

"Wait, what about Fang?" Jayde asked.

"I conjured her up before we even came into the Order Hall, remember?"

"Oh, right."

"Now, Jayde, I want you to imagine a bumbleberry pie," said Yow.

"Sure." Jayde closed her eyes. She then opened one eye to look back at Yow. "What's a bumbleberry pie?"

"What? What kind of little girl doesn't ..." said Yow. "Haven't you looked in any of the boxes that you have been delivering?"

"No. I was told just to take them right to their location," Jayde answered. Then she grinned.

"Oh, you little thief, I almost fell for it," Yow said.

"Yeah, I just happened to 'accidentally' lose a pie from time to time. They're really good. I see why everyone keeps ordering them," Jayde said.

"I want you to picture that in your mind. Keep your eyes closed. Imagine the pie. See it clearly in your mind. You can smell the aroma wafting up, see the berry goodness, and touch the smooth, delicious, crispy crust. Keep picturing it, Jayde. Keep that picture in your mind. Now very slowly I'll release the lock that I put on you with Fang. This will feel a bit odd, but just keep the picture in mind, and don't open your eyes."

Jayde could feel the block inside her releasing. It felt as if her whole body had been numb and only now was the blood rushing back through her.

"Hmm. Quite interesting. I wasn't the only one who put restrictions on your power. Oh, well, let's see what you can really do," said Yow.

She concentrated on the picture in her mind. The unnumbing sensation continued to gush through her. She could almost smell the pie, but again it became difficult to think with the tingling sensation all over her body. Slowly the tingling went away.

Pop!

"Open your eyes, Jayde," said Yow.

She did. The mass in front of her looked like the mangled insides of an exploded pumpkin. Stringy, lumpy dough looked floppy and uncooked on one side of the crust. The other side looked like a fried cheese-covered pinecone. It smelled like burned fruit. Mr. Li's grin lit up his entire face.

"I knew you were good, but, until I saw it for myself, I just wasn't sure. Well done!" he said, laughing.

"What do you mean? I made a burned-up slime pile. Maybe, if you cut out the part right in the middle, where the cold side meets the hot, it might be edible. I don't know," she said, but Yow was actually laughing. "Are you making fun of me?"

"Not at all, my dear. Oh, my, no. Jayde, you just passed the second test, and you have not even broken a sweat. Oh, how to explain? Where to start? You don't even realize how hard it is to do what you just did. You had bread dough and sauce, and let me see." He looked at the mess on the ground. "Blueberries and sugar and cinnamon and also icing on top. Not only that but you added temperature to cook it all and had a specific shape in mind as well. Having never conjured before, you managed not only to get all the ingredients but you also combined them and associated them all together! You did it just from my description. Without components you did it, with only your will!"

"I imagined a pie, Mr. Li. That's all," she said.

"No, you completely envisioned a complex completed project. You did it as your first actual Conjuring. In three centuries—well, actually, I have *never* had anyone have such a Conjuring for their first attempt. I have seen people try but never like this. The other part I neglected to tell you is that bumbleberries don't really exist. Well, they do, and they don't. They can be conjured, but there are no bumbleberry bushes or trees. They exist only in the mind of a conjurer. Yet you seem to have no difficulty creating them for your pie," he said, plucking one from the ground. He continued to grin.

"Well, what do people normally start with?" she asked.

Yow held out his hand. Jayde heard a small pop, and a round gray stone appeared in his hand. It had a swirl of white through it and seemed polished to perfection.

"Usually I have a person concentrate with something in their hands, and they conjure a replica."

He tossed the rock to Jayde. Jayde stared at the rock and concentrated. She could feel the tingling sensation just under the surface and released the energy.

Pop!

An identical rock appeared next to the other one and fell to the ground. Mr. Li picked it up and examined it with a grin.

"Well done again. Most novices actually do not begin with this rock," he said. "Most start with a tiny pebble, though you had no trouble."

"Well, it's easy to copy someone else's work," said Jayde.

"Oh, really? Would you like something more challenging?"

"Bring it on, old man! Uh, sorry, Master Li," she said. He laughed.

"Try this then," he said, followed by a pop.

He conjured objects of all shapes and sizes from the magic sand in the room. He made intricate wooden boats inside bottles. He made glass sculptures, ice sculptures, a lute, as well as a wall of stone.

Jayde copied each object perfectly.

He made ladders—some of stone, some of wood, some made out of string—all of which Jayde replicated. He made a wide array of weapons and clothing. After two hours both panted with exhaustion. Yow concentrated and conjured a tall glass of water; Jayde did the same. He then conjured a simple chair, which Jayde copied. They both then sat down and had a drink.

"That's an impressive start. Remember, though, that Conjuring outside this room will sap your energy, and this sand works as the perfect component to make anything. Thus, Conjuring here is much easier. Also do not try to conjure anything living," he said.

"Living? Like Fang?" she asked.

"Indeed. Don't worry. We will get there in time, but a living animal is much more complicated than a pie. I have seen dreadful creatures that do nothing but exist in agonizing pain. Whenever you create a familiar, which is what conjured creatures are called, you share a bond. If you create such a creature without honed skill, their pain will become yours. I do not recommend you attempt anything living until you are able to unconjure what you have made, and that takes many years of training," he said.

Jayde looked disappointed.

"Promise me this, Jayde. Take it slowly. I know this is all new and exciting to you, and you have more potential than anyone I have seen in my entire life. This also means you have more potential to hurt or even kill. Outside this room, for now, the most complicated thing I want you to attempt is a pie. One pie. Do not try to do more than that in a day. Please trust me on this. Until you can make one good enough to eat, don't conjure anything other than what we have made outside this room. If you feel the need to work on your imagination, you can continue practicing on Fang. Agreed?"

"Agreed."

They sat in their chairs, recovering from a busy morning of Conjuring. Jayde broke out into a laugh.

"What's so funny?" Yow asked.

"I'll be able to make anything, won't I? Anything I want?" she asked.

"With time you will only be limited by your imagination. For you, that seems to be hardly a limitation."

He looked around the room for the cat. The room now had objects of varied shapes and sizes strewn all over the place. In their busy morning of Conjuring, the cat had been forgotten. Jayde called out for her, and a tiny meow came from under a pile of conjured torches. The kitten had wormed her way under the assorted chaos and had been spending her time licking the middle portion of the pie Jayde had created.

"You have to make a pie good enough for *me* to eat, not her. Why don't you take a break with Mr. Norris outside for a little bit. We can continue training in about an hour."

Jayde walked from the room. As soon as she crossed the threshold, half the objects in the room vanished. Fang hissed as the pie she had been eating vanished in front of her. Yow walked over to the tiny cat and picked her up, talking to her as he walked out the door.

Chapter 25: Chosen

Sarah came into the shop at dawn, as she always did. Lucy accompanied her, and they discussed the street life of Grandeur while they walked. Kevin woke to her entering the shop. He got dressed in his small room and joined them, preparing the shop for the morning.

"So many people sleep on the streets on the weekend," Sarah said. "Most of them look like they spent the night fighting each other."

"They probably did, I reckon," said Kevin.

"How many fights do you think you've been in?" Sarah asked.

Kevin became serious. "Too many." Kevin seemed lost in thought for a second. "How about you? You ever been in a scuffle?"

"Me? Hardly. Not unless you count running from the wivari and a shayde," she said.

"What?" he asked, his voice suddenly serious.

"Nothing," she said. "I've just never been in a fight."

Kevin walked to her and stared. "When did you see a shayde?"

"When I came back from my trip with Thaddeus, we were attacked. I know I mentioned him before. Thaddeus was a pompous nobleman in the upper echelon," she said.

"When did you see a shayde?" Kevin repeated.

Sarah started from the beginning, when they left Haynis. Kevin listened carefully as she told the story of her trip home. He occasionally asked questions to clarify but otherwise remained silent, as she told everything that had happened.

"Wivari don't normally act like that. I don't know why a shayde would focus down one person like that either. I've never heard of them working together. And they don't hypnotize people. Something's off, but I'm not sure what," he said.

"Forethought," said someone with a rumbling voice behind Sarah.

Mullet had appeared near her sometime during her story.

"Don't *do* that! You're like a giant cat. How you can move so quietly is beyond me," said Sarah.

"Do not call him a cat! If anything he is a ferocious tiger to be feared," said a small pixie from his shoulder.

"Tali," Mullet said. The small pixie had become a nearly permanent attachment to Mullet's shoulder. Her wings had fully healed over the last month, but she still followed Mullet everywhere. It made for a unique relationship, since Mullet rarely spoke, and Tali never stopped.

"Wivari don't think ahead. You said they came at you from all sides in a split second. That takes planning. Also one of them tried to spell you in some way to prevent you from getting away," said Kevin.

"Well, like I said, John and Lucy mentioned it being a shayde," Sarah said.

"I reckon your encounter may not have been completely random."

"John and Lucy thought the shayde controlled the wivari," Sarah said.

"Agent," grated Mullet.

"I hope not," Kevin said. "Shayde's are intelligent creatures, and the Dark King has been known to use them. Someone wanted to make that whole scene look like a freak mistake. Even if it was a shayde, someone instructed the shayde to attack you. Someone tried hard to make it seem like a bunch of folks in the wrong place at the wrong time," Kevin said.

"Target?" Mullet asked.

"Well, that's the question. Who was the target? You think Sarah? It could've been one of the pixies."

John, the pixie who Sarah had almost crushed, joined in the conversation. "Why would someone want Sarah to kill me?"

"Maybe an agent thought you were a potential Chosen. It could be you were the target. But catching a pixie is like trying to catch the wind. But that doesn't make sense. Using wivari to kill a pixie is like using a bow and arrow to kill a mosquito. It's just the wrong tool for the job," Kevin said.

Mullet looked at Sarah and then looked at Kevin.

Tali piped in. "You think someone contemplated all these activities in order to get to Sarah?"

Kevin shrugged. "I don't know, but I think we should look at it through your eyes."

"What do you mean?" Sarah asked.

"Mullet looks like a meaty anvil, but he's an accomplished diviner. He just wants to see the events as they happened," Kevin said.

"It doesn't hurt, does it?" Sarah asked.

"No," Mullet replied.

Sarah sat in a chair, and Mullet placed his fingertips to her temples.

"Now just try to relax. Don't fight it. Just relax," Kevin said.

Sarah took a slow, deep breath. She felt the light pressure of Mullet's fingers on her temples. She slowly became light-headed and felt herself falling. After a minute of resting in quiet darkness, she began seeing vivid images. Her trip through Haynis passed in a blink. The trip away from Haynis sped by. The images then slowed.

She again saw her experience becoming a pixie. She gasped as she took flight. She felt the rush of the wind, as her legs lifted off the ground. Then she looked around. She heard the distinctive laugh of the hounds. She saw that same wivari on the edge of the forest, eyes glinting in the darkness. The images stopped. She felt something pushing in her mind, while the image remained frozen.

Slowly the images flowed again. She could see herself moving through the experience once more. She saw herself strike

John and watched him fall to the ground. Again the scene paused, and she felt that same pushing sensation in her mind, as the picture was stilled.

She felt herself moving forward. She saw John on the ground. She heard him pleading and looking up at her. Sarah wanted to scream, to cry out, and to do anything other than relive the experience. She felt Mullet pushing in her mind, while the image of her hurting her friend remained. She could feel John pushing against her foot, as the voice in her head told her to just stomp on the struggling bug.

Somewhere she heard the echo of a command. "Do it." She sensed the push in her mind again. Suddenly she felt a snap. The images then flashed by quickly through the rest of the events, until she made her way back to Grandeur.

She woke up in the shop, gasping for breath.

"Well?" Kevin asked Mullet.

Mullet put his hands to Kevin's temples. He left them there for about fifteen seconds before removing them.

"Who hires a shayde?"

"An agent," Mullet said.

"What? What are you talking about?" Sarah yelled.

"Something wanted you hurt. I'm not sure why. That creature put a nasty spell on you, but you broke its spell. The creature left some connection in your mind even after you broke the link. Mullet removed the remnants of that connection," Kevin said.

"So now what?" Sarah asked Kevin.

"You hurt that shayde by breaking the bond. Most of the shayde's consciousness was in you when you shattered the spell. The real question is why'd it come after you in the first place? Any ideas, Mully?"

The giant paused in thought. "Seer?" asked Mullet.

"Hmm. Yeah. We *should* get her checked out. I hope the seer will let us walk in for a reading."

"What do you mean?" Sarah asked.

"An agent of the Dark King might be hunting you. Agents are killers. If you *do* have an agent after you, we need to know."

"Agent?" asked Sarah.

"A chaos agent."

"What are you talking about?" asked Sarah.

"Chaos agents work for the Dark King Zolf Heller. He's the king of Zantia. Somewhere along the line he started thinking of himself as a god. This notion gave him the erroneous thought that anything he wants to do is not only fair but also right," said Kevin.

"Insane," grated Mullet.

"But it goes beyond that. Zantia has a whole different culture. In Zantia, if you want to do anything, and I mean *anything*, you must go through the king or his representatives. They make it all sound real nice, but what ends up happening is that the king controls everything. People are puppets to him."

"So where do the chaos agents come into play?" asked Sarah.

"The king lacks ethics but not brains. The king's agents are everywhere. In Zantia, agents hide in the poor population looking for uprisings. Agents are scattered everywhere over the land, searching for all sorts of things. But what it comes down to is that the king had his future read by a seer. This is the real reason for his agents."

"A long time ago, a seer predicted that the king's reign *might* come to an end. Bah, I'm getting ahead of myself. Let me start at the beginning, Sarah," said Kevin.

Sarah nodded.

"The story is a bit fuzzy, since it's so old, but I reckon my version's about as accurate as any. A thousand years ago the world was in chaos. All the countries warred with each other continually. Life was war, no matter where you came from. Finally the leaders of the four great countries realized the constant fighting had to stop. Thus, they got their smartest wizards, witches, and Talented people at the time to come to a solution.

"They decided to create a group that could help settle disputes. Each country would have one member. This team would keep the peace. They would be the *ultimate* peacekeepers. The group had five members in it, one from each country, and a fifth to search out the next member, if and when one of them died. The group was called 'the Chosen.'"

"The Chosen existed above kings and queens, above governors and emperors. They were the ultimate authority. They were equally respected and feared, for good reasons. The Chosen settled disputes. Their words were law. They were above the law."

"Wait a minute," said Sarah. "What happened if one of the Chosen was corrupt?"

"The leaders at the time thought the same way. A powerful spell was cast over the Chosen. The spell prevented anyone lacking morals from getting into the group. How it ended up working is that no person ever got elected to be a Chosen. In order to become a Chosen, a member had to be *called* into the group. You literally had to be *chosen* into the group."

"Okay. So will you pontificate on the intricacies of how the Chosen are chosen?" asked Tali.

"That's the tricky part. No one really knows. The extra member somehow knew the next one, but how that works has been lost with time. We do know that each member had great skill in magic. Together they moved mountains. But it wasn't their magic that made them the Chosen, it was their ability to solve the big problems. All creatures in the group were gifted."

"Creatures?" asked Sarah.

"Sure. The group of five, the Chosen, changed from time to time. The members in the group could be male or female, human, elf, troll, or whatever," said Kevin.

"Even pixie?" asked Tali.

"The Chosen could be anything living. With one member from each country, it'd be rare for the members to be the same species.

"For a long time the Chosen kept balance in the world. The Chosen worked in the background, preventing wars and rebellions. Having members from all over the world, the Chosen had no alliances to one specific country or species. Their decisions were not always popular, but, over time, their decisions proved them wise. The Chosen were respected.

"They dethroned kings and appointed new leaders. They settled disputes for any who asked for their aid. The Chosen organized quarantines in cities to prevent the spread of disease. In some circumstances many people died, but, in the long run, the decision saved thousands of lives. They would help anyone—rich, poor, king, or peasant. They would go anywhere, to any country, to where their help was needed most. Eventually they became quite popular, and often entire cities would celebrate having the Chosen visit their town," said Kevin.

"How is it that I've never heard of the Chosen?" asked Sarah.

"Here's where the story gets interesting. Few today know of the Chosen because, well, they've disappeared," said Kevin.

"A little over two hundred years ago, a serious problem arose. Zolf Heller had just become king of Zantia. He has the Talent to sap life out of the country's population so he could live forever. Zolf steals life from the peasants and commoners who can't protect themselves. No one really knows how old he actually is. Over time he gradually changed from ruler to eternal king.

"He declared war against Tenland and has been slowly pushing the boundaries for the last two centuries. Shortly after the war began, the Chosen were asked to help."

"This King Zolf sounds lacking in mental fortitude," commented John.

"It gets worse," said Kevin. "The Chosen met with Zolf Heller. They barely escaped that meeting with their lives. The Chosen realized that Zantia's king had to be stopped. They met with the leaders of the other countries. Only war could end the king's madness. King Zolf had to be brought down by force.

"Now you have to remember things were different then. The countries had lived in peace with one another for centuries. The leaders thought the Chosen were too harsh. Thus, the separate countries ignored the Chosen's advice and decided to ignore the problem. This was the first time in centuries that people didn't follow the Chosen's decision."

"But Tenland has been at war with King Zolf for years," said Sarah.

"True, but only because Zolf kept expanding. Tenland had war pushed upon them. But let me finish about the Chosen. This is where the seer comes in. King Zolf knew the Chosen to be dangerous enemies. The king received counsel from a seer. The seer didn't tell him what he wanted to hear. She simply said that the end of his reign would come at the hands of the Chosen.

"You can guess the king's response to the seer. He created chaos agents to hunt down and kill the Chosen. Now don't get me wrong. The Chosen had skills and great abilities, but they had become accustomed to love and respect everywhere they went. They could handle an occasional rogue assassin, but they weren't ready for the assault of an entire army of agents trained solely to kill them. All five were killed."

"Whoa! That's terrible," said Tali.

"Now as I said before, once one of a member of the Chosen dies, he or she or it is replaced by another member. In the past when one member died, the Chosen would find the next member. No one alive today knows how the Chosen were picked. We hear stories of a new Chosen appearing, but only one at a time. The king's chaos agents have continued their hunts. They've destroyed all Chosen or even potential Chosen.

"We've seen them hang a ninety-seven-year-old woman who couldn't get out of bed. We've seen them throw a newborn baby down a well. They have no limits. They are focused on killing anyone destined, or potentially destined, to be a Chosen. The king especially despises magical creatures. He began a campaign to exile nonhuman species, which worked quite well. Currently the country of Zantia has pretty much only humans in it. His royal decree to destroy nonhuman species obviously offended other species in the world."

"Wait. So you think I might be one of these *Chosen*?" Sarah asked.

"We don't know, but there are a few ways to tell," said Kevin.

"How do you two know all this?" asked John, hovering nearby.

"Well," said Kevin, looking over at Mullet. Mullet nodded, and Kevin continued. "You see, Mully and I have a complicated past. We *are* trained fighters, but we're a bit more than that. You see, we're paladins. Our main purpose is to stop King Zolf's agents. Paladins have been trying to give potential Chosen the chance to take down the Dark King for years. We're outnumbered, poorly supplied, and have close to zero funding. We just don't have the resources that the Dark King has," said Kevin.

"So where does Sarah fit into this?" asked John.

"That's why we need a seer. All seers, well, all *real* seers will be able to give the same fortune to the same person. They can tell if someone has the potential. Somehow chaos agents can see potential Chosen like seers can. We're always a step behind," said

Kevin. He stopped to get a quick drink and realized Sarah looked terrified.

"I'm sorry, Sarah. I'm not trying to scare you. Most likely this will all come to nothing. Mullet and I really wanted to come to Grandeur to get away from the endless chasing for a while. We've been at it so long we imagine agents everywhere. Being a paladin makes us a bit paranoid at times. In all our travels, we've never once found a potential Chosen before the chaos agents did. Usually we track an agent and try to bring them to justice. It's just following the trail of dead bodies and then …"

"Kevin," Mullet said.

"Yeah?" said Kevin.

"Shut up."

Sarah had become ashen. She tried to keep straight the swirling thoughts in her head. The two hired guards apparently hunted and killed men for a living. Granted they hunted killers … but still.

"Listen, we'll get an appointment with a seer. It'll be all right," said Kevin.

Sarah went to the bathroom and vomited.

Chapter 26: Unveil

"Did you hear that?" she asked.

"Hear what, Mrs. Crass?" her burly minion answered.

"No, of course you didn't. If you never listen, how could you hear changes that small? I hired your muscles, not your brain. Still I know I heard something."

Mrs. Crass had scoured Grandeur, looking for evidence of the next Chosen. After her will had broken, her driving motivation was only to serve King Zolf. A Chosen had not been found in twenty years, which concerned King Zolf. His concern became Mrs. Crass's passion. She *had* to find a Chosen for the king.

"What? Like a burglar or something?" said her other henchman.

"No, not a noise, you idiot. I heard a change. Something shifted. This might be what the Dark King wants me to find. Hand me the list," said the crazy old woman.

The grunt walked over to the table and returned with a list of a couple hundred names of people. A few names had a circle around them, while others had a star by the name. Some names were all in capital letters, while others had been underlined. Only Mrs. Crass knew what the markings meant. Nine of the names had a thin red line through them. The thugs knew what a line through the name meant.

"Time to recheck a few leads, I think," she said.

"Aw, but Mrs. Crass, we've checked and rechecked all those people in Grandeur over and over again. Finn always says the same thing. 'No aura of significance,' whatever that means," said the thug.

Mrs. Crass walked over to the large brute. He continued to stare at her like a slug looking at a child with a container of salt. His partner had already moved to the other side of the room. One had learned never to question her orders, but some people learned slowly.

Some people might be surprised that an old woman with a wooden spoon could knock a large man unconscious.

"Time to recheck a few leads," Mrs. Crass repeated.

"Yes, ma'am," said the only conscious lackey.

The sleek midnight-black cat observed the interaction without interest. It leaped down from the cabinet and crept to the unconscious man. It sniffed the large goose egg growing on the man's head and lapped up the trickle of blood from the cut. It looked over at the other man and smiled, too broadly for how a cat should be able to smile. Its teeth had a dull red shine to them.

The man always did whatever Mrs. Crass asked. He had also learned to do whatever the cat asked. Otherwise, Mrs. Crass would wallop him on the head for disobeying. The cat would eat part of his soul.

The man, the bozrac, and the old woman went out the door and began their long night of searching for the next Chosen.

Chapter 27: Seer

After careful research and a few weeks of inquiring, Kevin secured a meeting with a seer. Sarah, John, Lucy, Kevin, Mullet, and Tali made their way toward the Thieves' District. They weren't concerned with all of them leaving the Picky Pixie at once as Mullet and Kevin had installed so many barricades that thieves would need siege equipment to break into the store.

With the booming success of the Picky Pixie, Mullet and Kevin had also convinced Jenny, the head pixie, to hire extra help. Kevin and Mullet researched the potential guards for the shop themselves, ultimately hiring the two nekarions from the tournament. The lizard creatures were actually brothers. Unlike most of the other competitors, the duo of nekarions had entered the tournament mainly for the job opportunity. They had considerable difficulty landing jobs in Grandeur. Even though the city had all types of creatures, a pair of nekarions still stuck out from the norm. Kevin and Mullet convinced Jenny that the brothers were the best match for the job. The two nekarions guarded the store while the others left to visit the seer.

The streets progressively became dirtier and the buildings less inviting as they walked. The three pixies, John, Lucy, and Tali, seemed completely unaware of the change in surroundings, as they continuously chattered in a mix of English and Pixish. They flew around while the humans walked. They peered in windows and shops, exploring new surroundings.

After an hour of walking, they were in the heart of the Thieves' District. Steel bars covered broken windows. Most of the shops had fortifications strong enough to repel a catapult. Kevin made a few absent comments about how they could improve their own security, but mostly they walked in silence. The pixies continued their idle chatter. Kevin yelled at Lucy after she flew through one of the broken windows only to come out a different window. He explained the potential danger, but the pixie just laughed.

Kevin pointed to a looming stone building and whispered something to Mullet. Mullet crouched down and concentrated. He put two fingers to each of his temples, and then looked back up at Kevin and nodded.

"I thought so," said Kevin.

"What is it?" asked Sarah.

"A bullet grog, about two hundred paces away. It's chained to the front of that building, but they're still meaner than frozen snot. I don't know why anyone would have a grog chained to a building. It's just plain stupid, even for the Thieves' District," Kevin said.

"A bullet grog? I don't see anything," Sarah said.

"They blend into their surroundings. It's a poisonous critter about the size of a small dog but looks like a mix between a frog and a cow. It may look funny, but they're dangerous. A full-size one could knock you unconscious for a few hours. Their saliva can paralyze a small child for days. They can shoot their tongues out as fast as you blink. We'll be fine on the other side of the street, but it's not me that I'm worried about," he said.

Mullet nodded. "Tali," he bellowed. The tiny pixie shot over instantly. "Stay here," he said, pointing to his shoulder.

"Okay, Mullet," she said and settled on his shoulder.

Pixies, for the most part, regarded advice with indifference. Tali, on the other hand, not only listened to Mullet but actually obeyed what he said. John and Lucy had flown over after seeing Tali fly away. Kevin explained again about the bullet grog. It took quite a bit of convincing to make John and Lucy stay with the humans. Tali, for her part, actually remained quiet, sitting on Mullet's shoulder.

The pixies reluctantly agreed to remain on a human shoulder. John sat on Sarah's shoulder, while Lucy rode on Kevin's. They made it past the grog without incident. The seer's small house stood just past the ominous stone building with the grog.

The seer's door opened immediately when they approached. They walked in. A table was set for three. One plate had a leafy green salad with big pieces of grilled chicken and a light oil dressing. The next had an impressive shank of pot roast coated with gravy and a heap of mashed potatoes. The third had a giant piece of blackened grouper and spicy rice with a slice of lemon. All three dishes looked delectable. The drinks in front of each also were different. The salad had an ice-cold glass of milk in front of it. The pot roast had a giant mug of ale. The grouper had a tall glass of water and an amber wine.

They looked at the food for a second before sitting down—Sarah in front of the salad, Mullet in front of the pot roast, and Kevin in front of the grouper.

"This is incredible," Sarah said. "This is actually my very—"

"—favorite food in the world? Yes, yes, Sarah, I know," said a woman from behind the door. "I'll be out in a minute. I'm just finishing a plate of *xiosha-nooters.*"

A few seconds later everybody's perfect grandmother came through the door. Her gray hair was rolled up in a tight bun, and she beamed with an honest joy seen in those who truly love what they do.

"There we go. We wouldn't want our pixie friends to be left out, now would we?" she said. She set a plate in the middle of the table where a much smaller table stood with three even smaller chairs. On that table she placed a tiny platter with what looked like tiny steaming loaves of bread.

"*Reeeeally!*" squealed Tali, who flew from Mullet's shoulder to the smaller table and attacked the bread. The other two pixies did the same, wolfing down loaf after loaf of the small bread.

"Eat! Eat! We'll get to the reason you're here soon enough. By the way, I am Madame Fiona," said the old woman. They ate and chatted. Madame Fiona asked about the pixie shop and how each was doing, as if she had known them their whole lives. She made an absent comment to Mullet about how his garden in the mountain was coming along, which caused the large man to laugh, the first time any of them had ever heard the bulky man chuckle.

After they had all finished eating, the old woman cleared the dishes and replaced them with smaller plates of warm chocolate cake. Sarah enjoyed the meal but was starting to wonder about the old woman.

"I bet you're all getting a little curious about me. Well, probably more you than the others, Sarah, seeing as Mullet and Kevin have visited seers before," she said. Fiona took a sip of her tea and continued. "There used to be hundreds of us in the past, but with King Zolf the Loony killing us off as fast as possible, well, it has become a profession that few desire."

"So you're a real seer?" asked Sarah.

The woman looked at her and smiled. "Did you need convincing? I figured giving three people and three pixies their favorite meals would be enough. That's the funny part about being a seer. People try very hard to find you and seek your advice, but when they finally make it to you, they need proof that you are who you say you are. I suppose it is just a sign of the times. Ah, well, you didn't come to hear me ramble. Let's do what you came here to do. But first I must ask why you have come to see me in the first place?"

"I thought you were a seer? Can't you just tell?" asked Sarah.

Madame Fiona laughed. "I can tell much about you. I can tell strong emotions and desires, like your favorite foods for instance. But I am always interested in hearing motives."

Sarah told her story. Kevin added the parts about his suspicion of chaos agents pursuing her, plus Mullet's explorations in Sarah's mind. Kevin explained his concern that Sarah might be marked, and that was the primary reason for the visit.

"Oh? So it is an aura reading you want? Not just looking for a fortune to be told?" she asked. She walked to the front, and shut and locked the door. She then closed the blinds. After this she waved her hands over the front wall, and a hum emanated from the wall.

"We don't want any passerby overhearing us, do we? Such a long way from Zantia, but the war comes here as well. No matter. Come with me," she said.

The seer turned, and the rest followed her into the accompanying room. Sarah sat in the chair across from the smiling aged woman. Madame Fiona rummaged through her closet and came out with a tall clear sphere. The ball had a tiny hole at the top. She placed the sphere on a small stand. She then took out an assortment of minuscule leather pouches and poured different colored sand into the small hole, while the others watched. At first nothing happened, and then a small haze appeared and made its way out of the hole at the top of the sphere, as if the globe gave off heat.

"Okay, Sarah, I need you to relax. Close your eyes. Relax."

"Wait," Sarah said. She felt for the note from her father in her pocket. She believed Madame Fiona, but she still hesitated before showing her note. The note said Sarah must be certain about who she showed this, but Sarah also had no one else to turn to. "Before we start, I need to give this to you. My dad told me to give this to someone important. I think that is you," Sarah said. She then handed over the note her father had given her before her house had burned down.

The seer kept the note closed and put it on the table. She then placed her hands on Sarah's temples. Madame Fiona took a deep breath near the sphere, sucking in the vapors and then slowly exhaled. When she did, a thin stream of silver smoke came from her mouth and surrounded Sarah's entire body. The seer continued to take deep breaths of the vapors from the sphere and exhaled smooth streams of silver smoke till Sarah became completely covered in it. The smoke clung to her skin. A cloudlike gray outline of Sarah could be seen. Through the gray smoke, tiny cracks of gold shimmered, as if under the surface trying to get out. Madame Fiona kept her fingers on Sarah's temples throughout the entire process. Only after Sarah was completely covered did she close her own eyes and appear to concentrate.

"I see that three others have been tampering with your mind. The first came when you were but a child, apparently hiding your aura. The next was a dark presence, a shayde. The third, a healing one. I must say that you did a fine job, Mullet," she said.

Mullet grunted in response.

"But that's not why I'm here," said the seer, taking another deep breath, again exhaling silver smoke. Slowly a faint gray glow came from the seer's fingertips. It spread through the smoke surrounding Sarah till it all glowed.

"Now let's open the door and see," she said. The gray smoke slowly changed color. A noise came from deep inside Sarah's body. It sounded like knuckles cracking, but it happened countless times in rapid succession. As the small cracking noises continued, the color of the smoke changed from gray to a deep golden. The gold color became brighter, and the smoke faded away, leaving a pure golden glow behind. The process took a full minute. When she finished, the seer's smile lit up her entire face. She had streams of tears pouring down her face, but she muttered quietly.

"Oh! Oh, I never thought! It can't really be, can it?" she asked the two men on the couch.

The two men looked at one another, then back at the old woman.

"What?" asked Mullet.

Madame Fiona's voice became quiet, yet had an even larger impact. "She is a *Chosen*!"

The two paladins both paled. Sarah remained in a trance staring ahead.

"Most people remain silver after I see through them. That of course means they will have no impact. Occasionally I have found some with a red aura. That means they might eventually come in contact with the king in their life. Those that are red have the potential to cause the King harm. It is no guarantee, but they *might*. Normally those with a red aura are hunted by chaos agents. Even rarer are those with the blue aura. Blues actually fight against the king's agents. You two are blue to the core. But no one truly possesses the means to actually stop him," she said. Her hands trembled as she took a sip of her tea, spilling some of it on her lap.

"The seer for King Zolf told of one with a golden glow who could actually stop the king. Like any reading, it comes with no guarantee, but this woman has the potential to change everything—everything or nothing. An aura is just a sign of potential, not a guarantee of the future. What is interesting is that her aura was silver at first and then changed to gold," she said. She paused for emphasis. "Someone went to great lengths to hide her."

"What should we do? We've been hunting agents for a long time but have never actually come across a Chosen. So what do you suggest?" asked Kevin.

"I ... I don't know," admitted the seer. "I opened the door. Her true aura is now revealed. Perhaps she may enlighten us when she comes out of her trance. She has a gift, something that has the potential to stop the Dark King's reign. Other than that, I do not know. Someone hid her aura. Who that is, I also don't know. More than likely having her aura shielded protected her from discovery until now. She emitted only the faintest hint of aura before I opened the door."

"Well, get her outta her trance."

"Oh, my, no. If I pull her out of it, the door may shut again and lock away her Talent. She must awaken herself. It usually takes from an hour to a day," said the seer.

"A day! She's comatose!" said Kevin.

"I know. Believe me. There is no one more curious about the potential of this girl than I am. Heed my advice. Act in haste, and all will waste!" said the seer.

"Okay, okay," said Kevin. "Now at least we know what we got, I guess."

"No. You don't. You have no idea what you are up against. You paladins may have hunted chaos agents, but that is not the worst of what is out there. If she's a Chosen, and I'm risking my life by saying that she is, the Dark King will not just send any chaos agent to kill her. No Chosen has been found in two decades. He has an army of assassins. The fact that a shayde already tried to kill her once is a sign that someone saw through her defenses. Someone must have been very close to her, most likely for a long period of time, to be able to detect that hidden glimmer of truth."

"But who? And what's her Talent?" asked Kevin.

"Hunter," said Mullet.

"What?" asked Kevin.

"The first will be the Hunter," said Mullet.

"Correct! But previous Hunters always knew. I don't know how she could be the Hunter and not know," said Madame Fiona. She then looked back to the table and remembered the note Sarah had given her.

The seer opened the note.

"Clever. Oh, what clever parents. They knew. Her parents knew! They also understood enough to hide her until she was older. Who they hired to hide her aura, I have no clue. Just look at this note," she said. The first letter of each of the phrases now glowed a faint gold.

"So what is the Hunter?" Kevin asked.

The two paladins looked at the seer, waiting for her to continue.

"Well, don't ask me! I don't know either. Your guess is as good as mine. No one other than King Zolf has found a Hunter in two hundred years," she said.

Mullet nodded.

"Stay true to your duty, paladins. This girl needs all the help she can get. She *is* a Chosen, and she is the Hunter. Now that her aura is clear, agents may spot her as well. No one knows how the chaos agents track down their prey," she said.

"Ma'am, we'll protect her with our lives," Kevin said.

Fiona suddenly looked sad. "Yes, I know you will."

Chapter 28: Excessive Conjuring

Marl enjoyed a wide variety of food. He could survive by eating pretty much anything. He could grind stone into small enough pieces just to savor the minerals, but he also enjoyed a nice cinnamon bun with coffee, which he took with one cream and two packets of raw gravel. Thus, late one evening, as Jayde concentrated and slowly conjured a bumbleberry pie, he waited with eager expectation. He found them to be quite delicious, despite their lumpiness and frozen edges.

Fang, now a three-foot-tall yellow tabby with hundreds of green whiskers, watched as Jayde concentrated.

For weeks she had trained hard under Mr. Li, learning different Conjuring techniques. He continued to state her progress was staggering, but she had become frustrated with how slowly he wanted her to proceed. She decided that, just this once, she would try to conjure a little more at home.

She concentrated for ten minutes, visualizing the finished product. She saw it up close and far away, and she could almost smell it. Only after she felt she could practically taste it would she release the door in her mind and conjure the pie. The first one actually looked quite good, compared to her previous attempts. But when she cut into it, she could see raw dough, while the edges gave off a faint charred odor. The second one she conjured took her another twenty minutes. Again she tried to visualize every detail, concentrating on each ingredient separately, securing the look, feel, and smell in her mind. She released her will. Pop! The pie formed in front of her. It looked perfect. Marl agreed, though she stopped him from devouring it to take a closer look. Some of the berries had a slightly undercooked appearance, and the crust on one side seemed a bit too brown.

Fang mewed after the second pie conjured into the room. She jumped into Jayde's lap and pawed at her stomach. Jayde wanted to try again; however, as soon as she concentrated, the tiny kitten again jumped into her lap and began purring loudly. Jayde picked up Fang and put her in her basket. She then put the basket in the dumbwaiter and closed the door.

The third time she concentrated even harder. She shut out all other senses and focused inward. She saw the finished product. She rotated it and viewed it from all angles in her mind. She could see it, and it appeared perfect again, but she did not release her will right away. She studied it in her mind, searching for imperfections. The pie popped into existence, but she found a few minute flaws. Jayde tried a fourth time, this time getting closer to a perfect pie but not quite there.

On her fifth attempt she cut the pie into pieces in her mind. She opened it up, examining it in her mind, and then put the pieces back together. She did this from different angles, reorganizing it. She felt a small click. Though she had thought it perfect mentally before, for some reason she knew it now fit just how she wanted it.

Pop!

The pie steamed with heat, evenly distributed and baked to a golden brown.

Cameron came into the kitchen right after Jayde had finished the fifth.

"You're cooking? When did you become such a good cook?" he said.

"I don't feel ..." said Jayde and collapsed to the ground.

"Jayde?" said Marl, bounding to her side. He picked up the girl in his massive arms, "JAYDE! Wake up!" bellowed the troll. Marl's eyes went instantly from concerned to frantic.

"Fix her! Fix her now!" he yelled at Cameron. The rock troll's voice boomed through the whole clinic.

"Get her to a cot, Marl. What has she been doing?" Cameron asked, as they hurried toward the closest clinic bed.

Marl ran past with Jayde in his arms. The clinic was extremely busy, and not a cot was available.

"MOVE NOW!" yelled Marl to a large man with an ice bag on his ankle.

The man took one look at the frantic rock troll and hobbled off the cot back toward the front of the clinic.

Marl gently placed Jayde on the cot while he explained what had been happening.

"She be make food pop from space," said Marl.

"What?"

"She pop food. It 'pop,' and food come out," said the troll. His eyes darted from side to side. "Fix her! Use dat thing you do and make her good!"

"Marie, come here please," Cameron said into the large room of the clinic.

Marl explained what happened again to Marie.

"She overexerted herself Conjuring," she said.

"What do we do?" asked Cameron.

"I don't know! You're the doctor. Find out what's wrong, genius."

Marl wrung his hands over and over, pacing back and forth. He looked at Cameron, willing him to have the answer.

Cameron placed his hands on Jayde and concentrated. He did so for a full minute and then opened his eyes.

"I don't feel anything abnormal," he said.

Jayde was a sickly shade of gray. Sweat poured off her face. She looked limp, and her breathing came in raspy chokes.

"No, no, no, NO!" bellowed the troll. He smashed the ground with his fist, sending small tile fragments everywhere. Amazingly the patients nearest the troll suddenly became much better and left their gurneys.

The front door to the clinic slammed open, and Yow Li came running in.

"Where is she? Where's Jayde?" cried Yow.

"Over here," said Marie.

Yow ran over to Jayde. He saw her on the cot, unconscious.

"I told her. I *told* her. Where's that cat? She shouldn't have let her try a third time, much less a fifth," said Yow to himself.

Cameron just looked at him.

"She overconjured. She has the Talent, just not the control. Oh, I'm sure she'll eventually acquire incredible stamina, but I told her to take it slowly. Okay. Where is it? Where's the last thing she conjured?" he asked.

"She pop food over dere," said Marl.

"Did anyone eat it, any of it?" he asked.

"No," they all responded.

He ran into the kitchen, followed by Cameron and Marie. Marl stayed with Jayde. Yow saw the pie on the table. He closed his eyes and slapped his hands together in front of his chest. His middle three fingers laced together, extending his thumbs and pinkies. Then he swept his arms out broadly and made two large circles with his arms as a gush of wind came from him. The pie faded quickly and then popped into nothing.

He walked back into the clinic. Cameron looked at Marie; her expression showed she had no idea what was going on either.

Jayde was sitting up in bed, groaning and looking ill, but at least now she was awake.

"What just happened?" she asked.

"You are a complete idiot. That's what happened!" yelled Yow.

Jayde looked at him, confused.

"What did I tell you? No more than once a day? What do you do? Not only do you do a second, but, after that, you do a third? A fourth? Then a fifth? You are lucky to be alive!" said Yow.

"She be good, right? She good now, yes?" asked Marl.

"She'll be fine. A bit hungry, perhaps, but fine," said Yow.

Marl picked up Jayde again, this time in a rocky embrace. "No do dat, Jayde. Please no do dat. Oh, Jayde. Please no do dat," said the troll.

"Care to explain what just happened?" asked Cameron.

Yow scowled. "Whenever you conjure, you have to put in a part of yourself, your will into whatever you do. With training and years of practice, you can learn to only put the tiniest fraction needed to accomplish what you want. Some things take more. Some take less. But when you start, partitioning your will is extremely difficult. That is why I tell my students never to conjure more than once a day. I need time to see how much of their will they use for each of their Conjurings." He looked at Jayde with a face that could melt stone.

Jayde caught her breath from Marl's stony hug.

"That way I can tell how many times they might be able to conjure. Teaching students how to partition is key. It is a slow process, thus my warning. Jayde apparently felt the need to put her entire will into making a stupid pie. Then she did it a second time. Luckily for her, she has the ability to recuperate faster than any conjurer I've ever seen. So after draining her entire will, she did it again after only a short time. Fortunately Fang gave me warning after the second Conjuring, so I made it over here as fast as I could. Unfortunately she had already finished her fifth before I could get here and stop her."

"So what does that mean?" asked Marie.

"Well, I was able to unconjure it. Whenever something is unconjured, most of the will goes back to the person who conjured it in the first place. Thus, Jayde is now doing much better. She's lucky to be alive, all things considered," Yow said.

Jayde held her head in her hands. "Why does my head feel like it's going to explode?"

"Because you're an idiot, that's why!" said Yow. "You just drained your entire will and then had it slammed back into you."

"I'm sorry," said Jayde.

"No, I'm sorry. I'm sorry I thought you could be a great conjurer. Great conjurers need more than just raw willpower. Great conjurers need discipline. Great conjurers need patience. Mostly great conjurers should be able to be trusted, and, if they promise something, they should keep their promise!" yelled Yow.

"So now what?" asked Jayde. She had tears filling her eyes but fought them back.

"Now you go back to pie delivery girl. There are five levels in training, first as novice, then apprentice, journeyman, expert, and finally master. In your weeks you already have more skill than some of the journeymen, or even some of the masters I have trained for years, but you *have to have discipline*! I thought since you could do lots of hard work and prove yourself, you were ready. Apparently I was wrong. Apparently you don't know how to listen. So you can deliver food until I feel you're ready to train with me," said Yow.

"You're not kicking me out of the order?" asked Jayde.

"No, girl, you have to do more than that. Conjuring is the bottom dweller of the order world, remember? You have too much potential for me to abandon you. You just scared me. I think you scared your rock troll too."

Marl nodded in agreement.

"You reminded me of my—" Yow stopped. He took a deep breath. "You reminded me of a bad experience I once had with another young conjurer," he finished.

"Thank you, Mr. Li," said Jayde.

"You're still an idiot. Now where is Fang?" he asked.

"I put her in the dumbwaiter," said Jayde.

Jayde got out of bed, but, after an unsteady step, Marl picked her up and plopped her back on the cot.

"Me get cat," said Marl. He walked over and opened the door. The tiny kitten jumped down and ran directly to Jayde and jumped on the cot. Seeing Jayde doing well, she began purring and rubbing against her mistress.

"I guess that means you forgive me for locking you in the elevator," said Jayde. "Ow!" The small kitten had bit her finger but then immediately began purring again.

"All right. Now, Jayde, you must truly promise me. One conjure per day. I released the bond that was once on you, so I cannot force you to keep the promise. To stop you from practicing would be stupid but only once per day. Got it?" said Yow.

"Got it. I promise, Mr. Li. I'm sorry," she said.

"Good. We'll see you tomorrow for your deliveries," he said.

"Thanks," she said, fighting tears.

Chapter 29: Pull

Sarah spent the first night in a trance. The second night she spent crying. She felt homesick. She had been on her own for quite a while, but much of that time she had been a servant. Now that she had freedom and independence she had never felt so alone. Thaddeus Gumble had provided constancy. It had been miserable, but at least she had had stability. Her life had been turned inside out.

When she thought back on it, Thaddeus had actually been terrible to her from day one. Sarah missed her parents. Her father had been strict, but fair. He educated her about virtue, hard work, and ethics. Kindness was not his strong suit, but her mother's kindness never wavered. Her half-dryad mother instructed her all about living in the woods and running a house. Her mother also taught her about the country of Suliad, as well as her own heritage. Sarah was half human, one-quarter dryad, and one-quarter something her mother never told her about.

Her childhood had been spent in a small cottage with her parents. She had some hazy memories of running away from a different place, before they settled on their tiny cottage in northern Suliad, but she had only been three at the time. Her father had made many trips to the distant villages and always came home with books. Sarah read everything she could get her hands on. She had learned about magical creatures but now realized how lacking her education had been. Wivari, vampires, pixies, and countless other species all had unique attributes and abilities she had never known of when she lived in her cottage.

The one topic her father rarely spoke of was the war. He wanted to leave that part of his life behind and wanted her to be safe. Then, that tragic night when Zolf's troops came, all sense of safety was destroyed.

She had experienced so much after fleeing her burned home. She had been chased and attacked. She had escaped a mind-stealing shayde. She had started a business and had run a tournament. She had hired two men who knew all about the outside world, yet she felt empty inside. Now she had a fleet of pixies, two paladins, and two nekarions as friends. Her life had new and interesting twists, challenges, and changes, but she felt a longing inside that had never been there before.

Sarah steadied herself, but she felt so strange. She could not place it. She could sense her surroundings differently. The longing sensation that had always been a part of her now felt stronger than ever before. She was explaining it to Mullet and Kevin, but she did not understand it herself. Kevin thought the sensation was from having the seer open her mind and it would resolve with time.

She looked at the note her father had given her. The word *Hunter* spelled in gold letters remained on the page.

Time passed.

After a week the feeling had not dissipated. The pull remained as strong as when she had woke up after visiting the seer. The last time she had felt it this strongly was the night of the tournament. She remembered it that night, but she had been so busy she attributed it to her being nervous.

Kevin explained that, years ago, a seer had revealed Kevin's aura to be the rare blue color of the paladin. He had vomited the entire next day, but, after that, he felt normal. For Sarah the sensation of longing only solidified. Sometimes during the day the feeling became much stronger and hit her in waves. She tracked the sensation to find some sort of pattern, yet none existed.

"I don't want to be wet leaves on your fire, Sarah, but maybe you're just sick," said Kevin.

"Maybe," said Sarah, unconvinced.

"Could it be just coincidence that you felt *off* after the visit to the seer? I don't know much about medicine, but staying in this little shop for a week can't be good for anyone. Right, Mullet?" said Kevin.

Mullet looked over from the corner and grunted at Kevin's comments. Mullet was playing chess with Tali, while John and Lucy watched. The set was gilded with beautiful pixie carvings, but that offered the tiny creature no advantage. Tali walked across the board with pieces as tall as she was. She tried to be sneaky and cheat while she played, and, for some reason, Mullet let her get away with it. Her cheating did not seem to matter, since Mullet won every match.

"Well, I don't think it's good for you at the very least. A Chosen hasn't been seen in decades, so maybe just being a Chosen makes you feel funny—but maybe not," said Kevin. "If you're feeling so lousy, maybe you should go visit that doc who cured Mullet's little pest over there."

"Hey!" yelled Tali in protest.

"That might not be a bad idea," said Sarah.

Tali zipped over to Kevin. "That doctor is amazing! He reconstructed my wings with astonishing skill. I really thought I would never fly again, but then he applied medicine on my wings and realigned them, at least that is what Mullet said, which really did not create agony as I thought it might, and then he …"

"Tali," said Mullet.

"Sorry, Mullet," she said and flew back over to the bear of a man.

"Well, why don't we finish up at the shop today and go this evening? I don't even think that clinic opens until after dark," said Kevin.

"Considering the doctor's a vampire, I suppose that makes sense," said John.

"Excuse me?" asked Kevin.

"We actually met him a long time ago, when we traveled with Sarah to a small town. He repaired the obese man who Sarah aided," said Lucy.

Kevin looked at Mullet. "Did you miss him being a vampire on your recent trip to heal your chattering little friend?"

Mullet did not respond.

"Don't get me wrong. The few vamps I've met have been charming and courteous, until they want to make a withdrawal."

"Wait. John, are you serious? He's the same one?" said Sarah.

"Yes, Tali took us to the clinic a few weeks ago, and both Lucy and I were surprised to encounter the same vampire doctor as in Haynis," said John.

"He's wonderful. Just because you humans believe nonhumans are untrustworthy does not mean that you can condemn unjustifiably. He repaired my wings when I had lost hope, and pixies *always* have hope!" said Tali.

"Now calm down, little miss. I just get a little nervous when I'm not at the top of the food chain, that's all," said Kevin.

"He's good. I checked him," said Mullet.

"You checked him? How could you check him and not realize he is a vampire? Wouldn't that be pretty obvious? I ain't the sharpest sword on the wall, but we know Sarah is something of a wanted commodity," said Kevin.

"He's good, Kevin," said Mullet again.

Kevin looked at Mullet. He rarely said names; it was his way to emphasize a point. "I guess you're sure then. I suppose you and Blabberoni will come too?"

"Blabberoni? Who's Blabberoni? I know you are not pontificating about me, since, if you were, I do not believe I would allow you to get away with it. In fact I might just—"

"Tali," said Mullet. The pixie settled down on his shoulder but stuck out her tongue at Kevin.

"Fine. We all can go see this wonderful doctor. Who am I to think going to a vampire doctor's office at night with the first Chosen in two decades might be a bad idea?" said Kevin.

Chapter 30: Assassins' Order

Jayde woke up from her late-afternoon nap. Her shift delivering food started at six at night. Marl did not approve of nighttime deliveries. He had become greatly more protective of Jayde since her brush with excessive Conjuring. Thus, he had appointed himself as her personal bodyguard. Jayde liked to have Marl along at first, but it became tiresome quickly. He did not let her take any shortcuts. He did not let her leave the main roads unless the delivery required it. He especially watched her to be sure she did not attempt any Conjuring unless in the Order Hall under Yow Li's direct supervision.

"What do you want me to do?" Marie asked.

"Make him stop following me!" Jayde pleaded.

"Have you asked him?"

"About a thousand times," said Jayde. "It's like talking to, well, a rock. Watch." Jayde yelled over to Marl, consuming an enormous roast beef sandwich, with extra sand. "Hey, Marl. Any chance I can do my deliveries alone tonight?"

"Is der chance you stop ask me same stuff?" answered Marl, as he took a monstrous bite.

"You see? He won't let me out of his sight! I've yelled at him a bunch of times, but the best I have gotten is for him to stay about fifty feet behind me," said Jayde.

"Would it help any if I told you that he had been following you to and from the Order Hall every day before you had your little near-death adventure?" asked Marie.

"What?"

"Marl takes his job as your protector very seriously. He has been watching you much closer than you realize. He's been training extremely hard to perfect his camouflage. Rock trolls can shape-shift to a degree, and Marl has been training just to allow you to keep your perceived freedom. That is no small feat. He has been tailing you quite some time now without your knowledge," said Marie.

"I didn't know."

"I didn't think you did. He truly cares for you, Jayde. I don't think Marl wants you to know he's been protecting you undercover," said Marie.

"So why does he have to be right next to me now?"

"You have to remember that Conjuring is new to him as well, and it terrifies him. You should have seen him when you overconjured. He was a mess," said Marie.

"No. Really? No. I mean, nothing scares Marl. He's not afraid to get hurt or maimed or punched. Since we've been here, I've seen him jump into three bar fights just to work on his training," said Jayde.

"Yes, he is very brave. But bravery does not mean you can't be frightened. Bravery means that you can face fear without it crippling you. He's not scared for himself, but he's terrified of something happening to you. He feels as if he failed you when you overexerted yourself. He feels that he somehow should have stopped you."

"Well, that's just dumb. How was he supposed to know I'd collapse?"

"Exactly. If you didn't know, how could he? Unfortunately he feels guilty about it, and this is his way of compensating for what he sees as his failure. If you want my advice, I'd just let him go with you and try not to harass him for it. He does it because he cares about you. We all do," said Marie.

"Oh," said Jayde. She shouldered her backpack. Jayde tried to remember the last time someone had told her that they cared. Seeing her move, Marl lumbered behind her. "Thanks, Marie."

"No problem."

Jayde started her normal route toward the Conjurers' Order Hall. Marl lagged behind her. Jayde stopped and looked back. Marl did an excellent job blending into the crowd despite his bulk.

"C'mon, you big lout. Walk with me," she said. Jayde saw movements from the shadows materialize into Marl. He practically skipped up to her.

"You let Marl walk with you?" he asked.

"Sure. You'll follow me either way, right? At least this will give me someone to talk to other than Fang. She's a great listener, but she doesn't say much." The tiny cat mewed in response.

Mr. Li met them both at the entrance to the Order Hall.

"Good evening, Jayde. Good evening, Marl," he said.

"Hi, Mr. Li. You got deliveries waiting already?" she asked.

"Just one, Jayde. Just one. You're going to a shady part of Grandeur tonight, so a little intimidation factor might be nice. Your delivery is to an old friend of mine. It seems that I am not the only one in Grandeur who has noticed your abilities. He stated that he has been watching your skills develop as well.

"He wants to meet you in person, so let me warn you. He is a bit odd and perhaps a bit intimidating, but he is one of my closest friends. Tonight you're going into the Thieves' District, so I thought you should have a little extra help. Brutus will join you tonight," he said.

"Brutus?" asked Jayde.

"Yes. Brutus! Come here please," said Mr. Li.

Jayde initially thought a bear had stepped out of the hall. On second look, the creature more closely resembled a dog, though this dog must have weighed over five hundred pounds.

"This is Brutus," said Mr. Li. "He is a modified mastiff, one of my very favorite familiars. Brutus, this is Jayde."

"Nice to meet you, Brutus," Jayde said, taking a step back.

"A pleasure to meet you as well, Jayde," said the dog.

"Whoa! You talk?" said Marl.

"Indeed. Don't all thinking beasts talk in some manner or another?" asked the dog.

"Yar, I guess," said Marl.

"I'm glad we all get along so well," Mr. Li said. "Brutus is loyal, kind, and strong. Also, in case you are blind, he can handle just about anything you are likely to encounter. Since he is my familiar, he can keep me updated on what you are up to on your deliveries too."

"What? Fang's getting demoted?" asked Jayde.

"Well, she's become more loyal to you than me, even though I made her. The fact that she allowed you to attempt a second Conjuring should have clued me to this. I don't want you to get hurt. Please see this as an old man looking out for a favorite student, not as someone spying on you," he said.

"The more the merrier, but will Fang get along with such a large dog?" she asked. When she looked for Fang, she saw the small kitten rubbing her nose against the dog's large paw, purring.

"I think they'll be fine," said Yow.

"If you don't mind, Yow, I think I might appear a bit overbearing for the streets, don't you?" said Brutus.

"That's kind of the point, B," said Yow.

"Well, then just make it so that I can return to form if I have to," said Brutus.

"No respect from my students … my cat likes Jayde more than me, and now my dog is telling me what to do," Yow said dramatically. Yow then performed a quick gesture, and Brutus decreased in size. He still looked like a massive two-hundred-pound dog, but at least he did not look abnormal.

"Say hello to Slicy for me," said Yow, as he walked back into the Order Hall.

"Can I say hello by biting off his arm?" Brutus growled for emphasis.

"Be nice. That clown has saved all our hides more than once, despite his biting disposition."

"I'll bite him right in his disposition," grumbled Brutus.

Jayde walked around to the rear of the Order Hall and picked up her night's delivery. Jayde had tried to make friends with everyone in the order. This became much easier after her fall from greatness with her accidental excessive Conjuring. A few members rejoiced at seeing the new upstart taken down a peg. She picked up her food for delivery and the address.

"If he's so worried, why doesn't Yow just come with us?" Jayde asked Brutus.

"Yow is head of the Conjurer's Order. He wouldn't be allowed where we're going. By sending me, he is looking out for you."

"I can keep Jayde safe," said the rock troll.

"No doubt you could, my rugged friend, but I can instantly call for backup if needed. What I see, Yow can also see. Plus Yow has been around for quite some time. I have accompanied him on most journeys, so most should recognize me as an extension of him. He is well respected, so I doubt we will come across any trouble," said the dog.

"*Oi*, you smart pooch," said Marl.

"Thank you. Also, Jayde, you might want to make Fang slightly more intimidating as long as we are going to the Thieves' District," said Brutus, a line of slobber stretching to the ground with his grin.

Jayde nodded. She concentrated, and Fang enlarged to a black tiger with white stripes. Fang roared in approval.

The delivery consisted of several meals, as well as a few pies, which caused Jayde to grin. She looked at Marl, and he laughed.

"Dat what got you in dis mess in the first place." He laughed again.

"Let's go," she said.

The girl, rock troll, cat familiar, and dog familiar took off into the night. Jayde had learned the local neighborhoods quite well by now. She also knew most of the back roads and shortcuts to get around the city. This address, however, was deep in the Thieves' District.

She made idle chatter with Brutus and Marl, as she walked toward the rougher side of town. Jayde felt much happier about her decision to keep Marl close. As they traveled, fewer people walked the streets. The people still outside hid in their cloaks, trying not to make eye contact with anyone around them.

Brutus had stopped talking some time ago, without Jayde realizing it. She looked over at the dog and started to say something, but Brutus glanced at her quickly and shook his head. It then struck her. He wanted to appear to be just a dog, not a smart familiar that could enlarge in size and communicate with the most powerful conjurer in the entire country.

Jayde was good at reading looks.

A man staggered down the road. The foursome made their way to the opposite side of street. The man also tripped his way to the other side. Brutus stepped in front of the others and growled, staring right at the drunk. The dog grew in size. The man looked up at the large dog and suddenly became sober, walking without difficulty to the opposite side of the street.

"Punk," grumbled Brutus under his breath.

They made it the rest of the way to their destination without incident. The building added a menace of its own on an already intimidating street. The steel numbers of the address glinted against the black building in the moonlight. It was a fortress. The only windows it had were on the second and third floors, all of which were covered with thick bars.

The windows also had a black tint to them, which prevented anyone from seeing inside. Other than the numbers outside, the building had no markings. Everything about the edifice exuded a feeling of secrecy, deceit, and malice.

The doorbell, however, made a laughing sound when Jayde rang it.

A small slit opened in the door, a pair of eyes peering out. "State your business," hissed the man.

"Delivery for Slicy," said Jayde.

"Wait here," he said, followed by the slam of the slit.

After a brief pause the door opened, and the foursome entered.

"Follow me," said a man dressed in black.

Twenty dark figures in black cloaks stood by silently. Jayde walked down a hall, passing the figures; only their eyes could be seen. Not one made a noise. Not a whisper. Not a cough. Not a sniffle. Not even a scuffle of feet. The hall remained eerily quiet.

"Jayde, me not like dis place," said Marl, his voice a low whisper.

They followed the man down numerous turns. The halls in the building all curved, which quickly disoriented Jayde. The man came to a large black door. The door had thirty dead-bolt latches on the side. Each of the locks had a vertically oriented latch that could be turned either way. The man rapidly turned the latches, some to the right and others to the left in rapid succession; he then opened the door and continued. The group followed. The door automatically shut behind them, and they heard the snaps of all the locks going back into place on their own.

The man turned down various hallways. They followed through the twists and turns until they were hopelessly lost. Finally they came to a bizarre door. The door appeared to be made of clear gelatin. Suspended in the gelatin were hundreds of keys of all shapes and sizes with three keyholes on the left side of the door. The man in black recited a poem as his hand moved up, down, left, and then down, just short of touching the gelatin.

The man held his breath and slowly reached into the substance and pulled out a key. He inserted the first key into the top keyhole and turned it with a loud clack.

He repeated the procedure two more times, each time reciting a singsong poem that Jayde assumed helped him remember which keys were the appropriate ones. After the third key was inserted, the door opened slowly.

"Why so much security when it is *inside* your own place?" Jayde asked the man in black. He did not respond.

They finally entered a very small room. The man closed the door immediately after they were inside, including him. With the door shut, the room became dim; only a slight red light from the back of the room allowed any vision.

"What are you doing?" said Jayde.

The man again said nothing and walked to the rear of the room. Hundreds of small pegs stuck out from the wall, and he adjusted a few of them. Jayde felt the whole room shift. It was not a small room but a large dumb waiter. After a few minutes in the dark and the quiet, the dumb waiter stopped, and the door opened. They walked into an empty white room. The only things in the room were the elevator at one side and a black door at the other.

The entire room gleamed white except for the door. The door was covered in sticky, fresh black paint. A small knocker was the only other thing on the door. No hinges could be seen, nor was there a doorknob.

The man in black pulled back the hood that had been cloaking his face the entire time. He appeared extremely nervous. His acne-riddled, oily face glinted in the torchlight. He took a long deep breath, apparently to steady his nerves. With his index finger and his thumb, he grabbed the metal knocker and created a unique rhythm. It seemed as if he played a song known only to him, as he continued to knock fast, then slow, followed by hard, then soft, and pausing, only to start again with a different rhythm. Finally he stopped. The man stepped away from the door. The door melted away and faded into nothing. The knocker on the door fell to the ground with a clang.

The man pointed. "Go quickly. Just through the next door is your location. Do not come back this way," he said.

The group walked into the next room. The man in black picked up the fallen knocker. He held it in midair, when the sticky blackness reappeared. They were now alone.

"Okay, that was weird," said Jayde.

"Me still no like dis place, Jayde," said Marl.

"What do you think that stuff is?" said Jayde, walking toward the previous sticky door.

"JAYDE! Do NOT touch it," grumbled Brutus. The large dog had clamped down on the back of her pants and tugged her off her feet. She landed on her behind with a grunt.

"No need to bite my butt off. Jeez!" said Jayde.

"If you touched that stuff, I might have to! That's shadow ooze. If you get that on your skin, it burns, and it continues to burn till there is nothing left to consume. Even a small amount on the tip of your finger can be enough to work its way through your entire body. Just stay away," said Brutus.

Jayde retreated from the inky door.

They walked to the other side of the room where a plain wooden door with a normal doorknob stood. The door had a small piece of paper taped to it.

Jayde took the paper off the door and opened it. It had one phrase:

SHAVE AND A HAIRCUT?

Jayde flipped over the note. Nothing else was on it, just those words written in thick strokes in red. Jayde knocked on the door. The group waited. She knocked on the door again, with no response. She flipped over the note, looked at it once more, and knocked a third time: *knock knock kno-knock* **knock**.

"Hello," sang a voice as the door opened wide.

Despite the cheery voice, Jayde still expected a man dressed in a black robe, and he was. However, as he moved forward, she glimpsed under the robe, seeing myriad colors. Bright purples, yellows, and happy hues all clashed on his pants. His shirt similarly had a colorful diamond pattern of all colors. He quickly pulled the robe closed. His face had many white blotches. His left eye had a vertical scar through the top and bottom eyelid. If he was supposed to look like a clown, no one was laughing.

"Wonderful, the food has arrived. I have been craving a good pie for some time. Please come in," said the man.

"Are you ... Slicy?" asked Jayde.

"I, young lady, am the previous fool of the ill-mannered king with whom your acquaintance has not been met, yet, at the same time, whose destiny all our futures—including our very lives—may still hang in the balance. I earned a glorious reputation as the Sensational, Scintillating Slicy the Great, first of the Elite twenty-five, and the first to achieve a tenth-level blade mastery. And you, young lady, are lucky to be alive," he said with a bow.

Chapter 31: Hunter

Sarah locked up the shop for the night. Kevin and Mullet pulled down the immense front gates. A thief would need a year with a hacksaw to get through their gates. A small back door existed, which the pair had created as a one-way door. People could get out of the store quite easily, but only pixies could get back in. Two sets of glowing nekarion eyes glowed inside the shop. No one had broken in for quite some time.

Mullet and the ever-present Tali accompanied Kevin and Sarah on their trip to the doctor. The reptilian nekarions remained at the store to guard it in their absence. Sarah still did not think this doctor would be able to find anything wrong with her. The feeling of longing remained constant. She felt it pulling her, tugging at her mind like an itch that could not be scratched. She thought again about how much she missed her family.

John and Lucy joined the foursome, since they had originally designated themselves as "Sarah's" pixies. After discussing this with other pixies, they amended the title so that Sarah was their human, which the rest of the troop approved.

Tali lectured the entire group about Dr. Sangre. She droned on about his compassion and his empathy toward all living creatures. As the group approached the clinic, Tali saw two figures exiting the front door.

One figure physically threw a fat, balding man out of the clinic. The fat man landed in a heap. He was blubbering, while the other figure walked back toward the clinic.

"You don't understand. I *have* to have my *dilaudda*. It's the only thing that works, really!" said the fat man.

"*You* don't understand. I can tell when you are lying. I can literally feel your pain, but you don't have any. People like you *drain* the life out of honest workers everywhere. Don't come back unless you are bleeding or dying," said the doctor, and the door slammed behind him.

The fat man continued to roll around on the ground in apparent agony for another ten seconds. Then, without any intervention, he got up and calmly walked down the street.

"That was your compassionate doctor, wasn't it, Tali?" asked Sarah.

Mullet chuckled, while Tali, amazingly, said nothing.

Once inside, they wrote down Sarah's name, her medical history, as well as her magical history on a sheet at the front of the clinic. A few other patients waited with Sarah. A slim feline-faced creature yowled in pain. A large wood troll sat calmly reading a book, but it had seven crossbow bolts sticking out its left arm. Green sap slowly oozed from the bolts, but the creature seemed unfazed. A human mother looked over a small sneezing child, who also oozed green sap from a continuously runny nose.

After half an hour Sarah and her party had made it to the front of the line and got called back to a bed.

Cameron sat down next to her and introduced himself. He looked around the room and smiled at Mullet and Tali.

"I see you have made a full recovery," he said to Tali. The pixie beamed. "You know, you owe him a great deal for getting you here so quickly and taking such good care of you," Cameron said, pointing to Mullet.

"I think her gratitude is starting to kill him though," said Kevin.

Mullet smiled.

"I know you," said Cameron.

"We met at the tournament a couple months ago. You yanked a hunk of metal out of a rock troll's side and then patched him up. Mullet said you also did a fine job of fixing up the little chatterbox's wings as well," said Kevin.

"You look familiar as well," Cameron said to Sarah.

"We met maybe three or so months ago in Haynis. You took care of Thaddeus's firefoot," she said.

"Oh, yes," he said. "Well, what brings you in today?" He looked down at the chart. "Sarah?"

"Where to start …"

"How about the beginning?" answered Cameron.

Sarah told how she had been feeling homesick. She thought it felt like homesickness, but, now that she had thought about it for a while, it felt more like a longing. She felt a pulling inside her, almost an ache, but she had difficulty describing it.

"I see you marked 'other' under magical encounters. Anything you're leaving out that might shed some light here? I won't be able to help you unless I understand everything that's happening," said Cameron. He relaxed in his chair, giving her the time to tell it in her own words.

Sarah looked around nervously and then asked if they could go somewhere they would not be overheard. Cameron just nodded his head and called out. Marie appeared. Cameron asked for an "*eye-eye*," and she disappeared. She reappeared seconds later with a purple metal circle. She put the circle on the bed.

"Do you have any problem with the people here listening or just strangers nearby?" asked Cameron, motioning toward Mullet and Kevin.

"No. I just don't want anyone nearby listening in. They already know the story," said Sarah, nodding at Mullet and Kevin.

Cameron pressed down on the purple metal. A sphere of purple light slowly grew from the circle and passed over the small group. When all in the group were inside the sphere, he released the disk. The sphere stopped growing at that point, surrounding only the group. The silence inside was immediate and absolute.

"Whoa, can we get one of those to put around Tali?" asked Lucy.

"Now no one outside the sphere can hear you, so please continue."

Sarah looked at Kevin and Mullet. Kevin still seemed nervous. He stopped Sarah before she spoke and asked Mullet to take one last look into Cameron. Mullet sighed and looked at Cameron questioningly.

"If that's what it takes, go ahead," said Cameron.

Mullet again gazed into Cameron's eyes and concentrated. He scanned Cameron for ill intent or for any possible link or allegiance to King Zolf. He found nothing. He also tried to find anything pertaining to him being a vampire, but Cameron pulled back as he prodded.

"Find everything you needed?" asked Cameron.

Mullet nodded.

Sarah told the whole story. The only thing she left out was the seer's declaration of her being a Chosen. Cameron listened quietly as she told of her visit to the seer.

"But the weird thing is, ever since the seer did … whatever she did to me … well, I just feel this pull. I tried to explain it to the guys, but I really don't know what it is myself. It's as if I need to go somewhere. The feeling changes from day to day. Yet I can feel it pulling. I don't know. Maybe I'm just depressed or simply feeling weird, having found out my aura is special or something like that. I don't know," said Sarah.

"Hmm. Well, Kevin could be right. You might just be coming down with the flu, and the timing is all coincidental, but I doubt it. I want to run a few baseline tests, but I expect them to come back negative. I think I know what is happening, but I need to rule out all other possibilities first," said Cameron.

The nurse came back and drew some blood samples. Kevin smiled at Marie.

"So you help people, and, if you need it, you can have your nurse pound the lights outta anyone who causes trouble," Kevin said.

"We don't have repeat troublemakers here," said Marie.

She disappeared with the blood samples and the purple disk and Cameron. The noise of the clinic instantly returned.

They waited in their tiny room. Cameron returned a short time later. "Well, as I suspected, everything came back normal. Sarah, I would like to try something. It is a little out of the ordinary. One of my Talents is that I can experience my patient's symptoms. If you don't mind, I would like to do that, so that I can feel what it is you are trying to describe to me. Are you okay with that?" he asked.

"Does it hurt?" she asked.

"No," he said.

"It seems everyone else has been looking inside my brain. Why don't we just start a party in there? But if it can help figure out what's going on, go for it."

Cameron leaned close to Sarah and put his hands on Sarah's temples. A small flash of blue came from her eyes. They both remained still for a few minutes. Cameron appeared to be lost in thought, and Sarah looked completely blank. Sarah let out a slight sigh and then blinked a few times, her consciousness returning.

Cameron let out a shout of laughter. "I knew it! I never thought I would see it. Never!" said Cameron. He called Marie over, and she again made the barrier of silence with the *eye-eye*. The purple sphere of light again covered the group.

"What? What is it?" asked Sarah.

"Sarah, you are the Hunter, the first of the Chosen!" said Cameron.

Sarah paused. Kevin had wanted her to keep that knowledge private, but it seems the doctor had figured it out on his own.

"That's what they tell me, but I don't think I really know what the *Hunter* is," Sarah said.

"You feel the next Chosen. The group of five Chosen is trying to come together. You alone have the ability to find the other four Chosen. You can reunite them again. With the Chosen assembled once more, well, that could change everything, literally! You can find the people who can end the Dark King's madness," said Cameron.

Kevin looked at Mullet, who remained solemn.

"You sure about this?" Kevin asked the doctor.

"She is the Hunter foretold by every seer since the Dark King began his reign. She's the one who can end the war," said Cameron. "Let me show you."

Cameron left the room and came back with a shiny large black cube. He twisted the top of the cube, and it opened smoothly. From inside he pulled out a black leather-bound book with golden writing across the front in letters that Sarah had never seen before.

Kevin's eyes went wide. "Is that a copy of the *Soliatrela?*"

"It is," said Cameron.

"All copies of the *Soliatrela* were destroyed, weren't they?" asked Kevin.

"All known copies," said Cameron.

"Who are you, really?" asked Kevin.

Cameron ignored him.

"What is it?" asked Sarah.

"It is a copy of the original prediction made by the seer who told the mad king he would not reign forever. It is the prediction that his reign could come to an end. The Hunter is the first to appear. Only the Hunter can feel the pull of the location toward wherever the other Chosen are located. Only once the Chosen are reunited can we have a chance to stop the Dark King once and for all," said Cameron.

"Whoa, wait. Don't I get a say in all this? I mean, some loony lady says I have some undiscovered Talent and then casts a spell on me and now I feel homesick, so you guys want me to go fight a war?" said Sarah, her voice rising.

The two paladins looked at Sarah, and then at Marie and Cameron.

"You don't understand what this really means," said Cameron. "Marie worked as a war sage, gaining information to fight the Dark King. Your two friends are paladins. I'm sure they have told you what that involves to some small degree. But all of us, ALL of us are pawns. We can hardly even chip at the surface of the Dark King's march to power. His borders have been slowly expanding for decades, and nothing can prevent him from slowly taking over the world. This prophesy"—Cameron paused, holding up the small black cube—"told that there might be a chance to stop him.

"Very few know that the Hunter is able to find the other Chosen. When the Hunter finds all the Chosen, then they together can stop King Zolf's reign. But it all begins with the Hunter, which is not a job you sign up for. As far as we can tell, the previous Hunters have all been random creatures from all walks of life," said Cameron.

Sarah let out a choked groan. "Are you all crazy! What if I just say no?"

Kevin put a reassuring hand on her shoulder.

"There's no choice to make. Call it fate or luck or destiny or whatever, but you're the only one. There have been other Hunters before you. Often they don't even know they have the gift, but you, well, you found it out in the company of two paladins. You have a better chance than any Hunter before you," said Cameron.

"And what if I still say no?" asked Sarah stubbornly.

Cameron looked grim. "The pull only gets stronger with time. A Hunter eventually follows the pull or loses his or her sanity. Only one Hunter exists at a time. When that one dies, another one is born," said Cameron.

"What Cameron says is true. You're the Hunter. The time to keep you in the dark is past. There's a war going on, Sarah. Many have died already, but it's still just at the beginning," said Kevin.

"So why haven't these Chosen people stopped him then?" Sarah asked.

"The king's been hunting Chosen ever since he killed the five who met with him two centuries ago. As long as he prevents the Hunter from finding the rest of the Chosen, he's safe," said Kevin.

"Ha! What an idiot. He'd have to wait a lifetime for them to die off. Wouldn't that just mean he would be about to die as well?" asked Tali.

"King Zolf has ruled for over two hundred years now, and, from what I'm told, he still looks like he's a young man. He's been sapping life from his subjects for centuries," said Kevin.

"Hold on. You mean his plan could work?" said Sarah.

"No. His plan *did* work," said Cameron.

"But how will the Chosen stop him?" she asked.

"No one knows. With no Chosen for two centuries, their history has been muddled. The Hunter is the only one who can feel the Chosen. In the past, the Hunter might have to seek out one Chosen, maybe two during the Hunter's lifetime. Normally this would be a time of great joy and excitement, since anyone in the world could be the next Chosen. As soon as the Hunter finds a Chosen, their life is forever changed. But now, well, there are no Chosen, and you're the only one who knows who they are," said Marie.

"Unfortunately it also makes you a wanted person. The Dark King will want to capture you," said Cameron.

"Wait. I thought you said this king guy was some sort of ruthless person. Why wouldn't he just kill the Hunters, if he captured them?" she asked.

"You're exactly right. We paladins have heard stories, which I reckon have more than a shade of truth in them. From what I was told, he just killed the Chosen he caught at first, but, as soon as he killed one, another would be born to replace it. This is why we paladin have been trying to keep the Chosen safe," said Kevin.

"It's even worse than that," said Cameron. "The king learned that capturing a Hunter would prevent the rest of Chosen from coming together. Thus, if he captured the Hunter and kept them alive under lock and key, he would be fine. Remember, only one Hunter is alive at a time. King Zolf found a way to locate the previous Hunters, and since then he prevents each Hunter from dying under his watch," said Kevin.

"So the Hunters would just live out their lives in the Dark King's kingdom and never be the wiser?" asked Sarah.

"Hardly," said Marie. "As a war sage I learned much of the history of how the king handled his prisoners. The Hunters who get caught live a life of misery. The king does not care that the Hunter has no control over being chosen to their fate. He enjoys knowing that the one who has a chance of ending his reign spends their lives in helpless despair. He will occasionally torture a potential Hunter for hours at a time," said Marie.

"But I thought he wanted the Hunter to be alive for a long time," said Sarah.

"Oh, yes. Each would get the best health care of anyone in his kingdom, but that did not stop him from hurting them. The king has very talented healers. According to what I've been taught, the Hunters would beg for their deaths. But obviously the king wants the Hunters to be alive for as long as possible, since the death of a Hunter only starts the search for the next all over again," said Marie.

"So these Hunters would live long lives?" asked Tali from Mullet's shoulder.

"Not usually. Even with the constant supervision of healers, Hunters have died from the pull. They cannot seek the

Chosen. They feel the spell guiding them toward the other people they need to find. Each day would be slightly worse than the previous. With time, the simple fact that they were not allowed to search for the other Chosen drives them mad. Hunters usually die during their imprisonment despite being fed and cared for," said Marie.

"So they kill themselves?" asked Sarah.

"Well, in a way the Dark King kills them," said Marie. "By locking them up, they eventually lose their will to live."

"But I'm twenty-three. Wouldn't I have felt this pull long ago?" Sarah asked. She seemed numb to the information being thrown at her.

Kevin looked at her sympathetically. "The seer told us that somehow your Talent and aura were masked. With your Talent being cloaked, the pull must have been hidden as well. Your homesick feeling must be the pull leading you to the first Chosen."

"So what happens when I find all these people?" Sarah asked.

"No one knows. For over two hundred years, none of the Hunters have ever found all the people they needed to," Kevin said.

"Oh? Why is that?" Sarah asked.

"They all died first," said Cameron.

Chapter 32: Slicy

"I'm lucky to be alive?" Jayde asked the white-faced man.

"Indeed, my dear girl. Though aren't we all?" said Slicy.

"Slicy, since when did you speak in double-talk and riddles? Isn't all that 'beneath' you?" said Brutus.

"Ah, Brutus, you overgrown, mangy mongrel, long time no maul. Why be succinct when you can confuse as eloquently as I can?" said the man.

"I take it you know this guy, Brutus?" asked Jayde.

"Oh, sure," answered the white-faced man. "The giant *dogmiliar* has tried to pee in my yard before."

"*Dogmiliar?*" asked Jayde.

Brutus sighed. "He means me. I'm a familiar, and a dog, thus *dogmiliar*. Slicy is the worst kind of clown, one who actually thinks he is funny."

"Ouch! You get one point for succinctness, but minus two for vernacular. I'm a 'fool,' not a clown, not an idiot, not a joker, nor a jester. A fool. Keep it straight, mutt, before I neuter you," said Slicy. A cruel-looking knife appeared in his hand and then disappeared just as quickly. "You, on the other hand, young lady, are something altogether different. You have been a topic of some contention in the order."

"What? Why?" Jayde asked.

"'How did she do it?' they asked? 'She just looked like a little girl,' they said. For some reason they didn't ask why send an entire decatroop for one little girl, but apparently the employer knew more than we did, didn't he? Yet you still eluded all them," said Slicy.

Jayde looked around, to be sure the man was talking to her. For some reason he seemed to be speaking to a crowd of people.

"I managed to do what now?" she asked.

Slicy's mouth did not move, yet she distinctly heard "Trust me. Just play along."

"Ha! No fooling a fool, right? I mean, you must have found out by now. Would you tell the Elite your story at least?" asked Slicy loudly.

"Uh, sure, I guess," said Jayde. She looked at her companions for support, yet all looked as completely perplexed as she was.

"Though it is completely up to you," he said quickly, while pulling Jayde into the room. "Then again, if the rest of the order finds out you waltzed into the inner sanctum on your first trip here, well, I'd like to say they'd kill you, but they can't do that, am I right?" he said with a grin. The four looked at him with blank expressions.

"You know what his talk mean?" Marl asked Brutus.

"I haven't got a clue, but I think we are about to find out," answered the dog.

Slicy led the confused foursome through the door into a lavish room. The room had dozens of people in it; yet, as they walked in, the chatter disappeared. Slicy walked to the front of the room with Jayde, Brutus, Marl, and Fang following. The people in the room were all dressed in black and had different ways of cloaking their faces. Most wore elaborate masks. A few others simply had large hoods. Not a single person, except Slicy, showed his or her actual face.

"After weeks of tracking and finagling, and much hard work and effort, I have found the one thing that you all have been looking for. That's right. I present to you our dinner!" said Slicy.

The Elite laughed. Jayde shrugged and handed out the boxes of food to each of the tables.

Jayde looked around. On the walls were murals of people from apparently all walks of life. Under each picture was a plaque. On each was a name and the word "Unkillable" and a ranking from first to sixteenth. Behind Slicy was another frame, but the portrait was covered by a tarp.

Every portrait showed a person of incredible strength and cunning. Jayde thought that each mural showed an amazing insight to the type of iron-willed survivor each of the persons must have been. One picture showed a man fighting off ten warriors with only a shovel. Another showed a large brute clearly in agony, yet crawling his way out of a horrendous pit of spikes. His clothes were drenched with blood and his face tortured; yet beneath him in the pit were other men, who she assumed must have fallen by his hands. The other murals depicted similar scenes of heroic survival. Slicy stayed at the front of the room.

"When I found the next Unkillable, I didn't believe it. I must ask that you not judge by appearances. Listen to the story. As you all know, I was lucky enough to witness the actual event. It surprised me as well, but, in our line of work, looks can be quite deceiving," said Slicy.

"Just think of a mere fifty years ago. Who of us would challenge Plimpo the Goblin? Who? I know I wouldn't. If any of you had seen a more miserable little puke walking down the street, well, you probably would think him hardly worth spitting on, much less being the most lethal assassin this Order Hall has ever seen," said Slicy.

Jayde looked around and could see shaded faces nodding in agreement.

"Our seventeenth shares many characteristics with our previous Unkillables. The first of which is a razor-sharp mind. I saw it with my own eyes, and, even afterward, I couldn't believe it. The trap was set. No escape could be possible. At least that's what this humble observer thought," said Slicy while walking around the room.

He made his way to one of the tapestries where two dark figures played chess. "Before my eyes, I thought I saw a certain checkmate. The king seemed to be the only piece on the board except for a few worthless pawns. However, this king had other plans. Each pawn turned out to be a powerful piece, skilled beyond reckoning. The king was still trapped, until the king revealed a secret no one had even guessed."

The dark figures sitting at tables around the room sat, breathless, riveted by Slicy's every word. For some reason his voice drew in all the observers, Jayde included. He slowly walked around the room, finally arriving next to Jayde. It made her uncomfortable to have the wicked-looking clown man stand right next to her while he gave his speech.

"But you did not come tonight to hear me blather, now did you? So it gives me great joy and extreme pleasure to introduce our next Unkillable. Judge for yourselves if she is worthy, though I have no doubt of your decision. Jayde the Conjurer!"

The room exploded into applause. All stood on their feet and hollered. They yelled, as Slicy slowly walked to his seat. The clapping continued and then dissipated. Finally it died out. Slicy looked back, seemingly surprised at the empty podium at the front of the room. He stood up and walked back to her.

"Jayde? If you would be so kind?" he said.

Jayde walked up to the white-faced man. "What do you want me to do?" she whispered.

"Just a little shy," he said to the crowd. "Tell the story! Tell how you managed to survive!" he said.

"Survive what? What are you talking about?" she asked.

"Tell. How. You. Beat. The. Assassins," he said, while smiling at the crowd.

He gently pulled her along, getting the crowd to clap again now that she had taken the podium.

"Uh, hi," said Jayde. The assassins? What assassins? The dozen crazy guys that shot needles that Cameron stopped? The guys that Marie had destroyed on the trip getting to Grandeur? What?

Jayde thought "dumb luck" might not go over well as her reason for thwarting the assassins.

"It was the night of the big tournament," said Jayde, her voice cracking. "I was watching Marie and Marl fighting, and then some guys came up and threw needles, but Cameron blocked them. He killed most of them, and then they threw some stuff that exploded. They are all dead. The end."

She stared at the crowd while a ten-second eternity crept by.

"What?" one shouted. Grumbling flared throughout the crowd, and a few got up from their seats, looking quite angry. Jayde glanced around and could see sinister glints of metal in the hands of some of the Elite in the crowd. Marl flanked her side instantly.

Slicy appeared at Jayde's other side with a broad smile on his face.

"Gentlemen, Ladies, and Slaarg, and Vehimoth and Knarr, please, perhaps it would be more illuminating if I told the story. I know that a few of you remember Grath the mountain man who was the sixth Unkillable. When he told his story, he used ten words total, and I quote, 'Me wamp 'em good. Wamp you too. Leave Grath 'lone.' Slicy's voice completely changed when he repeated Grath's words. It did not seem like he was impersonating another voice when he did this; it seemed like he had actually changed to another person.

"So let me try to do justice to this story, and then you may judge for yourselves."

More grumbling came from the crowd, but they took their seats. Slicy began his tale. Jayde thought it would start at the tournament, but it began instead back in Haynis. He told of an elite trio who had been sent there to dispatch a young thief. The description matched the rainy night perfectly. He spoke of a well-trained threesome, much more than a match for one little girl, or so they thought. The details of what had happened were vague, but all three had been killed that night without a scratch on Jayde.

The next trap had been dispatched and had set up an ambush. They knew the girl was coming through the woods, only accompanied by a middle-aged woman. This time they had taken no chances and had hired a group of ruffians, as well as a rock troll. Slicy told the tale of the battle in the woods, and again how those seven had failed to dispatch their mark a second time.

He finally told the tale of the tournament. It was obvious that he had witnessed this event by his description. He included her trips to the gamblers' booth. He also made up parts about how Jayde had "sensed" something being amiss. Slicy knew his crowd. He explained her "sixth sense" about certain things, even though she did not even know an ambush existed.

Jayde watched from the back of the room, as her mind slowly put the puzzle together. She glanced around and looked closely at the Elite. They almost looked similar to the three assassins that had tried to …

How could I have been so stupid? she thought. She had been blinded by that stupid clown; he had caught her off guard. All of them were assassins. Catching people off guard was their business. That and killing people. Jayde looked toward the door they had come through only to see that it no longer existed. No exit could be seen; the room was sealed.

"As I said before, Jayde's a conjurer. If you know most conjurers, then you likely think of them as people with a few party tricks and nothing more. Most conjurers can make a green sheet turn red, or change a short piece of string into a long one. Some more talented conjurers have been known to even be able to change an apple into an orange. Rarely a few conjurers can change the benign into the bizarre. She is one of the 'true conjurers,' so to speak," said Slicy.

"Even now she has two familiars with her. Perhaps some of you recognize Brutus, the fearsome familiar of none other than Yow Li himself. I have seen this beast in action and know his brilliance in battle. But Jayde has her own familiar as well, don't you, Jayde?"

Jayde nodded and reached into her pocket. She had miniaturized Fang upon their arrival at the building. Carefully she pulled out the tiny purring cat. Fang had been sleeping in her pocket and stretched out in her hands. A few in the crowd laughed at the diminutive creature. Jayde became angry at their dismissal of Fang, who was a force to be reckoned with.

"What a joke!" one snickered near Jayde.

"Pathetic," said another.

That's it! Jayde thought. She put Fang on the ground and linked minds with her. In a blink the tiny cat expanded into a gigantic white lion. Fang released a terrifying roar over the crowd, and the laughter stopped. Jayde smiled and then conjured Fang into a cute pink kitten. Fang bounded into her hands and began purring again.

"Did you think I was lying? Did you think I would lamely promote someone unworthy to the title of Unkillable?" asked Slicy, while smiling broadly at Jayde.

The crowd hung on his every word. He embellished and exaggerated, making it seem like Jayde had orchestrated the location of the assassin attack to an area that favored a conjurer's skills.

"She had detected their strengths and weaknesses by clandestine trips to and from the gambling hut, each time obtaining small but critical pieces of information about those who she had realized were tracking her.

"She never claimed to be the best conjurer ever, but I have spoken with Yow Li, the head of the Conjurers' Order, who himself said he had never seen one with more potential. Being blessed with this skill, she worked hard to fine-tune it. She wielded her assets, imagination, and quick mind, more deadly than my knives." As he said this, he emphasized the point with five knives that appeared out of nowhere in his hands, spun in a rapid series of twists in the air, then again vanished.

"You, the Elite, can understand the importance of ingenuity and cleverness better than most. To a conjurer, these skills define them. Versatility is key. Is it not, brothers?" said the harlequin-faced man.

"As I was saying, her ally had nearly reached his limit. How one man could block one needle assassin baffles me, much less twelve at a time, but all men have limits, and he had reached his. Nine assassins had been vanquished. But the remaining three were vigilant," he said.

"This rock troll aided her by destroying one of the three, and the trio was down to two. Then, in an effort that would surely kill their target, the two remaining drew out their secret weapons. They pulled out a pair of needle bombs," said Slicy.

The audience became hostile. Several commented about how needle bombs were outlawed and not allowed in the order. Others stated how no one could ever survive a single bomb. Slicy held up his hands, and the group again became silent.

"Indeed, how could anyone survive not one, but two, bombs? Needles from those bombs explode on contact. Unless they embed into something, the target dies. Jayde had only seconds to escape the perfect trap. I watched this all from a safe distance. I must admit, I was sure it was over. I don't say this often, my friends. … I was wrong.

"As the bombs reached their peaks, Jayde and her friend's tremendous efforts were in vain. They were dead. They just did not know it. If she conjured a rock shield, the first needles would explode through it, and the next would find their mark. So what did she do? What was the perfect choice? She had seconds, yet, even in this room with all the time in the world, do you think you could avoid death in that situation? Still she found the solution—something so simple, so elegant, and so perfect.

"My brothers, she conjured a giant potato. I know. I know! Don't laugh. Think about it. What else was firm enough to take the hit of multiple exploding needles without causing the needles to rupture? Name one other item that could be made in a flash that would do the same. Could you, my brothers, under similar circumstances find the solution to such an impossible situation? In less than a second? And save all your comrades? Our fallen brothers were not as lucky. Thus, yet again, I present to you, Jayde the Conjurer," said Slicy.

This time, when he said it, he pulled down the large drape over the last mural. In the picture was an extreme close-up of Jayde's face in silhouette. It was perfect. Overlapping the outline of her face was the tournament in amazing detail. The mural showed the assassins impaled with their own spikes. Jayde stood proudly under her protective potato coated in spikes. Jayde had her arms up with a mysterious, magical-looking mist coming from her hands to create her shield. Both arms raised confidently, her friends cowered in fear under her protection.

Jayde was again brought to the front. This time the assassins cheered their congratulations. Slicy asked for them to put it to a vote. A unanimous aye came from the crowd, and she was elected an Unkillable.

"I know we have other orders of business tonight, so please continue the meeting without me," said Slicy. "I plan to educate our newest member, and I'll personally escort her out."

The Elite continued to cheer, as Jayde and her group made its way out of the room. The foursome followed the white-faced man through a hidden door in the rear of the room, while the other twenty-four assassins went about their business.

Jayde looked ashen. She had assumed the assassins had been after Cameron. He had even implied the same.

"So three separate groups of assassins tried to kill us?" Jayde asked.

"*Us?* What *us?* Three separate squads had been assigned for you, young lady," said Slicy.

"But ... why me?" she asked.

"Uh-uh. An excellent assassin never reveals that information, especially when he doesn't know. All you need to know is that it will no longer occur. You just received the highest honor any nonmember could receive," said Slicy. "Now no questions till we get outside." Slicy continued to navigate through a maze of identical-looking corridors.

"What's this 'honor' you're talking about?" Jayde asked. Slicy remained silent.

Slicy led them up a winding staircase, then turned down a long twisting hallway. Finally he walked to yet another nondescript door, but, when he opened this one, it led them outside to the street.

"It does get so stuffy in there, doesn't it?" asked Slicy.

"What just happened!" demanded Jayde.

"Jayde, you just became promoted to Unkillable, meaning no one can put a hit on you. Ever. Well, at least not through any Assassins' Order that I know of."

"What?" Jayde asked.

"Jayde, someone hired people to kill you. I don't know who or why, despite searching quite thoroughly. Yow Li learned about one of the attempts and asked me to help. Yow has saved my biscuits more than once, so I owe him. I know I didn't explain any of this while in there, but inside the Assassins' Order is a bad location to tell secrets. Thus, I took it upon myself to do some digging. Yow was right. Someone's looking for you—and not a friend. Thus, making you an Unkillable created a solution to a problem you didn't know existed. Not only that but, as an Unkillable, you can have an assassin act as your bodyguard," said Slicy.

Jayde continued to walk, shaking her head, taking it all in. "Why would someone be after me?"

"The same question Yow and I have been trying to solve," said Slicy.

"Wait. First you try to kill me. Now you're 'protecting' me? How do I know that this isn't just some sort of trick to get close to me to finish me off!" she said.

Brutus looked over. "Assassins are rarely known for their ethics, but, in this case, what Slicy told you is true. Anyone who has achieved this status is revered through all their Order Halls. Any assassin that even accepts a proposition to do anything to you is punished by death. With an assassin as a bodyguard, someone would have to be crazy to attack you now, because it would bring the wrath of the entire Order Hall against them."

"I think I just want to go home. If Yow wants me to do more deliveries after tonight, he can just stick them up his nose," said Jayde.

They walked back toward the clinic. Slicy continued along with them. At first Jayde assumed he just wanted to make sure they made it out of the Thieves' District without any difficulty. Then she assumed he wanted to make sure she made it back to the Conjurers' Order Hall. However, he continued with them past the Order Hall as well.

"What are you doing?" she asked Slicy.

"Well, in my brain, I'm yodeling at an extremely fast tempo, but that's probably not what you meant," he said.

"Why are you following me?"

"I thought Sir Fleas-a-Lot made it clear earlier. You have achieved Unkillable status. That means that you can have an assassin bodyguard whenever you are in danger, and, believe me, you *are* in danger. When the other Unkillables reached this status, they found it amusing that they could appoint a bodyguard. But in your case I think this job might require a more personal touch," said Slicy.

Yow Li's voice came out of Brutus. "Slicy, you've worked your way to the top of the assassins' ladder. If you get too involved, won't this upset your standings?"

"Yow? How long have you been spying on me?" asked Slicy with a smile.

"Ever since your first visit from Zantia. You know that," said Yow through Brutus.

"Ooh, point for the crotchety old man. I've taken a liking to your little protégé. Maybe I just want to see her make another giant potato." The fool laughed.

"You used to be much better at lying, Slicy. Care to try your answer again?"

Slicy walked in silence for a bit. He slowed and walked next to Brutus. He pulled out two daggers, one blue and one red, and struck them together. He appeared blurry for a second and then disappeared completely.

Jayde heard his voice whispering to Brutus, "There's more to your friend Jayde than Conjuring skills. We'll talk about this later, Yow. I don't like talking about this on the street," said Slicy.

"Are you using some of your Talents that the Dark King taught you?" Brutus growled.

"She sticks out. If I recognize it, then I'm surprised a chaos agent hasn't," Slicy said.

"I released a lock on her Talent a while back. No one could possibly have known before then. We'll talk more about this later," Yow said through Brutus.

The rest continued their walk in silence for a short time. Slicy reappeared after a minute, yet still seemed excessively cautious. His casual talk about assassinations did not worry Jayde. His walking quietly did.

Slicy twisted quickly and whipped a knife down a side street.

"Stay here, Jayde. Normal-size time, Brutus," said Slicy.

The familiar nodded, and he grew to the size of a horse, fur bristling. He sniffed the air and paced around the rest of the group, who all stood clueless as to what was going on. Marl pulled Jayde close.

Slicy darted into the alley. His knife lay buried to the hilt in a board. The alley was empty.

He walked out, slipping the knife into one of the many pockets hidden in his outfit.

"Not sure what but something is following us. I could have sworn that blade went right through it, whatever it was. You catching any scent?" he asked.

"Nothing," Brutus answered.

"What was that all about?" asked Jayde.

"Not sure. Hopefully nothing. We should just keep moving."

They continued their trek back toward the clinic.

On the rooftop a black cat sat, calmly licking its paws. It stopped a second, then continued its routine of grooming.

"I thought you said that you could never be seen when you didn't *want* to be seen," said a haggard old woman.

"That patchy white-faced one has more skill than most I meet," answered the cat.

"Did you find out anything?" Mrs. Crass asked the black cat.

"A little. He cloaked himself before getting into anything too juicy, but that in and of itself tells me something is going on, something your master certainly would not like. Perhaps it's time for your last request?" asked the cat.

"Not until we know for sure, but we need to put an end to this before it gets out of hand. If any of them has even the potential of becoming a threat to the Dark King, they need to die," said Mrs. Crass.

The bozrac purred in agreement.

Chapter 33: Reunions

Sarah pointed toward where the pull seemed the greatest. She had been pacing rapidly for the last half hour. The direction did not change much, but she could feel the pull strengthening. She thought she could no longer bear it.

Cameron had closed the clinic. It had taken a while to get the remaining patients out, but using his Talent allowed him to quickly heal his patients. Eventually only Marie, Cameron, Sarah, Kevin, Mullet, Tali, John, and Lucy remained.

Time passed slowly for Sarah. She tried to leave the clinic to meet the pull. Cameron and Mullet kept her inside.

"I have a feeling this night is about to get interesting," said Cameron.

"It's driving me crazy! I'm sure it's getting closer. *Gah*! Just let me go out there," said Sarah.

"Dr. Cameron knows what he's doing. I reckon I trust him on this issue. You said you wanted to give him a chance, so give him one," said Kevin.

The three pixies amused themselves by playing a game. They sat in a circle and spoke rapidly in Pixish. Periodically one would throw a small glowing circle at another, which zapped the other; then they would all laugh, and they would continue.

The bell at the front door rang, and Sarah let out a yelp in surprise. She sprang to her feet, but Cameron and Mullet helped her back to her chair.

"Just relax. We don't know what will happen, if this is the first Chosen," said Kevin.

Sarah grumbled but sat down, while the door opened, and a few people—as well as a rock troll and a gigantic dog—walked into the room.

"Indeed, you do deserve some enlightenment, Jayde. Each and every time your life is in danger, would you like me to first have a discussion with you? There are times for discussions, and there are times for actions. I'm not very good at debating an arrow out of the sky. 'Excuse me, Mr. Arrow. Could you please not skewer my friend Jayde? She's ever so nice. ....' Oopsies, too late. Jayde splatter everywhere!"

"Well, no. But I don't like not knowing why you hurl a blade into some post," said Jayde.

"Welcome home, Jayde," said Cameron.

Jayde looked up and saw Cameron. His smile melted. He faced Slicy, poised to attack.

A pair of long daggers appeared in Slicy's hands, each of which gave off a faint blue glow. Cameron stood his ground, but the conversations of the room had stopped. The mood had changed from lighthearted to deadly in a heartbeat.

Brutus slowly, but deliberately, walked between the two, though neither Slicy nor Cameron gave any ground. Yow spoke through his familiar.

"I sense a bit of bad blood in the air here. How about you all put down your weapons, and we try to discuss this like civilized people. Nobody wants to do anything they might regret."

"Sure. That sounds like a realistic option," said Cameron. No one saw him draw them, but a pair of black swords had appeared in his hands. "Please, how rude of me to be worried when King Zolf's assassin strolls into my clinic. I must be mad to think that one of the deadliest creatures in the world is a cause for alarm!"

Cameron's incisors had already grown, and a faint red nimbus surrounded his body.

"Cameron, he's okay!" shouted Jayde.

"Jayde, stay out of this. I don't know what he said to you, but I would not believe a word from this traitor," said Cameron. His voice sounded lower, darker, and more ominous.

"You're the reason I've been on the run. They exiled me after you did it. You killed hundreds, thousands! It was mass genocide!" Cameron said.

Both Cameron and Slicy had begun to circle each other at a distance, while the giant dog remained between them, but they stared at one another as if Brutus was not even there.

"Cameron, please, *please* listen," said Slicy. His normally light and jovial voice was now soft. "I tried for months to contact you. You don't understand what happened. The king was already going to do it. I have played it out in my mind a thousand times."

"Spare me your reminiscing, traitor," spat Cameron.

"It wasn't my fault. How was I to know the king's plans?" said Slicy.

"Which king? The one you work for or the one you killed?"

"I was, key word, *was*, Zolf's fool. I tried to get word to you, which nearly cost me my life! Betraying the Dark King isn't done easily by the way! Your Majesty, do you think I really wanted to kill like that? Do you think I wanted to throw away our friendship?" said Slicy.

"I don't know what you intended. I just know what happened," said Cameron.

"No, you don't! Your Majesty, please, just hear me out," said Slicy.

Sarah, who had been sitting in the chair behind them, stood up. Her sweat-covered face showed pure exasperation. She screamed in frustration and launched herself at Jayde. Jayde screamed as the young woman charged at her.

"No! Don't touch her!" screamed Cameron. But it was too late. She reached Jayde and picked her up in a giant bear hug.

"Finally!" said Sarah.

As she embraced the young woman, a deafening ring sounded out. A single pure note echoed through their bodies like a shock wave. An explosion of energy shot out in all directions from Sarah and Jayde, knocking everyone to the ground.

"Oh, no," said Slicy and Cameron together, their intonation the exact same.

"We have to get out of here," said Slicy.

"Why?" said Sarah.

"What's going on?" asked Kevin.

"The Hunter just found the first Chosen," said Slicy. "Every chaos agent within a hundred leagues just heard that bell as clearly as we did, and they know what it means."

"Oh, that's great. Can someone tell *me* what it means?" asked Jayde.

"It means our trip to Grandeur has been cut short," said Marie, who had already grabbed random vials and powders from the cabinets. "It would be ever so nice, Cam, if we could stay in one place at least long enough to unpack."

"We don't have time to pack. We have to get out of here," said Slicy.

"*We?* There's no 'we,' Slicy. You can stay here and greet your buddies when they arrive, but there's no chance you are coming with us. Give my regards to the Dark King when you see him," said Cameron.

"I told you. He wants me dead more than anyone. I'm literally at the top of Zantia's hit list. I heard the bell. Don't you think, if I worked for him, I would have just killed the Hunter instantly? Your Majesty, I arranged to add Jayde to the Unkillable list!" said Slicy.

"Slicy, if you don't want to die, stay here. This is your only warning. Out of respect for whatever friendship we may have had, I will give you that. The next time I see you, I will assume you work for the Dark King and act appropriately," said Cameron.

"If chaos agents are in transit, we have to go," said Kevin.

"Walk quickly, but don't run. Stay close, and don't wander," said Cameron.

The group left the clinic. Marie muttered about all the good medicine they had been forced to leave behind. She had packed a small satchel of medicine which seemed to be able to hold much more than its size.

Sarah and Jayde remained wide eyed about everything going on.

"What did you just do to me?" asked Jayde.

"You're the second Chosen," Sarah said.

"Great. What does that mean?"

"I'm still learning myself," said Sarah.

Jayde and Sarah kept talking, asking a continuous stream of questions until Cameron gave them a look. The group walked in silence from that point on.

Cameron and Kevin took the front, while Marie and Mullet took the back. Brutus and Marl took the middle, completing the circle around Jayde and Sarah. The pixies flew above, periodically darting ahead to scout.

Cameron stopped long enough to look back to be sure Slicy was not following. The group moved quickly through the streets. The clinic was located in the middle of the city, which meant they still had leagues to walk to get out.

The group continued quietly for thirty minutes, pausing occasionally. Each time they stopped, the pixies dispersed in three directions and zipped back. Brutus sniffed the air, and Cameron shimmered briefly with a dim blue light. No one detected anything unusual, and they continued their journey. It took over two hours, and the city remained eerily quiet, but nothing stopped the group's progress.

They made it to the walls, though all could sense the apprehension of the group. Brutus growled, then said, "Cameron, something smells wrong," he whispered.

"Could you be a little more specific?" Cameron whispered back.

They had arrived at the edge of the city. The large city walls loomed nearby.

"I'm not sure. It's all over the place, not just one direction," the giant dog said.

"Check it out," Cameron said to the pixies.

"On it," said Tali, and she disappeared in a flash, followed by John and Lucy.

The group waited in silence.

"Sarah, come here a minute," said Cameron.

The young woman came to his side.

"How do you feel?" he asked.

"So much better," she said.

"I figured as much. You are the one who can tell where the next in the group might be. I want you to close your eyes and see if you can feel that pull again, like you did with Jayde. It'll likely be a faint pull, but see what you can find."

"I'll try," she said. She closed her eyes. After just a few seconds she opened them again.

"I can feel it. Wow, that's odd. It's the same pull but really faint. It's that way," she said, pointing. "And it's really far away. I would guess maybe a thousand leagues, maybe more. I don't know how I know that, but that just feels right," said Sarah.

"Good work," said Cameron. His voice, however, sounded as if he disliked the direction she had chosen.

The pixies still had not returned.

Brutus's fur slowly raised on the back of his neck. "Something's coming. Something from inside the city," said the dog.

"Time to go," said Kevin, and the group continued the last bit through the gates and out of the city.

"No guards," said Marie in a way which implied she did not think this was a coincidence.

The group continued into the night. Outside the city the evening seemed much darker and colder than expected. John was the first pixie to return.

"They are coming from all sides! Wivari, hundreds of them, along with something else. They're coming exceedingly rapidly!" shouted the pixie.

"We'd be better off in the city against those monsters," said Cameron.

As if in response to this statement, the city gate's crashed closed behind them, locking them out.

"We walked into that trap like a bunch of empty-brained farm boys," said Kevin. "What's the plan, Mully?" Kevin asked.

Mullet seemed lost in thought for just a few seconds.

"Three groups. Marie and Marl take left. Paladins take right. They'll have us pinned against the wall, but that will prevent being flanked. The dog and the vampire guard the girls, if they break through.

Cameron's eyes widened at being referred to as "the vampire."

"Be vocal. If you tire, pull back and let someone replace you," said Mullet. "Who made him boss?" said Jayde.

"He may seem like a giant brute, but don't doubt him as a tactician," said Kevin.

Mullet had already pulled out an enormous mace covered with long metal spikes.

Cameron nodded to the giant man's plan, and the others had already positioned themselves.

"Right," said Kevin. "Like Mully said, this'll be chaos, so stay vocal. If you need help, let others know. If you get tired, pull back and let one of the two in the rear take your spot. Don't fight till you're exhausted and useless," said Kevin.

Seconds later Lucy flew back to the group, yelling that the wivari were coming. Marie and Marl spread out a short distance, while Mullet and Kevin did the same. The sound of sinister laughter could be heard.

The first wivari came out of the thick forest that bordered the road to Grandeur. It stopped and looked at the band in front of it. The mouth split the face of the beast in half down the middle, as a hollow laughter poured out. Several rows of teeth glistened in the moonlight, but it did not charge. It looked toward what at first appeared to be nothing but blackness, but then the faintest outline of a black cat could be seen. More wivari had now joined the first, and they all waited in a line.

A high-pitched voice came from the darkness. "Kill them all but the Hunter."

The wivari charged in a mindless fury. The first hound met the end of Mullet's mace. Even though it came at a dead sprint, the blow knocked it backward into a tree with a bone-crunching snap.

Marl and Marie worked seamlessly together. Marie had darted ahead of the troll and met the onslaught of the creatures alone. Marie danced between the creatures in front of Marl. Many ran past her without stopping, but most snapped at her, wanting to rip her to pieces. She avoided the attacks by inches, each time landing a blow on the creature. She appeared to be punching and kicking the creatures with minute blows; however, each creature that passed her limped and yelped in pain, which made it an easy target for the devastating blows from the troll. The rock troll used his long club and hammered the wolflike creatures. By dazing creatures as they passed her, Marie made them easy targets for the blows from the massive troll.

Wivari poured out of the forest. Kevin and Mullet worked efficiently against the swarm to the north. Kevin's sword flashed in the night, severing limbs and heads. Mullet had replaced his mace with an ax and hacked through creature after creature.

Cameron waited by Jayde and Sarah patiently, trusting the skills of his group, his black swords drawn. A few wivari had made it past the foursome, which he dispatched easily. Brutus growled that he should leave some for him as well, to which Cameron said he hoped he would not have to.

Still more creatures poured from the woods. The bloody carnage of the onslaught continued to pile up, as Marie and Marl took the brunt of the onslaught. Despite their strategy now being obvious, the wivari were slow learners, and Marie's "daze and pound" tactic continued to be effective. Bodies of dead wivari covered the ground.

Kevin and Mullet had been pulled farther and farther away from Marl and Marie as the wivari spread out from the woods. Cameron moved Jayde and Sarah farther away from the city gates in an attempt to stay between the four fighters.

"Me no can keep dis up for long!" yelled Marl through the noise of the battle.

Kevin chanced a glance, while darting under one of the creatures and smoothly sliding his sword through its center.

"Troll, fall back and guard the girls. Cameron can give you a break. Marie, you'll have to go for killing blows till they switch!" boomed Mullet.

"Got it. Here comes the time to switch!" yelled Marie. She pulled out two vials from her cloak and slammed them into the ground, while at the same time bouncing backward from her place at the front of the onslaught. The vials released smoke for a few seconds, then exploded, sending wivari flying. This gave Marl time to spring back to Jayde and Sarah. Cameron appeared at Marie's side.

Cameron noticed she had several large lacerations on her arms and one long one on her leg. Punching anything with that many teeth could not be done without consequences.

Jayde had seen Cameron move quickly before, but she had difficulty following his movements now. In the moonlight she watched as his black blades disappeared into one wivari only to reappear out the side of another. For a short time not a creature got past him as he single-handedly annihilated the creatures. He slowly worked his way back to Marie's side, and they worked as a team. Again and again, wave after wave of the twisted creatures charged.

Marie began to tire and yelled out to Kevin and Mullet. Communication was difficult to hear with the wivari's' continuous barking laughter. The twosome charged to the front and assisted. Slowly the four were pushed back by the seemingly endless beasts. Brutus and Marl had spread out from Sarah and Jayde, as more and more wivari slipped past the first line of defense. The enormous dog bounded to the side of a wivari and bit down on its neck with a crunch. Brutus then whipped his head to the side, and the body of the creature went flying.

"We have to do something!" yelled Tali to the other pixies. She then flew to the front of the battle by Mullet. She attacked a wivari with a tiny pin sword, but the creature just ignored her and kept on charging.

Mullet, however, held his blows, trying not to strike the pixie, and three creatures pounced on him in a flash. They tore at his side and his arms. Kevin darted to his side and slew the creatures, but Mullet's arm was a mangled mess. He stood, but his left arm flopped to his side, oozing blood.

"Tali, go back!" said Mullet.

"Sorry!" she said and sped back to the group.

Mullet replaced the two-handed ax with the mace he had used previously.

"You need a machete, my friend," said Kevin.

Mullet grunted in agreement, but in the middle of a battle, a weapons seller is rarely found.

"Ask Jayde," said Cameron.

Mullet looked at him with a raised eyebrow but did not argue, and he ran off to Jayde's side.

A sharp pop was heard, and he rejoined them with a wicked-looking machete in his hand, larger than normal but perfectly sized for him.

"Nice," said the giant.

The onslaught of wivari stopped as suddenly as it had started.

Marie and Mullet looked the worst, both openly bleeding, though the entire group showed signs of exhaustion. Brutus padded over to the foursome, tail wagging. Marl lumbered over as well. Kevin and Mullet walked toward the forest to be sure no more waited in hiding. The pixies joined them to scout from the sky.

Sarah and Jayde stayed at the wall, trying to figure out exactly what had happened. They had not conversed much since leaving the clinic. For some reason the heat of a battle with twisted snarling beasts did not seem the appropriate place for casual talk. Relief flooded them as the battle finally seemed to be won.

"That was a cool trick, making the machete," said Sarah.

"Thanks. I'm training to be a conjurer, but I guess that'll be put on hold for a while."

"Meow," said Fang.

"This is Fang," Jayde said with a grin. "She's my cat, sort of. Mr. Li gave her to me to practice my Conjuring, but, after a while, Fang liked being with me more than him. So he let me have her, even though he conjured her in the first place. Want to see a trick?"

"Sure," said Sarah, smiling along with the girl.

Jayde looked down at Fang and concentrated. The cat grew from the size of Jayde's thumb to a large puma with pointy tufts of hairs coming from its ears. Its fur changed from striped gray to a glistening white. Fang seemed unperturbed by all this and continued to clean herself, happy to be out of Jayde's pocket for the time being.

"This is Sarah, Fang," said Jayde.

The cat looked up, seemingly surprised to see a new person in front of her. She took a few steps forward and nuzzled against Sarah, while purring.

"Affectionate, isn't she?" Sarah said.

The cat's ears perked up, and she turned toward the city gate and hissed. The two women looked in that direction.

A humanoid creature moved toward them from the city gate. Neither Jayde nor Sarah made a noise. Jayde told her brain to scream, but she seemed paralyzed, as she continued to stare at the black-cloaked creature floating toward them.

Fang hissed again, but the two women remained transfixed. The cat jumped into Jayde's chest, which knocked her down. She shook her head and then screamed.

Marie, Brutus, Cameron, and Marl looked back.

"A shayde!" screamed Marie, who took off running, followed by the others, but they were over a hundred paces away. The creature was too close to the young women. They continued to run forward, but the shayde already had a curved scimitar drawn. Jayde's friends would be too late. The two girls stared helplessly at the creature, as it closed the distance. The creature pointed at the cat, and it was thrown backward, leaving nothing between them. The shayde floated toward them, its blade already raised to strike.

Time slowed for Jayde. She could see the hideous creature closing in, but she could not move. Fear paralyzed her, and she could feel a tear run down her cheek. She knew she was about to die but could not even turn her head as it approached. The creature was no more than five feet away.

Suddenly from the center of the creature's chest appeared a blade. The creature stopped its slow movement forward. Jayde could only watch, transfixed. The creature slowly turned to the side. The blade protruding from its chest was covered with a thick black sap. Under the sap, etched in the blade, she could see the outline of a smiling court jester. The creature collapsed.

Jayde inhaled for the first time in over a minute.

"Slicy!" Jayde yelled and ran to the man behind the now dead shayde. She wrapped her arms around him in a big hug, which he accepted with a grimace of pain. Only after she released him did she realize that he dripped blood.

"You're hurt!" said Jayde.

Slicy groaned and slumped to the ground. "I've felt better."

"What are *you* doing here?" said Cameron.

"Saving my life, that's what," Jayde said. "I don't know what happened in the past, but I do know he just saved my life, Cameron. If not for him, I would be dead. Dead!"

Cameron looked at the shayde, then at Slicy, then at the shayde again.

"What's your game, Slicy?" asked Cameron.

"I like cards, hi-lo, and the occasional game of me versus twenty wivari. I'll try just about anything once," he said. He coughed a few times and spit out a bloody clot.

"Cameron, please," said Jayde.

Cameron glared at the bleeding man. Slicy had slumped to the ground, but, despite his wounds, he released a wheezy chuckle. "Have I ever mentioned how much I despise shaydes? I always thought they were a rarity, but they seem to be popping up everywhere nowadays."

"All right, Slicy, it's time for you to leave. You may have helped Jayde here, but I still don't trust you."

Someone spoke from the woods.

"Yes, Slicy, I am sure the king would love to hear exactly why you decided to betray him," said the man. The group collectively turned toward the voice. Slicy was the first to respond.

"Blubbo?" said Slicy.

"I told you never to call me that!" yelled the man.

"Thaddeus? Thaddeus Gumble, is that you?" said Sarah.

Thaddeus looked at Sarah. "Ah, my servant, care to join me for another trip?"

Sarah just looked at him, shocked to see him standing in the woods. Five wivari stood by his side, and two shaydes floated eerily beside him.

"What happened to you?" Sarah asked.

"After you somehow got away from the initial wivari attack, I had to figure out another way to take you down. But the shayde you met did not tolerate your escape very well. How you knew the interaction between pixie and shayde magic, well, I think you just got lucky," said Thaddeus.

"You work with that thing?" Sarah said, pointing at the shayde.

"I work for the king. Your little disappearing act threw me off, but I see someone finally broke down the walls in your mind. I suspected from the start you had potential, though I never fathomed you to be the next Hunter," he said.

"In case you missed what happened, we just slaughtered your little puppy army. It'll take more than five goober-dogs and two floaters to take us down," said Slicy.

"Always so cocky, despite winning by sheer luck," said Thaddeus, staring daggers at Slicy. The fat man then looked over at Jayde.

"You're also one hard brat to kill. When I made my trip to Haynis, that rancid hole you call home, I expected to find my assassins with one dead little girl. Instead, I find out some stupid vampire saved her. Apparently she made some friends and got some protection, since the second set of assassins also failed on your trip to Grandeur," he said.

"You? You're the fat man with the firefoot?" asked Jayde. He ignored her question.

"Unfortunately I was too late in realizing your true importance. But, with my new friends, I can clean up the mistake," said Thaddeus.

"Wow, fat, delusional, and arrogant—a triple threat," said Slicy.

Thaddeus continued. "Granted I would have preferred to capture the Hunter and leave the rest of you mangled in a bloody mess, but, no matter how it is done, killing off a Chosen will secure a reward with the king," said Thaddeus.

"How much is a shallow worthless soul going for these days, Blubbo?" asked Slicy.

"Slicy, that mouth of yours will get you killed one day," he said. He then looked into the shadows. "Kill the girl."

The wivari charged, while barking their horrible laughter. Kevin's blade destroyed one of them, while Cameron split two before they could even get to a full run. Marie kicked one under the chin hard enough to launch it into the air. While coming down, she kicked it again with a brutal roundhouse kick that sent it spiraling into the forest. The last wivari ran directly at Mullet. The giant man casually raised his machete and, with a single stroke, cut the creature in two.

"That's it?" Slicy said. But when he looked, Gumble was gone.

"No. That is not it," a new voice hissed from the shadows. "You humans always rush to congratulate yourselves."

Everyone looked toward the edge of the forest. A silhouette materialized from the blackness, revealing a small cat.

Slicy cursed and spat out another bloody clot, while he forced himself to his feet. Cameron and Marie walked between the creature and where Jayde and Sarah stood next to the city wall. Kevin and Mullet quickly flanked them. The cat sat calmly and licked its paws.

"We be scared of small cat?" said Marl.

"That's no cat. That's a bozrac," said Slicy. "It is a demon from the Abyss. They are cruel, deadly, and hungry. The main problem is that they can't be killed."

"Great. What's the good news?" asked Marie.

"Who said there was good news?" said Slicy.

"Any ideas, Cameron?" she asked.

"Normally I'd say run, but none of us are in any condition to get far, and, if what Slicy says is true, I don't think it would matter much anyway," he said.

Mullet and Kevin slowly advanced toward the cat, which seemed either to not notice or not care about them.

"Nothing can kill it?" asked Marie.

"Nothing but another bozrac," said Slicy. "You wouldn't happen to have one on you, do you?"

Mullet and Kevin continued their slow advance.

The cat looked up and smiled a tooth-filled grin.

A second voice, that of an aged woman, came from the shadows. "Stop playing and finish them."

The black cat sneered at the shadows. It looked at Mullet and pounced. The giant man reacted instinctively with a swing of his machete. His aim seemed true, but somehow it passed through the creature. The creature passed through his arm, and Mullet collapsed to the ground. The bozrac bounced to the side and pounced at Kevin.

Kevin dodged the attack and struck before it landed on the ground. His swords flashed in the moonlight, but the cat danced through the blades unfazed. The blade passed through the cat. Yet the creature sprung at Kevin and went through his chest. Kevin screamed, and a stream of white light followed the cat as it appeared from the other side from his body. Kevin gasped for air for a few seconds, then was still. The cat casually walked toward Sarah and Jayde.

"Don't fill up on the appetizers. You need enough strength to actually *kill* the girl," said the voice from the shadows.

The cat continued to walk toward Jayde. Marl walked toward the cat.

"Marl, stop!" yelled Jayde.

"Dat t'ing want to kill you, Jayde!" he yelled.

"Marl, please listen to me. Just get out of its way," she said. The rock troll ignored her. Cameron and Marie joined the troll. Brutus lumbered up to their side as well.

Jayde watched as the small cat slowly strolled toward the foursome. The cat crept deliberately to the group. Jayde racked her brain for an answer. She looked around and saw Slicy catch her eye. He winked at her, as he slowly caught up with the other four. Mullet made it back to his knees, but whatever the cat had done to him had sapped him of all his energy. Kevin remained on the ground.

Then she had an idea.

She hoped Cameron would not be too mad. Jayde cleared her mind and thought about the giant potato again. Jayde picked up a large stone and hurled it over the group. Her thoughts were clear. She concentrated. The picture in her mind had no flaws. She made it even bigger than before and released her energy.

Jayde had expected the familiar popping noise. This time, a thunderous boom accompanied the appearance of the gigantic spud. The group did not have time to move before it completely covered them. The cat jumped back, surprised for the first time. Jayde screamed at the cat.

"You're after me, right? You stupid cat, you think that we walked into a trap? Don't you know that you're the one walking into our trap!" said Jayde. She then took off running.

Jayde sprinted as fast as she could, leaving Sarah by the wall and the rest of the party behind. The bozrac recovered quickly from the appearance of the giant potato and instantly gave chase. Its earlier casual approach had disappeared, while it sprinted after the girl. Despite being the size of a small cat, it quickly closed the distance. This young girl was the only obstacle in the way of his freedom from the bond to that horrid Mrs. Crass.

Jayde sprinted away from the group. The bozrac chased, closing the gap. Jayde chanced a look back and saw the creature gaining on her. She could see Mullet as nothing more than a large mound in the distance. The even larger mound of the potato she had conjured was in pieces, as the foursome underneath quickly forced their way out. However, by the time they were out, this would all be over, one way or another.

Chapter 34: Running Away

Jayde sprinted across the flats just outside the city of Grandeur. Many months earlier she had jumped across rooftops, running for her life. At that time three trained assassins had pursued her, to kill her because a fat man had suspected she might have potential. If that man had known how much potential she really had, he would not have sent three assassins; he would have sent an army. Jayde had spent her life thinking she was to remain a street urchin, just scraping by. Her new friends had given her insight that perhaps she had more to offer.

She chanced a glance backward to see the bozrac had narrowed the gap to less than fifty feet and continued to close. Jayde stopped and turned to face the creature. Her sudden movement caused the bozrac to slow its approach.

"Didn't I tell you that you were walking into a trap?" Jayde asked.

"Oh, do your worst, little girl. The other fools may manage to survive, but your time is up."

The creature ran straight at Jayde. It smiled in anticipation of the kill. Jayde stood her ground as it closed the distance. She thought of Slicy. The time for words had ended; only actions remained.

The bozrac pounced straight toward Jayde's chest. In that moment time slowed. Jayde lifted her hands. She did this not to protect herself but to bring up her weapon.

The bozrac had killed hundreds in its time. It saw its prey raise her hands to defend herself, but it could slide through physical defenses easily. The taunts from this creature meant nothing. The defense of the creature meant nothing. No trap could stop a bozrac. The white-faced man had stated truly: only a bozrac could stop a bozrac. It pounced, and, in midair, it realized that, this time, its prey actually had a trap ready.

In Jayde's hands she held her tiny weapon. Instantly Fang, the tiny familiar, expanded into a pure-white bozrac. The previous boom from the conjured potato was nothing compared to the deafening explosion of the conjured bozrac. While the creature continued its path toward Jayde's chest, Fang entered the black bozrac's body first. Jayde jumped, as the creature continued, but she could not move in time.

It plunged into Jayde's chest. Instantly Jayde could not breathe. She felt like an icy fist had grabbed her heart. Pain shot through her whole body. Jayde yelled out, twisted, and turned, and rolled on the ground, but the pain continued. She could not breathe. She had no doubt. Her plan had failed; she was going to die. No matter how hard she tried, she could not take in a breath of air. Her body hungered for a single breath that she could not take. Her body vibrated with pain.

After ten seconds Jayde felt like a weight within her had been lifted. Jayde gasped several deep breaths. Just the simple act of breathing had never felt so good. Her body still ached, but the intense pain eventually lifted. Her vision slowly cleared. She lay on her side and opened her eyes.

A white bozrac sat in front of her, cleaning its paws.

"Fang?" asked Jayde between gasps of air. The white cat watched her, purring.

"Who else?" it said.

Jayde groaned; her body ached everywhere.

"You can talk," she choked out between breaths. Then Jayde groaned and realized that her chest still hurt. "What happened to the bozrac?"

"Dead," said Fang.

Jayde turned and saw a mass of rumpled black fur.

The rest of the group quickly caught up and surrounded her. Marl cried openly at his failure yet again to protect his friend. Cameron took a medical approach, checking her out from head to toe. He also used his Talent to scan her from the inside out, but, other than a few scrapes, Jayde had no injuries.

"I'm okay, Cameron, really," Jayde said, followed by a groan she couldn't muffle, all while still on the ground.

"But why, Jayde? Why did you do it?" he asked.

"Well, I didn't have time to do anything else. That thing was after me—not you, not Marl—*me*. I wasn't going to let anyone else get hurt over me. There was nothing anyone else could do. You said it yourself. You didn't know how to stop that thing. Slicy was the one who gave me the idea," said Jayde.

"Whoa, whoa, whoa!" said Slicy. "I didn't say go potato crazy and then run off to fight a bozrac by yourself. I knew you were nuts but not insane."

"How did you know it would work?" asked Marie.

"I didn't," said Jayde.

"It should not have worked actually," said a newcomer. The voice came from Brutus, but it was Yow, the Conjuring master, speaking. "All her previous transformations had been just in shape or color. This time she conjured for real. She actually changed Fang into a real bozrac."

"Conjuring a familiar is one thing. Making familiars is the second-highest level of Conjuring possible. The only higher form is to actually give a familiar a life of its own. It seems that Jayde managed to do that, amid the chaos of the moment no less," said Yow.

"Well, at least she chose a form in which I can speak," said Fang. The cat looked over its pure white fur. "I think she did a fantastic job, though I will miss being changed into a panther to scare Cameron. I truly enjoyed that."

"Hilarious," said Cameron.

"Kevin," said Mullet.

They all looked back to see his lanky form still on the ground.

The group ran back. Cameron arrived first. He shook his head. Kevin was dead.

"No. It can't be," cried Sarah.

"He's dead, Sarah, and, though I am truly, *truly* sorry, we have to go. Now," said Cameron.

Mullet lumbered over to Cameron's side. He still appeared quite pale from his interaction with the bozrac. He remained silent for a few moments, kneeling by Kevin's still form. Cameron kept his eyes closed, laying his hands on the man and using his Talent to feel any spark of life.

"I'm sorry," Cameron said, taking a deep breath. He scanned the group, looking at each individual. Slowly he shook his head. The group stood in silence for a minute for their fallen friend.

"I know we'd all love to relax after our ordeal, but more trouble will be coming soon. We have to go," said Slicy.

"*We?*" said Cameron. "I already told you. You are not part of the 'we,' Slicy."

"Cameron?" said Jayde.

"What?"

"He has to come with us. I don't know how to explain it. I don't know what past you two have had, but he saved my life, more than once today. You're the leader of this group, but he *has* to come," said Jayde.

Cameron sighed. He looked over the members one at a time. All eyes were on him, waiting for him to lead.

"If I'm in charge, then my word is final. I need not only your respect but your loyalty. If I say something, you must obey, even if you disagree with it. I've made some mistakes in the past. Maybe this is my chance to make up for them. But all of you"—he looked at Slicy—"ALL of you must respect what I say as a command. Can you … will you all do this?"

He looked around the group. Each person nodded when Cameron looked him or her in the eye. Each of the pixies did the same, as well as the familiar Brutus. Cameron stared at Fang for over a minute.

"I realize free will is new to you, Fang. But, if you are to be part of this group, you also must agree," he said.

The cat looked up at Jayde miserably. "Do you know what you are asking of me, Cameron? Do you really know?" Fang asked.

"A bozrac's oath is bound by its life," said Slicy. "Nearly any creature can break its oath, but a bozrac cannot or it dies. You're asking Fang to go from a creature that has not only just gained life but also freedom and to return to a life of servitude," said Slicy.

"I'm sorry to do this to you, but this is the only way. Will you follow me?" Cameron asked again.

The bozrac looked again at Jayde. "This is the only way I can stay with Jayde?" Fang asked.

"It is," Cameron answered.

"Then I agree," said the bozrac.

Slicy spoke up. "Your Majesty, may I make a suggestion?"

Cameron glared at Slicy but let him continue.

"Being a creature of the Abyss, a bozrac is part demon. Now I know we all just love our cute little white kitty here, but she has the potential for disaster. Might I suggest that part of her oath be that she never kills? One kill, a single taste of a human soul, would be enough to corrupt her. After that first taste, I doubt any of us would be able to stop her," said Slicy.

Cameron again looked at Fang.

"I give you my oath, I will not kill anything or anyone … without permission," said the cat.

"Fine. First order of business is you, Slicy," Cameron said.

"Cameron," said Jayde. He silenced her with a look.

"Against my better judgment, a *Chosen* has demanded you stay in the group. We have a long ways to go. With a group this size it may take months to get to our next location. You tell us everything about you, from the beginning. You will leave nothing out. After they learn everything, and I mean *everything* about you, we can all decide if we want to keep you as part of the group or not," said Cameron.

"Everything?" Slicy asked.

"From the beginning," said Cameron.

"Your Majesty? Can I leave out my little run-in with the mermaids—"

"Everything pertinent, Slicy. From the beginning," said Cameron.

"Well, if this is the only way I can be part of this little suicidal adventure, so be it," said Slicy.

"Slicy, why do you keep calling Cameron, 'Your Majesty'?" asked Jayde.

Slicy looked down at her, then up at Cameron.

"You didn't tell them? They don't know?" he asked.

"No," said Cameron. "Now let's collect what we need. We have a long trip ahead."

"None of them know?" asked Slicy again. He seemed really amazed by this.

"Include it in your story, Slicy. Now let's get going," said Cameron.

"Where are we going, Cam?" Marie asked.

"Verrara," said Cameron.

Gasps came from the group, but no one disagreed with the choice. Tali mentioned something about changing her vote for the leader.

"Believe me. This would not be my first choice either. That is where Sarah feels the pull for the next member of the group, so that is where we go," he said.

"Um, Cameron, isn't that where the vampires live?" Sarah asked.

Cameron gazed toward the horizon, lost in thought for a second. "Yes."

"That's what I thought," she said.

Chapter 35: Slicy's Tale

Three hours later, after hastily assembling supplies, the group began their journey along the High Road out of Grandeur. A physician by the name of Cameron led the group. Marie, his assistant, who happened to be a trained warrior, a war sage, rode next to him on her horse. A young girl named Jayde rode a horse for the first time. Marl, a rock troll who seemed happy to have a friend, ran alongside her. Inside Jayde's saddlebag, a small white cat that could pass through solid objects groomed itself.

An enormous giant named Mullet rode a monstrous warhorse. His head hung low as he rode, for his closest friend had just been killed. On his shoulder, Tali the pixie, attempted in vain to lighten his spirits. The man had not cried in two decades, but tears poured from his eyes.

In the middle of this group rode a man with a white face bearing a wicked scar, named Slicy. A young woman, Sarah, rode with John and Lucy, two small pixies, flying nearby, also mourning the loss of their friend Kevin.

As they rode away from the city, a monstrous dog watched them leave. An old man leaned against the dog, as the group disappeared on the horizon.

The group traveled in silence the first day. Mullet's mood had slowly infused the group.

The next day the group plodded at a steady pace, passing multiple groups approaching the enormous city of Grandeur. It took quite some time, but eventually Cameron's group had no one around them but themselves.

"Well, Slicy?" said Cameron.

"I suppose it's time," he said.

"My story is one of darkness. This is a fool's tale, in more than one sense of the word. But I can't start off there. I'll let you make your own judgment. All I ask is that you try to put yourself in my situation. What would you have done? What would you do when faced with the same situations?" said Slicy.

"I was born in the Dark Kingdom of Zantia, in the city of Munk," Slicy began.

This ends Book 1 of the Jayded series.

Acknowledgments:

Thank you to my beloved wife. Thank you even for the "you gotta change this, you totally stole this from..." It was occasionally painful, but you made the book infinitely better, thank you, I love you always.

Thank you to my mom for, well, everything.

Thank you to my dad, for being unwaveringly encouraging and positive, and actually being the first one to read the book despite not being the first one with a copy.

Thank you to my cover designer Lindsay Wakefield. Thank you for all the tweaks and changes and for creating such a beautiful cover!

Thank you to Quiana for giving me a motivational kick in the behind exactly when I needed it!

Thank you to my awesome Street Team. Your help in editing, reediting, and re-re-re-re-re... well, you get the picture. Thank you to:

Becki Dykstra	Bill Clifford	Cinnamon Mellema
Cory Denuyl	Evan Kowalski	Greg Hayes
Jessica Crawford	Judy Soderquist	Julie Balgoyen
Kathleen Sypien	Laura Millimon	Lynell Averett
Adam Anderson	Martha Johnson	Meagan Beitn
Meghan Bronkema	Patrick Alinger	Quiana EagleTail
Rebecca Nelson	Robert McDaniels	Robin Rose
Sandra Morse	Stacy Meulenberg	Lindsay Shults
Sueann Unger	Wendy Vriesman	Jordyn Vriesman
Sarah Rasmus	Candy McKenney	Kristi Diephouse

Sarah Vuillemot	Michelle Wyniemko	Heather Titmus
Jenna Scheele	Amelia Meares	Beth Way
Elizabeth Gladstone	Drea Brown	Randy Elenbaas

For more information about the next book, character insights, and sneak peeks, please visit my website at **BrandtTrebor.com**.

Thank you,

Brandt Trebor